CLASH OF CULTURES

The Al Gordon Story

by Robert Miller

Edited by Donald MacLaren

This is a novel. The persons depicted are all fictional except for those historical figures, whose interaction with the fictional characters, is a product of the author's imagination.

Any resemblance to any other person, living or dead, is entirely coincidental

© 1998, 2001 by Robert Miller. All rights reserved.
No part of this book may be reproduced, stored in a retrieval system, or transmitted by any means, electronic, mechanical, photocopying, recording, or otherwise, without written permission from the author.

ISBN: 0-7596-3678-8 (e-book)
ISBN: 0-7596-3679-6 (Paperback)
ISBN: 0-7596-3680-X (Hardcover)

This book is printed on acid free paper.

1stBooks – rev. 06/26/02

Part I

Robert Miller

CHAPTER 1

October, 1934

Al Gordon had been told that the Jews were a minority in the world. But growing up in New York City's teeming borough of The Bronx, he was never quite able to bring himself to believe it.

For all of his eighteen years, Al had been surrounded predominately by the sights, sounds, smells, and shops of this Bronx Jewish neighborhood. Most of the people he knew were first and second-generation immigrants from Russia and southeastern Europe. His parents had moved from the ghetto of the lower east side into Harlem soon after they married and, later, progressed farther north to the more middle-class Bronx. They were not strictly observant Jews. And Al had long before decided that religious ritual held no importance for him. A few hours after sundown on a brisk October evening, Al stood outside the Mount Eden Synagogue, waiting impatiently for services to end. He waited outside, quietly defiant.

"Want to go bowling tonight, Al?" asked Hy Wasserman, who paused momentarily as he walked by.

"No, I'm waiting for my grandmother. I have to take her home, then I've got a date. You guys always make me look bad when I bowl, anyhow," Al responded, half-joking.

"I suppose you're covering the game tomorrow at Yankee Stadium for the NYU Bulletin. Having a big time reporter in the neighborhood is great. I'll know who to ask for passes," Hy replied.

Al's attention was caught by shouts from a group of girls playing potsy on the sidewalk of the building adjoining the synagogue. One girl's foot had just come down close to the chalk lines on the sidewalk. An argument had instantly erupted among the girls as to whether she had touched the line. Two elderly, bearded men at the synagogue door tried vainly to quiet the shouting girls. As the congregation started to file out, Al watched for his grandmother. She tended to linger, gossiping with the other older women. Heading inside the nearly empty synagogue, he saw three elderly women remaining in the U-shaped balcony that overlooked the Ark and Covenant. Grandma Sewat, who had come from Russia forty years before, and now was seventy-five, stood less than five feet tall; her hair was white and her skin a soft but wrinkled alabaster. Her piercing gray eyes always tried to focus on people, but her extreme nearsightedness kept faces a blurry vision.

Grandma's face lit up with joy on seeing her grandson. She kissed him and bestowed her Friday night blessing wish of "Good Shabbos" on him.

"Come, Grandma," Al encouraged, as he respectfully, but firmly tugged her arm. He wanted to complete his familial duty by escorting his grandmother home. Al said his good nights to the other two elderly women and carefully guided her to the steps.

The wall clock showed almost 8 P.M. when Al finally opened the door and helped his grandmother inside the Gordons' comfortable three-bedroom apartment. Al's mother and Aunt Molly sat at the kitchen table in unshakable concentration, like human bookends, as they played casino. Loud snores came from the living room where Al's father practiced his nightly ritual of falling asleep in his favorite over-stuffed, forest-green chair.

Al maneuvered the coat off his grandmother, gave her a quick kiss, and hung up her coat. As she walked over to sit in the bare mahogany kitchen chair, Al gave his mother and Aunt Molly each a kiss without saying a word. Al had no intention of staying home on Friday night. Even his fifteen-year-old sister, Shirley, was out playing with her teenage girlfriends. He made a smooth turn towards the door.

"Where are you going, Al?" his mother asked quickly. The question was like a net trying to catch a fleeing fish. Her brown eyes still stared directly at the cards straight in front of her nose.

Al knew his mother would not let him out without an answer. A feisty nice-looking woman, now of medium size with a natural reddish tint to her brown, but graying hair, watched over her children.

"Out. I'm going bowling," Al said casually.

"You're not going to see Selma again, are you?" his mother questioned without looking.

"Mom," Al groaned slightly. "Her parents only let me date her one night a week." Al looked at his mother and at Aunt Molly, who said nothing. Aunt Molly was a somewhat shorter, thinner version of her sister. Her brown hair now had traces of gray. Unlike Al's mother, she smoked cigarettes, always Raleighs, so she could save the coupons to buy some appliance every seven or eight months.

"Al, please. Why do you bother with her?" his mother asked, picking at her cards. "Couldn't you find a better class of girl than one who works in her parents' fruit store?"

"Mom, she's good-looking and an honor student at Hunter College High School." Al defended his choice as he opened the door. "But, still. I'm just going out. I'll see you later."

As Al slammed the apartment door and started through the dark hall. He wasn't sure where he was going. He'd told Hy Wasserman he had a date and couldn't go bowling, and he'd told his mother that he was going bowling and didn't have a date.

He had called Selma at her parents' fruit store earlier to ask for a date. "Al," Selma had said, "you know my folks won't allow it. We're going to the movies tomorrow night. I want to stay home and wash my hair." Selma had rattled on about what she had been doing that day. The conversation was pleasant, until she mentioned that Howard Peskin had just stopped at the store, so she would have to hang up.

Now it was after eight o'clock, and as Al reached the street, he wasn't sure where he was going. He wanted to do some walking and thinking.

Robert Miller

CHAPTER 2

Al found his feet automatically turning south to 174th Street, then east toward Crotona Park. Fifteen minutes later, he passed by Weinberg's Fruit Store and noticed Selma working. Selma Weinberg, about five feet two with brown hair, had large green eyes. She was not thin and not fat. She had a build the Jewish boys would describe as "zaftik," firm and fully packed with apple-sized shapely breasts.

Mischievously, Al decided to cross the street before Mrs. Weinberg or Selma had seen him. He walked cautiously, keeping an eye on the Weinbergs, entered the corner candy store, and went straight to the back into the phone booth. He sat down, deposited a nickel, and dialed the store's number.

"Weinberg's Fruit Store," Selma answered.

"Hi, Selma."

"Allie, what a surprise! I didn't expect you to call. I just stopped in my parents' store for a minute."

"Well, I just wanted to say hello. I was thinking about you. Oh gosh, hold on a second, will you?"

Al dashed out of the phone booth and the store, sprinted across the street, narrowly avoiding being hit by a passing truck, and into the Weinberg's store. He walked stealthily behind Selma, still waiting at the phone.

"Al, what are you doing here? Wasn't you just on the phone?" Mrs. Weinberg asked, looking away from her customer. Mrs. Weinberg was about forty, but appeared to have never been young. Already wrinkled and white-haired, she had been burdened by a difficult life in difficult times. She gave Al the unspoken look that seemed to ask, 'What is he doing here tonight?'

Selma turned around. Her face flashed from a shocked look into a relaxed smile. "You nut! What are you doing here? Here I am holding the phone for you. You made me feel like a jerk."

Clash of Cultures - The Al Gordon Story

"I had to see Abe Steinberg about something, but he wasn't home. I thought I'd stop over and say hello. Maybe you can take a little walk with me before you wash your hair." Al tilted his head and raised his eyebrows with a smile.

Selma looked at her mother. An expression passed between them that Al couldn't understand.

"No, Al. I told you I couldn't see you tonight. But, if you want to, you can walk me home." Selma turned to her mother and said innocently, "Momma, I'll be at home if anybody looks for me. Okay?"

Mrs. Weinberg shook her head yes and gave Al a cold stare.

As they started down the sidewalk, Al's hand touched hers and their fingers intertwined. "I just had to see you. I was feeling so good today. There was so much to tell you, and tomorrow night seemed so far away," Al said anxiously.

"Tomorrow night's date may be further away than you think, Allie. If my father had been in the store, he would have been mad as anything. He probably wouldn't let me go out with you tomorrow. He says seeing you once a week is enough." Selma reminded Al he had to play by her father's rules, which were to be followed strictly if Selma were to continue being Al's Saturday regular date.

"Where is your father?" Al asked.

"He went to some kind of meeting with my brother, Joey."

"You mean there's no one home now?" Al asked, brightening.

"That's right. Don't get any crazy ideas. Cause you're just walking me to the door and we'll say good-bye. That's all there is," Selma said with a tone of authority. Every nice Jewish girl in the Bronx knew never to give in to a boy's temptations.

"Honey, your mother will be in the store until ten, and I promise that I'll leave fifteen minutes before ten. That gives us almost an hour together," Al pleaded.

Selma stopped and looked at Al. Her hand gripped his tighter. "Allie, darling, there's nothing I'd like better, really. I can't." She hesitated in order to prepare Al for the truth. "Howard Peskin is coming over. He should be here now. We're going to the movies. I didn't want to make a date with him, but he asked me to go to the RKO Fordham in front of my mother when he came to the store this afternoon. When I started to say no, you should have seen her glare at me. I told him you were taking me to the Fordham tomorrow. He asked me to the show at the Crotona. I had to say yes!"

Al felt he had been hit in the stomach. "Oh," he hesitated, trying to hide his pain, but blurted out, "Go to the Fordham or to the Crotona, if you want. I don't care. I'm not even sure about tomorrow night. With the football game and all. Go on. Have a big time. I'll call you tomorrow. Maybe."

By now they had arrived at the entrance to her apartment house. Al let go of her hand and started to walk away.

"Allie," Selma called softly.

"What?"

"Don't be mad, honey. I couldn't help it. Come upstairs with me for a few minutes till he comes." Selma offered Al the best come-to-me look she had seen in the movies.

Al sullenly walked back to Selma. He opened the unlocked front door of the five-story apartment building. They walked up the stairs together saying nothing. At the landing, Al suddenly grabbed Selma roughly, pulled her to him and kissed her. Selma responded with a soft, yielding kiss. The kiss would have lasted longer, but the sound of the door opening and closing downstairs startled them. As they broke apart, Howard Peskin bounded up the stairs. At the landing, Howard gave a surprised look when he saw the two of them standing close together. Howard was Al's opposite, being taller than Al, blond, stiff, and with a more buttoned-up personality.

Selma broke the awkward moment by giving Howard a big smile. "Hello, Howard. I wasn't sure whether you said you'd be at the store or at the apartment. Al stopped by and walked me home. I'm ready now. Shall we go?" Selma turned and looked Al in the eye, offering him her best innocent, bright smile. "Good night, Al," she said pointedly, and then with only a very slight questioning tone in her voice asked, "See you tomorrow night?"

Al watched as they went down the steps. Only after the door had closed, did Al start down. His steps gave off a lonely echo in the staircase hallway. Outside, Al watched as they walked away, then turned in the other direction. By the time he had walked four blocks, he realized he had had only one quick kiss with Selma. He had not said a single word to Howard. Selma had been with him for a few minutes and gone so quickly that Al wondered if he had been dreaming this sudden reversal.

Al and Selma had been "going steady," for a year, which meant the relationship had developed into something more serious because they were supposed to see each other once every weekend. Howard Peskin had intruded on what had been an acceptable arrangement, although maybe not fully accepted by Selma's parents. During that time, Al had gone out a few times with other girls and wolfed around at New York University, where he had just entered his sophomore year working towards a journalism major. The snag remained that Selma had one more year to finish high school. Her parents wanted their daughter to meet other nice Jewish boys, just as Al's parents stressed that he should try to meet other nice Jewish girls. Al had been trying to persuade Selma that he was crazy for her. With all his bravado, Al still felt a nagging doubt about whether Selma was a girl he wanted to eventually marry. And marriage was something that Al knew he could not even begin to think about for many, many years. Now her parents had the audacity to encourage her to go out with Howard Peskin. Alone again, Al walked along, convincing himself that he really did love Selma.

By the time he had passed Claremont Park, his moods were jumping around like a checkers game. Love. Hate. Anger. Anguish. His love and hate for Selma bounced around, depending on how he perceived what she said, what she meant, and what she might be doing with Howard Peskin. He hated Howard. He wanted to tell them both off, but he never wanted them to see his conflicted anguish.

As Al walked slowly, he kept thinking, I won't call her tomorrow. I'll just let her sit and wonder whether I'll show up or not. She needs to be taught how it feels to worry about someone you love. The hell with her. Who needs her?

Robert Miller

CHAPTER 3

Al knew he could not go home to his parents looking and feeling ruffled, like he had lost everything. They would not understand nor empathize with him over Selma. He decided his best medicine was to walk the Concourse a few more hours. He fought hard to take his mind away from Selma, but kept wondering if Howard Peskin would be trying to kiss Selma, and if she would let him. He tried to keep his mind on the break he was getting by being assigned the Rutgers-NYU football game the next day. Sports thoughts offered the only salve to his ego. He pictured himself in the press box at Yankee Stadium and writing the enviable front page by-line story in the next issue of NYU's campus paper, *The Bulletin*.

By 11 P.M., Al gave up the lonely, austere walk and arrived home. Time seemed to have stood still in the Gordon apartment. His mother and Aunt Molly still sat peering at their cards, without looking up. His father remained asleep, snoring in the same position in his deep, fat upholstered chair in the living room.

"Allie?" his mother called out.

"Yes, Mom."

"A fellow named Tom Delavito called three times. He says it's important, and you should call him whenever you get in... no matter what time. Who is Tom Delavito, Allie?"

"He's the editor of the university paper. He's never called me before," Al wondered about the surprise call.

His mother motioned with her finger without looking to a piece of paper on the counter. Al picked up the paper and deciphered some numbers scratched there. He dialed the numbers and waited as the phone rang four times. Someone said 'hello'.

"Tom? Hi. This is Al Gordon. Did you want me?"

"I'm glad you called back. You're going to cover tomorrow's game, right?"

"Yep."

"'Al, when you write the story, can you bring it over to my house tomorrow afternoon?"

"Sure, Tom, but I promised Fred I'd bring it over to him so he could take it to the printer when they publish the paper on Sunday," Al explained.

"Fred Hyman's sick. He won't be able to come down to the printer on Sunday. Can you go there with us and help us make up the sports page?"

"I guess so," Al said, hesitating. "Fred's always done it. I don't know what to do. I'll sure try."

"Be at my house after the game. I'll tell you what we're doing. See you tomorrow. Say, Al, have you ever been to Texas?" Tom asked after a pause.

"No. Why?"

"I shouldn't have mentioned it. Fred has pneumonia...and won't be able to take the trip to the Texas A & M game. A damn shame. He's waited four years to go. I don't know who will go. Maybe you'll be the lucky one."

"Holy mackerel!" Al exclaimed. "Wouldn't that be something?"

"It's the kind of thing they always send a senior to," Tom said calmly, not promising anything to Al. "Like I said, you might just get lucky. Write a good story and I'll see what I can do to assign you to cover the game in Texas. Talk to you tomorrow, Al."

Al sensed a slight nervous tremor in his hand as he hung up the receiver. Ever been to Texas? The question echoed inside him. Hell, I've never been further from New York than Atlantic City. The answer rebounded inside. The best Al had hoped for was a trip with the football team for the next year or two to New Brunswick, New Jersey, or Easton, Pennsylvania.

Al went to bed smiling and thinking about all his new possibilities. Selma and Howard had evaporated from his thoughts. His mind filled with wild west images of Texas.

Robert Miller

CHAPTER 4

Saturday morning dawned bright and warm, and Al was up early, dressed, and before noon had his portable typewriter under his arm and was on the subway headed for Yankee Stadium.

He passed a battery of phone booths at the subway station and thought of calling Selma.

"The hell with it," he decided, and climbed into the empty press section set up along the third base line.

He was greeted by the school's P.R. man, Joe Beagle.

"Mr. Beagle, I'm Al Gordon and I'm covering the game for the downtown Bulletin," Al told him.

"Sure, Al, how are you? Where's Fred Hyman?"

"Oh, he's down with the flu, and I'm covering this game."

"Okay, then sit over here," Joe instructed this new sports writer, pointing to a corner seat in the third row. "You'll be sitting right next to Dan Parker, sports editor at the *New York Mirror*. By the way, would you like a hot dog?"

"Sure," said Al.

In a few minutes, a man brought Al a tray of hot dogs. Nothing like getting the royal treatment, Al thought and then offered to pay for the food. Al's eyes lit up when the man told him the dogs were on the house, and Al became greatly impressed when the man told him all the coffee and Cokes were free, too. This sports writer's life is quite the good life, Al told himself before ordering a Coke. When the man left, Al tasted a few bites of his on-the-house, mustard-laden hot dog. The flavor of the dog put him in the mood of a fan ready for a good football game.

Al had aspirations to one day be a famous New York sports reporter. Not more than an average athlete himself, he simply loved the smell and excitement of the games and the adventure of sniffing out a good sports story.

Clash of Cultures - The Al Gordon Story

By the end of the game, the sky had become overcast, the wind brisk. Al's fingers ached from the cold as he finished his story in the now empty ballpark. He packed up his typewriter and headed away after a solid win for the NYU team.

The sun had set while Al rode the Lexington Avenue subway underground to downtown Manhattan. Street lights beamed dull white circles on the streets where Al walked along Eleventh Street to Tom Delavito's apartment. He found the number over the door, walked to the fourth floor and knocked on the door.

"That's timing for you. You're right in time for dinner," Tom Delavito said, waving Al in and smiling broadly. Tom, six-feet-two inches tall, stood four inches over Al. His somewhat sallow complexion contrasted with noticeably thick black hair. The two enjoyed getting to know each other better and Al offered his assessment of the day's game.

Al, a sophomore, held Tom Delavito, a senior and the editor-in-chief of *The Bulletin*, in awe. After a meatball and spaghetti dinner, Tom read over Al's story.

"Pretty good lead, Al," Tom mused. "I don't think Fred could have done it much better." Tom leaned back in his chair and speculated. "It's a damn shame for Fred he's sick. I spoke to Dean Wilbur about who should accompany the team to Texas. You're the logical next choice, but...you're only a sophomore."

"Well, what's the verdict?" Al asked anxiously.

"I'll talk to the dean again. The team leaves after practice on Monday."

"Do you think I have a chance?" Al asked, hoping for reassurance.

"It's between you and Joe Blane."

The possibility of Joe Blane startled Al. "He's the Assistant Business Manager of the paper. He's never written a line of copy!"

"That's true. However, he's on the Associate Board and he is a junior." Tom smiled at the confused look on Al's face. "Relax. Don't despair. Meet me at the print shop tomorrow morning for the make-up of the paper. We'll call the dean from there."

Al left Tom's apartment as if determined to hold his breath until the dean's decision the next day. When he reached the street, his watch showed almost eight o'clock. *Oh, damn! I had a seven o'clock date with Selma and I've forgotten to call her.* The cold reality sent a wave of guilt through him. He knew Selma, would not stand for being stood up. If he were to rescue the night he would have to find the first candy store and make an emergency call to Selma. Al found a phone booth within a few minutes and dialed her number.

"Hello, Weinberg Fruit Store," a hoarse voice answered.

"Mr. Weinberg, is Selma there?"

"Al, she's home. She's waiting for you there. Wasn't you supposed to be here long ago already?"

Robert Miller

"Yes, Mr. Weinberg. I'm still downtown. Will you tell her I'll be there by nine?"

"Sure. I'll close the store, run two blocks and up three flights of stairs, and tell her! Don't be stupid! If she comes here, I'll tell her. If she doesn't come here, I won't." Mr. Weinberg's bluntness carried a subtle, honest undertone of humor that typified a no-nonsense Jewish father.

"Okay. If she comes by, tell her to wait for me. I'm on my way!"

Forty minutes later, Al got off the subway and ran over to the fruit store, lugging his portable typewriter, and into the back of the store where Selma frowned upon seeing him.

"You have some nerve," Selma scolded. "I thought I was stood up. We'll never get to the movies now. They'll be jammed!"

"Selma, I'm sorry," Al apologized, while he delicately led her out the door. "Let's forget about the movies. Let's just take a walk."

"With your typewriter? Do you always carry your typewriter around with you, or just when you're on a date with me?" Selma seemed ready to make a bad scene.

"Let's drop it off at your house and then we can walk." Al could almost feel the angry quills rise up on her back, but he dared to ask, "Did you have a good time last night?"

"I did, if you want to know. Howie took me out to the movies. Then for a soda. And I got home at a reasonable hour without having to go through a wrestling match like I do with you."

"What kind of a crack is that? Were you disappointed? Or, are those so-called wrestling matches so unpleasant?"

Selma raised her eyebrows and gave Al an insulted look for asking her, a young lady, such questions.

They continued to walk slowly down the street. Al mulled over the unexpected changes in the last twenty-six hours since they had walked the same street. Neither Selma nor Al said anything more, but both were trying to sort out their thoughts. Al had a premonition that something had already changed in their relationship, and wondered if she thought the same.

Outside the Weinberg's apartment, Al reached over to touch Selma's hand.

She stiffened. "You think all you have to do is...oh, damn!" Selma quickly gave up the reprimand and, instead, yanked her hand away.

At the third landing, Selma asked Al to wait a moment. She opened the door, set his typewriter down, and locked the door behind her. She turned to Al with a questioning look, "Allie, I don't understand you. Something has happened. Tell me. What's eating you?"

"Selma, so much has happened since yesterday. I thought you were my girl. Now, I find you're seeing Howard Peskin. If it wasn't for the football game today, I'd have gone clear out of my mind wondering about you two."

"Did NYU win?"

"Yes. And next week they play Texas A&M at a place called College Station, Texas. It's possible that I'll be going to Texas to cover the game."

"Go to Texas? You? Just like that? I don't believe it."

"Yeah! And, if I go, I'll be gone almost two weeks." Al's excitement to be going to Texas could only be clouded by the one painful thought that shot through his mind. "Will your father let you see Howard Peskin on Friday and Saturday nights?"

"There you go again. What's Howie got to do with anything? I thought we were talking about you. Come on, I don't want to fight over Howard. Let's go and stop talking about him," Selma said firmly.

Al's face showed a strained smile, but he still had unanswered questions about where he stood with Selma and where Howard Peskin fit into the equation.

CHAPTER 5

Sunday was an important day in Al Gordon's life. He finally got to see how NYU's Bulletin was put together, and with his own by-line on the front page.

He watched quietly at first as Tom Delavito and the other members of the paper's Executive Board edited copy, marked proofs, and laid out the newspaper page by page. At first he felt lost, but he began to feel confident in a few hours, and started making contributions. By the time the group stopped to eat the sandwiches a deli delivery man had brought in, Al's self-perception had changed from walking-in-the-door vulnerability to being a working member among the very seniors from whom he had felt so isolated. While everyone sat talking and finishing their sandwiches and sodas, the phone rang. Al's head raised straight up to look at Tom.

"It must be Dean Wilbur. You'll know in a few minutes," Tom said softly to Al, just before reaching for the phone.

Al heard Tom answer yes and no a few times. When Tom hung up, he turned to Al, "You're Acting Sports Editor until Fred gets back. You'll leave for Texas sometime tomorrow after the team practice."

Al sat stunned and motionless, as if he just experienced a miracle. Tom's quick answer left Al stuttering for a response. Congratulations went around the table. Al managed to give each one a strong handshake and a big thank-you smile. Just as quickly and without further congratulations, everyone got back to work.

The next day Al stopped at Dean Wilbur's office for an envelope full of train tickets and various things he had never seen before, everything he would need over the next two weeks. The package contained vouchers for meals and statements for each of his teachers, explaining that he would be out of class and asking them to give him work assignments to take along.

By 4 P.M., Al had boarded a train that would take him far away from the style of life he knew in the Bronx. The trip offered entirely new experiences. The world would become a little broader for Al.

He found he would be sharing the Pullman berth with Marvin Pearlman, the Sports Editor of the University Heights edition of NYU's Bulletin. Marvin was a short and somewhat squat senior, with coldly intense brown eyes and a shock of dark brown wavy hair.

Dinner was served in the dining car immediately, so it could be cleared for other passengers by 6 p.m. Eating in a dining car with the NYU football team, the coaches, and members of the press came as a small taste of sports heaven for Al. The clean white tablecloths, the long menu with exotic-sounding dishes, and Negro waiters in white coats reminded Al of the scenes he had seen only in movies. The meal of steak, mashed potatoes, and pie that almost everyone ordered, Al thought of as one of his best meals ever. For Al, the time on the train meant living like a movie star.

During what turned out to be long hours of riding through state after state, Al developed the habit of staring out the window most of the way west into St. Louis.

"Hey, here's Big Chief Nose in the Window. What in the world do you keep looking for out there?" joked Marvin Pearlman.

Al looked around to see Marvin sitting down next to him.

"I can't believe what I'm seeing! This is a different world. I haven't seen an apartment house since we passed through Yonkers. I can't believe the things I've seen, and we're about to cross the Mississippi." Al turned to look out the window again. He imagined himself extra lucky to be living every sophomore's dream to be traveling like this and at NYU's expense.

"Com' on, Al," said Marvin. "Does St. Louis really look a lot different from New York?"

"It's not just that. I'm taking in everything that's new," Al said, turning back to Marvin. "Look. I'm only used to an automat, a cafeteria, or a deli. Here I am on my way to Texas. Things are all new. I'm the sports reporter for the New York University football team at the Texas A&M game. I'm eating on a train. And the food! It's great. And, I'm traveling with reporters from well-known New York newspapers."

"Listen, take in the sights. Who knows when this team will get back to Texas again." Marvin broke into a smile. "Or, if you'll even want to get back to Texas. A big city guy like you."

Al and Marvin enjoyed a laugh. Al turned again and looked out the window. He felt amazement and rejuvenation in wanting to be a sports writer. He saw himself in the future traveling like this and having the prestige that comes with being a great reporter. For the moment, he was simply a boy, much like a Huckleberry Finn on a train, instead of on a raft going down the Mississippi. He felt humbled by all he had to see and learn, unlike some sophisticated snob from the big city. He imagined what might awaited him in the wild west on the other side of the Mississippi. He dreamed up the sight of cowboys, horses, and gun fights like he had seen in the western movies.

Settling down to his writing, Al squeezed in a brief interview with Coach Stevens. The coach, about fifty, a quiet type who, although tall and a former athlete had gained weight around the stomach and under the chin since his playing days. Al had to ask Coach Stevens the pointed question, "Do you think NYU is ready for a powerhouse like Texas A&M?"

"Man for man, we're as good as anybody. However, we don't have the reserves they do. We've got to keep our first team on the field sixty minutes to stand a chance. Our problem is that they have a second team as good as their first and can rest their players. I can't do that," Coach Stevens said candidly.

Al knew the coach trained his players to be the best, but NYU would be on the field against one of the Goliaths of football. As the hours and scenery rolled by, Al took advantage of his semi-prestigious position. The players talked to him, gave him interviews, and told him stories. To his thinking, he was beginning to become an insider with the team.

By 9 P.M., the train slowed down through Missouri. As the train came to a stop, Al left his dreamy thoughts and saw a yard worker in overalls carrying a lantern walking alongside the train. Al lowered the window and called out, "Where are we?"

The laconic reply was "Springfield."

Tony Beretta, an NYU tackle from Holyoke, Massachusetts, who sat next to Al, jumped up and hollered exuberantly, "Fellas, we're in Massachusetts!"

The railroad man, hearing him, turned back and said, "No, you're in Springfield, Missoura."

For some reason that none of them could explain later, the car full of football players and the rest of their entourage called out hilarious hoots and rolled around with laughter.

The train started its monotonous clacking as it rolled along after the Springfield stop. The team players dutifully went off to bed to get rested. Al sat alone in the smoking room adjoining the lavatories, opened the window, and peered out onto a rural scene that left his mind boggled at such complete darkness. He could not imagine so much space without a street light. The train sped westward through southwestern Missouri and into Oklahoma. The sun came up as the train crossed the Red River, which seemed more like a creek to Al, and finally entered Texas. A couple of hours later they could see the Dallas skyline growing taller in the distance over the plain. The clouds and sky were speckled gray and white like a Texas mare.

The train pulled in for a brief stop in Dallas. Al took advantage to browse through the terminal and bought the local newspapers. He found new pleasure in goggling at the abundance of blonde Texas girls walking past him. He finally rejoined his traveling companions waiting alongside the train and pronounced with great excitement, "It is true. The girls in Texas are beautiful!"

"Now, here's a great reporter! He's got the real scoop on Texas!" Tony Beretta teased Al, with a big grin.

CHAPTER 6

The train finally brought the NYU group to its final destination, Bryan, where they received a big greeting from a group of officials and reporters from Texas A&M University. After the welcome, they were put on buses and taken to a dining hall for a Texas-style lunch of tacos and guacamole salad. Al first picked gingerly at the Mexican food. Once realizing its great taste, he devoured several tacos, smeared with the green guacamole, in minutes, as if feasting on Coney Island hot dogs.

A student, wearing an Army cadet uniform, came up to Al and Marvin. "Hi, there. I'm your host, Jim Allen Bates. I'm the sports editor of *The Eyes of A&M*, the campus newspaper. Welcome to Texas," Jim Allen said exuberantly. He was tall, thin, with blond hair cut in a cadet crew cut style.

Jim Allen explained, "Everybody in Texas is named Jim or Bill or Bobby, so we use first and middle names together all the time down here. There are a few Als, but I don't think I ever met a Marvin before. Where are you fellas from?"

Al got the immediate impression that he was a typical Texas Aggie and that all the Aggies liked to talk a lot.

"I'm from the Bronx," Al said.

"So am I," Marvin added.

"I've heard of a Bronx cheer," Jim Allen said. "I never heard of the Bronx."

Al and Marvin took quick glances at each other. They realized how far away from home they were when people told them they never heard of the Bronx.

"Let's stop and have a beer," Jim Allen suggested. "They'll serve us in Bryan, but a cadet can't buy a beer anywhere in College Station. I've got my car, so we can go down the road."

Al and Marvin looked at each other with astonishment as Jim Allen pulled his car up to a grocery store and brought out three cold beers. After two sips of beer, he proceeded to drive over to Prince's Drive-In and order some hamburgers. Here Al had his second encounter with Texas girls. He goggled at the teenage carhops in short skirts, running in and out, and pleasantly serving the customers in their cars.

"We're a long way from the Bronx," Al said under his breath to Marvin, as Jim Allen gave the order to a young blond girl who smiled courteously at the three young men.

The dinner that night was served to the A&M cadets and the NYU people in the large A&M dining hall, where they had been for lunch. The meal consisted of Texas barbecue pork and beans.

Watching as Al and Marvin picked at their food, one of the A&M cadets taunted in a southern drawl, "Is that food a little strange for a couple of Jewboys?"

"Yeah, it sure is," Al said. "But, I'm going to try it!" Al raised a pork rib and took a bite. After swallowing, he shot back, "You guys come visit me in the Bronx and I'll see how you like herring and kasha varnishkes!"

"Kasha what?" hooted a student named Tex.

"Tex, you might die eating that," another A&M cadet called out.

"What part of Texas are you from, Tex?" Al asked.

"I'm from Shreveport, Louisiana," came the proud answer.

"If you're from Louisiana, why do they call you Tex?" Al asked innocently, taking the bait like a fish.

"Cause I don't want to be called Louise!" Tex hollered.

The whole dining room erupted in laughter. Al enjoyed the joke, but he also realized that Tex and some other A&M cadets might have suspicions about the strange "Jewboys" from New York. But Al and Marvin tried the local food without making a scene, and their hosts showed the boys from The Bronx more curiousity than animosity.

Back at Jim Allen's car, Jim handed the car keys to Al. "I've got a headache, Al, why don't you drive us back?"

Al kindly handed back the keys, explaining, "I don't know how to drive."

Jim Allen looked at Al with incredulity and gave the keys to Marvin. Okay, you drive," Jim Allen said.

"I don't know how," Melvin mimicked Al's answer.

"Oh?" Jim Allen said before sighing. "I'm getting myself some aspirin. Wait here. I'll be back." When Jim Allen returned, he still did not feel great, but he had Al and Marvin get in to drive them back to their sleeping quarters.

"I can't believe that you guys don't drive a car," Jim Allen said, frowning from disbelief and the pounding headache.

Al and Marvin explained about New York subways and why people in the city don't need cars.

"If you don't have cars, where do you New York fellas get laid?" Jim Allen wondered.

Robert Miller

Al and Marvin looked at each other sheepishly. Al ventured an answer. "Hey, Jim Allen, we fool around plenty in the parks, on the roofs, sometimes on the stairs between floors of apartment houses. You have to understand we go out with nice Jewish girls who will sometimes let you feel them up, but they save what they've got till they get married. Us New Yorker fellas don't get laid very much unless we want to go to a whore. She'll cost two dollars, at least. Maybe a dollar, if we find someone to drive to Scranton, Pennsylvania."

Jim Allen let out a loud whoop. "Hey!" He calmed down to explain, "We have a bunch of girls coming down tonight and staying over for the game tomorrow. The real action is the girls who go to the University of Texas, but they're at another game this weekend."

"Oh, well, we'll see how the weekend goes," Al said in a noncommittal tone, as he glanced over at Marvin. "This isn't like the Bronx," Al mumbled to Marvin, adding a mischievous twinkle.

CHAPTER 7

Clyde Youngblood, the Texas A&M University press officer, a tall, burly giant of a man, looked Al over suspiciously as Al lugged his portable typewriter into the press box. But when Al introduced himself as the NYU sports reporter, Mr. Youngblood broke into a broad smile and greeted him with the handshake grip of someone used to pumping fifty-pound barbells. Al was only used to pounding on his typewriter. He directed Al to a seat in the third row of press seats.

"Young Mr. Gordon, did New York University really send you all the way down here to see Texas revenge itself on New York for the War Between the States? We've waited over seventy years for this day. Now, I'll try to make the lamb as comfortable as possible before the slaughter. Sheeit! We're going to do some Yankee bashing this day!" Clyde let out. His voice calmed to a whisper, "No hard feelings, boy."

Al smiled uncomfortably as Clyde walked away. I hope NYU doesn't do that bad, Al thought, trying to regain at least a facade of confidence.

An hour before game time, the Texas Aggie band marched into the stadium to the tune of "The Eyes of Texas." Al watched in awe as all the Texans in the stadium, including those in the press box, stood up at attention and fervently belted out the anthem.

> The eyes of Texas are upon you
> All the live long day
> The eyes of Texas are upon you
> You cannot get away.

Hearing the song for the first time, Al simply stood in a pose of reverence as he listened to the entire stadium of Texans proudly sing their anthem. As soon as the song ended, the Texas A&M team roared onto the field and the crowd went wild. NYU's squad, about half as many as A&M, ran onto the field. They really do look like lambs being led to the slaughter, Al thought. By kickoff time, Al felt thoroughly intimidated by the frenzy of the crowd and felt assured the NYU team knew the same feeling.

In the first half, after a Texas A&M touchdown, NYU launched a long drive to score a touchdown and tie the game at 7-7. Then NYU intercepted an Aggie pass and was threatening when the halftime whistle ended the NYU drive. The underdogs from New York ran off the field enthusiastically with the score still tied at 7-7. The Texas crowd appeared thunderstruck at their team's inability to dominate and destroy the upstarts from New York. Al and Marvin were in a state of euphoria. They spontaneously hugged each other and Al shouted, "Wasn't it fantastic?"

"I can't believe it?" Marvin beamed back at Al.

In the second half, three Texas A&M touchdowns followed in quick succession. Al could only sigh and wonder what terrible abomination had taken over the NYU team. Two minutes into the fourth quarter, the Texas Aggies scored again to make it 42 to 7. The Texas coach now played third-and fourth-stringers against the exhausted New Yorkers.

Al was depressed and embarrassed when he noticed something happening on the other side of the field. Behind the NYU bench, a girl in a violet outfit somersaulted and exhorted the crowd to cheer for NYU. Thinking this might be an interesting story, he closed his typewriter case, picked up a small note pad and left the press box. He made his way down the stadium's steps to get across the field to try to talk to the unexpected NYU partisan.

The score was 49 to 7. The girl drew a few cheers from the Texans to support the disheartened NYU players. As the final whistle blew, Al went onto the field to talk to the girl.

When the brown-haired girl turned around to say hello, Al could not believe he was looking at the single, most beautiful face he had ever seen in his life. She had pale white skin, with hundreds of freckles dotting her face. Her penetrating blue eyes, radiance and bright smile simply startled him. Maybe a beautiful creature like her lived in New York City somewhere, but certainly she was unlike any of the Jewish girls he had seen in the Bronx. Al thought her milk and honey skin texture could only come from the pure pasture land of Texas.

"Hi," Al stumbled in his greeting. "I'm Al Gordon of the NYU Bulletin. Are you an NYU cheerleader?"

"Shucks, no," said the vision, whose deep blue eyes sparkled back, surrounded by the pale, freckled face. "When I realized my outfit matched NYU's colors and NYU was being beaten so badly, I decided I had to do something. It's a shame these poor NYU boys came so far for such a licking." Her Texas drawl added a sweetness to her voice.

"Do you go to Texas A&M?"

Clash of Cultures - The Al Gordon Story

"Don't be silly. There are no girls at A&M. I go to TSCW."

"What's TSCW?"

"Texas State College for Women. We're the sister school of A&M in Denton, Texas. It's about 200 miles north of here. I was invited for the weekend by Billy Joe Patton, an A&M football manager. He may not be happy with what I did on the field, but I sure felt sorry for these poor NYU boys."

"What's your name?"

"Mary Jean Monahan."

"Are you from Denton?"

"No. I'm from Houston."

"Do you mind if I write about your cheering for NYU?"

"I don't mind. Why should I?"

"If you give me your address, I'll send you a clipping."

"Sure. It's simply. P.O. Box 1674, TSCW, Denton, Texas."

Al kept staring at her. She looked into his face, and then broke into the biggest, warmest, and most gorgeous smile Al had ever seen.

"Mr. Gordon, it was nice to meet you. I'd better go and find my date."

"Mary Monahan, it was great to meet you. I'll mail you a copy when I get back," Al said awkwardly.

"Thanks," Mary said. She walked away a few steps before she turned, giving Al another gorgeous smile, and waved good-bye.

Al forgot where he was and stood there smiling like he had just seen a rainbow for the first time.

CHAPTER 8

"Hey, Al!" Jim Allen called out. "We were just starting to send out a search party for you. We're on our way to have Ating beers."

"Eighteen beers?" Al asked. "Who can handle that many?"

"No, not eighteen. Ating beers. I'm celebrating, and you and Marvin are commiserating. Hey, don't be so downhearted. You really didn't think your team stood a chance, did you?"

"I did until the start of the second half," Al moaned. "I never expected things to fall apart so quickly."

"Al, for being a good loser," Jim Allen teased, "we're going to Bryan for the beers, then I'm buying you fellas dinner, and after that we're going to a party at the Varsity Club, where you'll meet some TSCW girls."

"I met one already," Al brightened. "She led cheers for NYU during the second half."

"I saw her," Jim Allen said. "Who is she?"

"A real beauty. Her name is Mary Monahan."

"Mary Jean Monahan!" Jim Allen exclaimed. "My Catholic cousin. You won't stand a chance with her. I've heard they call her Virgin Mary. There's more action to be had elsewhere."

Before dinner, Jim Allen celebrated with four beers, which had no effect on him. He enjoyed partying and giving a commanding performance of how he could master bottles of beer one after another. Al started wobbling after two beers, but this was to be expected since he was initiating himself to drinking beer.

At dinner, Al's thoughts floated back to that beautiful face he met today. For him, she was a living Cinderella named Mary Jean. "Is Mary Jean really your cousin?" Al asked Jim Allen. "Are you from Houston, too?"

"No, I'm from Mexia," Jim Allen began to explain. "Mary's mother and my mother are first cousins. What does that make us? Third cousins or first cousins, once removed? My family lived around Mexia just about a hunnert years. I'm probably related to half the people there. Some moved to Dallas and Houston like Mary's mother."

The talk drifted to sports writing. Jim Allen said the only thing he envied about New York was that they had so many newspapers and a profusion of great sportswriters. Jim Allen went on talking about sports and rodeos. "Some day," Jim Allen boasted, "we'll have major league baseball and football teams in Texas." The New Yorkers just laughed. Not a chance, Al and Marvin thought, glancing at each other. "Okay, some day you'll see." Looking at his watch, Jim Allen began slowly moving his body to stand up. "Hell, enough about sports! Let's go over to the Varsity Club and find ourselves some women to dance with!" Jim Allen said strongly. He then let out a whoop before standing up.

At the A&M victory dance, Al's eyes widened with excitement. He thought that luck smiled on him again when he saw Mary Jean in the crowd of seven hundred students.

"Who's that with her?" Al asked Jim Allen. He nodded his head towards Mary Jean.

"That's her date, Billy Joe Patton." Jim Allen puckered his lips before going on. "He's one of the managers of the football team, and a pretty mean guy. I don't much like her being with him to tell you the truth."

"I'll cut in on him to get a dance with her. If he cuts back in on me, I'll cut back in on him again," Al said.

"Not permitted. You can't cut in on a guy who cut in on you," Jim Allen responded authoritatively.

Al looked at Marvin Pearlman. "Marvin, will you cut in for me?"

"I don't know how to dance," Marvin pleaded.

"Go on, you won't have to dance. I'll cut right back in on you," Al reassured him confidently.

Marvin and Al walked up behind Billy Joe and Mary Jean. Marvin tapped Billy Joe on the shoulder and cut in to dance. Marvin took two steps with Mary Jean. Right away, Al tapped Marvin. Mary Jean, offering an unexpected look at what was happening, suddenly found herself dancing with the sports reporter from NYU. She came happily into Al's arms, pulled closer to him, and they danced away from Billy Joe.

"Al, I enjoy dancing with you," Mary Jean said. "But please don't ask me again tonight. Billy Joe is upset. He's been drinking and he's threatening trouble. Send me the clipping, if the story appears. And write to me. But, please don't look for problems tonight. Neither of us needs that."

Al and Mary Jean parted on the dance floor. Six hundred young men milled around, and maybe a hundred girls had come to the dance, of whom only about twenty really danced. The dance wore on for Al. It was no celebration dance for him, while he glumly thought about Mary Jean and all the lost chances to dance with her again. He entertained himself just walking around. An hour later as Al

Robert Miller

headed across the darkened floor, he heard someone running behind him. Al braced himself, expecting trouble behind him from an A&M cadet, but he saw Marvin approaching.

"That girl you were dancing with came back. She came up to me. She's looking for you. You've made a hit with her!" Marvin shouted in Al's ear over the loud music.

"Where is she?" Al asked exuberantly.

"With Jim Allen!"

Al turned and made his way back to Jim Allen where Mary Jean stood next to him, looking distraught.

CHAPTER 9

As Al approached, Mary Jean broke into a broad, happy smile that brightened the whole world for Al.

Mary stepped toward Al. "Dance with me, Al! I'm so glad to see you. I was afraid I'd never see you again."

Al held her close and tried to do the only dance he knew, the Two-Step, to a western-style song that a vocalist was calling out. "If I came home tonight, would you still be my darling, or have I stayed away too long?" the vocalist sang without a great deal of success.

"What happened to your date?" Al asked.

"He tried to get me into his car, where he had a bottle of bourbon. When I wouldn't do what he wanted me to do, he curled up with the bottle. By now, they should be off in Dreamland together. He turned out to be a pig and a bore. I'm glad I got to meet you, Mr. New York Sportswriter. What do you think I should tell my Aunt Lucille when she asks me about Billy Joe?" Mary Jean asked, smiling.

"Tell her he was a pig and a bore and you preferred a Jewish sportswriter from New York."

"You're Jewish?" Mary Jean's eyes widened with wonderment. She looked amazed to realize she was being smitten in the middle of a dance by a Jewish boy.

"Does that make a difference?"

She reared her head back and laughed. "Why should it? We're not going to get married, are we? I've heard about Jews for years, but never met one. Now, I'm dancing with a Jew."

"It's hard to believe you never met one. Maybe there aren't any in Texas. You ought to come to the Bronx. There are lots of us there."

"Oh, there's some Jews in Texas. They own stores downtown and live in a section called Waterview." Mary Jean's eyes twinkled. "I once heard it called Bagelview." She giggled innocently.

Al had not thought that it was a big deal to meet or to dance with someone Jewish. He never thought of himself as "different" and had given little thought to his heritage while in Texas. Mary Jean represented the purity of a young girl from Texas. Her religion was simply unimportant to him.

"Would you like something to drink?"

Mary Jean threw her head back and laughed again. "Oh, no! Do you have a bottle of bourbon in your pocket too? If so, you won't be the first fella to try to get me drunk. Anyway, like I told Billy Joe, I don't drink."

"I was thinking of punch," Al said. His face had turned brick red with embarrassment, but she only saw the embarrassment in his eyes. "I hardly ever drink myself."

"Sure. I'm very thirsty. I'd prefer a Dr. Pepper."

Al saw Mary Jean relax. "I'll ask Jim Allen."

"We can ask him together," Mary said as she took hold of his hand, as they broke away from the dance floor to search out their friend.

Jim Allen smiled and shook his head as he saw them holding hands. Al explained that he and Mary Jean would like to buy a Dr. Pepper. Jim Allen knew of a place two miles away. He ended up pulling out his car keys and handed them directly to Mary. "Mary, take my car, but you'll have to drive. Would you believe that Al doesn't know how?"

Mary gave a big smile to Jim Allen, and Al nodded thanks as they headed out of the dance.

At Prince's Drive-In, Al sat close to Mary in Jim Allen's car. Tonight he did not have to goggle the waitresses in short skirts flitting around the cars. His eyes focused on only one pretty Texas girl, Mary Jean, who sat in the driver's seat.

"So, Mr. Sportswriter from the Bronx, tell me how you like Texas," Mary Jean said with a twinkle in her eye.

"I don't know all about Texas, but I think I'm about to fall in love with you."

Mary Jean's face turned to the car's roof, and she began to laugh. Al, embarrassed by her response, slumped back in the seat. Her laughter turned to a giggle. She leaned over and kissed Al on the cheek.

"Allie Gordon, you are the strangest, silliest, most foolish, and most interesting young man I have ever met, and you sure know how to get a girl's attention." Mary Jean let out a soft laugh.

Al reached across her waist, pulled her toward him and kissed her softly. Her lips lingered with his, then she pulled her head back. She only had a moment to look into his eyes. Al's lips found hers again. The second kiss became longer and softer, and her arms went around his neck. Slowly, maybe reluctantly, she pulled back.

Clash of Cultures - The Al Gordon Story

"Yes, you surely know how to get a girl's attention," she said softly. She caught her breath. "My father certainly knew what he was talking about when he told me to beware of men from the north and east of Ohio."

Al noticed how innocent and happy she looked.

"Al, you're a Jew from New York who's going home tomorrow. I'm a Catholic girl from Houston who'll never see or hear from you again after tomorrow. Don't complicate my life. Finish your Dr. Pepper and let me take this car back to Jim Allen and find where I'm spending the night," Mary said softly.

"Mary, who says you'll never see me again? I told you I'd write to you. I have your address don't I? It's twenty after ten now. I don't have anything to do until 12:10 tomorrow when my train leaves for New York," Al pleaded before pausing. "Except to get to know you better."

"That, young fella, is exactly what's not going to happen. You know me as well as you ever will. It has been fun. And did you say you are catching the 12:10 train? So am I. But, please don't give me any trouble tonight. Just take me back to the dance before my reputation is totally destroyed."

"You're the one who's driving," Al said softly with a smile. "You have the car keys."

Mary gave an embarrassed giggle and blinked the lights for the hop to take away the tray. She kissed Al on the lips before the surprised Al had time to get his arms around her waist again.

"Al, you are absolutely the most interesting boy I have ever met. I don't think I'll ever forget you or this night."

Mary Jean started the car and backed away from the drive-in. Al kept looking at her and forgot about the sexy car hops moving around outside in their short, ruffled, blue-and-white uniform skirts.

Mary Jean smiled at Al's innocence. She knew this young man from New York showed her respect. Unlike some of the Texas boys who wanted to conquer this virgin, he did not frighten her. She kept seeing something in his eyes. He may have been from the great sophisticated city of New York, but he treated her with a loving, patient tenderness. His eyes also made her smile. His eyes showed that special luminosity when he looked at her.

CHAPTER 10

The first Sunday in November at College Station, Texas, reminded Al of a perfect August day in New York. Al had gotten up early to walk the Texas A&M campus. He compared the campus to Van Cortland Park in the Bronx, except that the campus had buildings and a football stadium. After the walk, Al ate breakfast before the others and went back to the room to wait for Jim Allen to stir.

"Hey, good morning. Will you drive me to the railroad station in Bryan?" Al asked Jim Allen excitedly. He calculated he'd better get Jim Allen moving, if he was to have a few extra minutes with Mary Jean this morning.

The groggy Jim Allen looked at the clock. "It's nine o'clock in the morning! There's no train until 12:10. Don't you have a bus that'll take you there?"

"Your cousin Mary said she'd get there early. She's taking the same train," Al explained excitedly.

"My God, Al! You're stuck on Virgin Mary. God help you! You'll have to kiss the Roman ring to get to first base with her. My goodness! The Jewboy from New York and the Holy Mother of the Fisheaters! What a combination! What about Marvin?" Jim Allen groaned out as one eyelid closed.

"He can take the bus," Al said calmly. "I want to be alone with Mary," Al explained with a new tone of urgency.

Jim Allen hooted. "Alone on a train full of TSCW virgins and a horny football team. That's a laugh!" Now, both eyelids were open, staring with disbelief at this New Yorker who had some illusion of hope.

Around eleven o'clock, a full hour and ten minutes before train time, Jim Allen pulled his car into the Missouri Pacific depot in Bryan to drop Al off. Al scanned the station and went inside the ticket office. His face wore a disappointed look when he returned to Jim Allen and took a seat in the car.

"Tell you what. If I find Mary at the university, I'll give her a lift," Jim Allen suggested. "If not, Al, have a good trip back and come see us again. It was nice to meet you."

Al clasped Jim Allen's hand. "What a four days this has been! You introduced me to guacamole, taught me to drink beer, and I met your cousin, the most beautiful girl I have ever seen. Thank you for putting up with me and bringing me here early. If this is what they call Southern hospitality, I am grateful for it," Al said graciously.

A taxi suddenly drove up. Mary Jean Monahan and her friend, Mary Sue Baker, got out. Al saw Mary Jean scan the station. Her face lit up when she saw Al waiting in the car.

"Mary Sue," Jim Allen called out. "How about taking a short spin with me. We'll leave these two lovebirds for a few minutes. I'll bring you back before the train arrives."

Both boys watched as the two Mary's looked at each other. Mary Sue walked over to the car. Al got out and closed the door for her when she got in.

Mary Jean Monahan's eyes sparkled, but she gave Al a frown as he walked up to her. "Is there no end to the embarrassment you'll cause me? 'Lovebirds' indeed! Have you been boasting to all the boys at A&M that I let you kiss me last night? My reputation is ruined. I was up half the night wondering what kind of girl you thought I was." Her blue eyes peered intensely at Al.

"I think you are without doubt the most beautiful, exciting, bedazzling creature I have ever met." Under the bright Texas sun, Al looked deeply into her blue eyes.

"Like I said last night, Al, you do know how to get a girl's attention. Do you expect me to believe your Yankee line?"

"That is no line, Mary. I have never met anyone like you. Never."

Al took Mary's hand, and they walked over to the shaded bench where he had left his bags. Sitting down, Al hung tightly to Mary's hand. He studied her hand, observing it was the smallest, whitest hand with the tiniest fingers he had ever seen. She turned out to be the sweetest surprise he could have had in coming to Texas.

They sat, shaded from the sun, asking questions, learning about each other. Mary described herself as a devout Catholic girl, who never kissed a boy on her first date, until last night with Al. Al described himself as a not-so-devout Jewish boy from the Bronx, who had never been far from the Bronx.

Mary Jean took Al's hand in hers and pressed it to her chest. Al felt the rise of her breasts. She leaned forward and brushed his lips with a brief kiss. She pulled away when he tried to put his other arm around her.

"Here's your team bus. It means the train must be coming soon. I have to sit with the girls from TSCW, but I'll save a seat for you. Will you join me there?" Mary asked.

"I can ride with you to Dallas. Then we go to St. Louis and then to New York."

"We change trains in Dallas, too, but we'll be going on towards Oklahoma City. We'll have to say good-bye in Dallas. I still don't know if I'll ever see or hear from you again. If I don't, I want you to know it was exciting to meet you, Allie. I never expected anything like this to happen to me. I'll remember this weekend all my life." Mary gave Al a longing look with her blue eyes, as if she could cast a spell on his heart.

"Mary Jean, I'll write you as soon as I get the clipping. Listen, I'm only eighteen and have two and a half more years of college. I don't know when I'll ever get married, but... I know now that I've met the girl I intend one day to marry." Al smiled the smile of a happy man in love.

"Do you mean that?"

"I sure do."

"It would mean agreeing to become a Catholic." Mary Jean took his marriage idea as literal truth. Her Catholic religion would play a role with whomever she married. Al gave little thought to religion. He was simply lost in the innocence of love. It did not matter if Mary Jean might be a shiksa, as a non-Jewish girl would be called. Labels didn't mean a thing to the young, innocent Bronx boy, who, himself, unawares, sometimes carried what could be twisted by some people into the disparagingly label of "Jew."

"Is that something we have to talk about right now?"

"Maybe not, but I want you to know where I stand."

Al sensed an inner strength in Mary's determination not to be dissuaded from certain things, especially her religion and her reputation.

Al and Mary, oblivious to their surroundings, looked up, fully aware now and surprised to see Jim Allen and Mary Sue standing a few feet away.

"Well, if they ain't lovebirds, they sure act like it, don't they?" Jim Allen taunted. "We've been standing here for over ten minutes, and neither of them looked at anything but each other. Who should I feel sorry for? My kissin' cousin from Houston or this innocent Yankee?"

"Don't feel sorry for either one of us. We're the two happiest people you've ever met and we have two hours to spend on the train to Dallas before we have to part," Mary said with a giggle.

Al and Mary got up to board the train. Nothing could stop them from gripping each other's hands as they walked, while their other hands struggled to carry their bags.

Al had not expected to find love in Texas. Like other major events, love can happen very suddenly. By accident or some preordained plan, he found himself spiraling hopelessly in love, and Mary Jean spiraled with him.

CHAPTER 11

On the train ride to Dallas, Al showed Mary Jean the Texas map he had been given for the trip. Towns with names like Hearne, Calvert, Franklin and Kosse dotted the map.

"Do you know any of these places?" Al asked as they sat pressed against each other.

"I was born in Kosse," Mary Jean pointed to the small town on the map. "My grandfather is the mayor. Do you want to stop there and say hello? I think you'd like each other. He's an atheist," she whispered. "I couldn't tell that to anybody, except a not-so-devout Jew who says he might marry me some day. He's entitled to know the skeletons in my closet."

Al moved closer to Mary and gave her a quick kiss. His vision of paradise would be to have this beautiful, playful woman with him all the time.

"Tell me about your family. How did they get to Texas? How come you're Catholic and your cousin, Jim Allen, is Protestant?" Al asked.

"There's so much to tell. It was still Mexico when my great-great-grandfather and his brother came here from Illinois in 1831," Mary began.

My people were still in Russia back then, Al thought.

"My great-great-grandfather's wife was half-Indian and my mother's mother is supposed to be half-Cherokee. My father was Irish Catholic from Ohio. He came down to Kosse with an oil company twenty years ago and ended up marrying my mother. He gave up his Catholicism to marry her. My little brother died of scarlet fever ten years ago. He was only three. My father blamed himself, made confession and rejoined the Church." Mary's voice took on a sad tone. "My mother converted to Roman Catholicism. They remarried in the Church, so I actually got to attend my parents' wedding. I've gone to Catholic schools. I like being a Catholic. It makes sense to me. It's important to me."

"Your brother died? How terrible," Al said softly.

Robert Miller

"My brother's death almost destroyed my parents. It was devastating for me too. I was only seven. Little Jim and I loved each other so much." Tears formed in Mary's eyes.

Al leaned closer and took her tiny hand in his. No words had to be spoken. Al wanted to protect and comfort this delicate, amazing girl, whose heart still mourned for her little brother ten years later. Mary found solace in Al's quiet, earnest and serene nature. She leaned over and caressed Al's arm.

Al finally broke the silence, "When I was just a little younger than three, I had pneumonia and diphtheria. They thought I might die. I was saved with blood transfusions. That's my earliest memory."

Mary cried more, thinking about her lost brother and Al's story. "I'm so happy you lived to make me happy. I'm so happy to have met you and I'm terribly afraid that I'll never see you again," Mary confessed softly.

As the train approached Dallas, they held hands tightly. The need to cling to each other heightened. Hopelessly lost in their new love, they were desolate at the prospect of parting.

Standing on the platform at the Dallas station, Al and Mary kissed good-bye. Al felt her kiss soft and tender. Her lips came slightly apart and he danced his tongue into the opening. His tongue caused her to give off a low moan and she moved even closer to him. His hand moved down and gently squeezed her buttocks.

"Ooohh, Allie. Please, don't spoil everthing."

"Mary, I'm not going to spoil anything. I'm going to kiss you one more time. Then I'm going to get on a train and have this last moment to remember...until I see you in June."

"In June?" Mary asked wide-eyed.

"Of course. I'll come to Houston in June and find a summer job. We'll be together."

"You mean it?" Mary's eyes remained wide open.

"Now that I've found you, do you think I could ever let you go?"

The conductor's call - "All aboard!" - finally broke their last kiss. Al scrambled to get aboard at the last minute.

"Al Gordon!" Mary shouted as Al's face appeared at the window. "Don't disappoint me! I expect a letter from you very soon and I'm expecting to see you in June. It's a commitment!" She waved as the train moved away.

Al stuck his head and arm out of the raised window to wave back to her for as long as he could see her.

By the time Al got seated in the train, his brief kissing session with Mary on the platform had become the talk of the football team.

The normally taciturn Coach Stevens nudged Al as he passed by and said, "We had a tough day yesterday. You may have scored more than anyone."

"I met a lovely girl," Al said with a blushingly. "I'm falling in love, but I in no way scored anything."

"Don't tell that to anyone else, Al," Coach Stevens teased. "It might ruin your reputation. It seems as though everyone on this train has suddenly gained great respect for you. Your girl is very pretty."

Al thanked the coach. He turned away to look out the window. Mary's face appeared in his memory. He wished he had a picture of her. With so much to tell Mary, Al pulled out a pen and paper to write a letter. Two hours later as the train crossed the Red River he had not stopped writing. At dinner time, Al walked into the dining car like a veteran traveler. The team members greeted him with hoots and calls like a lover boy hero. They all knew him, knew about his girlfriend and had watched their last kiss on the platform. Al enjoyed his sudden celebrity status, where less than a week before he had boarded the train and had been treated as an outsider. He savored the steak dinner and all the talk about Mary. After everyone had gone to bed, Al sat alone looking out the parlor car window. He sped north and east, now, back home to familiar surroundings, but away from his new love. He had left the Bronx to see the bigger world, only to find he had left part of his heart back in Texas. He would never have imagined that such strong feelings would overwhelm him in Texas, and for a shiksa at that, as he could hear his mother saying now. The train's rhythmical metallic beat through the plain's virgin darkness brought melancholic thoughts about Mary. A new meaning of loneliness had taken over Al's heart.

CHAPTER 12

Al opened the office door and gave his mother a warm, confident greeting. She had just come back in from an errand and finished taking off her hat to get settled in to do the bookkeeping and administrative work at the two-person Gordon Advertising Agency.

"Allie!" Mrs. Gordon said, coming alive and giving her son a big hug. "Were you really in Texas? You didn't write." Her voice became more serious. "You didn't call. I was so worried about you."

"I'm fine, Mom. It was a wonderful experience. What a country this is! West of the Hudson, it's a different world! I'll tell you about it tonight."

"Aren't you late for school?" his mother worried.

"The train just got in."

"It costs a lot of money to send you to NYU, and you've already missed six days of classes and you'll miss half your classes today. I don't understand why they let you go."

"Mama, I think I learned more these past ten days than I did the whole year and two months I've been in college!" Al knew his mother might keep him stuck there by asking a hundred questions. He quickened his tone, "I've got to run! See you later!" Al gave his mother a quick peck good-bye.

Al headed right for the NYU Bulletin, where the offices happened to be deserted. He smiled, satisfied to see that his story from Texas was set up as the lead story on page one and his short feature on the impromptu cheerleader, Mary Jean Monahan, was featured on the sports page. Al sat down and wrote Mary another letter. When he finished, he walked it over to the post office. Looking around, Al thought, For the first time, New York looks dingy. Now, he could compare everything with the clean air and the wide spaces on the plains. There were not seven million people jammed together there, as in New York City.

Back home in the Bronx, Al was confident, feeling the bravado of a New World explorer who has just found land in the West. With no one else to visit, he gave Selma a call. She still represented someone to talk to, a friend. He called the Weinberg Fruit Store. Selma answered the phone politely.

"Selma, it's Al. I'm home! How are you?"

"Fine. Did you really go to Texas? I can't believe it. Did you find the time to send me a postcard?"

"Of course I did." Al thought it best to tell her a white lie, "I thought of you all the time. Can I come over tonight? I've got so much to tell you!"

"No, Al, I've got homework to do. I did miss you, Allie. Call me tomorrow. I'll see you on the weekend."

Al felt let down as he hung up the phone. He had forgotten that back in the Bronx, Selma was only his Saturday night date.

On Saturday morning, Al found an airmail letter in the apartment building's lobby mailbox. The letter came from Denton, Texas. His heart jumped. He opened it excitedly, began to read it, and then stuffed it into his pocket to finish on the subway.

Dear Al,

Your letter arrived. I was thrilled to get it, but I could not read very much of your illegible left-hand scrawl. Anyhow, I want you to know what you have done to me. As I calculate it, we have spent a total of four hours together, and those four hours changed my life. I have fallen in love with you! (Is that something I neglected to tell you when I was with you?)

Al lost himself in the pleasure of Mary's words. The letter gave him encouragement that he and Mary remained connected. Her love had not evaporated.

You wrote of coming to Texas in June to find a summer job. Maybe you ought to come down for Christmas and look around. You must think me wanton, but I DO want to see you again soon. Also, can you type your letters on your portable typewriter in the future?

Al read the letter three times before he got off the subway at 161st Street in the Bronx. As he walked into Yankee Stadium for the football game that day, his thoughts transported him back to Texas. He wondered what Mary would be doing tonight, and if she had other dates. They loved each other, but could he expect Mary to sit home every Friday or Saturday night, like a Catholic nun, while waiting for him to come back?

That night, Al took Selma on their prearranged Saturday night date to see a movie at Loews Paradise Theater. They talked little, but held hands.

"Allie, is something the matter? I thought you'd be bubbling over with tales of your train trip and Texas, but you seem to be withdrawn," Selma said, with a mixture of worry and gentle rebuke. She even felt neglected that Al was not grabbing at her and seemed too solemn to kiss her.

"I'm just thinking," Al said, coaxing her along with a gentle smile. He guided her across the street to Krum's, where they each had an ice cream soda. There was no denying that Al was thinking about Texas, but many of the thoughts about Texas were too secret to be shared. After leaving Krum's and engaging in minimal conversation, they walked home hand in hand through a cold wind, along Fordham Road towards Selma's parents' apartment. Al finally told Selma that he might go back to Texas.

"You'd go to Texas for the holidays?" Selma gasped. "How will you get there? What about our time together New Year's Eve? Howard Peskin asked me to go out with him New Year's Eve and I told him I was committed to you."

Al remained calmer this time at her mention of the name Howard Peskin. "I'll hitchhike, if I go, and stay with Jim Allen and his family. I shouldn't have said anything."

"Shouldn't have said anything? Sure! Why not let me know on December 30th? I can't understand what's come over you, Al. You've changed."

"Yes, I've changed. It's different out there." Al's voice sounded like he was in two places at the same time.

"Well, how about the girls you met in Texas? Did you tell them about me?" Selma watched Al closely for his answer.

Her question pinned him down, but he diplomatically decided it was not time to say good-bye to Selma. "If I'd met any girls in Texas, I would've told them about you." Al decided a white lie was better. He laughed off her question. "It was a terrible game. All I thought about all the way home was getting back to you and holding you in my arms again."

Selma smiled contentedly, trying to believe Al, as they continued their walk.

They reached Selma's apartment building and went inside to sit on the steps. She opened her light topcoat. Al pulled her close to him and kissed her. He didn't try to understand himself. He just didn't want to say any final good-byes to her. Selma responded to his kiss. A moment passed as she let him fondle her breasts, but then she pulled his hands back to refrain them by holding them.

"What is to become of us?" Selma asked. "Do you really know me?"

What kind of talk is this from a seventeen year old girl and right at this moment? "I know you're beautiful and exciting, and that I always want to be with you. I know that you bring out the beast in me. I want to touch you everywhere and I want you to touch me. I do enjoy being with you." Al tried to kiss her again, but she rebuffed him. "Okay, if I go to Texas, I'll be home for New Year's Eve. I promise. I'll see you then."

Selma leaned forward and gave him a quick, accepting kiss. "Allie, I may not understand you either, but I care for you more than you'll ever know. But I know it's time for you to go now. We'll see each other next week."

The walk home seemed colder to Al. Selma seemed to be able to rebuff and frustrate him. With each stride, Al's thoughts turned towards warmer and happier days in Texas.

There are loose ends in my life. Sure I'm a shit for lying to Selma. I'm captivated by wanting to see Mary. Will she remain true to me? Will she walk away suddenly with somebody else? Will there be another Howard Peskin in her life? Which one of us might be the first to give up on the other?

Al found it curious to be caught between the melancholy sadness of a dying relationship with a Jewish girl and the excitement of a new relationship dawning with the beautiful and entrancing girl he had met so briefly in Texas.

CHAPTER 13

December, 1934

Six weeks after returning from his first exciting trip out of the Bronx, Al busily packed his bags again, working under the intense scrutiny of his mother. She kept asking if he had enough underwear, warm clothes, a raincoat, and a present for his hostess, whom Al only described as, "The mother of a cousin of my new friend." It was a convenient white lie.

Al left Thursday morning, after borrowing $20 from his mother, to add to the $30 he had saved and the $20 more he expected to collect that day for three weeks of work at the school library. Seventy dollars was more than Al had ever had in his pocket at any one time in his entire life. He felt quite rich.

At the entrance to the Holland Tunnel in Manhattan, Al began his hitchhiking journey across country to get back to Mary. His first offer of help came from a truck driver who gave him a ride to Pennsylvania. At a toll booth, a priest gave him a ride to Harrisburg, plus advice about marrying a Catholic. "Marriage is okay," the priest concluded, "but only if the Jewish party to the marriage agrees not to interfere with the spouse's religion and agrees that all children of that union be brought up as Roman Catholics." It sounded like a memorized answer from one of the Church's rule books.

The next day another trucker gave Al more advice, more on the fundamentals of survival on the road. "Truck stops are good places. The food is good. You can rest there. Tip the girl who serves you coffee a nickel and tell her where you're going, and more often than not she'll line up a ride for you."

The idea worked at the next truck stop. The waitress got Al a ride and he splurged by tipping her a quarter.

Clash of Cultures - The Al Gordon Story

"How long have you been on the road?" the truck driver asked Al.

"I've lost track of time. I left New York on Thursday afternoon, and let's see, I've been in Pennsylvania, Maryland, Virginia, West Virginia, Tennessee and now Alabama," Al recited, as he moved each finger to count off the states.

"You go to NYU?" the driver quipped. "Isn't that school full of Jews and niggers?"

"Lots of students are Jewish. There are only a few colored people in our school. Not many. But we don't have separate schools for colored people in New York."

"We do here," the driver said firmly, giving Al a glance. "And we always will. This is God's country, Alabama. White man's country too. If our niggers are respectful, they get along just fine. If not, they find trouble."

"Listen, I don't want to fight the Civil War with you. And you might as well know that I'm Jewish. If that makes a difference to you, you can stop and let me out. I'll get another ride," Al said with a tone of exasperation. He had no idea what trouble the driver might give. He knew he was in Ku Klux Klan territory, but he had never faced a life-threatening situation because of his Jewish heritage. It didn't make sense why people had to go around hating others, but he had seen newsreels at the movies showing Hitler's and the Klan's effrontery trying to convert others to their hate groups.

The driver only chuckled. "Aren't we touchy?" He took his right hand off the wheel and stretched it out to Al. "My name's Ed Boyle. I'll take you as far as Tuscaloosa. And we refer to what you call the Civil War as The War Between the States."

Al nodded, smiled and shook his hand, thinking maybe the man only wanted to test this young university student's ethical strength.

By Saturday night, Al found himself a truck stop in Carthage, Texas about 300 miles from Houston and desperate for a ride the rest of the way. About 2 A.M., a station wagon with Arkansas plates pulled up and a dark, short chubby man got out to stretch his legs. Al came up to the man and they talked a little.

"You're from NYU? Are you a meshugah? Hitchhiking in the middle of the night in country like this?" the chubby man asked with alarm. He extended his hand and introduced himself. "I'm Abe Gold. I went to the City College of New York. Why in the world is a nice Jewish boy from New York here in the backwaters of Texas in the middle of the night?"

"I'm going to see the most beautiful shiksa in the world," Al beamed.

Abe woke up his wife, Shirley, so she could move to the middle of the seat and let Al sit by the door. Their small son slept in the back seat against a pile of suitcases. Shirley's legs straddled the gearshift, as she proceeded to play the role of Al's surrogate mother, giving Al her best Jewish advice.

"Mary Monahan you're going to see? Oy vey! You want an Irish girl? You can't find one in the Bronx? You have to go all the way to Texas? Jewish girls

Robert Miller

aren't good enough for you? I know Jewish boys fool around with shiksas when they have a chance, but to get mixed up with a Christian girl is to abandon one's own people. Believe me, I know. Three years I've lived in Little Rock. It's a whole different world from the Bronx. Even the few Jewish people in Arkansas are goyim. Abe thinks I'd like Texas better. I want to go back to the Bronx where I belong. If you want a shiksa, you deserve to be left here."

Abe hadn't said a word since they left Carthage. He rebutted his wife's idea with a raised voice, "We couldn't leave him out here. He could get himself lynched or robbed. Besides, this is America. New York is a ghetto. This is where the future is. This is where we can become real Americans."

"Oh, Abe. Be quiet or you'll wake Sheldon," Shirley retorted. "I don't know where he gets his ideas. He's a Bronx guy, too. He took me out of the Bronx, but he can't take the Bronx out of me."

Al smiled and shook his head in agreement. He was too road-weary to get in the middle of any family squabbles tonight.

By sunrise, Al waved good-bye to Abe and Shirley. He smiled at Shirley and told them that he hoped to see them in the Bronx or in Texas someday.

By the time Al walked into the Lamar Hotel in Houston, he was extremely hungry. He stopped in the coffee shop where he fortified himself with a glass of milk and a vanilla iced donut. Every few minutes he checked his watch, waiting for 8 A.M to call Mary. It had taken Al only two and a half days to hitchhike from New York to Houston, Texas.

CHAPTER 14

At exactly 8:00 A.M., Al called Mary's house from the hotel's phone booth.
"Hello, is Mary there?" he asked the female voice who answered.
"This is Mary. Is that you, Al? Where are you?" Mary asked with growing excitement.
"In the lobby of the Lamar Hotel on Main Street."
"You got here so quick! How did you do that?"
"I've been traveling night and day."
"Just stay where you are. I'll be there in twenty minutes!"
In less than ten minutes, Mary drove up in her father's black Chevrolet. Al looked in the car and saw Mary's beautiful face beaming with a broad welcoming smile. She wore a dark green satin dress. She got out of the car and ran into Al's arms.
They kissed on the sidewalk, but, as Al tried to hold her closer, she wiggled out of his arms and laughed. "Save that for later. It's Sunday morning. I made confession yesterday and I'm going to take Communion at ten o'clock Mass. Please don't put any unholy thoughts in my mind. Certainly, not until after Mass and I receive Holy Communion."
"You're going to church this morning? I just got here," Al exclaimed in an exhausted voice.
"Especially this morning, silly. I have so much to be thankful for. I want to thank God that you're here!" Mary's logic was to thank God immediately for Al's safe return to Texas.
"What should I do while you're in church?"
"I want you to come with me. You might even like it. Don't be afraid." Mary tugged at Al to get him to move.
Al wasn't afraid. He was overwhelmed with the joy of being beside this exuberant, beautiful girl who seemed happy just with his presence, no matter how tired he looked after all the days hitchhiking and having had no shower. In an

Robert Miller

easygoing way, Mary was determined to take care of God first and show Al how to do the same.

Al let himself get lost in enjoying her company and excitement. He had never met someone who showed such enthusiasm for both him and her religion. In the church, sitting next to her, he watched as Mary Jean dropped to her knees at the pew and prayed. Al marveled at how lovely and pious she seemed. After a few minutes, she rose and, seated herself next to him. She seemed to brighten the entire church with her smile.

On the way home, Mary stopped at a drugstore where she knew there was a phone booth. Al's mother had called Mary several times already, worried that she hadn't heard from him. Al called the operator and asked to make a collect call to New York City. He was surprised how fast the call went through. This was his first long distance phone call. Al made the call brief, but reassured his mother that everything was fine.

"You didn't tell me that my mother also spoke to your mother," Al said hesitantly, hanging up the phone.

"I forgot that. But they got along fine. Two worried mothers," Mary Jean smiled with a shrug of one delicate shoulder.

"What's your mother worried about?"

"She worries about me. About what kind of boy I invited to spend Christmas with us. About how you'll have to sleep in the dining room in our apartment."

"Does she worry about me because I'm Jewish?"

Mary began to giggle. "I told them you weren't Catholic. But, I haven't told them yet that you're Jewish. It didn't come up. I didn't think it was important." Mary took hold of Al's hand and pulled him out of the phone booth back out to the car. "Let's go over to Hermann Park. We can walk through the gardens."

Al smiled. Any other questions about worried mothers vanished from his tired mind with Mary's innocent smile.

After church, Mary and Al toured the gardens at Hermann Park. When they sat on the bench, Al sat tightly against her. Now that they were together again, Al could not wait to savor her sweet aroma and kisses. He pulled her closer. She let him kiss her, but pulled back.

"Now, be good. I know a lot of people in Houston. I'm not going to let you spoil my reputation like you did at the Dallas railroad station," Mary teased. "Just close your eyes. Hold my hand. Take a little nap. I'll be right here. I can't tell you enough how happy I am that you're here. I want my parents to love you. Just relax."

Al complied with a smile and gently nudged his head at just the right spot on Mary's soft shoulder. Al's brain was already dulled by exhaustion. No more thinking. No more worrying about the parents. No more worrying about being Jewish. Nothing mattered, except the feel and smell of Mary Jean Monahan.

CHAPTER 15

After a brief rest in Hermann Park, Mary and Al walked through a narrow apartment hallway into the living room where Bill Monahan, Mary's father, sat reading the Sunday newspaper. He was a short trim man with rimless glasses that gave him a distinguished look. Seeing them approach, Mr. Monahan immediately put aside his newspaper, stood up and displayed a genuine, personal warmth. He greeted Mary with a kiss and shook hands with Al.

"You're the sportswriter who wrote such nice things about Mary when she was acting silly and making a spectacle of herself cheering for the wrong team. You made some impression on my daughter. Welcome to Texas. It's nice to meet you," Mr. Monahan said, welcoming Al.

Al thanked Mr. Monahan for his hospitality as Mary steered him toward the kitchen. Mary introduced Al to her mother, who flitted from one spot to another in the kitchen, while preparing lunch. Mrs. Opal Mae Monahan was a short, matronly woman, about forty, similar to his own mother. There was a dark hue to her skin, high cheek bones and a somewhat hooked nose that seemed to reflect her Indian ancestry. Her eyes were almost a neutral gray. She smiled at Al, wiped her hand on a dishtowel, and extended it to him.

"We've heard so much about you, Al. Mary Jean seems quite taken with you. She's talked of nothing else since she came home from Denton. We're delighted to meet you and to have you here with us. Did you call your mother? She seemed so worried about you." Mrs. Monahan's friendliness seemed tempered by caution, wondering why this young man came all the way from New York City to visit her daughter.

"Yes, I did call her. Thank you very much."

She turned to Mary and said hurriedly, "Dinner is almost ready. Your Aunt Cora is coming. She should have been here by now. We'll sit down as soon as she arrives."

Mary nodded in agreement. She took Al's hand and led him out of the kitchen.

"I love my Aunt Cora," Mary spoke softly. "She's my mother's youngest sister, closer to my age than my mother's. But she's high-strung and outrageous. I really didn't want you to meet her so soon, but there's nothing we can do about that now, is there?"

Al got the impression that Mrs. Monahan had sent for some reinforcements, namely her sister, to get another person's assessment of this Al Gordon from New York City. Al and Mary sat waiting impatiently in the living room and tried listening to Mr. Monahan talk about things he had read in the Sunday paper. As Al looked around, he felt comfortable in this five-room street level apartment, which reminded him of similar homes in the Bronx, except for the stuccoed exterior.

There was a bustle at the door as Mr. Monahan opened it for a package-laden Aunt Cora and her husband, Nick Scalia, whose darker complexion revealed his southern Italian heritage. He was tall, burly man, with thick black hair and dark eyes set in a thin face, and a developing middle-age spread around the center of his body.

Cora appeared to be about thirty, and seemed in many ways to be halfway between her sister, Opal, and her niece, Mary, in size, color, and demeanor. Her eyes were bluer than Opal's, but not as blue as Mary's. Facially, she resembled her sister, though her skin was lighter. Cora greeted Bill and Mary with a flash of her exuberant, flighty personality and then turned determinedly to Al.

"You must be that New York boy who Mary invited down. We've been hearing nothing but how you met her at a football game, and wrote an article about her, and how she's fallen for you hook, line, and sinker," Cora said in a straightforward manner. With that, Cora grasped Al's hand and leaned over to kiss him, not quite kissing, but putting her cheek against his and smacking her lips. She introduced Al to her husband, Nick, who stood quietly, letting Cora do all the talking.

Cora looked Al over carefully. "Lord, New York must be an exciting place to live. But, I couldn't stand to live in a place where the nigras can sit down right next to white people on the buses and trains and where there are so many Jews and Italians. Nick has lots of relatives in New York and New Jersey, but we don't ever see or hear from them. How do you like Texas?" Cora's talking gushed out like a fountain of nervous energy. She waited anxiously for Al's response.

"I love being where Mary Jean is. I'm happy to be here. But I don't have any problems in New York either. Some of my good friends are Italian. And my parents and sister are all Jewish."

There was a hush in the room. It was frightening for Mary, not sure how to predict anyone's reaction to the absolute truth Mary was in love with a Jewish boy. Mary squeezed Al's hand and smiled up at him.

Clash of Cultures - The Al Gordon Story

"I certainly didn't mean any offense," Cora replied. "Nick is Italian and I work for Jews. The Jews and Italians here are all Texans. But, from what I hear, the Jews and Italians in New York are all foreigners." Cora had a knack for antagonizing. Whether she said everything from a subtle bigotry or sheer stupidity, Al was not entirely sure.

"I hope I don't look like a foreigner to you, Aunt Cora. I was born in this country and so was my father. Certainly, both of my parents are citizens. Maybe I'm a Yankee in your eyes, but I'm as much an American as anyone," Al added confidently.

Mr. Monahan twitched in discomfort. He hollered out to Opal, "Is dinner ready?"

Al lingered in the living room with Mr. Monahan and Nick as Mary and Aunt Cora disappeared behind the closed kitchen door. The few minutes of silence dragged on before the door opened and Mary emerged. She took Al's hand to lead him away, saying, "Al, can I talk to you privately for a minute?"

In her parents' bedroom, Mary kissed Al on the lips and smiled. "Al, it's my fault. I never told my mother that you are Jewish. She made a pork roast and now she's worried that you won't eat it. She's also mad at Cora for what she said. Do you think we're all crazy?" Mary Jean gave Al a bewildered look for what had happened in the past ten minutes.

"I've eaten ham and I've eaten bacon. I ate pork at Texas A&M. I'll try your mother's pork roast," Al reassured. "Did I do the wrong thing to tell Cora I'm Jewish? I felt it had to be said."

"You did right. I should have told them first. Just kiss me one more time and let's go in and have lunch."

At the meal, Mr. Monahan said a brief grace, crossed himself and started cutting the pork roast. There was an awkward silence. If Mary's relatives appeared concerned that Al might be indulging in some spiritual lapse by eating the meat, Al did not. He was very hungry and had no desire to skip any part of this good meal. To him, God would want him to eat the food and the dessert. Mr. Monahan broke the silence by starting some trivial talk about baseball.

Al looked around the table. They were much like his own family, but there were small differences. These people were quieter. Instead of a loaf of rye bread in the center of the table, as Al was accustomed to, there were six slices of white bread. Instead of a few tomatoes and a head of lettuce cut in four quarters set in a bowl, there were individual salad plates. There was a big pitcher of iced tea and the water glasses sat empty.

One word explained the general mood of everyone at first: uncomfortable. With a seeming self-centeredness, Aunt Cora began talking about problems at her job behind the first floor perfume counter at Sakowitz's department store. Everyone listened without comment. Nick had not said a single word since being introduced to Al.

Under the table, Mary's hand reached over to Al's leg. She smiled at him, as if to commiserate with him for whatever discomfort the family's Sunday dinner might be causing him.

Aunt Cora went on about not understanding why Jews were so different from everyone else and why they didn't eat pork. Mr. Monahan glared at her and rebutted, "Maybe for the same reasons that Catholics don't eat meat on Fridays! You have to make allowances for different people's habits, laws and beliefs."

"Don't tell me about Catholics," Cora responded. "You Catholics are different, and the Italian Catholics are something else again. Nick agrees with me. He married me to get away from his mother and sisters and become one of us. Didn't you, Nick?"

Nick glared at his wife, then smiled at Al. "You have to forgive her. She doesn't know what she's talking about. If I could teach her to shut up once in a while, she'd be the perfect wife." He tried to warn Al that Cora gave her own opinions excessive significance. If Al could dismiss her opinions, nothing she said should bother him.

Al smiled at Nick, but wanted to avoid getting in the middle of any personal criticisms.

Aunt Cora went right on talking, barely pausing to breathe.

Al looked around the table and realized there was no central focus on what was happening. Everyone's thoughts were elsewhere.

The dessert of pecan pie was something Al had never tasted. Mr. Monahan accompanied the cutting of the pie with a brief speech on a proper pronunciation. "This is pecan pie, with the emphasis on the second syllable. In Ohio, when I was a boy, we called it 'pee-can' pie and emphasized the 'pee'. Nobody likes peecan pie, but pecan pie, if you emphasize the 'can', is very good. And my wife's pecan pie is the best in the world."

Eyes rolled at his humorous comments.

"Daddy says that every time we have pecan pie, which is pretty near every other Sunday," Mary warned Al.

When the desserts were finished, Mary eventually guided Al through the process of saying good-bye to everyone on the pretext of showing him some more of Houston before it got dark. Mr. Monahan handed Al his keys to the Chevrolet.

CHAPTER 16

Outside the house, Al handed the keys to Mary with the reminder that he still did not know how to drive. Mary asked Al where he wanted to go.

"Somewhere where I can take you in my arms and we can do some serious kissing," Al replied.

Mary drove her father's Chevrolet back to Hermann Park. As soon as the ignition was turned off, she slid closer to Al. Their kiss seemed thrilling, almost magical, as her lips opened and their tongues touched. Al heard her moan softly. She moved her head back.

"What's the matter?" Al wondered.

"Let me catch my breath. I'm a good Catholic girl. When you kissed me at the Dallas railroad station that day, it sent shivers through my body. I discussed it with some of the girls at college. College was a new experience for me." Mary looked down somewhat embarrassed. She hesitated and went on. "Once, I sat in the front seat of a car with a date when one of my roommates, a girl I really liked and respected, went all the way with her date in the back seat. Can you imagine what that did to my mind and sensitivities?"

Al listened quietly, aware of Mary's new honesty. She, too, was talking about life, sex and experiences that Al didn't think he and Selma had ever put into words back in the Bronx.

"The girls at college told me to loosen up. And the awful thing is that I tried. Two weeks ago, I was out on a double date. I let him kiss me, so I decided to experiment a little. I opened my mouth to let him French kiss me to see if he'd make me feel the way you made me feel. The truth is it disgusted me. I began to push him away from me."

Al was relieved to hear that. There could have been another Howard Peskin.

Mary went on. "I must tell you. I began to worry I would never, ever again feel the way I felt when you kissed me. Until just now. I like kissing you so much that it frightens me. Al, you're going to be here almost ten days and we're going to have to set some ground rules. We're going to have to promise each other a thing or two and keep our promises."

"What is it you want to promise?"

Mary Jean took both of his hands in hers.

"Allie, I don't want you to take advantage of my weakness. When you go home, I want to still be a virgin. My panties stay on and what they cover is off-limits. Is that fair?"

"Is there room for negotiation?" Al asked with a slight grin.

Mary Jean smiled back, but shook her head firmly to say no.

"I agree." Al recognized her strength and determination to keep everything well-ordered.

"I've been practicing that speech for two weeks, and I didn't say it the way I intended." She giggled momentarily before her face turned serious. "I hope you're not mad about my kissing John Ed Dickerson two weeks ago, but I had to find out whether it was soul kissing that I liked or kissing you."

"And?" Al wondered.

"I love kissing you. Your kisses turn me to jelly. And it's because I love you. Did I ever tell you that before? I want to spend the rest of my life telling you how much I love you."

Al started to open the top two buttons of her dress.

"Do you think that anything I just said gives you license to undress me, Al Gordon?"

"Only up to a certain point," he answered, and both of them started laughing.

"Let's hold the thought. I can't let you undress me in broad daylight here in Hermann Park. Let's drive around and talk." Mary moved back, leaving the buttons undone. She started the car with a glance to Al and drove off. She headed for the San Jacinto battlefield, where according to Texas history, the legendary Sam Houston routed the Mexican Army of Santa Anna almost a hundred years earlier.

By 6 P.M., it was too dark to inspect the battlefield. Al had fallen fast asleep on Mary's shoulder while Mary relaxed in the car. An hour later, Mary moved to position herself to drive back home.

"Where are we?" Al asked, squinting his eyes, stirring awake.

"On our way home," Mary said happily.

"What have you been thinking about?" Al asked casually.

"Those evil kisses of yours that turn me upside down and wear away my natural shyness and virtue," Mary Jean said with a mixture of truth and teasing.

One word caused Al to laugh. "I don't doubt your virtue, but I don't think of you as a shy person. Not a girl who'd jump out of the stands to lead 20,000 Texans in cheers for a forlorn New York football team."

"I am shy. I never did a thing like that before," Mary defended herself. "I've thought about that lots these past six weeks. Maybe God told me that you were in the press box and that leading those cheers was the way destiny intended us to meet."

Al reached over and kissed her as she drove.

She moaned and pulled back. "Maybe it wasn't God. Maybe it was the Devil." Mary Jean gave him her gorgeous smile.

Mary Jean decided to stop for hamburgers and sodas at Prince's Drive-in before they got home. Mary enjoyed her hamburger spiced with Texas chili while Al enjoyed his plain.

They sat there talking over plans for the next few days. Al said he wanted to visit the newspapers to see if there was a summer job available. Mary promised to drive him around and added how she had some Christmas shopping to do.

Christmas, oh, no. That means presents. I haven't even thought about gifts, Al thought and began to feel edgy.

Mary paid the carhop. She turned to Al, "It's time to get a bed made up for you in the dining room so you can get some sleep. Will you be all right?" Mary asked. When Al tried to get closer, Mary waved a finger to say 'no.' "More later. Let's go home and be polite to my parents."

Mary Jean smiled at the man she loved and started the car. Al could only imagine what else awaited him with this gentile family, but he felt at ease in the shelter of Mary's enthusiastic love.

Robert Miller

CHAPTER 17

Al and Mary returned around 10 P.M. to the ordinariness of the Monahan living room. Bill Monahan sat in the same puffy chair reading the Sunday paper with the finished sections of the paper spread out on the floor nearby. Mrs. Monahan turned off the radio and put aside her knitting.

"Please have a seat," Opal Mae said, inviting Al and Mary to relax. "We were starting to get worried."

"We sat in the car and then took a walk around the neighborhood. It's such a lovely night," Mary said self-consciously.

"I'm afraid it was a mistake to have my sister here for Sunday dinner. Cora talks so much. But, she's my baby sister. What can I do? It really spoiled our chance to get to know you. You do understand that we want to know all about the young man who seems to have swept our daughter off her feet," Mrs. Monahan said, trying to be pleasant, but a tinge of concern showed through.

Al nodded and replied, "I'm not exactly sure I swept Mary off her feet. I think it was the other way around. She captivated me as soon as I laid eyes on her."

"It sounds so romantic," Mrs. Monahan responded. She took a breath to continue. "Well, we are concerned. Mary Jean is seventeen years old. She has three and a half more years of college in front of her. You and Mary are from different parts of the country. You have different religions. We want you to be friends, but...you are are far too young to really consider a serious relationship."

Al looked intently at Mrs. Monahan, over to Mary Jean and then to Mr. Monahan. "I agree with everything Mrs. Monahan said. I'm eighteen years old and have few prospects. I understand your doubts and fears. I don't know what to tell you. I love your daughter. I want only the best for her. I want to look for a summer job while I'm here and then go back to NYU. I hope to graduate in three years."

"Tell us about your parents," Mrs. Monahan suggested.

54

Clash of Cultures - The Al Gordon Story

Al tensed slightly in preparation for the questions to come. He told the story about his parents having their own small advertising business in New York City. He talked about his goals of becoming sports editor at the NYU newspaper and then chief editor in his senior year. His parents had two children, him and his fifteen-year-old sister, Shirley. His mother was born in Russia and came here as a small child. She had gone to school here.

"Mother," Mary Jean interrupted anxiously. "Al hasn't slept in two nights. He's very tired. He doesn't need this interrogation."

"Interrogation indeed?" Mrs. Monahan laughed. "Al, I'm sorry if it seems like an interrogation. We're trying to get to know you and our daughter better." Mrs. Monahan gave her daughter a stern look. The unasked questions that still remained must have included why Mary Jean had fallen in love with a Jewish boy? Why couldn't she find a good Catholic boy as a boy friend?

Mary Jean reminded her mother that when she had met daddy, she immediately knew they were going to get married. Opal Mae cautioned Mary Jean to give herself time. Leaving some things unsaid, Mrs. Monahan moved to get things set up so Al could have a bed. As she moved chairs to make room, Mrs. Monahan tried making lighthearted talk by asking Al to help select the Christmas tree and hoping everyone would have a wonderful week together.

Al finally settled into bed for the night. He fell into a deep sleep, too deep to even be bothered with dreaming. In his sleep, Al sensed something. He woke in the dark and felt a finger on his mouth. He became aware of a form squeezing up against him on the sofa that had become his bed for the night.

"Be very quiet," Mary whispered in his ear. "I couldn't fall asleep knowing you were so close. I waited until I was sure my parents were asleep."

"What time is it?"

"Three thirty. Do I have to tell you to move over?"

Al moved over and Mary squeezed close to him.

"Don't forget the ground rules still apply." She kissed him with an open mouth. Soon her arms pulled out of the shoulder straps of her gown and Al had his hands on her firm breasts. Mary ran her hands all over Al. They held each other and thrust themselves against each other. Suddenly Al felt the pulsation of an immediate and premature ejaculation.

Mary apologized saying that she had become excited too and had lost control. She warned Al, "I'm going to have to get a washcloth and clean us up." She whispered with more anxiety, "They're going to hear you breathing. You're breathing so hard!" These were the last words Al remembered before falling asleep.

CHAPTER 18

Al woke to the sounds of Mary and Mrs. Monahan in the kitchen. The smell of breakfast cooking prompted him to get up and get dressed.

"Welcome back to the world, sleepy head," Mary said as she rose from the table and greeted him. "We're trying to plan our day, so you can visit the newspapers. Would you like some coffee? The bacon and eggs will be ready in a minute."

Later that morning, Al took his clippings to the sports editor at the *Houston Chronicle* building. He found out in a brusque way that there were no openings; none were expected, and summer help was never hired. He left and went on to the other Houston papers.

Five minutes later and across Main Street was the *Houston Post*. The Sports Editor there was somewhat more cordial. He looked at Al's clippings, asked him what he was doing in Houston, told him that there were a dozen applications for every opening. There was no chance of a summer job. He suggested that, if Al settled in Houston after graduation, that he'd talk to him then and accept an application. Al left discouraged, but was warmed by Mary's smile as he got into the car.

"Let's try the Press," she suggested. "It's not far away."

The sports editor at the *Houston Press* was impressed with the young man who had came all the way down from New York. He ended up introducing Al to Bill Wannamaker, the City Editor. Wannamaker was tall and broad with light brown hair and an almost blond mustache. Though a neat man in a suit, in the office, he wore his tie loose, his coat off, and his sleeves rolled up. He appeared the personification of the hard-driving city editor, but with a pleasant personality.

"I wish I had something for you. I can see that you're going to be a real newspaper man. We haven't hired anyone in years," Mr. Wannamaker said with regret.

Clash of Cultures - The Al Gordon Story

As Al got up to leave and they shook hands, Mr. Wannamaker said, "Just wait a minute. I've got an idea that might work for you this summer. We've got a former columnist who puts out a weekly publication in Galveston. The Hi-Lites of Galveston. She's an odd duck, but she might need someone to help her. Her name's Sally Hargrove. She's a crotchety old gal. You can tell her I recommend you. I'll get you her phone number."

Mary became excited when Al returned to her in the car and told her about the lead. She decided she would start to teach Al to drive right away, so he could drive around in Galveston.

Dinner that night was more relaxed with just the four of them. Having taken one of the four slices of bread, Al felt embarrassed when he found himself pushing the hard butter clean through the soft bread and spreading lumps of bread on the tablecloth. He explained apologetically to Mrs. Monahan that he was used to firmer, hard-crusted rye bread. Mr. Monahan asked if he'd ever eaten this white bread. Al explained he never had, though he liked the taste. He would have to learn how to butter the bread, just as he would have to learn to drive. Everyone enjoyed a laugh at some of the innocent things Al still had to learn.

Mary turned to the subject of Al's good luck in getting a lead for a summer job with Sally Hargrove. Al, she explained, had called and set up an interview with her for tomorrow.

Mr. Monahan laughed. "I don't personally know the lady, if she is a lady. Her columns in the Chronicle were scandalous and she was run out of town years ago. She was an intolerant biddy. I always thought she was a Ku Kluxer."

Adding comments like a running footnote to the conversation, Mary reacted by telling Al that her father called anyone he didn't like and who didn't agree with him a Ku Kluxer.

Mr. Monahan sternly admonished his daughter that she'd be foolish to ignore the fact that there were Ku Kluxers and others in Texas and all over the South who didn't like Catholics.

Al asked Mr. Monahan if he was against intolerance toward Catholics, was he against intolerance toward Negroes and Jews?

"Yes, I'm against intolerance, but that doesn't mean I'm against segregation. One has nothing to do with the other. There are many colored people that I like and respect, but, here in Texas, they don't go to school with us and they don't sit next to us on the buses. That's not intolerance. It's segregation. That's different." Everything sounded so clean, simple and orderly, but Al failed to see how the social blight that segregation left on people hindered the fulfillment of any society where it existed.

"If someone proposed that Catholics have their own schools and separate seats on buses, wouldn't you call them Ku Kluxers?" Al asked.

"Probably," Mr. Monahan said. "But we have our own Catholic schools, which are not supported by the state." He poked his fork in the air to emphasize his point proudly. "We pay school taxes to support their schools, but the Texas school system won't provide a single book to us. Do you think that's fair?"

"No, Mr. Monahan. I'm against intolerance. Intolerance toward Negroes, Catholics, Jews or any group is abhorrent to me and should not be encouraged in any form. Segregation is surely a form of intolerance."

The discussion could have turned heated as both the younger and older man tried to weigh into each other with his points. Mary interrupted by stating strongly that she hoped this table discussion would not turn into an argument. She wisely warned them she would not permit an argument to get started between two men she loved very much.

Bill Monahan laughed. "We're not arguing. We're having a discussion. I think tolerance means that people can disagree about something and still be able to talk about it. I like having another man around this house. I don't agree with everything you say, Al, but I like hearing what you say and enjoy having you here with us." Mr. Monahan paused for another thought, adding with a twinkle and a raised eyebrow, "Of course, I admit I'm a little uncomfortable hearing my daughter talk about two men she loves, which puts a boy like you, who has known her for six weeks, in the same class as the father who changed her diapers and has loved and supported her for seventeen years."

Mary again came to the rescue by bringing up the Christmas tree. Mr. Monahan took the new subject as an opportunity to give explicit instructions on what kind of tree to buy. There was one thing he could have control over and that was the tree. It was to be his blessed radiant tree, whether or not anyone else enjoyed it.

As Mary and Al finished their desserts and got up to help clear the table, Al acted a gentleman and thanked Mrs. Monahan for a fine dinner.

She smiled and explained, "Thank you, Al, for clearing the table. I'd like to be more comfortable with you, but I'm not there yet. We'll have to be a little patient with each other."

In the kitchen, Mary grabbed hold of Al's hand and squeezed it. "I think mother is trying to say that she hopes you don't get the job in Galveston and don't come back here this summer. Remember, she doesn't speak for her daughter. I want you to get the job and I want you to be here. I don't even want you to ever go back to New York. What do you think of that?"

Al gave Mary a kiss and started to fondle her. Mary pulled back and whispered, "Al, please. Not now. Move away. I have to readjust my clothes."

Al moved away with a mischievous grin.

The next day Mary drove Al to meet the infamous Sally Hargrove. She had arranged to meet him at the post office when she picked up her mail around 7 A.M.. With no formal office, she used the post office and the local cafeteria as her "office." After waiting about ten minutes, Al spotted a tall, gray-haired lady walking up to the post office. She looked between fifty and sixty, and had the purposeful plodding walk of a man. She carried her ubiquitous umbrella, along with a tote bag, a large pocketbook, and about three newspapers.

"Are you Mr. Gordon?" she asked when she approached Al.

"Yes, I am, Mrs. Hargrove. It's nice to meet you."

"Miss Hargrove."

"I'm sorry, Miss Hargrove."

"Young man, why do you think Bill Wannamaker suggested you call me?"

"I think he might have been impressed by some of my credentials. He didn't have a summer job to offer me, but he thought you might," Al said. He showed her copies of some of the stories he had written for the NYU Bulletin. If Miss Hargrove was impressed, she didn't show it.

"What makes you think a few stories about football qualify you to be a newspaperman?"

"I've covered more than football. I've covered all the other sports. Note the human interest item about Mary Monahan's leading cheers for NYU at the Texas A&M game. That's how Mary and I met."

"Opal Porter married a crude Irish Catholic pipeliner from the north and now their daughter is seeing a boy from New York, of all places."

Al remained silent and taken back by her attitude.

Sally Hargrove studied Al for a minute and then went on about the job in Galveston. It would require long hours and hard work six days a week, mostly getting ad renewals and collecting money. He would also have to report to her two or three nights a week back in Houston. The job would require little or no writing. He would earn ten dollars a week, plus bus tickets, but he would have to pay his own expenses. Miss Hargrove told Al she would let him know in early May, through the Monahans, if she would need him in the summer.

"You told me you were from New York, but you didn't mention that you were from the Bronx. Not that I blame you for not mentioning the Bronx," Miss Hargrove commented.

"Mary Monahan is waiting outside. Would you like to meet her?" Al asked politely, trying to be friendly.

"Why ever would I?" Miss Hargrove snarled. These were her last words and she left as abruptly as she had come.

Imaginary images of witches crossed Al's mind as he stood there stunned by the interview. Her cold, blunt, and heartless approach dismissed any idea of the spirit of "Southern hospitality" he had felt in others. He concluded the job could still be okay because a job was something precious in these times and he would not have to see her everyday.

While driving to get the Christmas tree, Mary worried about what it would be like working for a person like Miss Hargrove. Al had some trepidations, but he

Robert Miller

wanted to forget Miss Hargrove. He calmed Mary simply by reminding her the offer was only a "maybe" and that there was obviously no possible decision until May.

Mary turned to the lighter subject of picking out a Christmas tree. "I wanted you to come with me to pick out the tree and now I feel guilty about depriving my father of the pleasure he gets from doing that. He loves the Christmas season. We all do."

CHAPTER 19

That night, Mr. Monahan had to inspect the Christmas tree very carefully before it would be decorated. Al had dragged the tree into the living room. Mr. Monahan set up the tree in its stand, while Mrs. Monahan brought out the boxes of ornaments. Mr. Monahan conducted the orderly tradition of decorating, giving instructions on the proper placement of the red, silver and gold balls, tinsel and small angels. On the very top of the tree, a white satin and cotton angel sat, representing the angel who centuries ago brought the good news to the Virgin Mary that she would conceive a child, whose name would be Jesus. While the decorating progressed, Al explained his meeting with Miss Hargrove. Al noticed that the decorating of the tree seemed to give a tranquil mood to the senior Monahans. Mr. Monahan gave an admiring look at the Christmas tree. The decorations would actually culminate at the bottom of the tree where he would place the manger scene with the three Wise Men, Joseph, Mary, and the animals looking on the baby Jesus. Mr. Monahan admired his Christmas creation as though he had built a shrine in his living room. The Monahans looked adoringly at the glowing red and green lights on the Christmas tree. They seemed strongly spiritually bonded as they enjoyed the whole concept of Christmas in the living room.

Mary and Al moved into the kitchen to work on some refreshments. "It's his tree," Mary said, further explaining her father. "Christmas turns him into a little boy." Mary tried to explain to Al how to understand this Catholic family.

"And don't forget what happens under the mistletoe," Al added playfully, with his thoughts eagerly turning to the Monahans' beautiful daughter.

"Mistletoe has nothing to do with the Church," Mary retorted.

Al reached over to grab her.

"Not here! Not now! We have to act respectfully with my parents around," Mary said, wriggling away anxiously. "The good news is that my mother has a bridge game tomorrow afternoon and we'll have the house to ourselves for a few

Robert Miller

hours. Meanwhile, can you possibly keep your sweet hands off of me?" She blinked her eyes.

Was she enticing or rebuffing? Al got both messages and laughed along with her.

CHAPTER 20

The next morning Mary and Al spent time running around to different stores doing Christmas shopping after catching a bus into downtown Houston. At lunchtime, they met Mary's best friend from high school, Marjorie Leahy. The three of them ate lunch at Kelly's restaurant around the corner from the *Houston Chronicle*. Mary proudly displayed Al to Marjorie, who was pleasant enough, but Al thought her continual references to high school, the nuns, church, and related Catholic-oriented items were some kind of an implied, though unexpressed criticism. Al was learning to tune into messages being directed to Mary about her and Al's "differences."

Although Marjorie had offered to drive them home, Mary courteously declined the offer. Afterwards, Mary explained to Al that she did not want Marjorie to feel like she should stay and chaperon them until mother got home.

When they got back home, Mary put the packages down, excused herself and returned to the living room with her lipstick entirely removed. She wore a long-sleeved green dress with a high neck and buttons down the back.

Al sat on a corner of the sofa. Mary sat down very close to him and brought her face to his, initiating a kiss. Her mouth came open and their tongues touched, increasing their heat for each other. Al moved his hands to caress her breasts.

"I want this to be our perfect time together. We have at least two hours before my father gets home," Mary whispered. "Don't rush things. Just hold me. Hold me close. I'm so happy to be with you like this. I love you so much."

Without waiting too long, they began slowly unbuttoning each other's buttons. Al struggled longer with the smaller buttons on the back of Mary's dress.

"Let's go into the bedroom. But, please, Al, don't forget the ground rules."

Al kicked off his shoes, stepped out of his pants and followed Mary into the bedroom. Mary looked back at him and began to laugh. "You'd better bring your trousers and shoes with you." When Al returned and put his things down,

Mary gave him a come-to-me stare and removed her dress, lifting it over her head. She stood there before him in her slip.

Al, wearing only his socks, undershorts, and shirt, enfolded her into his arms, kissed her and moved his head back to ask, "Will you take off your slip? I want to see you naked."

"I won't take off my panties," she answered. "Remember your promise. I expect you to keep it."

Al entered absolute ecstasy as he gazed at Mary's breasts for the first time. She told him to lie back on the bed and she lay on top of him. Her legs were tight around his aroused penis. She apparently wanted to experiment with this position after another college girl at TCSW told her it would not harm her virginity. The sight of her half-naked and her slight movements were too much for Al. He gushed into orgasm.

After a few minutes of relaxing together, Mary suggested they take a shower. Al asked her to join him. She agreed, but reminded him that she would still be wearing her panties. "I'm still a virgin Catholic girl, no matter how close I try to get to you."

The warm shower water refreshed Al as he waited for Mary. After a few minutes, she joined him, clad in a bathing cap and panties. As the panties got wet, they became transparent. They gleefully soaped each other. Mary screamed with delight as she soaped Al's limp penis and watched it begin to rise in her hands.

After they dried off, Mary warned, "I think it best we're not here when my parents get home."

Al dutifully followed Mary as they exited the apartment thirty minutes later to walk toward Bissonette Street.

CHAPTER 21

Along the walk, Mary suggested they go to a movie. Her pace quickened which made Al ask if anything was wrong.

"Yes, Al," Mary replied somberly. "Something is wrong. I'm ashamed, embarrassed, and a little frightened. Mind you, I blame myself more than I blame you. Nothing happened today that I didn't expect to happen during your visit, but I really didn't expect things like this to happen so fast. I'm thoroughly ashamed of myself. I'm afraid of what you'll think of me. And I'm afraid God will punish me for my wantonness."

"Do you think I should leave for home now?"

"No, that's definitely not what I want," Mary stressed. "But," she hesitated, then pushed ahead. "If I lost my virginity I'd lose whatever self-respect I still have. Can you understand?"

Al thought about her expectations of herself. He knew she made what to her were very meaningful promises to herself and to God. God was very real in her life as was her despair that she might have failed Him somehow. "Of course, I understand," Al reassured her. "But, I'm also confused. Thirty minutes ago you made me deliriously happy, so it hurts me to see you so unhappy."

Mary slowed her pace, grabbed Al's hand and held it close to her body. "That's the trouble, Al. I don't know what I want from you. I love you very much. Your hands and body thrill me. But that frightens me. Maybe you'll just have to keep your hands off me for a while."

Al shrugged his shoulders and nodded his agreement. He had heard things like this before from Selma, too, although he had never had any orgasms with Selma. Mary seemed more like a furnace of hormones burning for him.

At the corner of Bissonet and West Alabama, Al saw a sign advertising "Texas Red Hot Coney Island Franks." That sounded like a friendly back-home taste of Brooklyn that could relax both of their jangled nerves. Al asked if she would like to check out the Coney Island frank.

"Why not?" Mary said eagerly.

They ordered two hot dogs, along with a Coke and a Dr. Pepper. After two bites, Al expressed disappointment with the flavor of his Coney Island red-hot frank, which tasted nothing like the kosher beef hot dogs he had bought so often at Nathan's at the real Coney Island.

Mary laughed at Al's disapproving expression. "Poor Al," she said consoling. "You came all the way to Texas to make me so happy and what am I doing? Criticizing you for doing some of the very things that have made me so happy and then thoughtlessly feeding you pork for Sunday dinner and again, just now. I forgot that frankfurters here are made of pork. Can you forgive me?"

Al laughed and, as a result, saw Mary's face light up again.

When they finished their franks, they were no longer interested in going to a movie just to pass time. They walked back home close together, slowly and in comfortable silence. This beautiful Christian girl now seemed more at ease with herself. Al imagined any final guilt would probably be removed somehow by her going to confession.

When they got home, Mr. Monahan offered to take everyone to dinner that night at The Plantation Restaurant. Al experimented with fried shrimp and southern style chicken, which he had never known in the Bronx.

Mr. Monahan seemed to enjoy having another man around, but Mrs. Monahan still remained defensive and aloof. When Mr. Monahan offered Al a beer, Al declined for two reasons. First, he didn't like beer. More importantly, Mrs. Monahan's face turned with glacial disapproval toward him and then with stark belligerence fixed on her husband who totally ignored the glare. Mrs. Monahan did not have to utter a word for Al to realize she was a fundamentalist teetotaler, so he graciously declined the offer.

"Maybe a nice Jewish boy like you would be better for Mary than an Irishman who loves his beer more than his home and family," Mrs. Monahan said sarcastically. "People tell me that, whatever is said about the Jews, they are family people who don't drink. I believe in sobriety."

"Jewish people drink wine on Friday nights and at Passover," Al tried to clarify. "Then again, most of the people I know like seltzer and soda more than beer and hard liquor."

This statement won an approving smile from Mrs. Monahan.

The next day and every day thereafter Mary took Al out in the car to practice his driving. Hour after hour he gained new confidence from these driving lessons. Al concluded his time in Texas was well spent in learning about life and people outside the Bronx and acquiring a new skill, even if it was one he'd rarely use back home.

Everyone seemed to have heard about this young man who had come over a thousand miles from New York City. People took an interest in meeting him, but tended to be reserved in their talk. One such direct encounter took place with

Mrs. Kelleher, the mother of one of Mary's friends. She was a tall woman with a wrinkled face, but her steel gray hair, piercing blue eyes and starchily straight back gave her a distinguishing look, much like a former school teacher.

Mrs. Kelleher bluntly told Al, "My daughter married a very nice Italian boy. I can't say we like it much, but at least there is the advantage that we all attend the same church." Al refused to be unnerved by the comment. Mrs. Kelleher went on in her opinionated best. "Of course, every Catholic family fears someone will marry a non-Catholic. Protestants are bad enough, but when it comes to Jews, well, I guess that some Catholics and some Jews have intermarried, but I doubt it ever happened in Texas."

Mary broke out with a laugh. "Mrs. Kelleher," she began, "Al and I are not thinking that far ahead just yet. He has two years of college to complete and I have three. Right now, we're enjoying the present, and I hope that is okay with you."

Mrs. Kelleher smiled. "Mary, you are a sweet and good Catholic girl and I have every confidence in your judgment."

"If that means you think it was wise of me to fall for Al Gordon, you're absolutely right. I fell in love with Al the minute he walked up to me at the football stadium, and I'll never love anyone else. Falling in love with him is the best thing I've ever done and I'm happier right now than I've ever been in my whole life, and you can tell that to anyone who is interested in my affairs," Mary affirmed strongly.

Al blushed and sat in silent wonderment at Mary's statement.

As Al practiced his driving on the way home, he finally had to ask Mary, "What was that conversation all about between you and Mrs. Kelleher?"

"Mrs. Kelleher was delivering a message from my mother and I gave her my answer. Mother will have heard what I said before we pull up at home. You can count on that."

Al drove on, quietly impressed by Mary's astuteness in picking up on the hidden messages circulating about him. He only wondered if these Christians were becoming frantic about losing one of their daughters to a Jewish boy from that strange country called the Bronx.

CHAPTER 22

Mrs. Monahan waited nervously until Mary and Al returned home from Al's latest driving lesson. She feigned innocence when asking about their dinner plans that evening. Mary explained that she and Al would have dinner out and then go on to babysit for the Johnsons, probably not arriving home until very late.

Mrs. Monahan's face expressed disapproval. "You'll be there alone?" she asked, knowing full well the answer and how much it bothered her.

"No, we won't. We'll have the baby with us," Mary answered. There was a long pause and Al could feel the weight of Mrs. Monahan's concern. Mary tried to soften it by adding, "And Marjorie said she might stop by. Does that make you feel better?"

Mrs. Monahan had waited for the right moment to lay out all her worries, even marginal ones, about this young couple's "love" and involvement with each other. She knew she had to be the iron chain holding down her daughter's happy-go-lucky feelings of her first real love.

"Mary Jean, do you resent my thinking about the propriety of the situation?" Mrs. Monahan turned to Al, and the very way she looked at him made his feet feel cold. "Please, Al, you're a nice polite young man and I really don't mean to offend either one of you, but I am the mother of a 17-year-old girl who has never been exposed to...," she paused a moment, then continued, "to difficulties in life, and I am terribly afraid for her...and for you too, Al. I really don't want either of you to get in over your heads. Should I apologize for that? I won't do it."

"It sounds to me as if there's a big 'but' coming," Al said softly with a pained look. His head turned slightly when he heard the bubbling sound of water boiling in a pot on the stove.

Mrs. Monahan remained focused on the pair, deliberately neglecting the pot, determined to go through with this conversation.

For the first time, Al saw the strong-willed similarity between mother and daughter.

"I'm afraid there is what you call 'a big but'," Mrs. Monahan replied. "In the first place, we're not ready to see our daughter fall seriously in love. She's too young and has too much school ahead of her to have her life complicated by anyone at this time. She should continue to play the field for at least two or three years before she settles on one boy. Even if you two were the same religion and had the same background, I'd be leery of either of you making permanent commitments at this time. You're both so young. You're too young. That's the nub of it." Mrs. Monahan frowned.

Al dropped his head, wondering what an appropriate response might be. Then he glanced up at Mrs. Monahan. Clearly, no response was necessary until she had finished spilling out her frustrations and worries, with a mother's straightforward honesty. The confrontation would not go away. Al knew he had to face whatever remained to be said and only hoped that Mrs. Monahan would not make this talk into a long diatribe. Oddly, both Mary's and Selma's mothers became strident when it came to protecting their daughters, but Al had never faced such a shockingly direct confrontation with Selma's parents because Selma had handled their relationship with restraint in front of her parents, never causing them alarm.

"You're of different backgrounds, from different parts of the country, with different religions. I'm afraid for you both. I look at you and I see how you can't keep your eyes off each other. I know how hard it is to keep your hands off each other. You're like two firecrackers ready to go off." Her eyes went back and forth watching them both, directing her words to both of them. "Don't look at me with such surprise, Mary Jean! It's there for all to see. In a few days, Al will be leaving and you're facing separation, heartbreak and unhappiness, and that's not what I want for my daughter." Her voice trembled.

Mary put her arm around her mother. "Mother, it may bother you that he's young, he's Jewish, he's far away, but it doesn't bother me. He's the man I love. I'm going to marry him and have his babies. Lots of them. But if you're worried about my chastity, you don't have to. Al is more of a gentleman than I'd like him to be. What do you think of that?" Too late, Mary realized the mistake she had made.

"I'm shocked to hear you say such a thing," her mother broke in, "but I'm happy to learn that Al has a sense of right and wrong, even if you don't. Mary Jean, are you deliberately trying to worry me more? I can't believe we are having this conversation in front of a young man you met only six weeks ago."

Al began to regain his composure. He turned to Mrs. Monahan and asked, "What do you want me to do? Do you want me to leave? If you do, I'll leave tonight."

Mrs. Monahan put her arm around Al. Her face turned wet with tears. Despite seventeen years spent carefully raising a beautiful daughter, she had still not prepared herself for the time when that daughter would be ready to fall in love.

"Al," Mrs. Monahan said, "maybe I'm beginning to see why Mary is so much in love with you. Yes, I might be more comfortable if you left, but, if you did, I don't think Mary would ever forgive either of us. All I ask is that you show respect for my daughter and know how much we love her and want to have faith in her. If Mary loves you, Al, then Bill and I will love you too. Let's enjoy our Christmas and then we'll all look forward to having you spend the summer with us."

Al instinctively put an arm around Mrs. Monahan's shoulder. She turned away only to step into Mary's arms. Al said nothing. He felt very alone as he watched mother and daughter hugging each other and crying. He understood that he was witnessing the steps mother and daughter had to go through in preparation for Mary's womanhood. Although he felt himself on the sidelines, he also recognized that this delicate transition included him and that if it were mishandled by any one of them, it would terrify him, and he would bolt right out the door.

Al's attention was distracted by Bill Monahan's quiet entrance.

Mr. Monahan brushed off his work trousers noisily to announce his arrival. Surveying the situation, he looked over at Al and asked half jokingly, "Who died?"

Mother and daughter began laughing. They went over and embraced the gawking Mr. Monahan who didn't know he had missed watching Mary stand her ground as a young woman.

"We've been having a mother-daughter heart-to-heart," Mrs. Monahan explained, with a smile while wiping away a tear. "And I'm afraid we frightened Al half to death. They are going out for the evening and leaving us to our own devices. Do you think we can find something to do to entertain ourselves until they come home?"

"I shouldn't be surprised," Mr. Monahan said, grinning. He winked at Al, as he headed for the bathroom to take his after-work shower.

Al finally managed a smile and sat down, trying to relax. His hands trembled. He knew there was nothing more to be said. No matter what the religion, he pondered, mothers were obligated to train their daughters about the "proper" balance between respectability and the realities of love.

In a few minutes, mother and daughter had finished discussing their plans. When Al got ready to leave with Mary, he found Mrs. Monahan more relaxed. She put the car keys in his hand, kissed him on the cheek, and admonished both of them to have fun. Her suddenly warm treatment surprised Al mostly because neither Selma's parents nor anyone else's had been this open towards him.

As he and Mary walked to the car hand in hand, Al mulled over what had happened.

Clash of Cultures - The Al Gordon Story

He drove slowly to the Johnson home. "Your mother is really something," Al said, with a glance at Mary. "First she makes me feel like a lowlife because she knows I want everything from her daughter, then she invites me to spend next summer here, kisses me and tells us to have fun." Al paused, then asked, "Are you sure your mother isn't Jewish? She looks a little Jewish and she sure knows how to turn a few happy hours we can spend together into a guilt trip."

"No, Al," Mary reassured, smiling. "She's not Jewish. She's a mother. Besides, Jews don't have a monopoly on guilt." She lowered her voice and asked, "Would you really have gone home tonight? I could have choked you when you made that offer. Here I am trying to figure out how I can cope with not having you with me until June, and you're ready to leave for home. Are you tired of me so soon?"

Al pulled the car to the curb and turned off the ignition. Slowly he took Mary into his arms.

"Just hold me close, Al. Hold me close. Don't kiss me. Don't touch me. Just hold me for a few minutes and I'll be all right," Mary said softly.

Al held her. Mary could not hold back her tears. They streamed down on his shirt as her shoulders shook and she rested her head on Al's chest. After a few minutes she regained her composure.

"Poor Al, maybe you should have headed directly home. I'll bet you had a life in New York. We've managed to complicate a bunch of lives here, haven't we?"

Mary raised her head and looked through the windshield. "Allie, start the car. We're going to be late."

The time spent at the Johnsons' home was more subdued than Al had wanted. For a long time, Mary had to hold the baby to keep it, and possibly herself, from crying. Al felt Mary had not completely thawed out from that conversation with her mother. The two of them spent a quiet night babysitting, listening to music on the radio, with no caressing or letting themselves go off like "firecrackers," as Mrs. Monahan had said.

When Al pulled the car to a stop in the Monahan's garage, Mary finally kissed him with passion. Her hands ran over his lap for just a moment. When he reached for her, she interrupted his attempt to kiss her. "Let's go in. I'll try to come to you tonight. Only this time, I'll bring a towel with me when I come." She giggled at her own double meaning with the word "come."

As soon as Al crawled into bed, he fell asleep imagining Mary's kisses, the touch and feel of her light body against his.

Al woke to find it was morning. Mary sat on the edge of the sofa fully dressed.

"You said you'd come back in the night," Al whispered as she leaned over and kissed him.

Robert Miller

She laughed aloud. "I did," she whispered back. "You were fast asleep. I kissed you and you didn't stir. So, I went back to bed." Then she went on in a normal voice, "Wake up, sleepyhead. Get dressed. Dad has already left for work and we're going to have breakfast in about five minutes."

Al felt momentarily confused by the time he got in the shower. What day is today? He finally remembered it was Saturday, December 22nd. He let out a sigh. He and Mary would not have much more time to themselves. Well, if I can't get to Mary any more, at least I can look Mrs. Monahan right in the eye at breakfast today with total innocence and she can read in my eyes that nothing happened to her virgin daughter, at least not yet.

CHAPTER 23

Al gripped the steering wheel with firm concentration as he drove Mary through the Christmas shopping traffic to the next store. He had managed to learn how to get Mrs. Monahan's Chevy under his control. Mary scurried in to buy the gifts — a carton of cigarettes for Uncle Glenn, a handkerchief for cousin LeRoy, and sundry gifts for others, each costing under a dollar.

By 1 P.M., Mary and Al arrived back home followed shortly by Mr. Monahan, who had left work early to start the holiday festivities.

"Merry Christmas!" Mr. Monahan said exuberantly, sounding like Santa Claus. "I'm through working till January third. Let's have some fun this afternoon!"

Mrs. Monahan looked him over closely and said in a reproving manner, "It appears to me you've been having fun already. I can smell the beer on you. Doesn't it embarrass you to come home half-drunk in front of your daughter and her young man?"

He laughed. "Lighten up, Opal! I had just one beer with the crew on the last working day before Christmas!"

"One beer my foot! Now you're going to sleep away the afternoon just when we have so much to do."

Mr. Monahan laughed and pinched her cheek. He slapped her bottom lightly and announced, "I'm not going to take a nap! I'm going to take a shower, get dressed and take you wherever you want to go! Mary and Al, too, if they want to come with us, though I imagine they'd be happier to stay here if we went out." He gave Al a wink.

Another grim look passed from Mrs. Monahan to her husband. "Of course they're coming with us. Nobody needs your remarks about what they might prefer to do."

Al wished he could hide both the embarrassment and disappointment he felt sure were revealed on his face.

Thirty minutes later, Bill Monahan, dressed in a fresh white shirt and muted striped tie, sat proudly behind the wheel of his Pontiac with Opal next to him, while Mary and Al wedged together in the back seat. Discussion centered on whether the family should go to confession that afternoon, allowing them, Mary explained to take communion at Sunday Mass. Mr. Monahan thought he might. Mrs. Monahan wasn't sure. Mary said she'd go to confession next week, after Al had left. Mrs. Monahan tilted her head but chose to say nothing this time. Al remained quiet, puzzling out what she must be thinking.

The first stop was St. Anne's Church where the elder Monahans decided to attend confession. Mary acquainted Al with the church and explained what the statues, the candles, the fount, and the poor box signified. Al was deeply struck with how much his Mary resembled many of the depictions of the Virgin Mary.

Mary, with a scarf covering her hair, became serene and pious in church. For a moment, Al thought back to the wild afternoon a few days before when she had taken a shower with him. He tried to come to terms with how this serious sedate young lady he accompanied in church could also be the alluring, loving young woman he had held, almost naked, in his arms. With that vivid memory in mind, he sensed an erection growing. Quickly, with puckered lips, he stared hard at a statue of yet another saint, hoping that would quiet down his excited hormones.

Al remembered hearing an explanation years before as to why Jewish women sat upstairs in an Orthodox synagogue. Someone said that though Jews were sexy people, they were supposed to keep their minds strictly on God and the Torah in the synagogue. But if a woman sat in front of a man in the synagogue, how could he help it if his thoughts wandered to that space and that sinuous form?

After the two Monahans emerged from the confessionals, Mr. Monahan drove them to dinner at a Mexican restaurant, where Al reacquainted himself with guacamole and chicken tacos that he had enjoyed at the A&M luncheon. Afterwards, all four went to a movie, but Mary and Al broke away to sit in the last seat of the balcony. The movie theater represented one more opportunity to be in semi-darkness and semi-privacy, where they could kiss, safely out of view of her watchful parents.

Once the movie finished, they stopped for after-the-movie sodas at an ice cream parlor and then toured the neighborhoods, enjoying the view from the car of Christmas lights twinkling on lawns, rooftops, and front doors of houses.

Al was awed by the sight of so many decorative lights, strung, he estimated, on three out of four houses. Innocently, he asked if the undecorated places were Jewish homes. Mr. Monahan roared with laughter at the idea.

"I doubt that there are many Jews in this part of town or any part of town," Mr. Monahan explained.

"The houses without lights," Mr. Monahan went on, "probably belong to people out of work, or those who can't afford the Christmas spirit." He paused to look at another house whose lawn was populated with glowing angels, Santa Claus and a nativity scene. "And, some people, Al, don't get around to decorating until Christmas Eve."

Al continued being fascinated by the different holiday displays.

When they arrived back home, Mary did not hesitate to put her own last-minute plans into action. She told her parents she and Al would go out again to Prince's drive-in for some sodas. Mrs. Monahan suggested they have sodas at home. Mary countered that she wanted Al to keep practicing how to drive so he could help drive them to Kosse to meet the relatives. After all, that was only two days away. Mr. Monahan gladly handed the keys to Al and, only after a glance at Opal, admonished Al not to keep Mary out too late.

In the car, Mary kissed Al quickly. "There'll be more of that later. Now, drive to Prince's. I'm dying for a soda and I know you're hungry. You didn't eat much of the Mexican food. I was watching."

"I tried to come to you last night," Mary continued. "Mother heard me walking around. I don't think she's been asleep since you got here." Mary giggled. Al smiled. "Such lovemaking as we're going to do between now and the end of your visit we'll have to do here in the car."

Al smiled again, but turned suddenly to keep the car on the road. That was the last thing he needed now — to have an accident and ruin the car.

The hamburger and Coke tasted good to Al, while Mary sipped her Dr. Pepper with satisfaction. When they finished, Mary suggested that they drive over to Hermann Park to look for a secluded spot. Once they found the right spot, they started kissing passionately. Al could not resist touching his Mary and moving his hands excitedly over her breasts.

At once Mary drew back. "Al," she said. "Go slow. Move over to this side of the car."

Al did as she asked. He watched, surprised, as she opened the buttons on her blouse and pulled it out of her skirt, then reached back to unsnap her brassiere and took it off. Al couldn't help staring with enjoyment at the naked contours of her delicate breasts. Then she moved toward him, leaned over to open the buttons on Al's fly, reached in and drew out his penis.

He let out a gasp and reached for Mary. She gently pushed him away, determined to do what she had already decided to do.

"Not just yet. Wait a second," she told him. She took a small towel out of her purse and wrapped it around Al's penis. She lifted her skirt high up and sat atop Al, firmly gripping his penis between her legs. They kissed with their tongues intertwining, slowly at first and then faster. Al's hand held her bottom and pulled her closer to him. He took turns kissing each breast and licking his tongue along her nipples. They could not stop their rhythmic movements to get closer.

Al gasped when his warm juices flowed into the towel held firmly between her legs. Mary reacted with a quiver.

"It thrills me to feel you come." She kissed him softly and backed away. "Now sit very still for a moment. I'm going to ease myself off you and try to keep us both dry."

"Stay where you are for a minute," Al pleaded softly. He got her to lean back. He ran his hands gently across her bare breasts. He pulled her close and put her left breast in his mouth. She gasped. He pulled her to the other side and put her right breast into his mouth and tasted her erect nipple.

"All right, lover boy," she said, with her teasing Texas drawl. She eased off him. "There'll be more of the same next summer, but we'll have to live on this memory until then." Mary had turned out to be so adventuresome and sexy. He knew she loved him and wanted to share all her love with him, but he couldn't help wondering how much of her experiment was drawn from lessons of her sophisticated college girlfriends.

When Al buried his head into the soft pillow back at the Monahans, he was already dreaming of Mary's movements atop him and the pleasures they had shared.

CHAPTER 24

Al felt he had barely been asleep when a fully dressed-for-church Mary awoke him. It was time to go to the morning Mass. Mary's piety now ruled.

At Mass, Al rose when everyone else did, but remained seated when the congregation knelt, which was often. His eyes were only on Mary, who once again seemed transformed in church into someone holy and virtuous as she alternately rose, sat and knelt. With her eyes sometimes closed and her face transfixed in prayer, she looked to Al like a fragile, holy, radiant beauty.

After Mass, Al found himself back at the Monahans home looking at the Christmas tree. With its green and red lights and silver, red and gold decorations, the tree dominated the living room. He reflected on how the number of presents under the tree kept growing. He wondered why he was feeling depressed while the Monahans were obviously having so much fun. Maybe some day I can get into the spirit of Christmas, he thought enviously. The difference in moods seemed to separate them, and that sense of separateness, too, began to weigh heavily on him. He became further depressed by his consuming love for Mary Monahan. He had never known anyone like her. On the one hand, she was an utterly free, almost uncensored sensuous spirit and, on the other, a devout, responsible, deeply religious Roman Catholic girl. His mood did not improve when he thought about having to leave her in two days.

The time hung heavy and dreary. He felt himself tumbling in a slow-motion, anticlimactic dejection after the first whirling, deliciously exciting days with Mary.

On Christmas Eve, the Monahans and Al exchanged gifts after dinner and then waited four more hours to go to midnight Mass. Al could see this was an important social event, with people gathering at the church long before the doors opened. People greeted each other with a hearty "Merry Christmas" wish. The Mass itself seemed more elaborate and certainly longer. When it was over, the

Monahans lingered briefly at the church and greeted people they knew, quickly introducing them to Al.

Back at home, Mr. Monahan reminded everyone they would have to get up at 5 A.M. on Christmas day to drive to Kosse, Texas. Still, Mary and Al stayed up as long as they could, using every available minute to kiss, hug and stay close together. The plan was for Al to travel with them to Kosse, then on to Dallas with Mary's Aunt Lucille and Uncle Damon, where Al then would be left on his own to hitchhike back to New York.

At 2 A.M., the only sound to be heard was a muffled snoring from Mr. Monahan in the back bedroom. Al and Mary sat side by side on the couch that had been made into a bed. For the two of them, thoughts were hard to express. They sat silently, holding hands, sharing a melancholy sadness about their uncertain future and, yet, wanting so much more time together. When Al kissed Mary, her lips were soft and inviting, but her hands gently pushed him away.

"Darling, you've only three hours to sleep," she said softly. "Who knows when you'll get a decent night's sleep again?" Then she added, as she rose and left him, "Good night my sweet love, and Merry Christmas."

Al watched his gracious beauty walk away and throw him a kiss before turning off the light. Al lay there smiling, thinking how glad he was after all that he had come to Texas for Christmas to be with his love.

CHAPTER 25

Al's introduction to Kosse, Texas started about 8 A.M. on Christmas morning after a two-hour drive north from Houston. The gray cloud-covered sunrise and the flat countryside made Al wish he was still back in bed asleep.

Kosse consisted of a few houses along a railroad track and one block of stores perpendicular to the railroad station. These included a drugstore, bus station, barbershop and a couple of grocery and feed stores. There were no buildings over two stories, no subways or the noises of millions of people and cars traveling into one anothers' paths.

A few plain houses lined the street just beyond the stores, all with front porches. At the far end of the street, the Monahan car pulled up to the home of Opal Mae Monahan's parents, Jim and Ella Porter. Once they heard the Monahans' Pontiac arrive people poured out of the house. Big Jim Porter, aptly nicknamed, was a tall, giant of a man, maybe 6-foot-3, only slightly stooped by age, heavy, with a weather-beaten face that revealed all his years out in the sun. His eyes squinted at everyone from under a ten-gallon hat. While Al thought many people might look ridiculous in such a hat, old man Porter appealingly embodied the image of the old historic native Texan.

As the Monahans and Al mounted the porch, Mary introduced Al to her grandparents. Grandma Ella smiled at Al and welcomed him warmly. She had a fair face with blue eyes, gray hair and soft wrinkled skin. Her stooped shoulders made her look shorter than she actually was. With a touch of roundness to her figure, she was still not as heavy as her daughter, Opal.

Grandpa Jim pumped Al's hand and turned to Mary to ask bluntly, "You like this feller?"

"Grandpa, I love him," Mary beamed.

"That's good enough for me," Grandpa Jim said, still pumping Al's hand. "Welcome to Kosse," he went on. "Mary's Aunt Cora has been telling us about you. I don't think she's exactly happy about Mary falling in love with a Jew-

Robert Miller

feller from New York, but I want you to know that I told Cora I think Mary has more sense than anybody else in this family because she knows what she wants and goes after it. We're about to sit down for breakfast. You sit next to me. Mary can sit next to you."

Al liked the old man right away. Large. Rugged. Forthright.

As they entered the dining room, it took a few minutes to give Al a quick introduction to all the relatives. There were Mrs. Monahan's three brothers — Uncle Damon, Uncle Pythias, and Uncle Lucien, and all their children, who were Mary's cousins and, of course, Aunt Cora and Uncle Nick.

Al counted 18 people around the table. They all seemed to be staring at him. He realized most of them had never seen a Jew before, at least, that they were aware of. Out here, Mary had told him, they might see a Jew, maybe a salesman, once or twice in their lifetimes, but to socialize with one was unheard of. Al put on his best manners and tried to act nonchalant as he helped himself to the scrambled eggs.

Grandpa Porter filled his own plate with eggs and then, to Al's astonishment, the old man sloshed a torrent of ketchup over his plate, turning the eggs from yellow to red. The ketchup then went around the table. While it circulated, the women kept up a stream of gossip about the visiting preacher who was to speak in church this Christmas morning.

Al noticed people got up from the table as soon as they finished eating. When someone rose, his or her place was cleaned and someone else would sit down and be served. He guessed some 30 people were being served breakfast on a rotating basis. This must be one of the largest gatherings of people in Kosse this morning, Al thought. Where are all these people coming from in such a small town? And all those staring youngsters, too.

When breakfast was finally over and all the dishes cleared, Al saw a newly energized bustle about the place as the women got dressed, primped their hair, dabbed on a faint touch of makeup, and got the children ready to go to the local church. For the first time, Al felt he had been totally forgotten in the hubbub around him.

Grandpa Porter leaned over to Al and asked cautiously, "Are you planning on going to church this morning, or will you set on the porch with me and watch all the hype-o-kritz walk by?"

"Sure, I'll sit with you," Al said, smiling at this exaggerated pronunciation of the term hypocrites, which made him remember Mary's warning that Grandpa was an atheist.

When everyone else had left for church, the old man led Al out to the porch, where they sat in old wicker rocking chairs. Old man Porter lit up his pipe and relaxed with puffs of smoke.

"I got no use for preachers or for churches. My daddy died when I was eight years old. My mother used to have the preacher come over for Sunday dinner once a month. When he came, there wasn't enough food for me or my brothers and sisters. And, my Mama would say to that preacher man, 'Have some more meat and potatoes.' He never said no. He'd eat a second and third helping, so there'd be nothing left over for us young uns. I made up my mind right then that I'd never go into a church." He paused to blow out some smoke and grin mischievously. "I broke that vow a few times for weddings and funerals, but not very often. My only fear is that someone in the family will hire a goddamn preacher to conduct the funeral when my time comes."

Grandpa reached down and pulled out a bottle of whiskey from a blanket under his rocker. "Take a drink," he said, then added, "Merry Christmas."

Al opened the bottle, took a sip and winced. He handed the bottle back with a contorted face. "You'll get used to it after a while," said the old man as he put the bottle to his lips and took a hearty gulp. After swallowing, he let out a satisfying "aaaaah."

"Al, you and I ought to drink the whole damn bottle ourselves and not save any for Bill, Nick, Damon, Pythias and Lucien. But, they'll sure need a swig after being cooped up with all those hype-o-kritzes in church. By God, Al, I can see why Mary likes you. She's the smartest one in the family and, even though she has become so goddamn religious going to that Catholic school and all, she picked out a feller like you who has the gumption to stay out of church and sit here with me on Christmas morning. I'm damn proud of her!"

Al leaned closer and asked, "Are you really an atheist? Mary told me you were an atheist."

The old man said he wasn't sure about God, but, as he saw it, all those preachers just took care of themselves, not God. He repeated to Al his demand that no preacher officiate at his funeral. He was not going to be reconciled to the preachers, nor to the hype-o-kritzes. Death was his business and nobody should get in his way. He had no need for churches and felt only contempt for all this organized religion business.

Al certainly didn't have the same strong feelings against all religion as Grandpa Porter, but wisely decided not to comment. Clearly, the old man had come to enjoy his reputation as the village atheist.

Grandpa Porter went on to talk about how very upset Mary's Aunt Cora had become over Mary seeing a Jew. He admitted that Cora had even asked him as head of the family to put a stop to it. Al was shocked at what seemed an unusually harsh step to propose. Unaware, the old man casually assured Al that he told Cora, his own daughter, to mind her own business. Others had tried to get him to stop Opal Mae from marrying Bill Monahan because he was a Northerner, an Irishman and a Catholic. "Even if I don't cotton to his religion, Bill Monahan turned out to be one of the finest people I have ever known and I'm proud to have him for a son-in-law."

I like him too, Al thought.

"Al Gordon, if you marry my granddaughter, I only want one thing from you. That you love her and be good to her. That matters a lot to me. What your religion is doesn't mean a thing to me."

The old man and Al sat rocking on the porch and looking out at the deserted street that disappeared into an empty landscape. From the porch, Al took in the vast openness and noted how the sky could be an overpowering force. There were no tall buildings, no throngs of people or machines, only the silent land that stretched to the horizon and on towards eternity.

Al listened to Big Jim Porter's long talk about the history of his family. He told how his grandfather and his grandfather's younger brother had come down here back around 1820 from Illinois. The territory was Mexican then. They had to fight the Mexicans, the Indians, the weather, the drought, the floods and everything else that came with the dusty, demanding land. When one of the Porter girls was kidnapped by the Indians and some settlers were killed, his grandfather returned to Illinois and didn't come back until Texas joined the U.S.A. in the mid-eighteen forties.

Grandpa stared ahead while he reminisced about family stories he had been told. His grandfather and father grew peanuts and watermelons. His father and his father's five brothers had been drafted into the Confederate Army, but only two of them came back. His father fought at Missionary Ridge, Tennessee, and at Arkansas Post. He had been wounded and captured by the Yankees in Franklin, Tennessee. He had survived the war but it had taken a toll on him.

At age 40, he simply crumpled over in the fields and died. Big Jim said he himself was a young boy at the time, forced by events to face many hardships along with his four brothers and sisters, while their mother struggled to keep the family and the farmlands together.

Al wondered for a moment whether, perhaps, Grandpa had not forgiven God for letting this happen to him. When the old man paused, Al asked if it was true there was Indian blood in the family.

The old man chuckled. "Yeah, lots of it," he said. His grandfather's mother was a full-blooded Indian and his own mother was a quarter Cherokee.

They watched from the isolation of the porch as people came out of the church. Al felt a pang of guilt over not accompanying Mary and her relatives to the service. They probably thought him derelict for not going.

Grandpa Porter sagely read Al's thoughts. "Whatever you do, Al, don't let Mary or any woman put a string through your nose and tell you what you have to think or believe."

CHAPTER 26

Mary and her cousin, Jim Allen Bates, were the first to arrive back. Hearing that Al was visiting, Jim Allen simply had to drop by after church and say hello. Jim shook Al's hand warmly. He kidded Al that word had spread all around the state of Texas that Mary had a new Jewish boyfriend who was coming up for Christmas. Jim Allen grinned and said when he heard the rumor, he knew it had to be Al Gordon.

When the rest of the family had gathered back at the house, Grandpa Jim had all the men, including Jim Allen and Al, walk with him to the barn where, out of sight from the house, Grandpa pulled out the whiskey bottle. The bottle passed from hand to hand as each man hoisted it, said, "Merry Christmas," gulped some down and gave it to the man standing to his right. Ultimately the men filed out of the barn and gravitated back toward the porch, where Grandpa ruled from his rocking chair.

Al now noticed knots of people who kept walking by the house. Some slowed their pace to congregate on the other side of the street and watch the people on the porch. Al leaned over and asked Grandpa what he thought the people were looking at.

"They're trying to figure out which one is you, Al. These people heard Mary had a Jew boyfriend and they never did see a Jew before. You're the big news in town, Al. They'll go away soon. Heck, there's some 500 people in this town and I reckon they'll all want to come and take a look at you sometime today. Aren't you glad you came?" He wagged his finger mischievously.

"Yes, in fact, I am. I may be a stranger here, but I feel very much at home with you and your family. I appreciate your kindness," Al said kindly, and meaningfully.

Al and Grandpa Porter read a special mutual acceptance in each other's eyes. Grandpa Porter squinted more and laughed. Al found his unexpected celebrity status a benign predicament and wondered what this east Texas town expected of him. Did they come thinking I'd be wearing a skull cap? Or, that I would have a black hat, a long black coat and earlocks like the Hasidim? Or, would I be wearing a prayer shawl? What do they expect me, a Jew, to look like? Swarthy with a hooked nose instead of my normal clean-shaven light-skinned self? Al felt uncomfortable being gawked at as the sole Jew for miles around.

Fortunately, the announcement that Christmas dinner was ready took him inside where everyone was set to enjoy the plates of ham, turkey, giblet gravy, fresh-baked biscuits and a multitude of homegrown vegetables. Al was taken aback by the constant high-pitched chatter of the women, while the men ate in virtual silence.

Aunt Lucille, who initiated a lot of the talk, was tall and hazel-eyed. Al saw her as a "club lady" who had come to life out of a *New Yorker* cartoon, but with a Southern accent. Sue Ann Porter, one of Mary's cousins, was very shy, somewhat younger than Mary. She had lovely ash-blond hair, but her body appeared extremely thin, accentuated by her height. She was still in that gawky stage between a teenager and a young woman.

Al took notice of Uncle Damon Porter, who would be driving his family and Al across Texas north to Dallas, where Al could start hitchhiking towards Arkansas. Damon was a younger version of his father, Grandpa Porter. He too was big and broad-shouldered, but unlike his father, he was very quiet, especially in the presence of his talkative wife, Lucille.

After dinner, Mary and Al had enough time to take a short walk down the by now quiet and deserted street. When they were far out of sight, Mary did a flagrant, unimaginable thing by kissing Al openly.

"There," she said drawing a deep breath. "That'll give the whole town something to talk about and it'll give me something to live on until June."

"But nobody's around," Al said.

"That's what you think!" Mary chuckled.

Back at the house, Mary's Uncle Damon, Aunt Lucille and their two children had already put their belongings in the car and were eager to leave. Mary helped Al carry his things from her father's car to Damon's 1932 Ford.

Al shook a lot of hands to say good-bye. He very courteously thanked them all for their hospitality. As Damon's family got in the car, Mary flung herself at Al one last time. She kissed him with her mouth open and her tongue exploring his mouth. As Mary broke away and stepped back, Al felt weak from the kiss and sheepish in front of her assembled family.

"Al," Mary said softly. "Please take good care of yourself. Please write to me. And come back to me in June. I can't wait."

He smiled as he nodded in agreement. Then he bent down and fitted himself next to one of the young daughters in the back seat.

Damon started the car and drove slowly down the street. Al turned and, through the back window, saw everyone getting smaller in a matter of seconds.

He watched Mary, her parents, grandparents and the rest, tiny figures waving farewell.

When the house disappeared from sight, Al turned to find Aunt Lucille had bent around to face him. Al asked her how long it would take to reach Dallas. She told him "about two hours." He expressed, once again, his appreciation for their helping him get to Dallas.

The two hours went by with Aunt Lucille doing most of the talking. She started out by asking a stream of questions. "Where do you live in New York? What do your parents do? What are you studying in college?"

Al thought that even if the trip were twice as long, Aunt Lucille would never run out of questions. Al answered carefully, reassuring her and whoever else would be hearing his responses repeated, that he wanted to finish college and his main career goal was to work as a reporter or editor at a newspaper.

Aunt Lucille confided how worried she was about Mary. In fact, she had arranged a date for Mary with "that very nice Patton boy" a few weeks ago. "It didn't work out," Al heard her say to her husband because of that Catholic thing. Al knew the real story of how Billy Joe Patton brought along a bottle of bourbon and hoped to take advantage of her, but he disclosed nothing.

Aunt Lucille expressed her belief that when Opal and Mary joined the Catholic Church, following their husband and father, they were reducing Mary's chances of finding a suitable young man. Even though she had heard of one or two Protestants marrying Catholics, intermarriage was very rare. For sure, she said, she had never heard of Catholics, or Protestants either, for that matter, marrying Jews. Anyway, she had it on good authority that Jews stuck to their own kind.

"Whose authority?" Al wondered.

Al told Aunt Lucille that he and Mary loved each other very much, but they really hadn't seriously talked about marriage.

Aunt Lucille began to regale Al with details of her family tree as well as some history of the Porters. Al had slept only three hours the night before, but he knew it was critical for him to pay attention to Aunt Lucille's self-centered nonstop chatter.

With a half smile on his face and a disciplined composure, he drifted close to the twilight of half-asleep, while Aunt Lucille talked on and on. Most of what he heard seemed unimportant. Occasionally he pinched a hand to keep awake and wished he was still with Mary.

By the time they reached Dallas, it was dusk. Aunt Lucille suggested that Al stay the night with them. But Al had had quite enough of her talking. He graciously declined the offer and said he wanted to start his journey right away.

Uncle Damon drove Al to Highway 67, which headed east to Little Rock, Arkansas, about 300 miles away. Before they parted, Aunt Lucille gave Al their phone number and extracted a solemn promise that he would call if he didn't get a ride by 10. Damon got out of the car, shook Al's hand and wished him well. Aunt Lucille got out, hugged Al and kissed him good-bye as if he were her favorite young man. Al mustered his energy and felt relieved to be leaving Aunt Lucille.

Christmas and Mary's relatives were behind him now. He did an about-face and walked toward the truck stop diner. The lights inside offered a reassuring welcome where everything else was dark.

Sadness, relief and apprehension passed through Al as he realized how long the trip back was. Some 1500 miles of cement highways lay ahead of him before he reached home.

In the diner, Al ordered a hamburger and a Coke to combat his fatigue. Thinking about New York and the pending New Year's Eve party to come, he bought a postcard and addressed it to Selma. He told himself it was the right thing to do since he had promised to send her one. "After all, Mary and I are not engaged and things may never work out with Mary", he rationalized. He gave the waitress a tip and some money to put a stamp on the postcard. She promised to mail it the next day. Al asked if she could help him get a ride to St. Louis. She looked around the diner. No one was there, but she knew a trucker who might be stopping in on his way to Memphis.

Al left money with his bill on the counter, lifted his bags and wandered over to the telephone. After a second try, he got through to his mother. He told her with luck, he'd be home Sunday. He asked her to call Selma and tell her he would surely be back for New Year's Eve. His mother acted as though the request was an imposition, but finally relented and agreed to call Selma.

When Al looked back toward the counter, the waitress signaled to him. When he walked over, she told him that her truck driver friend, pointing to a man in the corner booth, had come in and would take him along as soon as he finished his meal.

That night Al relaxed in the cab of a tractor trailer, which carried somebody's furniture and possessions through the night to Memphis. As the truck rumbled along, the driver rambled on about his family and his trips. There were no revelations, but the conversation took Al's mind off his melancholy. He savored again the heady excitement of his first few days with Mary. The Christmas tree. The Monahans. The Irish Catholics. The Masses. Pictures of Mary's sexy enthusiasm, contrasted with Selma's warm demureness bounced around in his head. The six months till June seemed too far away. Would Mary wait for him or find somebody new? What would his own feelings be in six months? Life appeared unpredictable that far ahead, especially with all those miles between them. He only knew New York was his future for now. He wondered sleepily what awaited him there.

CHAPTER 27

Al opened the office door to his parents' small advertising agency on 34th Street just west of Eighth Avenue to find his mother engrossed in work at her desk. When he let out a hearty, "Hi!," Mrs. Gordon looked up in surprise.

"The world traveler has returned!" Al's mother gently mocked. "I thought you forgot your mother," she said as she rose and gave him an affectionate kiss. "Welcome home."

They sat while Al began reciting all the states he had traveled through during the last two months. Arkansas had been his 19th. Mrs. Gordon listened patiently, but soon voiced other concerns.

"Exactly who are the Monahans you stayed with? Why did you stay with them when you told us you were going to see your friend Jim Allen Bates?"

"The Monahans are cousins of the Bates," Al explained, trying to show some honest logic. "They live in Houston and have more room for a guest. They have a daughter Mary, who I met and wrote about in an article when I went to Texas with the football team. I think I'm in love with her and she says she loves me. What do do you think of that, Mom?" he blurted out, hoping the shock would not overwhelm her.

"Not very much. Not very much at all," his mother frowned. She was not ready to hear about a girlfriend that far away, or any serious girlfriend. "We're proud of you that you did get to write for the NYU newspaper. But, what do you do? You fall in love with a shiksa you meet in Texas, hitchhike down there, worrying us to death and stay not where you tell us but under the same roof as this girl for God knows what kind of goings on!"

Mrs.Gordon rolled her eyes in exasperation.

"Mother! I did see my friend Jim Allen Bates but his parents had other guests." A small lie would soothe, he quickly decided. "Mary Jean Monahan is a lovely girl who goes to Texas State College for Women. She's a lady. You'd like her very much. Her father works for an oil company right there in Houston.

Robert Miller

They have two cars and are a fine established family. You'd like them!" Al reassured in a raised voice. His hand touched her arm.

"Monahans!" Al's mother said with a disdainful shrug. "Irish. Your father might like them. He drinks all the time with the Irish downstairs in Riordan's Bar. I know I wouldn't like them at all."

Al kept his hand on her arm, relaxed and waited. He knew his mother was changing her mind, as she struggled to accept the idea. "Yes you would like them, Mom. Mary's mother is just like you. She even looks Jewish. She plays cards two or three afternoons a week."

"That's all she has to do?" his mother challenged. She turned on Al again. "And what about this little Jewish girlfriend right here who works at her parents' fruit store? Did you tell her about this Mary? Ah, why should I care? You have a gift, Allie, for picking unlikely girls." Mrs. Gordon shrugged her shoulders.

"Mother, Selma goes to Hunter College High School. She's an honor student there. She's the brightest girl I know, except, maybe, for Mary Monahan. Why do you demean every girl I take a serious interest in?"

The office phone suddenly rang. His mother left his question unanswered as she picked up the phone. Meanwhile, Al used another telephone at the opposite end of the office to call Selma.

"Weinberg's Fruit Store," Selma answered.

"Can you deliver nine apples, four tomatoes, twelve kisses and one big hug?" Al teased.

"Al, where are you?"

"I'm still in Texas. I'm going to hop on an airplane this afternoon and arrive at Newark Airport around midnight. Can you meet me there?"

"How can I meet you at Newark Airport at midnight?" she exclaimed. Then she laughed. "Al, are you fooling around with me again? Where are you, really?"

Al told her he was in Manhattan at the agency and wanted to come by to see her in the Bronx. She told him to call back in half an hour so she could check if it was all right with her parents.

"Selma," Al lowered his voice. "I told you I missed you. Didn't you miss me at all? Not even a little?"

"I'll tell you when I see you, Al. Bye."

Al had no clue as to whether Selma was extra glad to hear from him. He shrugged and turned to see his mother watching him.

"Don't you think I heard the things you said to Selma on the phone. 'Did you miss me?' What would she say if she knew you were two-timing her with your new shiksa sweetie in Texas? When I was your age, your grandma told me not to believe things men told me. Could she have been warning me about the man my own son would turn out to be? Shame!" Mrs. Gordon voiced her disapproval, but her eyes shone with love. He was still her only son.

"Mother, you're a gem. You never liked Selma because her parents own a fruit store. Now you don't like Mary because she's not Jewish. I can't believe how concerned you are with things that don't matter. I know it's because you only want the very best, the impossible, for your son," Al said with loving reverence for his mother. Al kissed her on the cheek, "If I'm not home when you get home, that'll mean I'll be with Selma."

Al's mother returned his kiss and hugged him. "I'm glad you're back. And I'm glad you had a good time. If you see Selma tonight, enjoy your evening. A Jewish girl, even if her parents run a fruit store, seems a little better to me now." She stepped back and gave Al her version of a wink. "Does that shiksa's family really have two cars?" she asked as if she was somewhat impressed.

As Al nodded yes, mother and son both giggled, as if agreeing that having two girlfriends at the same time might not be such a bad thing. Al picked up his bags and headed out the door up to home in the Bronx.

Al said a quick hello to his sister, Shirley, too preoccupied with his own life to ask about hers, took a fast shower, changed his clothes and was off on the 20-minute walk to the Weinbergs' apartment. Along the way, he phoned Selma and found out she would indeed be home.

Robert Miller

CHAPTER 28

At the Weinbergs' apartment, Selma opened the door only seconds after Al pushed the buzzer. Her brother Joey joined them in the living room. Joey was a tall, thin 20-year-old with blue eyes, blondish hair and a small, almost Hitler type mustache. Eagerly, he fired questions at Al. "Did you really hitchhike to Texas and back? Was it warm there? Did you see any cowboys?"

Al answered briefly, noticing Selma staring at him impatiently.

After Joey got the hint and left the apartment, Al came up to Selma.

She resisted his kiss. "Al Gordon, you can't leave me for two weeks and go gallivanting around the country and then come back and expect to find things exactly the way they were. You might as well know, while you were traveling around Texas, I had three or four dates with Howie Peskin and one or two with other boys. I didn't just wait for you to return. And I didn't hear from you, not even a postcard," Selma complained.

"You mean to tell me you didn't get my postcard? I sent it from Dallas last Tuesday," Al asked astonished.

"Al, tell me the truth. What did you go to Texas for? Do you have a girl down there?"

Al feigned innocence. He looked peeved, as if Selma had asked a question not worth answering.

"Is that what you think? Or is that an excuse for dating Howard Peskin while I was away?" Al still had feelings for Selma, who, in her own way, was his first serious love, but he needed time to sort out those feelings. Whatever her suspicions, he was not ready to admit there might be another girl. "Is this how you greet someone who cares for you so much that he has traveled night day since he woke up five-thirty Tuesday morning because he promised to be with you on New Year's Eve?"

"You haven't been in bed since Monday night?" she asked, sounding kinder and concerned.

"No, I haven't. Though I did sleep a bit in trucks, on the bus and on the train as I headed home to you. It's hard to sleep much when you're sitting up."

"Al," Selma's voice softened. "I did miss you," she confessed.

"You do mean very much to me, but I've never felt a bit of security in our relationship. Excitement, yes. Security, no. That's why I'm so vulnerable to a boy like Howie."

"Vulnerable?!" To Al, that was a strong word. How could anyone be vulnerable to Howie Peskin, with his beady eyes and rolling walk? To me, yes. People always say I'm good-looking. What happened here? Al panicked in his thoughts. "In what way are you vulnerable?"

Instead of replying, Selma kissed Al, seeing that he had become jealous. She put her arms around Al. Her mouth came slightly open. Al took advantage of the kiss to dart his tongue between her lips.

She drew back.

"Damn! I'm not vulnerable to anyone but you. You excite me and you also frighten me. Other boys give me more of a feeling of security and safety." Selma moved slightly away from Al. "We have to go by my parents' store and tell them we're going to a movie or else one of them will come by to see what we're doing."

They exited into one of those cold December nights when the Canadian air frostily blew down through New York City. Al enjoyed warming his hand in Selma's as they walked. After telling her parents their plans to stay out till 11, they continued with an arm around each other towards Tremont Avenue. Along the way, Selma admitted again she was glad Al was back and that she had missed him a lot, yet almost in the same breath she told him how other boys "treated her better," and took her to nicer places. They danced better than Al. They were more trustworthy. She ended by asking, "Why is it that I'm stuck on you, Al Gordon?"

"I can't figure it out either, Selma," Al said. "I guess we bring about the beast in each other," he added with a slightly smug grin.

Al had his arm around Selma all through the double feature at the Crotona Theater, and afterwards when they stopped at a luncheonette for ice cream sodas. They spent the hours quietly renewing their own bonding. Of course, Al knew Selma, on principle alone, would angrily and abruptly leave him if he told her about Mary, but Al, still, enjoyed her company and did not want to say good-bye. Now that he was with her again, he looked forward to New Year's Eve and more time together.

On the way home, Selma brought up the subject of what they would do New Year's Eve. Al suggested that they go to Times Square. Selma scoffed, saying that mostly drunks would be there. She bragged that Howie had invited her to the roof of the Hotel Pennsylvania. Al felt put down. Abruptly he stepped away, dropping her hand.

"Don't get angry, Al. But, you never have taken me to places like that. You take me to the movies and buy me a soda and think you have a license to feel me up for the next couple of hours. I don't mean I don't like kissing you, but, Allie dear, I sometimes feel taken advantage of. I would like to be escorted to nice places," Selma said wishfully.

Al turned to face her.

"Selma, I'd like to take you to nice places, but I don't have rich parents and I don't get an allowance. I can't compete with Howie on that level. If you'd like to go some place fancy with him New Year's Eve, you can. I won't hold you back."

They stood in silence, both thinking "perhaps I've gone too far" but neither willing to back off as yet.

Al stubbornly repeated in his mind: If she goes with Howie, that will be the end of our relationship. I could be more virtuous and not have to hide my relationship with Mary, but why should I? And if she sails off with Howie, what will I do on New Year's Eve? I don't want to be alone.

Selma took Al's hand back, raised it to her lips and kissed it gently. "Al, I'm sorry I'm giving you a hard time. You hitchhiked across America. You've said you're awfully tired and here I am almost baiting you. I've thought about Howie's offer, it's true, but you're stuck with me New Year's Eve. And do you know why?"

"Why?"

"Because I'm stuck on you." She kissed Al quickly on his lips.

When they reached her apartment building, they sat down on the steps inside. Selma opened her coat. Al reached in as they kissed each other eagerly, caressed her sides and then ran his hands over her breasts, which he knew had to be protectively covered by a brassiere and a slip under her blouse and wool jumper.

Al drew his hand back after a minute. "I'm embarrassed. I did take you to the movies and bought you a soda. You've said I think that gives me license to touch you. But that's not true at all. I touch you because I love touching you. It thrills me to touch you. I want to touch you everywhere. But, I don't want to offend you either. I don't know what you really want me to do. Do you want me to stop?"

Selma murmured to Al to stop asking foolish questions. She asked him to keep kissing her and explained that some things might have been said in resentment for his having left her.

They kissed again with mouths open. Al let his hand explore along her leg slowly. As their tongues touched, Al's finger found a hole in her panties. He moved his finger further until it reached the moist lips of her most private place.

She shivered in a spasm of ecstasy, as they kissed and his finger explored around. She shivered again and gasped. Then, she pushed his hand away.

"Oh God, something happened. I'm not sure what, but it thrilled me." She kissed Al for a moment. "I'm mortified. Your touching me there was so exciting. I almost thought I'd explode. But nice girls don't do that." She kept Al from touching her leg again. "Do you want to come inside and wash your hands?"

Al kissed her. "I'll make you a promise. I'll never wash that hand again."

They burst into giggles.

Al asked Selma if he could see her the next night or Saturday. Selma explained that while she had saved Monday night, New Year's Eve, for him, she admitted she had been uncertain when he would be back, so she had not saved every night. Al, confused, asked who else she had started dating.

"I think I love you. What more do you want from me?" Selma put him off.

Al took her hands in his and kissed them. Then he pulled one of them down to his crotch. She resisted. He explained that he wanted her to touch him. He promised, if she did, he would go home. He wanted Selma to excite him more and more.

She relaxed and moved her hand gently over the bulge in his pants. After a short time, she removed her hand, fingered Al's cheek and whispered, "Good night, Allie. I'm so glad you're back."

They got up and walked to her front door. She unlocked the door and kissed Al once more before going inside.

Al's feelings were mixed as he buttoned his collar. He and Selma had taken a step closer tonight in their intimacy, although Selma always managed to resist him far more than Mary. He wondered about Selma. Though he was back, she still went out on other dates, partly to keep her parents happy. He smiled as he remembered Mary. He pulled his collar closer to warm him on the lonely walk home, as he thought, a bit bewildered about the two girls in his life.

Robert Miller

CHAPTER 29

Around 10 P.M. on New Year's Eve, Al took Selma to the NYU Alpha Phi fraternity house. They were both looking forward to a party.

They found three couples there who were already into heavy necking.

Selma became uncomfortable and asked to leave. She wanted a real party where people danced, talked and had a good time.

Al then walked her over to the Lambda Delta House, another NYU fraternity, where there were indications of a party already in progress with drinks, snacks and festive decorations. Six couples had gathered and at least six young single university males roamed around without dates, including Howard Peskin. Howie immediately approached Selma and asked her to dance, ignoring Al. When they had finished dancing, Al quickly and firmly suggested to Selma that they leave.

A cold December wind met them outside. They had an hour and a half left before 1934 officially ended to find a party.

Al suggested they check out the happenings at Times Square. Selma agreed icily, more in response to her hatred for the crowd and not the cold air.

Times Square always guaranteed a crowd, a mix of good- natured people tooting horns and a few obnoxious drunks, who kissed girls as they passed by. When a stranger kissed Selma, Al nearly got in a fight with the youth and his buddies. Gradually, Al and Selma maneuvered themselves into the middle of the crowd at 44th Street and Broadway. They stood there with the others in the cold and watched the news bulletins, glimmering polka dots of lights rotating around the marquee of the building. Selma's nose began to run from the cold air. Panicking in a fearful phobia of the unruly crowd which pushed and shoved everyone back and forth, she turned to Al and suggested that they leave.

"Al!" she pleaded. "I'm frightened. I'm cold. Please get me out of here!"

Feeling the urgency in Selma's voice, Al grabbed her hand and pushed his way through the crowd toward the subway entrance. He suggested that they warm up at his parents' home. Nobody would be there. Selma nodded sullenly.

Near midnight, Al and Selma were in a fast-moving subway train full of people. Al whispered, "Happy New Year," and kissed her.

Selma did not enjoy the kiss. She had wanted Al to take her to a real New Year's Eve party, not a ride on the subway at the stroke of twelve.

Inside his parents' apartment, they drank milk and munched on cookies. Selma ate the cookies, but hid any signs of disappointment. She followed Al into the bedroom where they lay down and began to kiss. She seemed to let Al do whatever he wanted. Al took advantage of her compliance by loosening her clothes and reaching under the sweater and bra towards her breasts.

Selma didn't resist.

But she did resist when he tried to reach up her legs into her panties. So, trying another avenue, Al moved on top of her, opened his pants and inserted his penis between her legs. She didn't resist and let him kiss her, but her kisses were without passion. Al's passion was enough for him to reach orgasm. Then he moved off her and brought her a towel to clean up. She got up, adjusted her clothes and headed for the bathroom. When she came out, Al tried to give her a reassuring kiss. She rejected his advance.

Selma told him she was not happy with him or herself. She felt like a "kept woman" for coming to his apartment and letting him do what he wanted, whether she wanted to do it or not. Al felt too exhausted and wanted to avoid any discussion about Selma's feelings. He only wanted them both to enjoy being with each other.

By 2 A.M. on the first day of January 1935, Al took Selma home on a streetcar along Tremont Avenue. They sat silently, listening to the joyous people around them.

At her parent's door, Selma kissed Al, wished him a "Happy New Year" and went inside quickly. Al felt snubbed and confused.

On the walk back home, Al became overwhelmed with sadness at mishandling his relationship with Selma. She wanted Al to take her out to nice places, but she always complained that Al only wanted to end the evenings by groping her body.

The incident brought Al a mixed sense of relief and regret. He enjoyed being with both girls, but he felt Mary loved him more.

He decided it was time to sit down and write a long letter to Mary Jean Monahan, professing his love for her and resolving to see her in June.

On New Year's Day, Al woke up late, but immediately resolved that he needed some New Year's resolutions. First and foremost, he promised to concentrate on his studies for a while. Second, he resolved to upgrade his reporter's skills. His final resolution was to make the last half of his sophomore year at NYU more successful.

Selma stopped seeing Al, but they did talk on the phone every week. His sister's friend, Monica, who was Selma's neighbor and classmate, gave him

Robert Miller

reports from time to time on Selma's dating. Al's "friends" at NYU delighted in giving him reports of their sightings of Selma and Howard Peskin at various places.

Al tried to date casually a wide range of girls at NYU and in his Bronx neighborhood. Most of all, Al wrote long romantic letters to Mary who replied with letters of her own. Together, they made plans for his impending trip to Texas — where he'd planned to work for the summer.

He also sent off a letter to Sally Hargrove about his expectation of working for her on the *Galveston Hi-Lites*, but, he received no response.

At the end of the spring term, there was a dinner for the NYU *Bulletin* staff at the Fifth Avenue Hotel. At the dinner, Al proudly heard the announcement that he would be appointed Sports Editor in his junior year. He would be the only junior on the paper's executive board. These opportunities would put him in position to become the Bulletin's Editor-in-Chief next year.

Al finally received a letter from Miss Hargrove asking when he planned to start work. He sent a letter indicating he would be ready to start on Monday, June 17th.

Al then went ahead and made plans with Mary about his living arrangements: He would stay a few days with her and then move into a ten-dollar a month garage apartment in Galveston.

Whatever plans Al ever had for Selma or for life in New York City were now on permanent hold for this summer. The closer it got to the time to leave, the more excited Al felt about seeing the enthusiastic Mary again and his new job in the state of Texas.

CHAPTER 30

In June, Al left New York City by hitchhiking to Texas. His first ride took him all the way south to Tallahassee, Florida, at which point he headed west. He marveled how in the first eighteen years of his life he had been in a total of three states. Now in the past eight months, he had been in seventeen states and would be in more new ones on this trip, making a total of twenty-three states. He resolved to someday visit each of the forty-eight states.

His next ride was with a young driver who became too tired to drive on and asked Al to drive. Al reluctantly agreed, afraid that he may have lost his touch after not having driven in the Bronx for six months.

"Drive carefully," the young man admonished. "We're a couple of Yankees in the deep south. If you're stopped by a policeman, tell him I'm teaching you to drive. The experience will help you. But, for God's sake, be careful!"

In his next series of rides, he traveled with truckers. After several rides, he luckily found one trucker who would take him nonstop to Houston, which would get him there as he had planned, by June eighth. Al climbed out of this last truck at a Humble gas station in Houston. He quickly found a phone and called Mary's home. Mrs. Monahan answered.

"It's Al Gordon, Mrs. Monahan, am I calling too early?"

"Goodness no, Al, just a minute. I'll get Mary. How are you? Where are you?"

"Not far away."

In a second, Mary's voice came through the phone. "Al, darling! Where are you? I'm so glad to hear from you!"

"I'm at South Main Street between the Old Spanish Trail and Kirby Drive. How far is that from you?"

"Not five minutes. Stay right there. I'll be right over."

Al washed, shaved, and changed his clothes in the men's room. He got back to the street just as Mrs. Monahan's Chevy pulled up. Mary, wearing a summery white frock, jumped out and ran into Al's arms. Her kisses were as sweet and warm as he remembered. He tried to push his body close to hers. She drew back and laughed.

"Slow down, big boy. You always seem to arrive here on Sunday morning after I have made confession on Saturday and expect Communion at Mass. Get in the car. We'll go to Mass together and I'll thank Jesus for sending you back to me. I'm so glad to see you!" She gave Al her gorgeous smile.

Mary drove straight to the Church. Al was too tired to resist. Besides he knew Mary had to go to church. Mary held Al's hand tightly as they walked in just in time for the 10 o'clock Mass.

Al remained seated in the pew as Mary knelt beside him. He looked at her and marveled, once again, at her beauty and piety. He compared the statues of the Virgin Mary to his Mary and was glad to have met his beautiful Mary. He thought she surely outshines the most beauteous Madonna statue. Al's eyes followed Mary as she approached the rail to accept Communion. He was awe struck by the reverent expression on her face as she returned to the pew after partaking of the wine and wafer that represented to her, with unquestioning faith, the body and blood of her Lord.

The Mass seemed to drag on for the tired young Al, who only wanted to hold this sweet and properly pious beautiful girl in his arms.

After Mass, Mary and Al drove by the fresh chicken market to pick out a chicken for dinner. Because there would be a forty minute wait to get the chicken slaughtered and cleaned, Mary decided they should use the time to drive to a secluded spot at Hermann Park. Al naturally reached over to crush her into his arms. She nudged him back.

"Whatever am I going to do with you?" she asked playfully. "I surely can't let you mess up my white dress just before we go home to have dinner with my parents. And I surely can't let you walk into our home with a bulge in your pants, can I?" Mary's eyes sparkled.

She put her small white hands over the bulge in his pants and opened the buttons of his fly. Al reached for her, but she moved back and said, "Al, let me take care of this wheedle worm. I haven't seen it in six months." Mary carefully took his penis into her hands as Al sighed with pleasure. She asked him for his handkerchief and carefully wrapped it around his penis and then began to rub it between her hands. As she worked, Al began to breathe more deeply and quickly reached a climax. He continued to breath hard, taking in gulps of air, as Mary moved the handkerchief to dry him off. When she was done, Mary pressed herself close to him and gave him a sweet, warm, open-mouthed kiss. Then she said, "Welcome back to Texas, my love."

Back at the apartment, the Monahans greeted Al warily after his six month absence. Instead of expressing any of their anxieties, they asked Al courteous questions about his trip.

Mrs. Monahan cooked the chicken that Al and Mary had bought to a crispy golden-hued brown. Al explained that he and Mary had chosen that chicken because it seemed the fattest. As they ate, Bill Monahan talked about the sermon by the Monsignor, in which he found little he agreed with. The conversation went on to Al's parents and all the Porter relatives at Kosse. Al found himself right at home again with the Monahans, though he struggled to accustom himself to their southern cooking of sweet potatoes, string beans and the watery ice tea, which made him think how much he'd prefer more familiar items like bagels, lox, and gefilte fish.

Al was quickly captivated by the beauty of the prim and proper-looking Mary Jean Monahan, who sat demurely on his left at the dining table. He wanted to reach out and hold her hand. His thoughts went back to their brief moment of passion in the car.

After dinner, the discussion came around to the concerns about Al's summer job.

"I've told people that you were coming down to work for Sally Hargrove," Opal Mae said with a tone of concern. "They all laughed and said nobody can work for that crazy woman. I don't say this to frighten you, but I think you should know what you are getting into and not be discouraged if the job doesn't work out."

Al gave her a confident smile. He told the Monahans not to worry. He would do whatever Miss Hargrove required. Yet, he was just a bit disquieted.

Mary had had enough socializing and announced to her parents that she and Al would be going out to see a movie and they left within minutes of her giving her mother and father a quick kiss, and before her mother could offer another suggestion.

CHAPTER 31

Once in the car, Mary changed directions and headed over to the San Jacinto Battlefield. As they walked around the battlefield, Mary explained proudly how brief the battle was that destroyed General Santa Anna's Mexican army. General Sam Houston's Texans had very few casualties, as they surprised the encamped Mexican army during the siesta hour one April day some ninety-nine years ago. This battlefield had become very significant to the Texans. San Jacinto Day is a very special holiday in Texas, very much like the Fourth of July.

On the drive back home, Mary told Al that there was a new Kosher restaurant in Houston called Schwartzenberg's and promised him that they would go there soon. Before they got home, they stopped over at the local favorite, generally inexpensive eatery, Prince's Drive-in, where Al enjoyed his usual order of a hamburger, a Coke, and fries. Mary ordered the Texas spiced chili and a Dr. Pepper.

They arrived back home by 8 P.M., which would be too early for everyone else to go to bed, so Mary arranged for Al to sleep that night in her bed, and she would sleep on the couch.

Al fell asleep in Mary's bed, breathing in her sweet scent that permeated the sheets. He slept for fourteen hours.

Al woke up to find Mary sitting quietly on the side of the bed.

She told him that her mother was fixing something for all of them to eat. Al showered, shaved, dressed and came to lunch feeling like a new person, after days on the road.

He lifted the white bread to inspect and smell the chicken salad sandwich, his first, and then ravenously devoured the whole sandwich, potato chips and iced tea.

Mrs. Monahan offered to drive Al and Mary to *The Houston Press* where he could visit the editor, Bill Wannamaker.

Clash of Cultures - The Al Gordon Story

Al's visit to the Press was pleasant. Mr. Wannamaker also warned Al that Sally Hargrove was a tough person to work for. After the meeting, Mr. Wannamaker invited Mary into his office and told her how impressed he had been with Al when he had first met him last December.

"If it doesn't work out with Sally Hargrove, let me know. Maybe we can work something out here when the vacation schedules overlap," Mr. Wannamaker said encouragingly.

Both felt buoyant from the meeting at the *Press*. Mary and Al drove over to the Motor Vehicle Department to schedule a driving test for Saturday morning. At this point, Al and Mary both felt more optimistic about Al's opportunities now in Texas.

At 9 P.M. Al finally reached Sally Hargrove on the phone, after several attempts. Miss Hargrove instructed him to meet her, right away, at 9:30 at Morrison's Cafeteria. Mary drove Al quickly over to the other side of town to the cafeteria and waited outside.

Al walked into the huge cafeteria at 9:40. He found Miss Hargrove sitting at a corner table sipping a cup of coffee and writing on a yellow legal pad.

"You're ten minutes late," she responded sharply when Al greeted her, the first time in six months. She gave a critical, somewhat poisonous, look and barked, "Sit down." She pushed the yellow pad at Al, as she completed her last entry. "Here is your bus ticket to Galveston and a return ticket." She pulled the tickets from her purse and thrust them at Al who took them. "I expect you to be on the 7 A.M bus, which will get you there by eight. Here is a list of people I want you to see. Each of them has an ad in the present book. You are to collect the money for these ads and find out if there are to be corrections for next week. I expect you to write down what you collect, and what you don't. Tell people that, if they don't pay in full, I may leave their ads out of the next issue. You finish the business, make every call, and meet me here tomorrow at 8 P.M. Do you understand?"

"Yes, I do," Al said. He wanted to ask other questions so he could be sure to do the job right. He was only too eager to prove himself on this first job. He replied with a series of rapid-fire questions. "Do you want me to try to sell them a bigger ad? Do you have a rate card? What shall I do if someone wants to change the ad? What if someone doesn't want to pay? Is there a place I can reach you during the day, if something is asked that needs an immediate answer?"

"You have my number. I have many places to be in Houston. You can keep trying me at that number."

Al asked about finding the addresses she had listed. She gruffly answered that he could find them in the centerfold map. She repeated the bus schedule, picked up her purse and promptly walked out of the cafeteria. That was the end of the meeting and his "training."

CHAPTER 32

Al returned to the car and sat down. He explained the assignment to Mary. He wondered for the first time if he really could work for Miss Hargrove. Her autocratic nature frightened him, he admitted. He said, "What will satisfy Miss Hargrove? She seems very demanding."

Mary laughed. "I wish you'd worry about satisfying me and not that old biddy." She smirked at another thought. "The way she stomps around even frightens me."

Al drove the car on home to take his mind off his fears, shifting his focus to practicing for the driving test.

At 5:45 A.M., a bleary-eyed Al got up, only fifteen minutes before Mr. Monahan arose, and prepared to go to Galveston. Mary drove him to the bus station and gave him her best "good luck kiss." Al sensed he was going to need lots of good luck to satisfy Miss Hargrove.

On the fifty minute bus ride, Al studied the current issue of *Hi-Lites* of Galveston Beach. It was a slick digest-size magazine that carried large ads from the major hotel in Galveston and many one-inch listings of rooming and boarding houses. Miss Hargrove apparently kept any hotel listings for herself. She had assigned him to visit twenty-eight "mom and pop" boarding houses that took in mostly summer boarders.

Al's first stop was four blocks from the bus station and eight blocks from the beach. A sign over the door read, ROOMS FOR RENT, DAY, WEEK, MONTH, SUMMER, INQUIRE WITHIN. Al knocked and waited a while, until a middle-aged man finally answered. He looked at Al suspiciously through the screen door. "What do you want?" he asked grumpily, as he moved the screen door half open, and blocking Al from seeing in or entering.

"I represent the *Hi-Lites* of Galveston Beach," Al said. "I'm here to renew your ad for the next month and to ask you for the eight dollars you owe for the last four weeks of advertising."

The man glared at Al in the bright morning light. He opened the door some more, apparently ready to do something.

"I told Sally Hargrove that ad didn't work because nobody came here and to take it out of the book! I told her that three weeks ago! I don't want no more ads! I won't pay for them!" He turned to close the door.

"The season is just about to start. Do you have rooms for rent? If so, this is surely not the time to be out of Hi-Lites," Al pleaded.

The man stopped and glared back. He reached in his pocket after a moment.

"Here's a dollar. That's all I can give you. Tell Sally Hargrove to cancel our ad! Don't come back and tell her not to come here! One dollar is what you get. And, I don't want to see or hear from you again! Do you understand?"

Al assured him that he did. He took the dollar and headed to his next stop.

Each stop was more or less a repeat of the first. He found himself entering a forbidding, harsh world of trying to collect money from angry people not interested in advertising. Many of the owners had told Sally Hargrove not to run the ad, but she continued to run them anyway. Al learned a quick lesson on salesmanship, that cajoling a customer by making ad change suggestions and trying to make the ad more appealing, could sway some customers to try one more ad. But, all too often, people told him that they did not want to pay the two dollars for the weekly ads.

By 6 P.M., Al had survived a blistering hot afternoon in Galveston talking to unfriendly people. He tallied his totals for the day: seventeen stops out of the assigned twenty-eight and thirty-one dollars collected. He was eighteen blocks from the bus station. He ran puffing all the way back to the bus station to catch the bus at 7:00 to meet Miss Hargrove at Morrison's Cafeteria back in Houston.

At the Houston bus terminal, Al saw Mary right away. She drove him over to the cafeteria. "You look absolutely awful for a man who has spent a delightful day on Galveston Beach," Mary said, frowning at the washed out look on Al's face.

"I never saw the beach," Al responded in an exhausted voice. "I only got within three or four blocks of the ocean, and all I got was tzuris."

"Tzuris?" Mary wondered.

"Tzuris. It's a Jewish word for trouble."

"Do you speak Jewish? I didn't know that."

Al explained that his grandmother spoke the language called Yiddish. He understood some of the words, but rarely used them. However, tzuris was precisely the word to express what he'd experienced all day.

Al arrived right on time to meet Miss Hargrove. She greeted him with a severe frown. She started right in with perfunctory questions. "Did you make the calls I listed for you? How much money did you collect? How did you do?" She snapped the questions at Al before he had a chance to answer.

Robert Miller

Al told her he took the 7 A.M. bus out of Houston and the 7 P.M. bus out of Galveston. He worked eleven hours and had seen seventeen advertisers, fourteen of whom wanted to cancel.

She counted the money, still frowning. There was one dated check. She quipped sarcastically, "Those Jews might close their account and move away by Friday."

"I had no idea the Sloanes were Jewish. They gave me no indication of moving anywhere. In fact, I suggested to them an improvement in their ad and they agreed to keep running it for the next few weeks," Al responded innocently.

"You suggested a change in the ad?" Her voice went high-pitched. "Do you know what it costs me to reset an ad? I didn't send you to Galveston to get ad changes. I sent you there to collect money, not cause me more work and more expense making changes in the listing. Do you think seventeen calls a day is a fair day's work?"

"Miss Hargrove," Al protested. "It was a long hard eleven hour day. I've been shouted at and told to go away. I got most advertisers to reconsider and run the ad again. I also walked about ten miles all over Galveston. I think I gave you a good day's work."

She looked at him fiercely. Al stared back.

"Maybe you did the best you could," she grudgingly admitted. She presented him with a list of twenty-four new advertisers to see the next two days. He was told he had to finish seeing those on the first list. She handed him two dollars from the money he had collected so he could buy two round trip tickets for the next two days. She instructed him to keep an account and make sure he got change to give back to her. Then she got up and walked out, leaving Al where he sat gawking at her.

CHAPTER 33

A few minutes later Al entered the car where Mary waited.

"Your nemesis just left," Mary joked. "That Miz Hargrove always carries an umbrella. A broom might be more appropriate."

Al thought about going back to do the same work in Galveston and quickly lost his zest for the job. He felt hungry, tired and disenchanted. Talking things over with Mary, he decided to give the job another try and planned to stay overnight in Galveston, preventing the exhaustion of long work hours and traveling time.

That night from his makeshift bed on the couch, Al was awakened by the sound of Mary's footsteps as she approached him in the dark. She stopped to kiss him warmly good night on her way back from the bathroom. She gasped as he reached for her. She put her lips against his ear to whisper, "The thought of spending the night together tempts me. Somehow, some way, we'll work it out one night soon, if you'll promise me that my panties stay on." With that, she kissed him again and was gone.

The next morning Al boarded the bus to Galveston again and was shocked to see Sally Hargrove already seated. "You're going to Galveston too?" His words stumbled out.

"Mr. Gordon," she said, "I don't have to report to you. You have to report to me. I have given you an assignment to see some twenty-four people today and add to that eleven you didn't manage to cover yesterday. That's thirty-five people. That is your responsibility today and tomorrow. Do you understand that?"

Al understood and explained courteously that he would be saving her one bus fare by staying overnight in Galveston. Having said that, he decided to sit near the back of the bus to stay discreetly out of her sight.

When he arrived in Galveston, he began his work immediately. He trudged from one boarding house to another just as he had the day before. He tallied up numbers in his head to keep an accounting of his visits: 19 stops this second day, $42 collected.

Eight people had told Miss Hargrove not to rerun the ad (which she did anyway). His costs: $1 to rent a room, sixty cents for a chopped steak dinner and twenty cents to call Mary.

Unlike the first two days of walking around under a blistering sun, Al trudged in rain all of the third day. He had neither a raincoat nor an umbrella, but he did have 16 customers to see. The third day also proved to be a repeat of all the same customers' complaints of the previous two days.

On the evening of the third day, Al rode the bus back to Houston. He was wet, tired and bedraggled.

Mary met the bus and drove him over to the cafeteria. "You look like a drowned cat, but am I ever glad to see you."

Al felt bone tired, but he smiled, happy to see Mary.

When he greeted Miss Hargrove, she gave him an appraised look and commented, "You look like a disgrace. Did you see my advertisers looking like you do now?"

"Miss Hargrove, it rained all day in Galveston," Al complained.

"Let's see what you accomplished," she snorted.

Al watched as she added up the totals. Al already knew the numbers in his head: 35 people contacted and $73 collected. He felt he had accomplished something.

"Thank you, Mr. Gordon. I'm being generous with you. I'm paying you ten-dollars for three days work." She quickly handed him the money and added, "Your services are no longer needed. I cannot have you represent Hi-Lites any longer."

Al sat up stunned. "You're firing me? Why? I've done everything you asked of me in hot weather and in rain. I've collected money from people who said they had already canceled their ads."

"I like clean-cut American people, Mr. Gordon. I don't like Jews," Miss Hargrove declared with a hiss.

"And I especially don't like Jews who don't tell me that they are Jews. I suspected you were a Jew because you come from New York and are dark, but it never occurred to me that Opal Mae Porter's daughter would have a Jewish boy friend, but then, if Opal Mae could marry an Irish Catholic, what could one expect from her daughter?" Miss Hargrove huffed out the words. She got up, pushed her papers into her purse, and strode out with her back straight and her chin sticking out.

Al froze in his seat and stared at her as she disappeared from view. He had been told he was less than a person by some woman who personified the meaning of the word bigot. He had to remind himself that what matters is that he was a good person, equal to anyone else.

Clash of Cultures - The Al Gordon Story

Al had only four words for Mary when he returned to the car. "I just got fired."

Mary laughed at the idea. She shook her head when she saw the hurt in Al's eyes. "You didn't want to keep working for that crazy old coot, anyhow, did you?" She consoled.

"I wanted to spend this summer here in Texas with you. Without a job, I'll have to go home. I'm shocked. I've never been fired before." He had wanted to make something of himself. The act of being fired was so demeaning. The reason for the firing, being a Jew, seemed so appalling.

Al gave Mary an innocent, shocked look that touched her heart.

Mary came closer and kissed Al. Her hands roamed over him, tantalizing him to forget the old bitch. Al responded and became excited. "Now you have been fired and fired up within minutes. I like fired up better," she cooed in her Texas drawl. "Let's go somewhere where I can really cheer you up."

Mary drove to a remote point beyond Hermann Park. When they relaxed, she started asking questions first. "Now tell me what you want to do? Are you hungry? Have you had anything to eat? Shall we go to Prince's?"

Al held her close and started to unbutton her blouse. He told her he had not eaten and was hungry, but right now he just wanted to kiss and caress her breasts.

Mary cooperated. As he put his tongue on her nipples, he could feel them harden. As she felt Al become excited, she opened his fly and pulled out his hardened penis.

"I don't want to put it in my mouth, but I will kiss it," she said. She ran her tongue along the top of it and kissed it again. She giggled nervously.

Al breathed deep and said huskily, "Sweetheart, I'm afraid I'll explode in your face if you kiss me there again."

"Give me your handkerchief," she commanded sweetly.

Al handed her the handkerchief, which was still wet from the rain. She wrapped it neatly in place around Al's throbbing penis. Al looked at his semi-nude beautiful Mary. He felt her strokes up and down on his organ. He held his breath as, shortly, he came. Mary smiled back at him as he sighed deeply.

"Was that worth getting fired for?" she asked. She cleaned up Al's wetness and continued talking. "I'm going to call Beth Johnson and ask her if she and her husband are going out. We might be able to babysit for them. What better way to celebrate your getting your driver's license than us being alone without anything between us, but one pair of the most sheer panties I have. What do you think of that?"

There was no answer. Mary turned to look at Al. He had fallen into a deep satisfying sleep.

She smiled at him as she buttoned her blouse to prepare to head home.

CHAPTER 34

The next morning Al called Bill Wannamaker at *The Houston Press*.
"Sally's a difficult woman. I knew I wasn't doing you any real favor when I suggested you get in touch with her," Mr. Wannamaker said. "How long did you actually work for her?"
"Three long hard 10-hour and 11-hour days."
"Did she tell you why she was letting you go?"
"She didn't want me to represent Hi-Lites, and that she doesn't like Jews."
"My God, are you Jewish?!"
Al said, "Yes."
"If I had known that I would have never asked you to call her. She's the most bigoted woman I've ever met. Al, come by and see me on Monday. I owe you something. I'll try to make it up to you for putting you in contact with that woman," Mr. Wannamaker said apologetically.
Al felt relieved as he put the phone down. If I had known that, Al reflected, why is it that I'm in some ideological 'thatness' - that my being Jewish creates such a conflict?
Back with Mary, Al got a look that said, 'What happened?'
"He asked me to come by on Monday. He feels bad about what happened with Sally Hargrove. I think he might give me a job on *The Houston Press*. What do you think of that?"
Mary's face brightened. She came over and kissed Al. Mrs. Monahan smiled politely at Al. He could not read her smile. She apparently was surprised that he should have such good luck. Al thought he saw more of a wince than a smile.
The decision was made that the three of them would spend the time letting Al practice his driving. Mrs. Monahan sat in the back seat giving what she considered her best constructive criticism.

Mary chose to finally break the tension by commenting, "No man should have to practice his driving on the day before his road test with his future wife beside him laughing and his future mother-in-law in the back seat making him nervous."

"Well, it is my car. Maybe I'm just a little nervous too," Opal Monahan admitted.

For lunch, Al announced he would use his pay to treat all of them at the new Jewish delicatessen, Schwartzenberg's. Mary and her mother readily consented.

Mary directed Al to a wooden house just off Main Street converted into a combination store and restaurant, but appeared nothing like the kosher delicatessens Al knew in the Bronx.

Al ordered a corned beef sandwich. The waitress asked him what kind of bread he wanted. He first looked at her as if she were crazy and then almost laughed, but he realized the Texas waitresses still had to learn from their New York "friends" how to eat Jewish food. He smiled and ordered rye bread. Mary ordered the same. Mrs. Monahan ordered the corned beef on white bread with lettuce. When Mrs. Monahan got her corned beef sandwich, she dabbed mayonnaise on it and declared it "delicious."

Al dabbed mustard on his sandwich and began eating. He said it was good, but not quite on a level with the corned beef sandwiches he'd had on Tremont Avenue. He told them corned beef sandwiches cost fifteen cents, a hot dog with sauerkraut cost a nickel, or a salami or bologna sandwich cost a dime.

As Schwartzenberg's filled up with customers, Mary kept nodding hello at people she knew.

"Do you know everybody in Houston?" Al asked in amazement.

"Not everyone, sweetheart. But, I've lived here all my life. I've gone to different schools, and I've met plenty of people. This is a small town, you know," Mary said.

"I'm absolutely floored," Al told Mrs. Monahan. "When I met Mary, she told me that I was the first Jew she had ever met, but it turned out she knew more Jews than she realized."

"Of course, we know some Jews," Mrs. Monahan reflected. "Houston has Jews, Syrians, Cajuns, Yankees, and various other forms of white people, and, of course, there are many Mexicans and nigras. There are two or three Jewish churches here. I know you call them synagogues, and probably two or three more in Galveston. There are many Jews here. We are tolerant of Jewish people here. But, we do think of them as different." She sweetened her tone to add, "At least we always did, Al, until we met you."

Al smiled and kissed her on the cheek. "Mrs. Monahan, now that you've met me, do you think of Jews as being more different or less different? And have you considered that I may be different from all other Jews or that Jews may be different from one another as Gentiles are?"

Robert Miller

"Gracious, Al, I've never thought that much about Jews at all until I met you. When one's only daughter tells me...mind you, tells her mother and father, not asks them...that one day she is going to marry this Jewish boy from New York, that makes a person think about that subject, doesn't it?"

Al nodded and smiled at Mrs. Monahan. Mary beamed brightly.

The driving lessons continued another two hours after lunch, until Mrs. Monahan finally approved and declared that Al had done everything correctly.

Back at the house, Al enjoyed the luxury of a glass of ice tea and Mr. Monahan's plush easy chair. Mary came in and nudged Al out of his nap to tell him that they would be babysitting for the Johnsons that night. Mary said, "I told her, 'Sure, I'll babysit, if I have Al to keep me company after her little one goes off to sleep.'"

Al thought he saw Mrs. Monahan wince again.

At the Johnsons home, Beth and Bob Johnson thanked Mary and Al for babysitting, allowing them to go out to a movie for a much appreciated change of pace. The baby had been put to sleep and was not expected to wake up.

"You two will simply have to find a way to entertain yourselves while we're away. We'll be back at eleven," Beth told Mary in a conspiratorial tone, just before following her husband out the door.

CHAPTER 35

Al and Mary sat in the living room feeling nervous about being alone in the quiet house. Al crossed his legs one way and then another way in awkward self-consciousness. Mary got up to peek in at the baby. Al got up and examined the bookshelves in the cluttered living room.

Mary came back, whispering that the baby girl was fast asleep. She relaxed then and put her arms around Al's neck as he stood in front of the bookshelves. She kissed him lightly a few times and teased him with her tongue. He relaxed more. His hands went down the back of her dress, fondled her bottom and then pulled it towards his body.

Mary let herself be pressed against Al for a few minutes and then backed off. "Take it easy, sweetheart. We've got hours before they come home. Let me make sure that all the shades are down and figure out where we can be most comfortable." She moved away from Al and went around the house pulling down shades. She returned and said, "We can go into the bedroom, if you want, but we'll have to be very quiet there. Or, we can stay here on the couch. Or, we can lie down on the floor. Which do you prefer?"

Mary's suggestions were direct and matter of fact without any apparent trace of guilt. Al did not answer. He simply pulled her to him and kissed her. His tongue roamed deep into her mouth. She gasped and stepped back.

"Take it easy, Al. We have a little time tonight" She turned her back and said, "Why don't you open the buttons on my dress and help me get my clothes off."

Al enjoyed her openness and helped with the buttons. It seemed Mary had planned what she wanted to do. The dress was well chosen. The eight large buttons that ran down from the collar to her waist were easy for Al to unbutton. She stepped out of her dress and went to a closet. He watched as she found an empty hanger and hung the dress from one of the light fixtures, explaining that she did not want to get it creased and wanted to keep it handy in case somebody

Robert Miller

came in. She then lifted her pink slip over her head and stood before him in her bra and panties. She had everything orchestrated for Al's enjoyment. She then turned off the lights, but left a low light on so Al could see her.

She then asked Al if he wanted to undo and remove her bra.

Al readily volunteered, saying that he needed the practice. She turned her back to him to let him undo it, but said that he was not to touch her yet. Al's hands trembled slightly. His fingers struggled in the semi-darkness to unsnap a hook that he could barely see.

"Should I do it myself?" she asked over her shoulder.

"Give me one more minute. You told me not to be in a hurry."

Mary smiled. She reached down to fondle the bulge in his pants. Al finally unhooked the bra, and as he did so, she slowly turned towards him, holding out her arms so he could maneuver the bra out and away from them.

"Now, let me undress you," she said, as she started to open his belt. Al's hands reached into the back of her panties and fondled the contours of her bottom. She stopped what she was doing and looked at him. "Al, you promised to leave my panties on and not to put your hands inside them. Please stop!"

"Sweetheart, I promised you that I would not remove your panties, but you never said that I couldn't touch your rear."

Mary turned her face up and kissed Al. "Do you want to discuss this further or do you want me to take your pants off and play with your wheedle worm?"

"Please," Al responded. "I want you to take my pants off and you can play with my thing all you want. You can call it whatever you want, but I'm not thrilled about your calling it some sort of worm."

Mary chuckled and knew her teasing had hit a sensitive nerve. She managed to get Al's pants and underpants down all at once. Al tried to step neatly out of his pants, but they got tangled up in his shoes, nearly throwing himself off balance. Then he tore off his shoes excitedly without unlacing them. Mary started unbuttoning his shirt buttons. Without a word, Al impatiently pulled the shirt over his head and threw it on the floor.

Mary came forward and started kissing him, on and around his lips, then working her way down his neck and over his chest.

Suddenly, a bell rang loudly. The noise startled them both, until they realized it was the phone. Mary ran to answer it. Al stood there naked and erect, wearing only his socks.

Al overheard her reassuring Beth Johnson that everything was all right and the baby was asleep. Al stared at the almost naked Mary, except for her sheer panties, standing in the semi-darkness. The low light bouncing off the shade gave her skin an orange hue, as she stood talking calmly to Beth Johnson. Al turned and took off his socks, moving his rumpled clothes into a small pile.

As Mary hung up the phone, the naked and erect Al walked over and hugged her. She grabbed his penis in her hand. They indulged in a lively discussion and a few quick ideas of what to call his excited penis, and Mary decided on calling it "my other sweet Al." Al accepted the title as being better than a wheedle worm, but he had the feeling that wheedle worm was a name that would stick in her head forever.

Mary got a towel out of her purse and spread it on the floor. She then lay on her back and beckoned Al to come toward her. Al thought again how everything seemed well planned. Al came down on his knees on top of her. She positioned "sweet Al" between her legs and pressed her legs close together. Without a word, Al moved back and forth and very quickly reached orgasm.

Mary remained still. Al stopped pulsating. Then she sighed and teased, "You have figured out how to get my panties off. You've made them all wet. I'll have to wash and dry them."

Al's fondest desire right now was to see Mary naked. She consented, adding that he had to be dressed when she came out of the bathroom, for their own protection.

As promised, Al dressed and waited for her to come out. When she came out, she walked naked towards him with a loving smile. Al's eyes took in every inch of her body. She came right to him and put her arms around him.

"Al Gordon," Mary said. "I love you. I am naked and humble in your arms. I want your body much more than you know. You're going to have to find a way to marry me very soon. Now, kiss me one more time and hold me close and then let me get dressed." Mary broke away after a long kiss and started to get dressed. Al pleaded to watch her get dressed.

"I'm very embarrassed now, but I wanted to show myself to you, too," she said. With uncharacteristic embarrassment now, she ran to the bathroom to put on her clothes. When she returned, she had Al help fasten the buttons on the back of her dress. They relaxed on the couch, sitting together as close as possible.

"I feel like a fallen woman," Mary mumbled her soft complaint in his ear. "We promised each other that whatever we do, I keep my panties on. And where are they now? They're toasting over a flame in the kitchen. I hope they'll be dry by the time Bob and Beth get home!"

Just as Al leaned over to give Mary a comforting kiss, the phone rang loudly.

Mary ran and answered it on the first ring. It was her mother. Mary explained how the baby had awakened but that it had just gotten back to sleep. She told her mother the Johnsons would be back home in an hour and a half. She promised that she and Al would come straight home so Al could be rested for his driving test tomorrow. Mary hung up the phone and returned to Al. She explained that her mother had called to make sure everything was all right.

"What if she knew I'm sitting here fully clothed, but with no panties on, or..." Mary hesitated. She grimaced and raised her eyebrows in anticipation of

Robert Miller

what her mother would do - probably put Al on a fast out-of-town, one-way bus back to the Bronx.

"Please don't keep reminding me of our promise or you'll drive me crazy," Al told her.

CHAPTER 36

Al could not resist reaching for Mary again. He put his hand on her leg and worked it up her thigh.

Mary gently took hold of Al's hand and held it where it was. She pulled his hand out with hers and kissed it. "Al, your fingers inside me thrilled me more than you can know. I can't let that happen again until our wedding night. Please respect my wishes." She took her hand away from his and got up. She walked to a chair across the room, sat down and asked Al if they could talk.

"Of course, what do you want to talk about now?" Al wondered.

"Religion," Mary said. She went on, seeing she had his attention. "Do you believe in God? What do you really believe?"

Al laughed from the shock of seeing her change from a sexy woman into a devout Catholic. "My darling, you sit there so prim and proper across the room from me without any panties on and you ask me if I believe in God! Sweetheart, I believe in love. What kind of question is that between two people who love each other?"

"For me, the first important question is whether you love me," Mary said. "The second most important question is whether you believe in God."

Al admitted to her that he believed in God, but he clarified his admission to say that he thought more about her than about God.

"Don't you think about my eternal soul? Am I only a plaything to you? Is that all I am to you, Al?"

Al smiled. "Mary, you're everything to me. Everything. I'll do anything for you. Anything. I'll even talk about religion, if you'll do one thing for me."

"And what is that?"

"When you retrieve your panties, will you lift up your dress and let me have a last look, front and back, at the sweetness you hide under those panties all the time."

Mary giggled. "Al Gordon, you are incorrigible, impossible, and something of a voyeur. You upset me sometimes because you won't be serious." Her tone turned more playful. "I might do what you ask, but you'll have to look fast because you'll get only a short peek."

When she got up, she walked towards the kitchen. With her back to Al, she lifted her skirt high. Then, she turned and faced Al for just a second. She saw him sitting there smiling as he gazed intently at her body. She turned and ran into the kitchen.

When she came out of the kitchen, she smiled radiantly as she stepped over to Al. "I have my panties back on. They are dry and even toasty warm. I feel safe enough to let you kiss me."

After a quick kiss, Mary returned to where she had been sitting and picked up where she had left off in the conversation about religion. She reminded Al that he had told her that he did not believe very deeply in Judaism. She told him she did believe very deeply in Catholicism. She felt he should know these things, and she wanted to ask him to share her faith with him. Mary explained to him that she was afraid his soul would be in purgatory a long time if he did not profess his belief in Jesus. Al asked her what purgatory was, since he had never heard about purgatory before. Whatever it was, it sounded ominous to him. She explained that Catholics believe that Jews and Protestants, who have led good lives, have to go to purgatory, a holding place between Heaven and Hell, before they can go to Heaven.

He asked her whether she had any doubts about her beliefs. He explained religions made him feel confused because there were so many and each one professed to be the only right way to God. "Mary, I was turned off by a religion that heaped praise on God in an ancient Hebrew language I didn't understand. Is God so vain that we must praise and exalt him all the time? If I really believed in all those prophesies about the Messiah, I might just believe that Jesus was the Messiah and that the Jews blew it. Mary, listen. I've turned my back on one religion that saddled me with ancient traditions, and prayed in a dead language. And now, you want me to join another religion, not too different from mine. I just don't think I can do that."

"It sounds perfectly logical to me, sweetheart," Mary said, as she brightened to his muddled look. "Catholicism is merely the culmination of Judaism. Jews, like Peter and Paul, traveled the world and told the story of Jesus and brought a modern Judaism in the form of Christianity to the world." She offered him a comforting, confident smile.

Al replied that he didn't want to change his religion because he would always think of himself as Jewish. He explained that, in the Reformed Jewish Movement, Reformed Jews prayed in English and lived modern lives not bound by foolish dietary laws of the Orthodox Jews. "It seems to me that the Roman

Catholics are the Orthodox of Christianity and the Protestants are the Reformed, just as the Jews have their Orthodox and Reformed groups."

"What a fascinating observation that is," Mary said excitedly. She beamed at Al's observations about religion. "The Roman Catholic Church is the one true church because it is built on Jewish faith and doctrine. If you could believe in that faith, you could be the noblest Jew of all, one who has come to realize that the ultimate fulfillment of Judaism is the belief in and love of Jesus."

Al sat amazed listening to her religious fulminations. He found himself impressed by her enthusiasm. Still, he hesitated. He knew he couldn't explain to her why changing his religion to Catholicism was not as simple as she made it out to be. He could not simply toss away his own Jewish upbringing. There were too many terrible uncertainties for him to become a Catholic all of a sudden. Al wanted those around him to accept and to respect both of them no matter their beliefs and allow them build a wonderful life together.

"Jesus told His disciple, Thomas, that he was blessed even though he had doubts," Mary encouraged. Her eyes sparkled with a radiance at each new idea she presented to him. It all made complete sense to her. "But, He told Peter that he was more blessed because he had more faith and no doubts."

Al sat there astonished. He reflected on Mary's fervent faith in someone she had never seen - Jesus. She spoke of Jesus, Thomas and Peter as if they were contemporaries and her friends, not biblical figures that lived almost two thousand years in the past.

Al's reluctance to accept Mary's stories made Mary more determined than ever to try and convince Al. Her reasoning about the link between Catholicism and Judaism seemed unique. While listening to her, Al never got the feeling, "I've got to get away from this fanatical lunatic." Her faith was not artificial; in fact, it was almost reassuring. Her faith was so strong. She lovingly persisted in trying to get Al to see how her God and her faith were so real for her. The passions and joys of running around naked were almost forgotten. They had not heard the Johnsons return, until Bob and Beth suddenly walked through the door. Their reappearance was the only thing that saved Mary and Al from staying up all night discussing the double, yet, overlapping lives and beliefs of Catholics and Jews.

By the time Al got settled into bed on the Monahan's sofa, he realized how special Mary was. Mary came by quietly and offered him her final good night kiss before she left.

Al lay in bed and breathed deeply. He began his nightly prayer to God. He had never shared with Mary the fact that he did pray nightly. He had not felt the need to discuss his relationship to God. Unlike Mary, he thought of his faith as too private a thing to share. Most of what he discussed openly were his doubts concerning the strict rules of religions. Tonight, he understood better that he was in a home and with a family where the Catholic faith was very precious and took

Robert Miller

on a larger-than-life meaning. Part of Mary's specialness was her faith. She prayed for him at church and at home. She prayed for his eternal soul. She thanked her God for him and his well-being. She did this freely, asking nothing in return. Al thought it only appropriate to pray tonight. He thanked God for the joys of this particular day, for the people who loved him so much, thankful to be away from the likes of Sally Hargrove, who was so full of hate.

His prayers finished, he felt a new peace and settled into sleep.

CHAPTER 37

After six minutes of driving, the portly middle-aged state driving inspector handed Al a temporary license. The inspector assured Al that a permanent license would be mailed from Austin in a week.

"The test was a snap," Al quipped, as he gave Mary a cocky smile. "You and your mother were tougher to satisfy."

"No matter what happens to our relationship, every time you get behind the wheel of a car for the next eighty years, you'll always remember who taught you how to drive," Mary said smiling.

Mary and Al decided to go to Schwartzenberg's for a celebration lunch. They each had a kosher special - hot dogs and beans. The lunch reminded Mary of knockwurst, a German sausage, but the term knockwurst was new to Al.

Al's conversation centered around his job plans. If Bill Wannamaker at the *Houston Press* would hire him for a few weeks, he could stay on in Texas. If Bill didn't, Al knew he would have to go back to New York City to work for his parents.

Mary's conversation centered around the Church. She told Al that she wanted to go to church in the afternoon so she could receive communion on Sunday.

"After you go to confession, are you telling me that will mean no fooling around tonight?" Al probed with a mix of fun and hope for another eventful evening.

"Didn't you have enough fooling around last night to last a while?" Mary asked. She smiled coyly, her cheeks blushing.

"Are you going to tell the priest exactly what we did last night?" There was a tone of astonishment in Al's hushed voice.

"I will confess to my sinful behavior," Mary said. "I surely hope he will spare me the embarrassment of having to give him every detail about what we did. He probably will. But, it is my duty to make confession now."

Robert Miller

Al's eyes had widened. The idea of confession bothered Al. He carefully weighed what to say to Mary. He didn't want to appear overly critical of the idea, but he also wanted to tell her how he felt about it. He was especially worried that Mary would be telling a priest what he and Mary did personally, that they constituted sins, but he did not consider their intimate behavior sinful. How could he face the priest, if the priest knew what he and Mary had done together? Al suddenly took the notion of confession very personally. He had never had to confess to a rabbi about the thing he'd done! He was not sure if he could ever be ready for such an experience, let alone, to have Mary confess.

"Can't you save your confession until after I've left?" Al asked. He twisted closer to Mary.

"Who knows, I may have something else to confess by the time you leave." Mary's flushed face and giggle helped take away some of the sting Al was feeling.

He tried to smile back.

"Al, would you do something for me just because I asked you to do it?"

"What?" Al asked.

"I'd like you to meet Father Reilly. He's the newest and youngest priest in our parish. I think you'd like him."

"Sure I'll meet him," Al said and added, "sometime."

"I'm talking about this afternoon. Would you do that for me?"

"I'd do anything for you, Mary. I'll meet with Father Reilly, but you may wind up being sorry you introduced us," Al replied.

Mary got up immediately and asked the cashier if she could use the phone. Al watched in astonishment. If anyone in New York asked to use the restaurant's phone, that person would be immediately and not politely directed to use a public telephone.

When Mary came back, she announced happily that they had a three-thirty appointment at the rectory with Father Reilly.

"It's only a little after two now. Why don't you let me drive you over to the park and maybe I can give you something more that you can confess to," Al suggested playfully.

Mary smiled, blushed and gave Al her serious frown. "Al, darling, there's a time for everything. Right now, I want to make confession. Then, I want you to meet Father Reilly, and then I want to receive Holy Communion tomorrow. I also want you to understand my motivation, my needs, my principles, and my beliefs. I don't expect you to understand everything I do, but I want you to respect what I believe in, as I will always respect the things you believe." Mary gave a comforting smile, leaned over, kissed him on the cheek and asked innocently, "Is that too much to ask?"

Al's answer was a silent shake of the head.

Clash of Cultures - The Al Gordon Story

Al had a new confidence and pride as he drove along Houston's streets with his new temporary driver's license. He remembered how easily he had passed the driving test. His confidence waned as he thought ahead to his next "test" in meeting with Father Reilly.

The darkness inside St. Anne's Church struck Al as disturbing after being out in the bright warm Texas sunshine. The church's imposing cool, dark strangeness cast a pall over his previous lighthearted thoughts.

Al compared the confession booths to phone booths he had seen in railroad stations. Three confessionals were in use. Each marked by the name of the priest hearing confession. Four people waited for Father Reilly, two waited for Father Simmons and no one was in line to confess to Father Walsh.

"You sit down. I'll get in line to see Father Simmons," Mary whispered.

"Why not see Father Walsh, you can go right in to him?".

"Father Walsh is old fashioned and awful. Nobody wants to go to him. I can't go to Father Reilly. It wouldn't be appropriate and might be embarrassing for both of us, if I confessed before our meeting. That leaves Father Simmons. You sit down and be comfortable. You can pray. Or, close your eyes."

Al sat feeling like an alien, an interloper. The big edifice was dark, with a high ceiling, and statues around the perimeter. Many candles burned, their lights flickering deeply in their red glass containers. Al counted about a dozen people scattered about, most of them kneeling and obviously deep in prayer.

Al watched Mary, now standing second in line to wait her turn. Her face appeared composed and serene now. Al thought about how much the Catholic religion meant to Mary. She seemed so comfortable when she was in church. He could only compare how strange and uncomfortable he felt being here.

Al looked again at Mary, now first in line. The look on her face had become somber. Still, her pious beauty outshined the lovely statues of the Virgin Mary that loomed over Al.

Al watched Mary intently as the door of the confessional opened, a lady came out and Mary entered the booth. Feeling alone, he wondered about Mary's experience of confession. Time dragged on. Al lost track of the time. When Mary finally emerged, she crossed herself, looked penitent and walked slowly towards Al.

"Did you catch hell?" Al whispered.

"I have to say many Hail Mary's between now and tomorrow," Mary replied in a serious voice. "I must be penitent."

CHAPTER 38

Mary reached for Al's hand as they walked out of the church into the bright sunshine and around the corner to the rectory adjoining the church.

"You'll like Father Reilly, Al," Mary reassured. "He's young. He may even be from New York. I want you to talk frankly to him and about your feelings. Then listen to him. He's understanding and tolerant. I really want very much for you to learn about my Church and my religion, so you can appreciate the way I feel."

Mary rang the doorbell to the rectory.

A forbidding middle-aged woman answered the bell and cracked the door open. Al could see only her face.

"Is Father Reilly expecting you?" the woman asked with a hint of a challenge in her voice.

After Mary explained they had a three-thirty appointment, the woman opened the door enough to let Mary and Al in. She excused herself and went to a table in the entry foyer. After pulling out an appointment book and checking it, she announced that Father Reilly would be back soon and motioned for Mary and Al to take a seat. Then she left.

The straight backed chairs were not comfortable. Mary started giggling at Al's unusual stiff and awkward sitting posture.

Father Reilly, a spry, young-looking, red-headed priest, greeted Mary effusively. He was tall and thin with blue eyes. Al thought him a handsome Irishman in a clerical suit.

Mary answered his questions and introduced, "Father, I want you to meet Al Gordon. He's the man I'm going to marry some day. He's not a Catholic. I wanted him to meet you and learn something more about the Church."

Father Reilly reached out and shook Al's hand. "Al Gordon, I'm happy to meet you. Mary is a wonderful girl. You're a very lucky man if you're the one she has chosen. Come into my office and tell me something about your plans."

Al and Mary found the plush chairs in the office more comfortable. Father Reilly sat behind his desk as he and Al began getting acquainted.

Al explained he was from New York City, where everyone seems to be either Jewish or Catholic. His own family isn't very religious, except for his grandmother, who lives with them; but the family keeps the traditions and celebrates the Jewish holidays.

"Mary has told me that Christianity is the fulfillment of Judaism," Al declared. "I've told her that, if I believed in the Jewish prophesies of the Messiah, I might agree that Jesus was the Messiah and the Jews didn't recognize him at the time. "But since I really don't hold with all those prophecies and find it hard to accept the Jewish dogma, I don't find it easy to accept the Christian viewpoint either."

Father Reilly frowned. He started speaking of Mary as the epitome of a bright young Catholic girl and devoted Catholic mother in the future. The priest suggested they had lots of years ahead to make up their minds.

"Father, I'm eighteen years old. My mother was married when she was my age. I know that Al is the boy I love and will always love and that there will never be anyone else for me."

Father Reilly frowned again. He tried a positive approach, saying "Al does come from a religious background."

He went on to note that Saint Paul was Jewish. Jesus's first disciple was a Jewish fisherman named Simon, who became Saint Peter. The priest wanted to give Al some books, including a copy of the New Testament, which he suggested should be rewarding reading.

"Are you telling me that I must become a Catholic if I am ever going to marry Mary?" Al asked anxiously.

"Darling, don't say if, say when," Mary corrected.

Father Reilly sighed, obviously believing that Mary could never be happy with a man who did not share her beliefs and devotion. He told Al that a couple could not be married at the altar of the Church, unless both were Roman Catholics. Even if a non-Catholic partner agrees that the children be raised Catholic, such marriages cannot be performed in the Church or celebrated with a nuptial Mass.

By the time Father Reilly finished his explanation, Mary had covered her face and cried, tears flowing freely. She wiped away a few and then spoke in a low voice.

"Father Reilly, many of the things you said are true. I would be very happy if Al could have the same faith I do. But before I would lose Al, I'd accept marriage in a rectory, or by a rabbi, or by a justice of the peace. Al, I want you to know that too. I love you so much," Mary said softly.

Then she suddenly got up and took Al by the hand. Al stood up, as did Father Reilly. Enough had been said to end the meeting for Mary.

Father Reilly smiled at Al, shook his hand, asked him to wait a minute and disappeared from the office. He returned with a New Testament and three pamphlets. The priest encouraged Al to read these, so he could understand Mary and the Catholic Church better. As the couple left, he invited Al to attend church tomorrow with Mary, saying he would be delighted to see them again.

Back in the warm sunshine, the world felt different to Mary.

"Darling, I'm sorry I brought you here. I really expected Father Reilly to be more understanding," Mary said despondently.

Al noticed how the tears had reddened her eyes.

"Al, I want you to know that you're going to marry me one day. There's no escape for you. You're going to marry me, not my parents, my family, my Church, nor any other baggage I may bring along. I love you." She paused to inhale. "Please take me home now. I think I want to go home, be by myself for a few minutes and have a good cry."

Al drove the two of them home, where Mary went to her bedroom and closed the door for two hours. Al sat in the living room to wait. Though assured by Mary of her enduring love, the Church appeared as a wall of restricting regulations.

When Mary came out, Al noticed the redness and puffiness around her eyes. Unless he were to become a Catholic right away, he felt there was no way he could help her.

"I guess you think I'm acting silly," Mary explained. "I've spent the last hour alternately crying, sleeping, and praying. I know now for a fact that, as devout as I am, I will not let anything or anyone drive you and me apart."

Al sat motionless, taking in every word as if he were hearing a confession.

"I want you to know that," Mary continued in an exhausted voice. "That's the primary thing. Right now, I need a little time and space to adjust my thinking about many things, but, Al, not about you."

At dinner that evening, Mary told the story about what happened with Father Reilly.

"What did you expect?" Bill Monahan wondered. "The Church's first goal is to perpetuate itself... Catholics marry Catholics... a person marrying a Catholic will convert. You're not thinking about marriage yet. I can't believe you brought Al to see a priest. Are you tiring of him and trying to get rid of him?"

The question presented too much of a shock to Mary. She began to cry. Losing her composure, she ran off to the bathroom.

A gloom settled over the table. Everyone ate without saying a word. Al waited nervously for Mary to come back. He felt too perplexed to offer any consoling words. They were all facing a harsh reality that he was different by being Jewish, a difference that could jeopardize the whole relationship right now and possibly even Mary's soul for eternity.

Clash of Cultures - The Al Gordon Story

Mary returned in five minutes. Her eyes had dried and she appeared more self-possessed.

"Daddy, I brought Al to visit Father Reilly because I am a devout Catholic and want Al to understand the depth of my convictions. I'm not tiring of Al. I'm going to marry him someday," Mary asserted strongly.

Bill Monahan pushed his fork into a piece of a potato and ate it. His eyes moved up to look firmly at Mary.

"I surely am," Mary said, challenging his look. "Al and no other. We'll get married somehow. But, he's going to be the father of the only grandchildren you're going to have. I expected this to be such a happy day. Why am I so unhappy now? It's because of Father Reilly." Mary nodded her head to reinforce her headstrong stance.

Bill Monahan let out a nervous laugh. He looked down as he began cutting through a piece of chicken. "Darling, you're confusing faith with the Church," he admonished. "Faith is what makes you believe as you do. The Church is an institution that always seeks to perpetuate itself." He paused before eating the piece of chicken. "You want to negotiate. You can't negotiate with the Church on some things! When it comes to God, we're all struggling with our faith. We're all trying to negotiate with God in one way or another every day."

Al looked over at Mary. She was on the verge of tears again.

Bill Monahan looked around the table. "I sat down to dinner in a good frame of mind, but now I'm surrounded by three sourpusses. I suggest we all go out to a movie. And, preferably a comedy!"

Al and Mrs. Monahan tried to smile in agreement. Their smiles had finally broken up their mutual severe stony silence during the delicate conversation between Mary and her father. Mary's emotions teetered between heartbreak and strong Irish determination.

Bill Monahan let Al drive the four of them to the movie. As Al steered the car, Mr. Monahan commented favorably on the way he drove, which Al much appreciated.

The day's experience only created more questions and doubts in the young man, but he feared to say a word about religion. He asked himself over and over again if these ideas of faith and Church regulations were all that important. He wondered what other "tests of faith" he would have to endure if he was going to marry his beautiful, pious Mary.

… Robert Miller

CHAPTER 39

Mary was already up and dressed when Al arose Sunday morning. He dug into a hearty breakfast, which he enjoyed, but Mary reminded him that she was fasting until she received communion.

Al came to the eight o'clock Mass slightly more interested than in any of the previous Masses he'd attended, now that he knew the priest in a more personal way.

Father Reilly had worn a black cassock when he met with them on Saturday. On Sunday morning, the priest was dressed in an elaborate white robe as he performed the Mass. Al alternately stood and sat with the congregation. As usual, he sat back in his pew, while the rest of the worshipers knelt in what had now become a familiar ritual for him. When Mary went forward for communion, Al could not keep his eyes off her. Her whole being seemed contrite and sanctified to Al, as she accepted what she firmly believed was the body and blood of her Saviour.

When Mary returned to the seat next to Al, she was a vision of saintliness in his mind. He pondered the mystery and contradictions of this girl. Her devotion to her Church was so much greater than he had ever felt for his own religion. He could never match her faith or devotion. How can I be worthy of her? How did a Jewish boy from the Bronx ever get so involved in such a situation?" Al asked himself.

When the Mass ended, Mary and Al stood talking to her parents. Mr. Monahan was pressing the women to go to the baseball game this afternoon, but without real success.

Father Reilly made a special effort to greet the Monahans and give Al a strong handshake. "Al, I was especially happy to see you in church this morning. I felt bad that our meeting yesterday ended so abruptly and unhappily. I'm glad to see that you're keeping an open mind. I want you to always feel welcome in our parish. Mary is very important to all of us at St. Anne's. If you are

126

Clash of Cultures - The Al Gordon Story

important to Mary...and I did get the clear message that you are...then you are also important to us."

Al thanked Father Reilly. His comments were meant to heal any friction and hurt that remained from yesterday. The priest then moved on to greet other departing and arriving parishioners.

As the Monahans attended the nine o'clock Mass, Al took Mary to Morrison's Cafeteria, where he bought her an after-Mass breakfast. As they sat down to eat, Mary cheered up. She reminded Al how his horrible experiences with Sally Hargrove started right here in this cafeteria.

"My Daddy seems to want very much for all of us to go to the baseball game today. How do you feel? It really won't be a lot of fun. It will be steaming hot out there and Mother will be grumpy all day. And, if you want to know the truth, I'd rather be someplace alone with you where we could take off our clothes, escape the heat of the weather, and maybe create a little heat of our own."

"That does it," Al said excitedly. "No baseball game for me! We'll stay home and find something to occupy our time!"

Mary blushed. She knew her young man, but she had to calm him down. "If you and I don't go to the game, my mother will be bouncing off the walls herself and nagging Daddy until he brings her home early. They'll come home and find us shamefully unclothed. I'll be disgraced. My mother will carry on and tell everyone. Daddy will get out his shotgun. So, we'll have to save cavorting in the nude for another time. It was just a silly idea."

"Shotgun?" Al let out a nervous laugh.

Mary got up and walked away to get another cup of coffee. Al focused his eyes on her departing figure. One moment she seemed so loving and wanton and then, quickly, she'd revert to the pious convent school girl. Then, when he least expected it, she would transform, once again, into a woman brimming with desire. Al decided he'd never figure Mary out, or know what to expect from her next.

Bill Monahan had the excitement of a kid at the ball game. He had managed to buy some bottles of beer and camouflage them in the picnic bag by covering them with ice, sodas and sandwiches. Opal Monahan acted like a dying swan in the Houston heat. She was appalled when Bill Monahan took out his secreted stock of beer and offered one to Al. Mrs. Monahan expressed her concern that, if Al drank too much beer during the game, he could lose control later that night, threatening Mary's virginity.

Al tried reassuring Opal Monahan that peanuts and beer went together at a baseball game. He also confirmed that Mary's virtue was, and would remain, pure. He told her that Mary was the sweetest young lady he had ever known.

Mrs. Monahan pouted and complained about having to sit in the hot sun and watch grown men play a silly game. Her blood pressure rose with each swig of beer that her husband and Al took. She declared she was not staying for the second game, even if it meant she had to walk home.

Bill Monahan made peace afterwards with his perturbed wife by taking everyone to the Plantation Inn for Sunday dinner. The Inn was an elegant old southern style restaurant, where black waiters in white aprons served fried chicken and fried shrimp. Al indulged himself by eating the fried chicken with his fingers. When Mary insisted that Al try one of her fried shrimp, he immediately developed a taste for the delicacy.

The hearty meal seemed to calm Mrs. Monahan, until Al made a suggestion. "After I return to New York, I hope Mary can come to visit a short time in the summer, fall or Christmas holidays."

Opal Monahan was aghast, and said in definitive terms she would never permit it. Her resistance only caused Al to react with a gusty courage about how serious he and Mary were about each other. Mary would one day have to meet his parents. Of course, Mrs. Monahan could come as her chaperon, Al concluded.

Opal Monahan gave Al a very appraising look and snorted that she would certainly accompany Mary, if Mary had not been properly married by then.

Al and Mary smiled at each other, but Al knew he would have to show he was a very responsible young man, especially to Opal Mae Monahan, if he were to keep seeing Mary in the future. That insight caused him to go from being relaxed and carefree on Sunday to aggressively jobseeking on Monday morning. He got up early, took the bus downtown to in *The Houston Press* office early enough to meet Bill Wannamaker as soon as that gentleman arrived at work.

CHAPTER 40

Mr. Wannamaker greeted Al warmly and reiterateded his feeling of guilt for involving Al with Sally Hargrove, though the word "Jew" was avoided. To absolve himself, the editor agreed to let Al work two weeks as a copy boy. Al would sub another two weeks for reporters who would be on vacation. His salary would then double, once he started working as a reporter.

"When do I start?" Al asked, trying to control his enthusiasm.

"How about now?" Mr. Wannamaker checked his watch before Al could answer and saw that it was 9 A.M. "You can work until 6 P.M. tonight. Beginning tomorrow, you'll work 6 A.M. to 3 P.M."

Al just offered a big smile and nodded his head "Yes."

Mr. Wannamaker called over the chief copy boy, Tommy John Stevenson, and introduced him to Al. Young, tall, thin, with ash blond short hair, Tommy was about a year older than Al.

"Walk Al around the city room, show him the ropes and especially how to handle the monitor board and where the tickers are," Mr. Wannamaker instructed quickly. "And show him how to strip the machines and what to do with the copy."

Whatever had been lost in personal worth and confidence with Sally Hargrove, Al regained doubly from Mr. Wannamaker. Al was proud of the editor's belief in him, and began to foresee a real career with a major newspaper.

As they walked, Tommy John Stevenson filled Al in on the details that Mr. Wannamaker would never take time to explain. To start, Tommy John gave Al the option of joining the American Newspaper Guild union. The union was tolerated at *The Houston Press* because it was owned by Scripps Howard, a national chain; but the other Houston papers were non-union.

Tommy John had been working at the Press for two years as a copy boy. The young man's attitude showed a subtle resentment, once he learned that Al would be advanced to be a reporter after only two weeks. But Tommy John rationalized

Robert Miller

his discomfort with Al's position by remembering Al would only be there for the summer.

Tommy John himself had been promised a permanent reporter's position by Mr. Wannamaker when something opened up.

As the day wore on, Al was mesmerized watching the reporters, rewrite men, caption writers, columnists, feature writers and Bill Wannamaker put the finishing touches on the evening paper.

By four o'clock, everything had slowed down enough for Bill Wannamaker to chat with Al. "I've had my eye on you all day, Al. You didn't stop moving. I like that. How did you like your first day on a daily newspaper?"

"It was overwhelming," Al said. His enthusiasm and adrenaline were running high. "I watched you, too, Mr. Wannamaker. You never stopped. You must have read, checked, corrected, and marked over a thousand pieces of copy. I never realized how complicated it is to put out a newspaper. I can't thank you enough for making a place for me."

"Someone did the same for me thirty years ago at the *Kansas City Star*," Mr. Wannamaker said nostalgically. "Maybe my helping you is my way of repaying a long overdue debt. So, come to me if you need help or advice. I'll always make time for you. I'll expect you promptly at six tomorrow morning. Mornings are the busy times around here." Mr. Wannamaker offered a faint smile, got up and shook Al's hand. Al turned and left the room.

Al's sense of amazement, that he had walked in and started working the same day showed on his face. By the time Mary came to pick him up, he had a copy of *The Houston Press* tucked under his arm. They drove over to Kelly's Restaurant where they had Texas-styled steak dinners to celebrate.

"I had some part in putting out this newspaper today. Articles I clipped off the ticker and gave to the cable desk are published here. I was promised four weeks' work and an opportunity of a bigger job at some future date," Al said in a happy, slightly bragging way. "The only bad news is that I start work at 6 A.M. I can't be disturbing your parents at four-thirty in the morning. So, I'm taking a room at the Hotel Cotton, two blocks from *The Press*, and it will give us a place to be together. Isn't that good news?"

"I'm not exactly sure," Mary said thoughtfully. "I wouldn't go to your hotel room. Remember the ground rules?"

"All right, Mary. You set the ground rules and I'll abide by them."

"The only thing is, Al, we'll have to tell my parents that you're moving in to room with a co-worker. They would never want me to go to a hotel to visit you."

Al agreed to whatever Mary said. He told the waitress to bring a piece of apple pie and convinced Mary to order ice cream, a little of which he stole to put on his pie.

Al read mixed emotions in the Monahans' eyes when Mary told them that Al had a four-week job and would move in with one of his co-workers because of his early schedule. Bill and Opal were surprised at the fast turn of good fortune for Al. Cautiously, they wanted to wait to see if this job really lasted before getting too excited for him. Besides, voicing too much enthusiasm for Al to stay meant encouraging Mary to continue seeing this strange boy from the Bronx. When Mary suggested that the next morning she would get Al up at 5 A.M. and drive him to work, Mrs. Monahan tilted her head and looked at her daughter with new amazement.

With a summer job at a daily newspaper in town, Al hoped that he could gain more respect from the Monahans. After Saturday's troublesome discussion with Father Reilly and Sunday's show of the Monahans' pesky hesitation about Al's relationship with Mary, Monday had proved to be as successful as he'd hoped. Al was almost at the point of thinking that Mary's prayers might be working some miracles. Maybe God does answer some of these Catholic prayers. In his new optimistic mood, Al considered it a humorous, but potentially worthy thought.

Robert Miller

CHAPTER 41

Early the next morning Mary drove Al to the front door of *The Houston Press* for the 6 A.M. shift. The new employee worked enthralled all day, running from the wire room to the cable editor, to the composing room, the reporters, the rewrite men, the caption writer, the city editor, and the photo editor.

Mary sat in her mother's car waiting faithfully as Al left the building at the end of the shift. He got in and sat down on the passenger's side, feeling his hormones still racing from the pace of work.

"Mother wants you to come back for dinner. She wants to hear about your day at work. Is that all right with you?"

"Sure," Al said, smiling confidently. "What a great day. But, do we have to hurry? I have to check into the hotel first."

Mary drove Al to the Cotton Hotel, where he got out and went in alone to prepay half of his monthly bill. Al exited by running down the lobby steps with his room key gripped in his fist.

As he got into the car, he quipped devilishly, "Wouldn't you like to see the room?"

Mary let out a nervous laugh. "Al Gordon, you know full well I want to see your room, that I want to be with you alone and lose all my inhibitions. But it wouldn't be proper or respectable for me to go to your hotel room."

"Didn't you say something about ground rules? Haven't I always abided by the ground rules you set?" Al pleaded.

"I'm not sure that I can continue to abide by this look-but-don't-touch situation we've gotten ourselves into. I can give you release with my hands, but I don't get any release. Can you be patient with me?"

She looked at Al's eyes and scanned down. The big bulge in his pants answered her last question. "I guess you can't." With a smile, Mary started the car and drove around the corner. She parked at an inconspicuous spot behind the hotel.

"What time is it?" she asked.

"Three forty-five."

"All right," Mary whispered in a deeper voice. "Let's go to your room, but we have just an hour. I promised mother I'd bring you home at five."

Al and Mary cautiously squeezed through a side entrance and scooted across the lobby to the elevator. They squeezed each other's hands nervously as they slowly ascended the elevator to Al's third floor room.

Once inside, Mary kissed Al briefly and stepped back. She began undressing first by opening her dress and lifting it over her head.

"Why aren't you taking your clothes off?" Mary wondered.

"I'm waiting for you to take yours off," Al told her.

"Al, darling, I'm going to take my clothes off, but not until you are no longer a threat to my virginity. You better get your clothes off and lie down on the bed."

Al did as she had instructed. Mary, in her slip, came over to the bed. Her tongue and lips kissed Al along his neck and chest. Her kisses and touch sent him wildly out of control, until he could not hold back.

"That excited me, Al," Mary told him. "It was like watching a volcano erupt." Mary's finger teasingly rubbed Al's chin as he lay exhausted. "Now, I'm safe." She eased back with a smile. "I'm going to take my clothes off. All of them. The minute that thing of yours starts rising, so will I. Do you understand that?"

Al nodded contentedly.

When Mary laid down naked next to Al, his hand began roaming the curves of her body. Mary's hand came to Al's hand and guided his fingers into a sweet, wet softness inside her. Mary moved her hand away and wrapped her arms around Al's neck. "Move your fingers faster," she moaned. Al watched as her breathing became harder. Her small breasts firmed and the nipples grew hard.

Mary kissed Al passionately for a long moment and tensed against him before letting go. He felt her body release. Mary became aware of his penis beginning to grow next to her leg. She kissed him one more time, got up and ran naked from the bed into the bathroom. A few minutes later Mary returned to find Al fast asleep.

Mary had all her clothes on when she leaned over Al's naked body, kissed his lips gently and talked sedately to him, "My poor tired hard worker and sweet lover. Now it's time to wake up, clean up and come to have dinner with my parents."

"Was I dreaming?" Al asked coming awake. "Mary, you bring me such joy."

"Al, darling, today, feeling your fingers inside me, you brought me to the point of my own explosion. It was absolute ecstasy. Can you imagine the joys we will bring each other when we are married?"

"Yes," Al sighed.

"You'll sit at the dinner table and talk about your job. But, I want you to know that all I'll be thinking about is how good it felt to be naked beside you - with your sweet fingers inside me and thrilling me so much," Mary added seductively.

Al smiled back and slowly rolled off the bed to take a shower.

Al and Mary managed to repeat their adventures in his room at the Cotton Hotel a couple of times during the next three weeks. Al described his work to Mary as exciting, but he playfully told her their time together always turned out to be more of a thrill.

Al spent two weeks as a reporter. This two week courthouse beat had turned out to be the most boring part of the job. But he still managed to get a few news pieces to the rewrite desk and proudly saw a couple of his articles in the paper later that day.

By the end of the fourth week of his summer job, Al took a few minutes to thank Mr. Wannamaker for all the experiences. The older man had been impressed with Al's work and enthusiasm. He described Al as part of the Press "family."

His words of praise to Al presented a strong and confident type of guarantee. Al would be welcomed back, not only to a summer job next year, but to a permanent job when Al finished school a year later. They shook hands and said goodbye, knowing they would not be seeing each other for some time.

Al sadly handed in his key to the hotel clerk, hating to leave the room that he and Mary could claim as their private place. He spent the remaining time Saturday and Sunday in the company of Mary and her parents.

Al brought up the suggestion again that Mary and her mother might visit New York City before Al came back next year, but Mrs. Monahan reacted unenthusiastically. She obviously still struggled with her own internal conflicts over the relationship and did not want to be seen as encouraging this long distance romance. She knew she did not want Mary entangled yet with those Northerners, or, possibly, those New York Jews.

Mr. Monahan appeared to have mixed emotions about Al's departure. He seemed to Al a genuinely nice man, though he probably would be happier if an Irish Catholic had been courting his daughter. Certainly he cared about Mary's happiness and well-being. Yet having lived so much in the company of women, Mr. Monahan enjoyed Al's male companionship as a son who balanced the strong females in the household.

The final farewells were said Sunday night.

The next morning Mary woke Al up at 4 A.M. She held him close briefly, wearing only a sheer nightgown. A fraction of a second later she stepped back and urged Al to get showered and dressed.

Clash of Cultures - The Al Gordon Story

Mary drove Al over to Route 59, where he would start hitchhiking back to New York City. Al kissed Mary a farewell that poured out his deep passions. Before he opened the door, they promised to see each other no later than December.

Al walked to the side of the road to position himself in the predawn darkness. He lifted his thumb to each passing vehicle. Mary waited across the street in the car. After a futile ten minutes of not getting a ride, Mary drove over to Al and rolled down the window.

"Can I give you a lift young man?" she asked with her Texas drawl.

Al's face broke out in a broad grin. "Take me to New York in your car and we'll travel via heaven itself."

Mary leaned back in the car and roared with laughter. "And spend eternity in hell for it," she responded quick-wittedly. "But, please don't think there is anything in the world I'd rather do, Al. Come in and kiss me one more time for luck."

Al got in. They shared their last kiss. Ten minutes later a pickup truck stopped. Al waved to Mary, got in and headed home.

Robert Miller

CHAPTER 42

Four days and about thirty rides later Al emerged from the Holland Tunnel. He thanked the driver who had brought him up from Trenton and walked to the subway entrance which would take him to his parents' office on West 34th Street.

Al opened the door to the two-room Gordon Advertising Agency. His mother looked up. She blinked with surprise. Without hesitation, she got up and embraced Al, ready to ask him a thousand questions.

"So, how was Texas? Did you have an enjoyable and productive time there? What are your plans now? How long is it until school starts again? Would you like to help us here this month?" Before Al could answer, she offered, "We could pay you eight dollars a week."

"I was making twenty dollars a week in Texas," Al said.

"What other job prospects do you have here?" she added with a tone of humor.

They both laughed. Al kissed his mother on the cheek again. "I'm hungry. Is it lunch time yet?"

Mother and son left right away for their favorite nearby lunch spot — the Coffee Shop at the Hotel New Yorker. Al's mother ordered a corned beef sandwich. Al ordered a ham and Swiss cheese sandwich.

"Ham and Swiss?" his mother snorted. "A month in Texas and you forget everything we taught you. Ham and cheese! That's double trafe! Ham by itself is trafe, but mixing any meat and cheese is trafe. And, ham and cheese together is triple trafe! What other bad habits did you pick up?" she asked frowning pretentiously.

Al laughed. "I learned to like shrimp, which is also trafe, and guacamole salad, which probably isn't."

"What is guacamole salad?" his mother asked suspiciously.

Clash of Cultures - The Al Gordon Story

"It's alligator pears or avocados mixed up and mashed together with some spices. It's really good. You might like it. I know dad would. He loves alligator pears. And, Mom, I have fallen in love. I have met the girl I will someday marry."

"Oy vey!" Al's mother exclaimed, raising her eyes up momentarily. "I knew it. You've fallen in love with that shiksa. She has swept you off your feet and gotten her hooks into you." Mrs. Gordon looked out at him from the corner of her eye. "Is she pregnant?"

"Mother!" Al expressed his disappointment at the suggestion. "Don't even think a thing like that. Mary is the nicest and most refined young lady you'll ever meet. You insult her and me by even thinking such a thing."

His mother laughed, apparently relieved. She assured him that she didn't mean to insult anyone. She wanted Al to understand love meant one thing and marriage meant much more. Marriage between two people with different religions and different ways of life was starting out with two strikes against it.

"You're trying to use a baseball simile to make me rethink," Al said, smirking at his mother's attempt.

"Allie, you might be very surprised at the things your mother knows." She raised her eyebrows and enjoyed watching a bewildered look cross her son's face.

During lunch, Al shared more stories with his mother about Mary. Al innocently and enthusiastically explained how wonderful Mary was. His mother probed with her typical questions and expected responses.

"What is her name?"

"Mary Jean Monahan."

"Mary Jean Monahan. Oy vey!"

"Mother, relax. You'll meet Mary one day. You'll like her very much. She's smart. She's beautiful. She's high class. You'll be impressed."

"Maybe," Mrs. Gordon mumbled.

Al smiled.

"Mother, you understand. Love is the greatest thing in the world. Love is unpredictable. Love shouldn't have to be within the same little group of people all the time. Right?" Al asked before biting into his ham and cheese.

"Huh!" his mother let out, looking at the sandwich and her son's bright-eyed look. "Love. Oy vey," she muttered again.

Al started working for his parents for the next two summer months. The Gordons' small advertising agency took various classified ads for a variety of newspapers and handled some commercial accounts.

Something new had been added recently, where a New York newspaper printed a coupon every day. Readers who saved six coupons could buy a book from the collection of *The World's Greatest Literature* for forty-nine cents. Because the readers' responses inundated the newspaper with coupons, the

Gordons became a station for distribution of the books, for which they were paid two cents on each book sold. The book distribution pumped in a new source of cash flow, bringing in $20 worth of weekly profits. The new revenue represented a small triumph during the days of slow business in the summer of 1935.

Al enjoyed the ambiance of 34th Street where he worked. Small storefront shops crowded along the street and shoppers bustled past each other, heading to unknown destinations. A few blocks away 42nd Street exploded with life, part of the heart of Manhattan, gaudy with movie houses and burlesque shows. Sometimes Al ate at the Greyhound Bus Terminal on West 42nd Street. He came not for the food, but to ogle the girls from the burlesque shows who would appear there for lunch with their heavy stage and eye makeup.

Al wrote to Mary almost every day. Mary mailed warm, loving letters in return.

Working at the advertising agency enabled Al and his mother to bond more closely, especially as they shared lunch three times a week. Al told her more and more about Mary Monahan, and her family, who sounded quite affluent compared to the Gordons. The Monahans' affluence impressed Al's mother. She never completely caved in to the idea of Al's romance with a girl who was not Jewish. She continually warned Allie about the complications of an "involvement," as she called it, between a Jewish boy and a Christian girl. Al found his father to be out of the office most of the time. When Al's mother brought up the "involvement" in the presence of his father, Al got the impression his father didn't much care.

During this period, Al fancied himself a lot more sophisticated for his daring hitchhike to Texas and back. Without Mary around, he started practicing his charms on some of his sister's friends who gathered at the Gordon apartment. Shirley did not appreciate her friends, who were mostly sixteen and seventeen, being bothered by Al's hovering about them. He had his playful fun in watching or teasing one or two girls who showed the slightest interest as he tried to wow them.

After a few weeks sitting at home on the weekends, Al had the urge to get out. One night he called Selma to talk about his trip to Texas. Selma informed him that she now dated Howard Peskin "regularly," but not "steadily." The distinction between the words meant that Howard could now be considered number one. That meant to Al that he could be an alternate on Selma's one-date-a-week list. Al mentioned to Selma that he had a "sort of a girlfriend" in Texas, but he did not elaborate on how intense the relationship had become. The call ended without Al asking for a specific date, but he implied that he would call again soon.

Al hung up the phone and thought about the conversation. Old feelings for Selma passed through him at the sound of her voice. She still meant something very special to him.

"If we get together, I can tell her more about Texas and *The Houston Press*." He didn't think about whether it was a dumb idea or not. I'd like to see Selma again. We could go out for old times sake. I'll impress her. Maybe she'll see that Howard Peskin's a dud compared to me.

CHAPTER 43

Al received a call from Jerry Edgar, who worked with Al on the NYU Bulletin. Jerry needed help. He asked if Al would find a date so he could go out with a girl whose parents did not want her to go out alone with Jerry.

"Al, if you aren't able to get someone to go with us, it will ruin my chances with Inez Weisblum. And, I really like this girl," Jerry pleaded. "We can all go on a picnic to Van Cortland Park on Sunday."

Al agreed to try to find someone and then he called Selma. Selma hesitated, but then relented by saying, "Why not?"

The trolley ride over to the park gave Al and Selma time to get reacquainted. Al looked forward to a good time. He and Selma balanced sodas, beer, fruit, blankets, a baseball bat and baseball gloves in their laps. His fingers managed to slip into Selma's hand as they sat close. She curled her lip and gave him a quizzical look before she let her hand relax into his.

"Are you still seeing Howard?" Al asked.

"Sure," Selma answered calmly. The she applied pressure on Al's hand. "Are you ready to tell me about your new girl in Texas?"

"Why not?" Al responded, then hesitated. This could ruin my whole day, besides any chances I have with Selma. What happens if Mary changes her mind? I'll have nobody, he thought.

"Well?"

Al talked superficially about Mary's cheers for the NYU team last November. He declined giving any more specifics.

"Howard showed me the article about Mary. He also told me that he heard you had quite a hot necking and petting session with that girl at a Texas railroad station," Selma said contemptuously.

"How did he know that?" Al asked.

"Apparently the whole team and even the coach saw the romantic goings on," Selma replied somewhat self-righteously. She laughed in a knowing way.

"Allie, Howard does keep me posted on your activities at NYU. He says you're the biggest wolf on the campus, and a very fast worker."

"And is he a fast worker?" Al wondered.

Selma laughed again. She let go of Al's hand for a few seconds. She returned her hand on top of his where it now rested on her leg. "Al, I've always known what you are. Howard is someone different. He may not be as exciting to me as you are, but he's steadier. More reliable. More dependable. The fact is I like you both very much. Can't we just have fun today and enjoy being together and forget about Howard and Mary, and see if we can still like each other? Can we do that?" Selma asked earnestly.

"Of course," Al agreed, and he squeezed her hand.

Jerry and Inez met Al and Selma at the park. Al introduced Selma to Jerry and Inez. The girls seemed to get along well together. They found a secluded spot. Al and Jerry threw a softball back and forth. The girls talked to each other and began to organize the food.

The couples made an interesting mix. Jerry and Inez warmed up to each other, though it was their first date. Al and Selma experienced a rewarming, after not seeing each other since New Year's. With old embers of feelings attracting them one or both held latent hopes for a rekindled romance. Each had been the other's first significant romance.

Al and Jerry relaxed on the blankets.

"It's too early to eat. We can't leave the food alone. What shall we do now?" Inez asked.

"Let's neck," Jerry suggested, smiling.

Inez laughed, leaned forward and kissed him on the cheek. "There. You've had a kiss. That's all of that sort of thing you can expect from me today."

They all laughed.

Al sprawled out on the blanket. "We all got up early today. Would you be upset if I took a short nap? Selma, do you dare lie down next to me?"

Selma giggled. "I dare all right. I might do just that, but not until you fall asleep. I'll stay here and watch Al sleep, Inez. You and Jerry can explore the park."

Jerry took Inez's hand and helped her up. They walked off, moving close together.

Al shut his eyes. He savored the thought of Selma beside him. With his eyes closed, he took Selma's hand. He squeezed it tenderly and ran his fingers along its softness.

"Selma, I have missed you very much, missed being with you. I'm glad that we're together today."

"So am I, Allie. I missed you too. I want to see you again, but we're going to have to define a new relationship."

"What do you mean?" Al asked softly without opening his eyes.

Selma chuckled nervously. "I'm not even sure myself."

Al's quiet presence encouraged her to go on.

"Al, you used to ask me if I loved you," Selma continued. "I was taught that you tell a man you love him if you are ready to make a commitment and be married for the rest of your life. I knew you were a flirt," she added in a deeper voice. "But, I chose to be with you. I let you do things to me and with me that I never let any boy do before." She paused and added pointedly, "Not before and not since."

Al caressed her hand, holding it to his face.

"Al, I had a love for you and I enjoyed what happened between us, until last New Year's Eve. I felt degraded, used, and like a kept woman. I was just unhappy."

Al lifted his head and smiled at Selma. "You used the term 'kept woman' on New Year's Eve. I had to ask somebody later what the term meant." He leaned closer. "I don't know what the future is for us. I only know I've missed you a great deal and that I have never wanted to kiss someone as much as I want to kiss you right now."

Selma leaned over and kissed Al. She made it a gentle, warm and lingering kiss. Both mouths opened and tongues touched slightly. When Selma sighed and lifted her head, Inez and Jerry stood beside them and started giggling.

"Jerry suggested we neck and I see that you two took up his suggestion," Inez teased. She turned to Jerry and added, "Maybe, after lunch, I'll be ready for a little of that myself. You'll have to wait to find out."

They all laughed and then started rummaging for the sodas, sandwiches, fruit, and beer. The outing, which had started out "iffy" in Al's mind, appeared to be warming up nicely. He and Selma had found old tinder ready to be ignited, whatever the terms might be. Inez and Jerry, starting out as strangers, relaxed, joked and hugged each other.

Selma and Al took a walk after lunch. Al brought the conversation around again to Howard. Selma explained that she enjoyed her casual dating with Howard, and that there was nothing more serious.

"Did you bring me here to talk about Howie Peskin, or did you bring me here to kiss me?" Selma asked Al boldly.

Al enfolded Selma in his arms and kissed her. She pressed her belly against his. Al moved his hands against her side. She reacted by drawing back and taking his hand in hers.

"Al, I'm happy to be with you." She paused and caught her breath. "I'm confused enough. I really didn't expect that your kisses could still turn me into jelly, but they do."

She turned and tugged at Al's arm to start walking.

"I really don't want to talk about Howie any more. I want to talk about your girl in Texas."

Clash of Cultures - The Al Gordon Story

"What girl in Texas?" Al asked coyly. "You have taken my breath away. Right now, I can't remember any girl in Texas."

Selma smiled, leaned over and kissed Al on the cheek.

A radiance of romance embraced both couples the rest of the afternoon. They gloried in each other's love, not knowing where their love would lead them.

Al began seeing Selma on Friday nights, with Howie Peskin seeing her on Saturdays. Al and Selma maintained a slight coolness towards each other, knowing this could not be considered an exclusive relationship. Still, their evenings together ended with a kiss outside Selma's front door. Selma would not allow much more.

Al wrote to Mary and was warmed by her letters. She wrote that she remained very hopeful that he would come down to Texas over the Christmas holidays.

Robert Miller

CHAPTER 44

Jerry Edgar, who was now the assistant sports editor, covered the NYU-Carnegie Tech game from the Yankee Stadium press box. Al had brought Selma to the Saturday game. They sat among the NYU students. At halftime, Al left Selma and went to the press box for a few minutes to talk to Jerry, and when he returned he found Howard Peskin in his seat sitting next to Selma.

"Selma is my girl now, big shot! And don't forget it!" Howard told Al angrily.

"When Selma tells me that and says she doesn't want to see me any more, I'll accept it. Don't forget you took her out when she was seeing me!" Al hollered back.

Howard and Al started pushing and shoving at each other. The only thing that calmed them down were the cries of people behind them calling out, "Sit down! Sit down in front!" Howard finally relented to the crowd and stomped away.

Al turned to Selma. Tears streamed down her face. She got up and pushed past Al.

"Where are you going?" Al asked as he followed.

"I don't ever want to see either you or Howard again. I feel thoroughly humiliated."

"Okay. I'll take you home. I have to tell Jerry Edgar something. We can go to the press box together. I'll take you home. And, please don't cry. It breaks my heart to see you cry." Al had a firm grip on Selma's hand. He turned her around and they headed to the press box.

Inside the press box, Selma's eyes popped wide as she saw the spread of hot dogs, sodas, chips, crackers, and buffet available to the reporters. Al gave Jerry new instructions and returned to Selma. He noticed a miraculous change. Her eyes were dry and she had a smile.

"I feel better now. I can stay until the end of the game. Is there any chance we can stay in the press box?" Selma asked softly.

Al made the arrangements for them to stay. While they sat there, Al pointed out the sports editors from the newspapers - Dan Parker of the *Mirror*, Jimmy Powers of the *News* and Bill Corum of the *American*. Al enjoyed Selma's upbeat mood swing.

"Howie was right about one thing. You are a big shot. I'm impressed," Selma whispered to Al.

On the way home, Selma gave some thought to Al's question about how she was feeling. "Maybe my problem is that I'm not ready to grow up. Howie is possessive and jealous. He wants me to be his girl. The fact is I'm not ready to be anyone's girl. I'd really be happier to see you both. You have your girlfriend in Texas. I don't have any security with you of any kind. I can't decide to see only you, unless I am number one in your life like I used to be." Selma grabbed Al's arm tightly. He felt the softness of her breast pressing his arm. "I don't want to see Howie tonight. Can we do something?"

Al stopped walking. He enveloped Selma in his arms.

"I'd like nothing better. I have a few dollars in my pocket. There's a kosher delicatessen on 161st Street. We'll have dinner there and go to a movie. Do you want to call home and tell them you'll be late?"

Selma decided she'd better call home. She also said she'd have to call Howie to cancel their date.

"Oh, Al, I'm a little crazy. I'm as happy this moment as I've been in the last year. Will you do one thing for me?" Selma asked.

"Of course, just tell me what," Al answered eagerly.

Selma looked up. Al looked into her scared face.

"Please tell me that you love me."

Al pulled her close. They stood embraced under the elevated subway tracks on the corner of River Avenue and 161st Street. Whatever it meant to their futures, Al and Selma wanted to forever remember the way-it-was. In their own way, they needed each other.

"Selma, I do love you. I love you very much," Al finally said. He sensed his love for Selma differed from his love for Mary. The two young women delighted him, but were as unlike as an apple and a peach.

Selma lifted her face and kissed Al warmly, passionately. She opened her mouth and let her tongue explore around his. Then caught her breath and pulled back.

"Allie, I love you, too. I love you. I love only you."

They went into the delicatessen restaurant. Selma ordered a salami sandwich and a cream soda. Al ordered a frankfurter with mustard and sauerkraut, a tongue sandwich, French fries and a Pepsi. Selma started to giggle. Al gave her a questioning look.

"You ordered a hot dog. When we were in the press box, you could have had all the hot dogs you wanted for free. Here you are ordering one you'll have to pay for. You are a big shot, Al." She softened her voice. "I am very happy today. I'm glad I've made up my mind. It's you that I love and I'm glad for this opportunity to tell you," Selma managed before another giggle.

After they finished eating, Selma addressed Al as "the Big Shot" and asked him for two nickels to make two phone calls. The first call was to let her parents know her plans for the evening.

"The second call is to Howie. I'll tell him I don't want to see him anymore." Selma paused so this new idea could sink into Al's awareness. A time to make a real commitment to Al had come. "Think it over, Al. You're going to be stuck with me. I'm never going to let you go. You're going to have to forget all about that girl in Texas. Do you understand me?"

"I do understand you. And, I can't remember any girl in Texas," Al replied. The words had come out, but his mind kept wondering if he should have said them. Should I be agreeing with her right now?

Al waited at the booth while Selma made her two phone calls. She returned teary-eyed.

"Howie told me that one day you're going to break my heart. He may be right. But right now, Al, I want you to take me to the nearest dark movie theater. I want to sit in the very last row of the balcony and kiss you and kiss you until I don't have any breath left in my body."

In the theater, Selma and Al spent a lot of time kissing. Al's hands explored her body. She purposely laid her coat over herself so Al's hand could reach under her blouse and slide around her breasts.

"Al, please relax. I'm your girl now. Let's just watch the movie. I'm so happy now. Are you happy, Al?" Selma asked.

Al said he was. The fact remained that he felt riddled with self doubts when he stopped touching Selma. Why am I taking such advantage of her? He analyzed, or, at least, tried to analyze what was happening. Selma had cuddled up to him to watch the remaining part of *The Barretts of Wimpole Street*. The movie showed Browning's courtship and love for Elizabeth Barrett in the staid period of Queen Victoria's rule. Guilty thoughts of Mary crossed his mind. What will I write to Mary?

In the course of the next weeks, Al continued to write to Mary, even continuing to profess his love for her, too. He found himself saying the very things to Selma that he had written to Mary. His letters began hinting that he could not be sure about getting back to Texas for Christmas. He blamed the problem on his busy schedule as sports editor of the NYU Bulletin, including a trip to Pittsburgh to cover an NYU basketball game.

As the weeks went by, Al found himself still writing to Mary almost every night. He knew new meanings of the word guilt. He was telling both girls how much he loved them. I'm not lying. It's the truth. I do love each of them! Why?

Al and Selma's relationship never reached the level as that of Al and Mary. They had no real place to be alone. For the most part, their sexual excesses were restricted to reaching into and under each other's clothes in the stairwell between floors in Selma's apartment building. They both felt their virgin status would not survive once summer came, for they would find new privacy in the darkness of the Crotona, Bronx, or Claremont Parks.

The specter of a summer separation still hovered. Selma knew Al had a job offer at *The Houston Press*. She also questioned in her mind whether Al had really broken things off with Mary, though he tried to tell her he had.

Christmas had come and gone. Al stayed in New York. Mary felt greatly disappointed that Al could not get down, but she resigned herself to keep waiting for him. The months of winter merged into spring and then summer. All the while Selma heard Al talking more about possibly working in Texas again.

She finally heard from Al that he had his confirmation. Mr. Wannamaker invited him back to work. Al assured Selma that he would be staying at the Cotton Hotel and not with Mary's parents. Selma announced to Al that she would start seeing Howie Peskin the following Friday night. Al was stunned.

As they walked in the park, Selma reminded Al one more time she loved him. She claimed she chose to go out with Howie as a way of relieving the pressures from her parents about dating only Al, and her own worries about what would happen with Mary, once Al got back to Texas.

"Why don't we get married now and you can come to Texas with me?," Al suggested.

Selma responded that he was only twenty and she was only 17 with another year of high school.

Al kissed Selma. His fingers crept up the inside of her light shorts and found the soft opening there. She moaned and pulled her head away to whisper, "Al, when we do get married, I hope you'll kiss me just like that and touch me just the way you are doing on our wedding night." She sighed and breathed deeply. "Then I'll be ready to give you everything. But, now you'd better take your hands away from me and help me protect my virginity until that wonderful night."

Al let her push his hand away from her, but he held on to her hand. He pulled it into his lap.

"What is it you want me to do?" Selma wondered.

"I want to open my pants so I don't make a mess."

"If you take my hand away, you could calm down and solve your problem," Selma suggested.

"I want you to solve my problem," Al said. After looking around the park, he lowered his trousers.

"You'll have to tell me what to do. I really don't know what to do or how to do it," Selma said in a hushed voice.

Al showed her where to position her hands and how to move them. She did as he said. Soon there was an explosion of wetness that startled the girl. She watched as another explosion came and then more semen oozed out. When Al became calm, they shared a handkerchief to wipe themselves off. Al stood up and readjusted his pants.

"What happened to that thing? It was so big a little while ago. Where did it go?" Selma wondered. She giggled. "Please keep that thing in your pants when you go to Texas. Tell Mary to keep her hands off it. That belongs to me. Will you do that?"

"I'm not sure if I'll ever see Mary again or that subject will come up," Al responded cautiously.

"Al, you spend the summer working and keep that thing in your pants when you're in Texas. I'll promise you more and greater pleasures when you come home to me."

"I hear what you're saying, but I'm not sure what you're promising," Al teased with renewed playfulness.

Selma laughed. "I'm making a commitment of some kind. I think I'm promising you everything, but my virginity. You'll have to wait until we are married for that. But, you can have everything else when you come back from Texas."

Al found himself in the predicament of having two girlfriends in two different cities. He had rationalized how and why he could be in love with each one. Enjoying the two different young women came to be like enjoying two fancy desserts at the same time. The only distasteful part was the guilt that came along with the fancy desserts. The guilt always remained while he kept talking about love to both of the girls. He laughed a little, but Selma did not know the thoughts that made him laugh.

CHAPTER 45

By the time Al left for Texas, his letter writing marathon to Mary had slowed down and cooled somewhat. His first intentions were to devote his summer to working long and hard at *The Houston Press*. Almost a whole year had passed since he kissed Mary good-bye. He expected she had another boyfriend by now.

With money saved up from his part-time work at the Gordon Advertising Agency and the NYU library, Al managed to buy a coach ticket on the Penn Texas to Houston. He remembered his previous Sunday arrivals. Mary had picked him up and swept him along with her ritual of attending Sunday Mass.

On this arrival, Al checked in first at the Cotton Hotel. He arranged for a three-month stay and paid his first week's bill in advance. Houston's heat and humidity had his clothes sticking to his perspiring body. The room felt stifling despite the electric fan overhead. After his first shower since boarding the train two nights ago, he flopped on the bed and slept the afternoon away.

When he awoke, he did not feel "normal." Hungry. Lonely. He identified his problems. He wrote Selma a long letter. He told her how he missed her — how he wished she had married him — how he wished she had accompanied him to Texas. Three months before seeing Selma again. She'll be dating Peskin again. Oh, damn. What to do? Al sighed to himself. Then he called Mary.

"Hello?" Mrs. Monahan answered. Her tone went to complete surprise on learning that Al was back in Houston. Since Mary would not be back home from college for another two weeks, Mrs. Monahan gave Al Mary's number at the college.

Mary seemed glad to hear from Al, though her tone sounded cool and distant. "I was hoping you could have been down around Christmas," Mary reminded Al.

"I really was busy as the Sports Editor at the Bulletin," Al defended himself.

"I know. But, the Al Gordon I knew last summer would have moved heaven and earth to be with me. That's when I knew things had changed," Mary added pointedly.

Al tried telling Mary she had been very special to him from the day he had met her at the stadium. She would remain special to him until the day he died. Al heard Mary's sigh.

"I was really in love with you, Al. In love. I was closer to you spiritually and physically than I've been to any other boy before..." She paused. "Or since," Mary reaffirmed how special Al had been. "You took advantage of me, used me to get a job here, and now, you don't need me any more and are ready to kiss me off."

Her words hurt. "Mary, how can you say things like that?" Al pleaded.

The operator interrupted to ask for more money.

Mary finally suggested that he could write to her and call her again. She added a "good-bye" and hung up.

Al had become sickened and depressed by the conversation. He knew, if he did not see Mary, he could go home to Selma with a clear conscience. On the other hand, Selma told me directly she will go out with Howie. She's not waiting around for me. I'm not a priest. I'm going out too...with somebody.

Al began the fast paced work at *The Press* early the next day. The reporters' rapid talk and Texas twang sounded like a foreign language sometimes. But he progressed quickly in getting back into the routine. Mr. Wannamaker assigned him to the rewrite desk when one of the rewrite editors called in sick.

During a lull, Al took time to send Selma another letter.

On one of the editor's rounds, Al's confidence and chest both rose when he received a pat on the shoulder and a compliment from his boss. Mr. Wannamaker asked Al if he had a car or access to one. When Al asked why, Mr. Wannamaker explained he wanted to assign Al to the police beat and he would need to run to the crime scenes. Al thought fast. He suggested his girlfriend Mary might help him, if he they made up.

Bill Wannamaker broke out in a broad grin. He joked with Al, asking whether his romance only hinged on using his girlfriend's car. Al had to explain their romance had cooled off in the past ten months.

"Women can complicate a man's life," Mr. Wannamaker quipped. "But, I had been much impressed with Mary's beauty and intelligence. You might have a long and lonely summer if you don't placate her...or find another girl." Mr. Wannamaker gave a fatherly pat on Al's shoulder to remind him he needed to act to recapture Mary's heart.

This time Al wrote a letter to Mary.

The letter iterated his disappointment in not finding Mary home. He reminded her of the happy times they had had together. He ended with a strong affirmation of his love for her.

After work, Mr. Wannamaker brought Al into his office. He opened a back door that led into a paneled private chamber. This inner chamber contained a big desk, a sofa, some easy chairs, and a cabinet, but no windows. Mr. Wannamaker had Al sit, while he opened the cabinet. He brought out a couple of bottles of Lone Star beer, opened them, and gave one to Al.

"Al, I just wanted you to know you've got the makings of a real newspaper man. I was stuck to put somebody on the rewrite desk, but you came through for me like a pro," Mr. Wannamaker observed. He took a long swallow on his beer. "Talk to me any time about our craft." With a twinkle in his eye, he added, "But don't ever ask me for advice about women. I've been married three times and fucked up each of my marriages. The only advice I can give you is to take your time, find the right woman, be damn sure, and then be patient with her and stick with her no matter what happens."

Al gave a slight chuckle, drank some beer and thanked Mr. Wannamaker again for the opportunity to work at The Press. They relaxed with small talk, finishing their beers. Afterwards, Al went back to his hotel.

Following dinner, Al decided he needed to talk to Mary. He called her, telling her proudly about his experiences at the rewrite desk and Mr. Wannamaker's compliments. He built up his nerve finally to ask Mary for a date on Saturday night. She gave a non-committal answer and suggested he call her later in the week when she arrived home.

"Don't think I have forgotten or forgiven you for how you treated me this past year. You've got a lot of explaining to do." Mary paused. "But, Al, I have missed you. I will be really glad to see you again." She confessed.

The conversation left Al confused, but relieved. He concluded Mary would begin to be happier towards him once she got his latest letter.

Things changed for Al when the rewrite man returned to work. Al was given the courthouse beat. He came back discouraged with no news. Mr. Wannamaker laughed, then chided him for letting the rewrite desk assignment spoil him. Al had to remember the rewrite desk got all the news. Out on the beat, Al had to learn to wait for something to happen or dig around to find a story. When Al was assigned to the sports desk, he cheered up. It gave him a sense of self-importance as he got the latest news off the ticker and then sometimes even had the opportunity to decide which stories to run.

On Friday night, Al called Mary's home. She answered right away and her tone had turned friendlier. She told him she received his letter, which Al felt explained her better mood. She made clear she could not see him tonight because she had just returned and still had to talk to her parents. Besides, she still felt miffed for missing his promised Christmas visit and for his lack of letters in the past months.

"If you had written me letters like the last one all along, I'd find it easier to forgive you. I'm really not sure I can now," Mary told him. "But, yes, I will see you tomorrow."

Al hung up the phone. He let out a long sigh. He had to wait and see what would happen.

Robert Miller

With no other plans, Al went upstairs to the small, lonely, hot hotel room. With unrelenting heat day and night, his clothes were wet and perspiration-stained. He lay down in his shorts on top of the sheets, falling asleep to the monotonous sounds of the electric fan blades spinning in the humidity-laden air.

CHAPTER 46

Back at work, Joe Bill Wheatley, the Sports Editor, gave Al helpful suggestions about putting the sports paragraphs together.

"Young feller," Wheatley added. "Bill Wannamaker is high on you. He thinks you could be a star in this business one day. But you have a lot to learn from him, from me, and from a dozen other old timers here. Remember that and you'll do okay."

Al thanked Mr. Wheatley for his help. As Wheatley left, Al decided that he would try to develop better relationships with the other reporters and editors. Al's thoughts turned to Mary.

He hoped to experience a pleasant, relaxing, and casual-dating summer with Mary. He ultimately wished to be free to go home to New York and date Selma for the coming year. To a young man who did not want to make any commitments until he finished college, his love life seemed in perfect order without any burdensome guilt.

Saturday afternoon Al had another déjà vu experience while knocking on the Monahans' front door. Mary greeted him. She appeared a prim and proper in a fluffy yellow summer dress. Al walked in and approached her to give her a kiss. She stepped back out of his arms, allowing only a brotherly peck on her cheek.

"Your parents aren't home?" Al asked looking around.

"I asked them to go out so you and I could have a talk," Mary responded. "They'll be back in one hour, and then Daddy offered to take us to the Plantation for dinner. I told him that depends on how our conversation goes."

"Exactly what is this conversation going to be about?" Al inquired.

"About marriage," Mary responded without hesitation. "About a Catholic marriage," she clarified.

Al swallowed hard. His face took on a startled look. "You want to get married? You want to get married now? What's your hurry?" His words stumbled out.

Robert Miller

"You listen to me, Al. You told me you loved me. I met you in November almost two years ago. You came down here in December and again last summer. I also told you I loved you. I gave you everything I can possibly give a man, short of marriage. Then what happened? Your letters grew cooler and fewer. I'm not going to let my emotions get the better of me this summer. I want to know if you are ready to make a commitment or not. It's that simple."

"May I sit down?" Al asked softly. He took a deep breath.

"Sit down, but don't make yourself too comfortable. I want answers. And, I want them now," Mary demanded authoritatively.

"Mary Jean," Al stammered. He realized he had walked into the force of her personality. He started by explaining he had a good job that lasted only for the summer and another year of college. "Doesn't it make sense to wait until next year before making definite commitments?" Al concluded.

Mary Jean's emotional state appeared to be set in one mental frame of logic. There had to be marriage or no marriage. Getting up from a chair she had taken across the room from Al, she stated forcefully, "I think you had better leave. I don't ever want to hear from you again." She spoke in a low voice. Her eyes watered.

Al suggested he could not quit college because she had taken this sudden whim about marriage.

"It's not a sudden whim. I'm fed up with college. If we get married this summer, you'd become a state resident and could go to the University of Texas. I'll find a job and support you."

Mary came over to Al and sat next to him. She started to cry. Her arms came around Al as in previous times. She tucked her head in his chest and began sobbing. "You have no idea what I went through this year without you. I was so humiliated. I felt abandoned. I knew you had girlfriends in New York and was convinced you were busy making love to them while forgetting about me."

Al pulled Mary closer. Her tears softened his heart. "Mary, why do you torture yourself so? I've never made love to any woman in my life."

Mary lifted her head, dried her tears and looked straight into Al's eyes. "Are you telling me that you've never had sexual intercourse in your life? You never told me that before."

"It's not something that a fella boasts about," Al answered shyly.

Mary tilted her head back to laugh. "I never imagined that. You seemed so experienced to me."

They hugged tightly. Al preferred her laughing to her sobbing and heartache.

"Al, you are here now and I never want to let you go. I love you very much. I want to cure you of your virginity and I want you to take mine. I want to do it soon. I want you to marry me now. It'll take three weeks until the banns can be read. Let's plan to get married on July Fourth. What do you say?"

Al didn't know how to respond. He ended up saying nothing. He just hugged Mary. He realized she had started making marriage plans almost as fast as a Bronx bookie could run his numbers.

Mr. and Mrs. Monahan entered the front door. Mary and Al drew apart to greet them. Bill Monahan offered Al a big Texas-style pumping handshake. The men settled down in chairs as the two women disappeared into the kitchen. When Mary returned, she approached Al and kissed him for the first time in a year.

Bill Monahan took everyone out to dinner at the Plantation Inn as promised. Everyone enjoyed a festive and happy dinner, especially Mary. By the time dessert was served, Mary was talking about the possibilities of a wedding on the last day of June.

"I don't understand what the heck the rush is all about," Bill Monahan said looking around at the other three.

"Daddy!" Mary interjected suddenly. "Now that I have Al back, I'm never ever going to let him go. I'm not going back to TSCW. And, I'm not letting Al go back to New York. He's mine. And, I want to make him all mine as soon as possible," she added with a gleam in her eye.

Al smiled and offered no comment, trying to stay within breathing range of the new wave of incredibly fast-moving plans.

Back home, Mary and her mother started making plans for a wedding. The talk circled around how many people to invite, what kind of dress Mary would wear, whether Al's family would be able to come and a rush of other details that Al found difficult to remember.

"Just hold on," Mr. Monahan counseled. "You're talking about a mixed marriage. You're going to need a dispensation. The Church will slow you down, believe me. Al will have to take instructions, even if he doesn't become a Catholic. You'd better forget the Church and think of a civil ceremony."

By the time the marriage talk had slowed down, Mrs. Monahan invited Al to stay overnight at the apartment. Al declined and said he would need to go back to the hotel to shower and have a change of clothes for the next morning. Mary told Al she would drive him back and pick him up for Mass the following morning.

"Do you remember how to drive?" Mary asked as she walked with Al to the car.

"I hope so," Al replied. "I haven't driven for a year."

Mary tossed Al the keys. He got behind the wheel, started the engine and slowly put the car in motion. When he felt comfortable driving, he reached over and held Mary's hand.

"Are you happy now, Mary?" Al asked.

"I'm getting there," she replied. "I want you to tell me you love me, that you really want to marry me now, that you're willing to consider becoming a Roman Catholic, and that you will surely agree to let our children be raised as Catholic."

Al pressed Mary's hand. "I do love you, Mary. I love you very much. You're the girl I plan to marry. I pride myself on being a free thinker. I'm not ready to say I'll ever become a Catholic. And, I'm not eager to ask my children, our children, to give up their Jewish heritage in its entirety in order to become Roman Catholics. If I can get a permanent job, I will agree to get married at once. I love you very much, Mary, and I do want to marry you now."

"Please say that again," Mary asked. Mary's hands grasped Al's arm.

Al parked the car on a dark street next to the hotel. He moved over and took Mary into his arms. He repeated several times how he much loved her. Al kissed her. Her lips were soft, open, and hinted at an invitation of more. Al felt Mary's shivers of excitement. He asked if Mary could come up to his room. She declined, knowing that her parents would be timing her trip to the hotel and back.

"Call me early tomorrow. We'll have breakfast and go to Mass together. On Monday, I'll pick you up after work. We can go to Schwartzenberg's for dinner and then to the rectory after that," Mary said. Her mind had already begun making new plans.

Within a few minutes, Al found himself back in his hotel room. He listened to the muffled electric fan blades blowing around the humid Texas air. I came into this room a single man. I'll probably be leaving as a married man. What's happening in my life?

Al watched the moon from his window. The tilted crescent-shaped moon would be changing from full to new, much as his own life, Al thought. He reflected on his changing circumstances. He might soon be finding himself a Jew, down here in the Bible Belt, married to one of the most beautiful, staunch, pious Catholic girls in Texas. He felt ready to leave the Bronx. Assimilation. The concept never crossed his mind. Being in love and being lucky. Only these concepts crossed his mind. He fell asleep after staring at the moon, the sticky, hot Texas air enveloping his body.

CHAPTER 47

During the ten o'clock Mass, Al remembered the other Masses he had attended with Mary. An uncomfortable feeling hit him when he sat, while the others knelt. He looked around and noticed a few others, like him, who did not kneel on cue.

The ringing of the bells cheered him. He remembered the bells signalled an approach to the end of the Mass. Al glanced down to see Mary, now on her knees with eyes closed, in apparent rapture as she prayed silently.

He marveled at the incongruity of where he was and what was happening to his life. All of these things could have happened with him and a Catholic girl in the Bronx, but didn't.

Out in the bright sunlight again, Mary, Al, and the Monahans tossed about ideas as to what to do on Sunday afternoon. It was decided that everyone would fend for themselves. Al and Mary decided on a lunch at Schwartzenberg's and then a drive to the Old Spanish Trail.

On the way to the Old Spanish Trail, Al suggested that Mary should drop by his room. She declined, reminding him again of their plans to be married in just a few weeks. When she asked if he could wait, Al moved her hand to the throbbing bulge in his pants. Mary laughed, kissed Al chastely on the cheek, and asked for his handkerchief. Al tried to keep his eye on the road while Mary ever so slightly unbuttoned the buttons on his fly, reached in and extracted his member. She covered it with the handkerchief and began to run her hand up and down.

"I can't keep driving," Al pleaded in excitement.

Mary had him pull off on a deserted street. Al quickly parked the car next to some vacant lots. Mary's strokes kept getting faster and stronger. Al exploded semen through the handkerchief and over her hands. Mary leaned over and kissed him.

"A wash cloth sure beats a handkerchief for this sort of thing," Mary observed. She used Al's handkerchief to try to clean up. "If we're going to do this sort of thing again, you'll need a wrapper."

"A wrapper?"

"I think I mean a rubber," Mary corrected.

"Where do you get a thing like that?" Al inquired.

"How should I know? But, I think they sell them in drugstores."

"How do you know that?" Al inquired again.

They both giggled over the unanswered question. They ended up going to the movies where they spent the afternoon watching *Lives of the Bengal Lancers*.

The next morning events worked in Al's favor. Mr. Wannamaker told Al he had a permanent job at the rewrite desk because another worker had quit to take a job with The Post. Al decided to approach Mr. Wannamaker with a hypothetical question that needed a real answer.

"Would there be a permanent job for me at *The Houston Press* if I decided not to return to college for my senior year, but stayed here in Houston?"

Mr. Wannamaker gave Al a quizzical look and broke out in a broad grin. "You've made up with your girl, haven't you?"

"Yes," Al answered. "We're talking about getting married."

"Good luck. You're the rewrite desk man now. I'll increase your pay to sixty dollars a week. Congratulations and...or commiserations," Mr. Wannamaker said. He beamed a smile at Al before walking away.

Al could not resist an immediate phone call to Mary.

Mrs. Monahan answered drowsily in her Texas accent that sounded to Al like, "Hailo."

Al realized the time was only 7 A.M., but Mrs. Monahan called for Mary to come to the phone.

"I've been up since five, working since six and now at seven I've got great news," Al bragged. "I've got a permanent job, my salary's been increased and I'm not going back to New York!

We can get married. Isn't that good news?" Al asked excitedly.

"It sure is!" Mary answered happily. "I love you!"

Al returned to his desk. He wondered why he felt unhappy. The answer came immediately. It was time to write a "goodbye" letter to Selma. Besides that difficult task, he also had to write a letter explaining everything to his mother and father.

Al's phone rang and interrupted his thoughts. A reporter began giving him the facts on a story about a murder the night before in Pasadena. Al's attention was suddenly diverted into putting together a good story.

By the afternoon, Al found time to write a farewell letter to Selma. He wrote about his new opportunities, his loneliness, the strangeness of Texas, the warmth of Mary's family, and the wedding plans for the next month. He concluded by telling Selma he would never forget her, and in truth he never would. He even took time to rewrite the letter to make it more legible. After that, he put the letter in with the office mail.

Checking his watch, Al realized he had made himself late to meet Mary. He raced down the steps and found her waiting in the car. Before visiting with Father Wall, they discussed where to eat.

"It could be Mexican or Schwartzenberg's. But, I feel, if I'm going to meet a Catholic priest and marry a Catholic girl I love so much, I ought to be fortified with a kosher hot dog and some kosher corned beef. Fair is fair, right?" Al joked.

"Fair is fair," Mary laughed in response. "Schwartzenberg's it is. We'll have a Catholic family and eat Jewish food. That sounds fair to me."

At Schwartzenberg's, Mary lost her humor and her tone became more serious. "Father Wall is something of an old fuddy duddy. I don't think he'll intimidate you in any way. Just tell him you're here to listen. Please remember you're marrying me, not the Church. All that I want is their blessing. It's important to me, just as you are important to me. Do you understand, darling?"

"I do," Al assured. "Don't worry, Mary. I have burned my bridges. I'm yours. We are going to get married. I know the Catholic Church is important to you, so I'll make my accommodation with it."

Mary ate a spoonful of her baked beans. She regained a sense of humor by suggesting that the powerful little beans would not be the wisest thing to eat before meeting with Father Wall. "My stomach is rumbling right now. With both of us eating these baked beans, we could bomb him out."

Mary and Al began their meeting with Father Wall in a more somber tone. The priest was a small, chubby, pink-faced man with sparse light hair around his balding temples.

Mary explained the situation. They hoped to have the banns read for the next three weeks so they could be married in July.

When Father Wall found out Al was not Catholic, he pulled out a yellow tablet and began writing down Al's answers to a series of questions.

"When and where were you baptized?" Father Wall asked.

"I was never baptized. I'm Jewish," Al said.

"I must write down that you're a heathen," Father Wall said as he made a notation.

"I am not a heathen. I'm Jewish," Al said respectfully, though firmly.

"I'm sorry, Mr. Gordon. According to our teachings, if one has not been baptized, that person is a heathen. I am simply stating a fact as we see it. There is no reason for you to become hostile," Father Wall replied, after giving Al a sharp look.

Al looked at Mary. Remaining silent, she appeared very tense while gazing directly at the priest.

"I really don't mean to be hostile, Father," Al responded. "You have taken me aback by calling me a heathen. The fact is I do believe in God and don't consider myself a heathen. And, I don't fancy being called one, either."

A series of questions continued for both Al and Mary. Father Wall finally asked Al if he would take instructions in the Church. The instructions were mandatory for any non-Catholic who wanted to marry a Catholic within the Church. Al explained that he had already agreed with Mary to participate in the instructions. The priest then produced a paper for Al to sign. Al read it and signed it.

"Thank you, Mr. Gordon," Father Wall said. He reached out to shake Al's hand. "And, good luck to you. Will you now step outside and excuse us for a few minutes. I wish to speak to Mary in private."

Al finished shaking Father Wall's hand and went outside to the forbidding waiting room in the vestibule. He seated himself in one of the tall, uncomfortable chairs and wondered to himself again what he was getting into.

Mary emerged with a downcast head and tears in her eyes. Al rose to embrace her, but she took his hand instead and guided him outside.

During the drive home, Mary alternately cried and talked as she explained the problem they faced with the Church. "There's no way they're going to give us a dispensation in time for us to be married next month. When a Catholic marries a Protestant, the Bishop can grant a dispensation. In the case of a Catholic marrying a Jew or other non-Christian, it is referred to the apostolic delegate in Washington, D.C., and only they can give a dispensation." She caught her breath and wiped her eyes. "I told Father Wall that I thought that was prejudice of the worst sort. I asked him why they didn't get approval from the Bishop or Cardinal in Berlin. In Germany, there are laws against Catholics marrying Jews." Mary chuckled cynically. "Father Wall has no sense of humor and, for that matter, no sense at all, surely no sensitivity." Mary hugged Al's arm. "You were a perfect gentleman. You were like a lamb being led to the slaughter. Will you please take me to see a rabbi and see if he will marry us?"

"I'm afraid we might get the same kind of treatment," Al said. He squeezed her hand. "We better find a Justice of the Peace and get married right away."

"Al, you have the knack of saying exactly what I want to hear," Mary said.

"Where shall we go?" Al asked.

"Let's drive around for a while," Mary said. "I'm still in a bad mood. I want to cheer up and relax a bit. Then I want to go with you to your room. And, I want to take off all my clothes and all of yours and get as close to you as I possibly can."

"You're actually going to take off your panties and act like this is our actual bridal night?" Al asked with raised eyebrows.

"The answer to your first question is yes and to the second is no," Mary said smiling. "The only thing I'm going to let you put inside me tonight are your fingers." She leaned over and kissed him. "Why are you still driving around aimlessly. Head towards the hotel, now.

Al clearly heard the emphasis on the word now. He made an abrupt turn and smiled devilishly at Mary. Mary grinned back.

Robert Miller

CHAPTER 48

Al woke up in his room from a deep doze. He lay naked and spent. He reached over to touch Mary, but she was not there. He peeked open an eye to see her sitting at the mirror, now clad in her slip and putting on lipstick.

She turned to look at him and gushed mockingly, "There's my lover, so big and so eager one minute. Then, pop goes the wheedle worm and it just shrivels up and off he goes to sleep. I took off all my clothes and enjoyed cuddling against you, but you, my sweet love, were totally out of it."

Al rose and came over to Mary. He began to work his hands down around her breasts. Her hands came up and restrained his.

"It's time for me to go home, darling," she said.

"It's barely 9 P.M. I'll get washed and dressed and we'll get something to eat," Al said, running his hands along her neck.

Mary consented.

At Prince's drive-in, Mary and Al reflected on their meeting with Father Wall.

"Al, I'm Roman Catholic. I always will be. According to my Church, if we are married by the Justice of the Peace, it will be like living in sin. The Church will not consider us married nor our children legitimate. I will still be able to go to church, but I won't be able to take communion or receive the sacraments. I am willing to do this," Mary said softly. "But, you have to understand that one day I hope you and I can make peace with the Church and be remarried in it. In the meantime, I want our children to be raised as Catholics. Can you agree with that?"

Al pulled Mary close. "Sweetheart, I've already signed a paper agreeing to let you bring up our children as Catholics. I'll keep my word. If you want me to go back and kiss Father Wall's butt and admit that I'm a heathen, I'll do that too, if it will make you happy."

Mary started laughing. She leaned over and kissed Al. "You always have a way of saying the right thing, Al."

After dinner, Al drove back to the Cotton Hotel and got out. Mary slid over, kissed him good-bye and drove off. Al continued watching until the red tail-lights of the car disappeared. He looked up and saw the glitter of stars. He felt a sense that everything would be all right.

Before Al fell off to sleep, the phone rang. Mary called with more news.

"I told my father about our conversation with Father Wall. He's angry and is going to call the Monsignor. Daddy's on our side. He got sore when I told him Father Wall called you a heathen. He liked what I said about sending for a dispensation from the Bishop of Berlin. He said he's going to ask the Monsignor if the Church has taken notes of Hitler's racial laws since they have established separate dispensations for Protestants and for Jews. He's also going to ask them if they've forgotten that Jesus was a Jew!"

"Will he really say those things?" Al wondered aloud.

"Probably not all of them," Mary chuckled. "But, he surely will get off some barbs. He may not be exactly one-hundred percent happy with my choice of you as a life partner, but he is a dear and will make the best of it, and he will fight for me when he has to. And, I think that means fighting for you, too."

Mary later asked if Al would call his mother with the news. He replied that he planned to call her the next day.

At work, Al's thoughts returned to the reality of the daily news: a bank robbery in Rosenberg and a shooting in Prairie View. He managed to avoid the usual vices of the other reporters - cups of coffee, cigarettes, and donuts. His work day meant plowing through notes they called in and putting the pieces of information together into comprehensive news stories.

After work, Al forgot the day's stresses and deadlines by planning dinner with Mary. While they were together that night Al found a phone booth to call home to tell his mother the "good news" about his coming marriage. Mary waited outside the booth. He made the call by reversing the charges.

"Hello, Al, are you all right?" his mother asked when she and her son were finally connected.

"Yes, Mother! I'm fine, and I have some great news."

"What's that?"

"Mother, I've got a permanent job at *The Houston Press* and they're paying me sixty dollars a week," Al told her, still building his nerve to tell her the rest.

"Sixty dollars a week?"

"Yes! Sixty dollars a week," Al repeated. "And, Mother, Mary and I are going to get married," he blurted boldly.

"What?" she asked incredulously.

"I said, Mary and I are going to get married, maybe later this month or next month. I'm going to stay on in Texas. I'll probably finish college down here."

Robert Miller

"My God! You're not going to finish college and you're going to marry that shiksa!" Mrs. Gordon exclaimed. "You call that good news?"

"Mother, it is good news. Mary is not 'that Shiksa.' She's a beautiful, young woman who you are going to love as much as I do. I promise you that."

"Don't be so sure of that, Allie," his mother answered cynically. "Tell me, is she pregnant?"

"Mother, please! Mary is a delightful, religious, sweet and very good girl. You'll be proud to have her as a daughter-in-law."

"I don't think you're ready to be married. My God! You're barely twenty. Live a little!"

"Mother, please! Don't begrudge Mary and I happiness. I called to share some good news with you and Dad."

"Allie, please come home before you do this. I want to talk to you."

"Mother, I can't. I'm working," Al pleaded.

"What about Selma? Did you tell her?"

"I wrote her a letter. She should get it in a day or so.

"That poor girl," Al's mother sighed. "I should get on a train and come down there to find out for myself what's going on."

"No, wait. Let Mary and I work out the details. Maybe you and Dad can come for the wedding."

"Maybe you should marry Selma."

"Mother! You never liked Selma. Come off it. You're going to love Mary. Please. This call is costing you a fortune. Tell me you're happy for me and wish Mary and me well."

"I do, Al. I really wish you both well, but I'm so worried. Write to me and call me in a few days, son. But please, think about what you are doing, Allie. Good-bye."

Al felt drained as he slid open the phone booth door and looked at Mary's expectant face.

"You told her?" Mary asked, incredulously.

"I told her," Al sighed.

"What did she say?"

"She said congratulations and wished her blessings on us both," Al said.

Mary's face brightened with happiness.

"What took so long?" Mary asked.

"First she told me we were both too young. She also asked if you were pregnant."

"She asked that?" Mary exclaimed. Her face flushed.

"I told her that you were pure and devout, and that she would come to love you," Al explained. "Now that we've made up our minds, what are we waiting for? If we have a civil wedding, you can still be a June bride."

"That is the most appealing thought," Mary responded in a low voice. "But, let's wait a couple of days. Remember Daddy's going to meet with Monsignor Ryan." Mary gave Al one of her radiant smiles that seemed to exude greater happiness on this particular night.

CHAPTER 49

Bill Monahan entered the Monsignor's office and was greeted warmly. The Monsignor motioned to a comfortable chair and the two men sat down. He listened patiently as Bill Monahan told him what a good, devoted Catholic girl Mary was and how upset she was by Father Wall's recent treatment of Al Gordon.

"Do you really want Mary to marry this Jewish boy?" Monsignor asked seriously.

"What I want isn't the issue here, Monsignor," Bill Monahan said. "The simple fact is that Mary loves this boy and is bound and determined to marry him. She very much wants the Church's blessing."

"And, she will get it," Monsignor Ryan reassured. "But, she'll get it in the Church's own good time, after the young man receives instructions and completes a proper waiting period."

Bill Monahan explained that the young couple had their minds set on a wedding in June or around the Fourth of July.

"That simply isn't possible. Mary is a young lady of beauty and piety. We respect her wishes and even her choice of a future husband. But, he'll have to devote an hour or two each week to studying our religion for 2 months. Tell her to plan a wedding around Labor Day and I'll see that she has her dispensation."

Bill Monahan assured the Monsignor that he would relay the message. However, he also told the prelate that Mary has threatened to get married by a rabbi or a Justice of the Peace. He ended wondering whether that would bar a later reconciliation with the Church.

The Monsignor warned that Mary would not be allowed under those circumstances to receive the sacraments. He hoped she would see the wisdom of waiting until September.

As Bill Monahan stood up to say good-bye, the Monsignor expressed another concern. A marriage by a rabbi could complicate her later plans to get married in the Church. Of course, being married by a Justice of the Peace was also not considered a true marriage in the Church's eyes. The Monsignor reminded Bill that he had also married a Protestant girl, who became a Catholic. They were later married in the Church, after ten years of a civil marriage. The Monsignor asked again if Mary could be convinced to wait until September, so she could be married in the Church; however, it would not be a Nuptial Mass, unless Al became a Catholic. A civil ceremony would be the best alternative, not a religious one as performed by a rabbi. He ended by asking, "Do you see eye to eye with me on that?"

"No, your Grace. I really don't. I don't see why you can't skip the banns and let Al take instructions for four nights this week and four nights next week. Let these kids have their rectory marriage with your blessing in two or three weeks."

The prelate sighed and shrugged his shoulders. The two men shook hands for the final time.

Bill Monahan returned home and sat down in the kitchen to report back to his wife, Mary, and Al. Opal set a big bowl at his place filled with extra large scoops of vanilla, chocolate, and strawberry ice cream, his immediate reward for the ordeal with the Monsignor.

"What happened?" everyone asked at once, while Bill tasted a spoonful of the chocolate ice cream.

Bill Monahan explained all of the Monsignor's comments, plus his one agreement to give a dispensation if Al received instructions over an eight-week period.

Al let out an exasperated sigh. The grueling heat of Texas had felt unrelenting to him. Now he was facing the grueling nonacceptance of the Church.

"Mary, it's up to you. I've already signed a paper with the Church promising not to interfere with your religion and allowing you to bring up the children as Catholics. If you want to wait until September, that's fine. If you want to wait to get married by a rabbi, my guess is that they'd give us the same load of bullshit." Al cast a shy look at Mary's mother. "Excuse me, Mrs. Monahan." Then Al turned to Mary and continued. "We can get married right away by the Justice of the Peace. Then, in our own good time, we can have a Catholic ceremony in September." Al reached over to hold Mary's hand. "Would you rather wait until September and get married in the rectory?"

Tears formed in Mary's eyes. "I'm not sure what we should do." She wiped away a tear. "Please understand, even if we were married by a Justice of the Peace, I will continue to be and think of myself as a Catholic, even if I am not able to receive communion in the Church. I will want, someday, to be married in the Church. I will continue to go to Church every Sunday to hear Mass and I will expect you to live up to your promise to raise our children as Catholics. Is that clear?"

"Does that mean you're saying "yes" to a civil wedding?" Al asked.

Mary broke into a broad smile. She leaned over in front of her parents and kissed Al on the cheek.

"He seems so eager, doesn't he?" Mary murmured to her parents.

"She turned to Al and said, "No, I'm not saying 'yes,' but I'm not saying 'no' either. Now, sweetheart, finish your ice cream and I'll drive you downtown to your hotel."

The four of them went on to relax by enjoying the ice cream treat. Al talked casually about the excitement he felt at work hearing reporters call in their stories about bank robberies, murders and shootings. Then, he quipped that he was finding similar excitement just trying to get married.

When Al arrived at work the next morning at 6 A.M., he saw Tom Davis, the cable editor, sitting at Mr. Wannamaker's slot on the long table.

"Where's Bill Wannamaker today?" Al asked him.

"He's taking a few days off. Is that all right with you? Or will you miss your patron too much?" Tom quipped.

Al noticed his smirk, and the remark troubled him. He remembered an earlier remark about "mixing in with everybody." Bill Wannamaker had favored Al, but Al saw it as Mr. Wannamaker's way of encouraging Al's potential as a newspaperman.

Al quickly returned to his desk and kept up a busy pace fielding assignments. As the day ended, Al evaluated himself as having done a creditable job. He received no approbations from Tom Davis, as he often did from Bill Wannamaker, but he received no complaints either. Al left the building wondering how well he really did that day.

"Did you have a good day?" Mary asked, as Al got in the driver's side to drive her to dinner.

"I don't want you to think I'm blasé about my job. It's exciting, but every day I'm dealing with the same human mess. Two murders, four accidents, three fires, and two robberies. It gets to be ho hum." Al's attitude changed. "That's where you come in. I can't help feeling that the best part of my day is having you in my arms." Al's eyes twinkled more.

"Think how much better it will be when we're married."

"To be married to you boggles my mind," Al said with an added grin. "Can we stay naked from the time I get home at night until I leave for work in the morning?"

Mary blushed at his openness. "We'll have to dress for dinner."

"Only when we have dinner guests, and that won't be too often during our first weeks of marriage. By the way, have you picked our wedding date?"

"I'm still trying to decide about the Church. I do want to marry you as soon as possible. Give me a couple of days. Can you do that, Al?"

"I think so. I'll wait for your decision if you'll come up to my room and cavort with me in the nude for a while," Al said.

"Then, why are you driving down South Main Street heading for Schwartzenberg's?" Mary asked flirtatiously. "Why don't you turn the car around and head back to the hotel? Only promise me that you'll obey all the ground rules. I'm more vulnerable than you know."

"I'll promise you anything, everything," Al said, smiling. His hand caressed her leg and then ran up under her skirt to touch the bare skin over her stockings. He enjoyed touching her bare skin all the way back to the hotel.

Robert Miller

CHAPTER 50

Conditions in the office were like the hotel room - hot, humid, and sticky. Fans blew the humid air around, but Al felt no noticeable relief.

Mary remained unsettled about whether to obtain a civil or Church marriage. She had arranged for Al to receive instructions by Father Wall at 8 every Tuesday evening for the next eight weeks.

On Friday afternoon, Bill Wannamaker returned with news that startled everyone. He had been appointed Managing Editor of the *Rocky Mountain News*, the Scripps Howard newspaper in Denver. Bill went on to announce that Tom Davis was taking his post as City Editor and Joe Pete Thompson would be the Cable Editor.

Al became concerned about his own job security under Tom Davis.

When Mr. Wannamaker came over to Al's desk to say good-bye, Al thanked him for all his help, the inspiration he had provided and told him that he would never be forgotten.

"You won't get a chance to forget me, Al. I need a cable editor at the *Rocky Mountain News*. The job is yours, if you want it. It will pay eighty dollars a week. And, I want to tell you that prices and wages are lower in Denver than here in Houston. You'll love it there," Mr. Wannamaker assured.

Al stood next to his old wooden desk feeling flabbergasted. "Can I give you my answer tomorrow? When do you want me to start?"

"Yes to your first question, but I'll need an answer by mid-morning tomorrow. The answer to your second question is right away."

Hearing Bill's emphasis on right away, Al did some quick calculating. He grabbed his calendar and thought out loud. "I may get married first. If I do, I'll get married a week from Saturday. If that's June 27th, I'll have to take my wife to meet my parents. I could start July 13th. Would that be okay? If I don't get married, I'll start June 28th. I'll let you know what I'm doing tomorrow."

170

Mr. Wannamaker began to laugh. "You're a young man who makes up his mind fast. I like that. I'll tell them you'll work here one more week. I'll put you on the payroll in Denver effective June 28th. If you get married, you'll have two weeks off with pay for your honeymoon. How do you like that?"

"Great! Thanks!" Al shook Bill Wannamaker's hand with added exuberance. After Mr. Wannamaker walked away, Al grabbed the phone and called Mary.

"Hello?" Mary answered sleepily.

"Mary, this is Al! How soon can we get married? I've just been offered the position of Cable Editor at the *Rocky Mountain News* in Denver at $80 a week. Bill Wannamaker's going to be the Managing Editor there. He wants me to start right away!" Al was breathless with excitement.

"Really?" Mary said.

"Bill will give us two weeks with pay as a wedding gift. We can see my folks. I'll take instructions in Denver and we can have a rectory wedding in September. What do you say? Why should we wait? We can get married next week and live happily ever after!"

"I can't believe you just accepted the job without asking me first," Mary finally stated.

"I accepted the job thinking only of you and a wonderful chance for us to get married right away," Al defended. "I'm proposing to you. I'm asking you to marry me. Will you marry me? Will you marry me next week?"

"Yes, yes! Of course, yes. But, I'm due to get my period next week," Mary said anxiously.

"How long does your period last?"

"About four days."

"When is it due?"

"Any day, probably Sunday or Monday."

"That works out fine," Al said without pausing. "Pick me up at four. We'll talk and make some definite plans, then set a time and place. We'll take your parents out to dinner and let them in on the big news!" Al said in a final burst of energy before saying goodbye. When he hung up the phone, he inhaled rapidly to catch his breath. This moment was very special.

He sat and contemplated making love to Mary in Denver.

The dinner conversation was dominated by a renewed urgency about wedding preparations, which quickly dulled Al's early morning enthusiasm. He endured sitting and listening as Mary's father and the two Monahan women discussed endless options and angles for the wedding. After dinner, Mary decided to go home with her parents to finalize some plans. She instructed Al to find out if his parents would be coming to the wedding or whether she and Al would visit them on the honeymoon.

Robert Miller

When the Monahans had left, Al suddenly felt quite alone and rather superfluous to the whole planning. "What have I gotten myself into?" he pondered on the walk to his hotel room.

Shortly past 8 P.M. Houston time, Al entered the phone booth to call his parents. After more conversation than was necessary, his mother finally accepted the collect call.

"How are you? Is everything all right?" Al's mother asked immediately.

"Better than all right, mother. I've got some good news and then some more good news."

"What good news? You broke up with that shiksa? That would be good news!"

"Ohhhh," Al groaned. "Please stop calling Mary 'that shiksa.' You're going to meet her very soon and you're going to love her as much as I do. We're going to get married a week from tomorrow night. And, I have a new job. I'm the cable editor of the *Rocky Mountain News* in Denver, Colorado, and my pay has gone up to $80 a week. How do you like that?"

A sigh came from the other end. "That I like. A new job in a new place. Why don't you leave that shiksa in Texas and call Selma? She called me the other day. I think you've broken her heart. Now that her schooling is almost over, she might even come to Colorado to see you, if you ask her."

Al knew he had to work hard to convince his mother of Mary's uniqueness before she was willing to accept the ultimate reality.

"You're marrying that shiksa," she went on. "You want your father and I to close our business for a week, spend two days on a train to crazy cowboy country to see you down on your knees in a church marrying a Catholic girl; then have us travel back home for two more days? What is your hurry? Are you sure the girl isn't pregnant? How can you let yourself get trapped this way?"

The word trap struck a nerve with Al. He could not accept the idea of being trapped. Al kept defending his decisions.

"Allie," his mother said. "I'm your mother. I love you. I'm really not prejudiced against Christians. But, are you aware of the difficulties that are inherent in any marriage, much less a marriage between two people of totally different backgrounds, from different parts of the country, with different religions? How old is Mary?"

"She was nineteen last month," Al answered.

"You're both babies!" his mother exclaimed.

After a while, Al's mother softened her tone and she ended with the promise to welcome Mary with open arms. His mother promised to love Mary, so long as Mary honestly loved Al. "I promise to love her," she finally agreed.

"Thank you, mother," Al said before hanging up. He had tried to explain everything carefully while remaining as positive as possible.

After the call, Al experienced new confusion. He called Mary's home just to hear the sound of her voice. He also needed her encouragement and her words to tell him he was doing the right thing. The line was busy.

Al kept calling every five minutes for the next hour but he could not get through.

When Al exited the phone booth, perspiration soaked his body and clothes. He felt exhausted. With a feeling of disappointment, he retreated upstairs to bed. A monologue kept running in his head, Am I doing the right thing?

CHAPTER 51

Saturday morning Al reported to work at the Press by 6 A.M. He and Mary had set a wedding date. Al found it difficult to communicate with Mary while she and her mother were busy getting everything ready. He felt like the "forgotten man." He had no idea what she was planning.

At work, Al found himself amidst a buzz of rumors as his co-workers discussed the latest new appointments and their effects on job security at the newspaper.

Tommy John Stevenson approached Al. "Congratulations! I heard you're going to be at the cable desk in Denver. It's a break for you."

"Thanks. It sure is," Al said. "But, I'm putting down roots here. That is, at least, I'm getting married here. Bill Wannamaker promised me two weeks off for a honeymoon, and then Mary and I will set up housekeeping in Colorado, where it should be cooler."

"Wow! You're one helluva New York Jewboy on the make, aren't you?" Tommy John exclaimed. "You were here one month last summer and one month this summer. You've gone from copy boy to rewrite desk and now have a big new job on the cable desk in Denver. And not only that, you've walked away with one of Houston's prettiest girls. I stand in awe of you."

"I don't know if that's an insult or a compliment," Al teased, sharing a laugh with Tommy John.

"Listen, Al. I'm not insulting you. I admit I may have been jealous when Bill put you on the rewrite desk while he kept me a copy boy. But, I also know Bill thought you could handle the assignment while I wasn't quite ready. I was your first friend when you got here and I want to be your friend when you come back some day. Who knows? Maybe you'll be the managing editor."

"That'll be the day," Al responded. He and Tommy John reminisced and enjoyed a few laughs. Al appreciated Tommy's recognition of his abilities, although Al still felt more like a stranger at the Press.

Later in the morning, Al had the opportunity to speak to Mary. She assured him that they were going ahead with the marriage plans.

Al relaxed again, feeling confident that Mary seemed very capable of getting everything organized on time.

As Bill Wannamaker cleaned out his desk, Al approached him to tell him he would be ready to start his new job on July 13th. Al had one other question to ask.

"Will you still be in Houston a week from today? I'm getting married next Saturday and I'd be honored if you'd agree to be my best man," Al said.

Bill Wannamaker shook Al's hand vigorously as he laughed. "Okay. So, you've gone ahead and done it. You proposed. She accepted. Congratulations! I'll be glad to be your best man. Do you know when or where?"

"Not exactly. Can I call you later about that?" Al responded with a shrug. Al almost blushed for not knowing those important details. Mr. Wannamaker gave him Al his phone number.

After work, Al tried repeatedly to call Mary only to hear the phone ring with no answer. After he gave up on reaching her, he walked over to the Union Station to buy their train tickets to New York and back to Colorado. From the train station, Al finally reached Mary in time to make dinner plans with Mary and her parents. Mr. and Mrs. Monahan seemed to prefer chaperoning them until the wedding day.

Mary drove up in her father's Chevrolet exuding a bubbling good humor. Her white summer dress and straw hat matched perfectly with her soft cream-colored skin.

She moved over and let Al drive. "I've so much to tell you. Also, I need to know your full name for the wedding announcements. I have no idea what your middle name is."

"My name is Alfred Emmanuel Gordon. My Jewish name is Avram Mordechai after my two grandfathers. I got my first name after my father met the New York State majority leader, Alfred E. Smith."

"My father will like that. He was a big supporter of Smith when he ran for president in 1928. He's Roman Catholic, you know," Mary said. "Where are you headed?"

"I'm heading for West Alabama Street to get your parents."

"Not necessary."

"They're not going to chaperone us?"

"Not necessary." Mary smiled. "I got my period this afternoon. My mother figures my virginity is safe until our wedding night." Mary gave a hearty laugh. "That means that my period will have passed by our wedding night and I'll be ready for anything you have to give me. How do you like them apples?"

"I like everything about you, sweetheart," Al said.

"Will you always love me, Al?" Mary asked.

"Always and always," Al promised. Al pulled the car over and took her into his arms. They kissed long and hard as other cars drove past.

The days flew by for Mary as she finished preparing all the details for the wedding.

The days dragged by for Al. His status at the Press became that of a lame duck. He was relegated to stripping wire copy off the tickers and bringing the copy to various writers and editors to write the articles.

Mary kept Al abreast of Bill Monahan's conversations with Monsignor Ryan. There would be no dispensation until Al received instructions in Denver. A church wedding could be performed after Al's instructions. Mary could then receive communion and, once again, be considered to be free of sin. Al asked Mary if this upset her. She responded that nothing in the world and, presumably the Church, could upset her now.

In his last four days at the Press, Al made a new friend unexpectedly. With two writers out, Tony Sabella, the Sports Desk Editor, found himself with too much sports news to cover alone. After Al volunteered to help out with the sports copy, Tony soon came to realize why Al was called Bill Wannamaker's speedy wonder boy. They worked fast together and soon became fast friends. By Friday, Al invited Tony to attend his wedding the following afternoon.

The wedding had now been scheduled for 5 P.M. with the reception to follow.

Early Saturday morning at 6:30 Al was jarred out of his sleep by the ringing telephone.

"Al!" Mary sounded frantic. "We thought of everything, except getting a marriage license."

"My God!" Al sat up in bed. "Is it too late to do that now?"

"I don't think so," Mary said. "I think the marriage bureau is open on Saturday mornings. Can you meet me at the Harris County courthouse at 9 A.M.?"

"How about breakfast together first?" Al suggested.

"It's not lucky to see each other before the ceremony, but we'll make an exception to get the license. Okay." Mary relented, "I'll pick you up at 7."

Al hurriedly jumped out of bed. "I'm getting married! I'm getting married!" he shouted and jumped around to wake up. "I can't believe what I'm doing!"

CHAPTER 52

Mary and Al enjoyed looking into each other's eyes on this special day. Mary had an English muffin and coffee. Al had orange juice, toast, and milk. Both were silent. Then, simultaneously, they began to giggle.

"What are you laughing at?" Mary asked.

"I'm just thinking how wonderful it will be to have breakfast with you every morning," Al responded.

"Are you nervous?" Mary asked.

"I'm too stupid to be nervous," Al said, smiling. "But, I'm happier than I have ever been in my life."

They discussed their honeymoon plans. Al had forgotten to plan where they would be staying tonight, but Mary reassured him she had made already arrangements at the bridal suite of the Warwick Hotel.

"Do you want to hear a secret?" Mary teased.

"Yes," Al said with a hesitant voice.

"My secret is that I never expected to keep my virginity right up to our wedding night, but I have done so and I give you the credit for that."

Al gave her an astonished look. They both burst out laughing.

Mary patted Al's hand. "I'm glad we waited. I'm proud of both of us." Mary stood up. "Oh, gosh! It's time to get over to the courthouse. Let's get the license."

As Mary and Al approached the door, Miss Hargrove came through the door of the cafeteria. She gave Al a surprised look.

"We're getting married," Al said as he passed Miss Hargrove.

"Huh!" Miss Hargrove said with a disdained tilt of her head.

When Mary and Al left the cafeteria, Mary asked Al with a wide-eyed look, "Why did you say that?"

"I would have liked to have said more. I just wanted her to know her hostility couldn't scare me away," Al said firmly.

Robert Miller

"I'm glad she didn't scare you away either," Mary added. "Come on. Let's go. We've got a license to get." She took a hold of Al's arm to head back to the car.

Al and Mary walked hand in hand up the courthouse steps and found their way into the door marked "Marriage License Room." A bored looking middle-aged man handed them applications to fill out. He asked Mary if she had proof of her date of birth. She produced her driver's license. Then he turned to Al and told him, "You'll need permission from your parents since you are under 21."

"My parents are in New York. You can call them on the phone and they'll give you permission," Al said anxiously.

"We need it in writing," the clerk said with a deadpan look.

"I can get them to send a wire. It can be here in an hour. Will that be all right?" Al asked anxiously.

"Look here," Mary injected. "We're getting married tonight. The mayor is performing the ceremony. One hundred people are invited. You have to give us the license."

"Little lady, I don't have to do anything. I don't make the rules. I follow them. A man needs his parents' permission to get married until he's twenty-one. That's the law. There's nothing else I can do about it."

"Al is twenty-one. He wrote down the wrong year by mistake. I can get someone from *The Houston Press* to verify that for you," Mary told the clerk.

"You'd better fill out a new form and get someone from the Press who can verify your age to come over in the next hour, if you want the license and want to get married today," the clerk said perfunctorily.

Al and Mary walked outside into the sultry morning air and over to *The Houston Press* building. They found Bill Wannamaker packing the last of his belongings and saying his final goodbyes.

Bill looked up and saw Mary and Al. "Behold the bride and groom on their wedding morn," Bill announced.

"There won't be a wedding tonight, Bill, unless you can help me," Al said with discouragement. He explained that he needed Bill to go over to the courthouse with him and swear that he had checked the records at the Press and, indeed, Al was twenty one.

Bill looked askance at Al. "Young man, I have given you your first real job. I've hired you for a responsible job in Denver. You asked me to stand up as your best man at your wedding tonight. Now, you want me to go to the courthouse and lie for you! I certainly won't do that."

Al's faced dropped, and he turned pale.

Bill Wannamaker rubbed his chin thoughtfully at the predicament the young couple now faced. He had to consider the likely complication that Al might stay in Houston to be with Mary.

"Do you think I would hire a man as my cable editor in Denver who was under twenty one? I will gladly go with you to the courthouse and tell them you are twenty one. But, first I must produce some evidence to that effect."

Mr. Wannamaker sent a courier to the payroll department to get Al's payroll card. He then called in a staff artist to change the date of birth. When he was satisfied with the result, Mr. Wannamaker held the card aloft and told everyone in a loud voice, "Now, we are ready to deal with the bureaucrats at the Harris County Courthouse, and see that you get your license this morning and are properly married by sundown."

Mary clapped while flashing her radiant smile. She gave Mr. Wannamaker a quick hug, and then hugged Al.

Still holding the personnel record over his head, Bill Wannamaker marched out of the news room with Mary and Al trying to keep up with his fast pace. The three of them had not noticed that six other newsroom employees had tagged along behind them.

Eight people trooped into the marriage license office in the wake of Bill Wannamaker. "I want to see the person who denied these two fine young people a marriage license," Bill bellowed.

"Just who are you, sir, to come into this office and start shouting?" the clerk asked belligerently.

"I am William T. Wannamaker, city editor of *The Houston Press*. That's who I am. I am to be the best man at the wedding of Al Gordon and Mary Monahan this evening. A wedding which, incidentally, will be performed by the honorable mayor of this fair city. It will be an embarrassment for me as the best man, and for the mayor; not to mention the bridal couple and their parents, if we do not have a marriage license. But, it will make one terrific story in Monday's *Houston Press*," Bill announced. The clerk was not intimidated by Bill's bluster.

"This young man told us he was twenty years old. Now he tells us he is 21. We need to see proof."

"Here is your proof. Here is his payroll card from the Press," Bill Wannamaker said. "It clearly shows his birth date. That makes him 21 years, three weeks and four days old."

The clerk scrutinized the payroll sheet and grudgingly added, "I'll accept this as proof of age and issue the license. Somebody has to pay me $1.50."

Bill Wannamaker reached into his pocket and produced two, one-dollar bills. He addressed Mary and Al, "Let me pay this as my wedding gift to you both."

Mary and Al thanked Mr. Wannamaker profusely.

Mr. Wannamaker reassured Al that what he did was no special favor. He simply counted on Al to do a good job for him in Denver.

Within a few minutes, the clerk came out of the back office and handed Mary the marriage license. All the people in the room let out a cheer. Mary and Al were congratulated by everyone, while the clerk waved impatiently for everyone to clear the room.

Outside, Mary quickly gave Al a kiss. She then hugged Bill Wannamaker once again and thanked him for all he had done. She waved goodbye and headed for her car. Al was to meet her at Kelly's Restaurant at 4:30. He checked his watch and saw that he had a long five and a half hours to wait. Bill Wannamaker and the other men walked back to the *Press*.

Al went the other direction to take care of one last thing. He walked into the back of a drug store and waited patiently until the other customers had left. A woman came up to stand beside him. Al turned to the pharmacist and suggested he wait on the lady first. When the woman paid for her purchase and left, the pharmacist turned to Al again and asked if he could help him.

With his throat dry and parched, Al whispered for the first time in his life to a pharmacist, "I want to buy some rubbers."

"How many?" the pharmacist asked.

"How many are in a package?" Al inquired.

"We have packages with three or with twelve."

"I'll take one with three," Al responded.

The pharmacist reached under the counter, quickly put the tiny package into a bag and discreetly handed it to Al. Al promptly paid the pharmacist and walked away holding his breath.

By the time he breathed outside, Al realized he had made a mistake. Three would not be enough for the honeymoon. He stood in front of the pharmacy thinking, but too embarrassed to go back inside. He headed for another drugstore that was less busy. Again, Al whispered his request to a pharmacist and promptly received a package of a dozen rubbers.

When Al walked back to his hotel, he had an air of confidence that came from being prepared for his wedding night, as well as the two nights on the train en route to New York City.

He and Mary had discussed the subject of birth control. Mary talked somewhat ambivalently about that phase of her Catholic doctrine. She would be delighted to have a baby right away. However, she felt she would not be committing a great transgression if Al used rubbers during the early months of marriage. Mary said she found out from her married Catholic friends, even those fervent in the faith, that they still bought "rubbers like they buy groceries."

Al clutched the neck of the small pharmacy bag tightly, making sure his treasures would not fall out onto the street and become the source of an embarrassing public scene.

CHAPTER 53

Carrying his suitcase along the Houston street, Al had new feelings of apprehension, as well as intense loneliness and desolation. He could not remember the last time he had felt such nervousness. He walked automatically to Kelly's Restaurant.

Inside the restaurant, Al saw a small sign, MONAHAN-GORDON WEDDING. An arrow pointed up a staircase. Before Al ascended the stairs, he asked one of the employees if there was a checkroom where he could put his suitcase. The man took it and inquired who he was.

"I'm the bridegroom," Al told him.

"Well, congratulations! I'm Ed Joe Connelly, the night manager here. I'll find a place for you to leave it upstairs and let you know exactly where it is," the man said enthusiastically as he pumped Al's free hand. "Why don't you go upstairs now. There's quite a crowd there and your bride will be here in just a couple of minutes."

Al walked up the stairs into a room full of strangers. As he got into the room, a young lady, who appeared vaguely familiar to Al, came up and pinned a white flower on his lapel. She introduced herself as Mary's cousin, Sue Anne Porter. She gave Al a peck on the cheek. Suddenly, Al found himself surrounded by Mary's grandparents, other members of the family, Mary's friends and former co-workers from the Press. Al guessed he shook hands with about a hundred people.

Al gradually worked his way through the smiles and handshakes. Bill Wannamaker broke through the crowd to introduce Al to the mayor of Houston, who would perform the ceremony.

The mayor greeted Al warmly and told him he had heard great things about him from Bill Wannamaker, then lamented that both Bill and Al would be leaving Houston for Denver. The mayor reminded Al that he would always be a son-in-law of Houston.

Ed Joe came up the steps to announce the arrival of the bride and asked everyone to take a seat.

The mayor, Bill Wannamaker and Al took their places up front. A man at a piano and another man with a violin started playing, "Here Comes the Bride." At that point, everyone's head twisted to look for the bride. Bill Wannamaker nudged Al to face in that direction too.

Al was stunned to see Mary enter the room veiled in a beautiful white bridal gown as she was guided by the arm of her father. Al could not yet see her face, but he was dazzled by her dress.

The ceremony was mercifully brief. The Mayor made a short speech about the joys and sanctity of marriage. He bade Mary to remember that her roots were in Texas and he proudly predicted that Houston would have one million citizens by 1945 or surely by 1950. He then turned to the bride and groom and had them exchange vows and rings.

"I now declare you man and wife under God and the laws of the great Lone Star State of Texas," the mayor exclaimed loudly. "You may kiss the bride."

Al, who was making a valiant effort to remain calm, noticed his hands trembling as he lifted Mary's veil to find her blue eyes gleaming at him. He leaned over to kiss her. Their lips seemed to brush each other and not quite meet. Mary regained her composure and started to laugh as she threw her arms around Al, inciting the assembled group to give the couple a hearty Texas-size cheer.

The next couple of hours passed for Al as if he walked around in a dream. He kept shaking hands with people he barely knew. Everyone offered congratulations and best wishes. Many people handed him envelopes and his pockets were soon bulging. He thanked them. Al and Mary deposited their envelopes into a large bowl which was surrounded by presents stacked on the table and on the floor.

The smell of food at the buffet brought Al back to reality. As Mary and Al sat at a table, someone had kindly brought them each a plate of food. Al noticed his plate heaped full with roast beef, meatballs, salad, and smoked salmon. Mary tried the smoked salmon and made a face.

"You don't like the lox?" Al asked her.

"What is it?" Mary asked.

"Lox is a Jewish word for smoked salmon. Now that you're married to a Jewish boy, you're going to have to learn to enjoy some Jewish food, or at least tolerate it," Al whispered.

"Is that a requirement?" Mary teased. "Why didn't you tell me that before?"

"Sweetheart, I did," Al responded. "But, I did it with subtlety. That's why I took you to Schwartzenberg's."

Mary laughed and gave Al a quick kiss. "Sweetheart, you are subtle. You only told me about corned beef and pastrami, not lox."

Clash of Cultures - The Al Gordon Story

Bill Monahan approached Mary and Al from behind to speak with them. He handed Al a thick envelope and car keys, while vigorously shaking Al's hand, congratulating him again. He then kissed and hugged his daughter. Turning to Al, he said, "Please take good care of her. Mary has been my most precious possession. Now, she's yours. Please, always treat her as a precious possession."

Al noticed tears in Mr. Monahan's eyes. Al put his arm around Mr. Monahan's shoulder and assured him that he would always love Mary. By now, Mrs. Monahan had come over and started hugging her daughter and Al.

"What are we all crying about?" Mary asked, wiping a tear. "This is the happiest moment of my life." She turned to Al. "Sweetheart, it's time for us to leave. Let's get out of here."

"They have to serve the wedding cake!" Mrs. Monahan exclaimed. "You can't leave until they serve the cake. I'll see that they do it right away!"

Al and Mary sat down again and waited for the wedding cake.

The guests seemed to be enjoying the time eating, drinking, and talking. The tired young newly married couple seemed to have nothing to say to each other. Al quietly began wondering about his parents, grandmother and sister and what they were doing.

"How are you feeling? Are you all right? Have you been drinking too much?" Mary interrupted Al's thoughts.

"I'm fine. I haven't been drinking. Maybe, one beer last night and just a sip of champagne at the toast. I never had champagne before. I'm not sure I like it."

"My sweet Al, this is a time for new experiences," Mary said, as she patted Al's leg in a provocative way.

As Al leaned close to kiss Mary, the cake arrived. Flash bulbs began popping. Someone handed Mary a knife to cut the cake. Their moment of being alone had passed. They were thrust, once again, into their uncomfortable roles of bride and groom for what seemed to be another long hour.

After cutting and eating the cake, Mary and Al said their final "thank you's" and farewells. Ready to drive away with his new wife, Al found himself squeezed compactly and uncomfortably into the front seat by Mary's bridal dress.

At the Monahan's apartment, Mary peeled off her wedding gown and was ready to leave in less than 5 minutes. Al followed behind carrying her luggage.

On the way to the hotel, Mary sat very close to her new husband. As he put his arm around his bride, the car weaved momentarily along one of Houston's dark streets.

Mary laughed. "I can just see the headlines in the paper. Lover boy takes hand off wheel and crashes on the way to his bridal suite on his wedding night."

"You'll never be a newspaperwoman," Al teased. "Your headline would probably be one of the longest in history."

"Can you write a better one?"

"Sure. How about 'Wedding night crash, bride and groom splash!'"

Mary tilted her head back and broke out laughing. She started running her hand along Al's leg. "Okay, lover boy, keep your eye on the road and get us to the bridal suite."

Al smiled as Mary looked at him with those gorgeous blue eyes that had brightened his life for almost two years.

CHAPTER 54

The bridal suite looked to Al like a grand Hollywood movie set. His old room at the Hotel Cotton would have fitted in just the bedroom here at least twice over, and then there was a spacious elegant adjoining living room, besides, where two tall champagne glasses awaited him and Mary on the table. And nearby was a bottle of champagne in an ice bucket, along with a massive basket of fruit.

Al approached the champagne. "Shall we open it?"

"Let's open it, sip just a little and maybe pour the rest down the sink," Mary said with a look of mischief on her face.

Al and Mary took their glasses and a piece of melon with them into the bedroom. They sat close on the edge of the bed where they sipped the champagne and nibbled. Then Al put his glass down and brought out the envelopes to begin counting the money.

"There's six hundred dollars here, plus a couple of checks! We're married and we're rich!" Al exclaimed. He reached over and pulled Mary into his arms. She quickly put both her champagne and melon down. In a moment, the two of them rolled exuberantly over all the five, ten, and twenty-dollar bills on the bed.

Al's hand roamed over Mary's body. His fingers explored her panties and towards the sweet opening those panties covered. Mary gasped and pushed Al aside.

"Please, sweetheart, wait just a few minutes more. I have a special wedding night outfit to wear. Please give me a few minutes to put it on," Mary whispered.

"You can put on your special outfit if you like, but I can't promise how long it will stay on." He pressed her hand against the bulge in his pants and told her, "Both of us are getting impatient."

Mary put Al's hand back between her legs where he had been exploring a minute earlier. "That makes four of us being impatient - two newlyweds and two under utilized sexual organs." With that, she freed herself from Al's hand and ran to the bathroom.

Robert Miller

Al occupied his time by taking out the pins in his new set of pajamas and putting them on. He nibbled on a pear, while he continued waiting.

When Mary came back into the bedroom, her hair looked longer than Al had ever seen it, draping down now to her shoulders. Al's eyes roamed down the pale blue transparent gown that almost matched her eyes and on to the enticing short transparent negligee.

Al became transfixed, gazing.

"Do you like what you see?" Mary asked.

"Mary, I love what I see. I can't believe all this beauty is mine. All mine. I love you, Mary. And I promise that I will do everything I can to make you happy for the rest of your life."

Mary came over to Al and started kissing him. They fell back easily onto the bed. Al caught his breath. Mary's fingers opened the string of his pajamas. The fancy gown and negligee slid down to her waist. Mary moaned as Al's fingers explored the delightful wetness between her legs.

"You're driving me crazy, sweetheart. I'm ready to have you inside me. If you have a rubber, put it on your sweet thing." She added one last word with emphasis, "Now."

Al got out of bed and tripped over his pajama bottoms which became twisted around his legs. He came back to look at Mary lying across the bed with one breast exposed. Her gown had crumpled up to her waist, exposing her beautiful shape and nakedness.

"Sweetheart, why don't you take everything off? Let me see you in all your glory?" Al asked.

"It's too bright in here for me to do that." Mary smiled at him shyly. "I'm just a little embarrassed. Why don't you turn off the lights and then I'll take my gown off."

Al complied. He found himself struggling in the dark to open his package of condoms and then trying to figure out how to put one on, as it was the first time he'd ever tried. He left momentarily to go back into the outside hallway to see what he should be doing.

Al returned to the dark bedroom. Mary carefully lifted her gown and negligee off. Al struggled to get the rubber over his penis. There seemed to be too much of an overhang. Al tugged at the top like a sock. The condom suddenly snapped apart. He heard a giggle in the dark.

"I hope you have more," Mary's voice said softly.

Al assured her that he did and went back to the dresser drawer to get another condom. He positioned it on as best he could and returned to his waiting Mary.

Again, their hands roamed over each other. Al felt Mary's fingers pull back when she touched his penis.

"I'm not sure I like touching that rubber. I think I like the real thing better," Mary explained in a whisper.

Al said nothing. His fingers started exploring inside her.

"I want it there, inside me," Mary moaned.

Al rolled over onto her and tried to insert his penis where his fingers had just been. He could not find the right position. He pushed. She moved to accommodate him. He tried again. Al told her to open her legs wider. She tried. He still could not make the entry. He pushed the head of his penis into the opening, but made little headway.

"The damn rubber is chafing and scraping me," Mary complained. "I don't like it. I'm going to take it off of you. I want you inside me and I don't care if we have a baby or not!" Mary said with a rising, impatient voice.

Mary rolled over and started rolling the rubber off Al's throbbing member. Just as she got the rubber off, Al's semen exploded all over her hands, the bedclothes and their bodies.

Al was mortified and began apologizing immediately.

Mary hesitated for a few seconds of disbelief and frustration, but soon started laughing hysterically. "It's a good thing this bed is big enough so we can sleep on the dry side and still have lots of room."

Al mumbled something to her again about being sorry and quickly fell asleep.

Mary, still naked, got up and walked over to turn out the light in the hallway. She came back and lay close to her new and naked husband before surrendering herself to sleep in the bridal suite. Her virginity, so far, had remained securely intact.

CHAPTER 55

Al awoke alone in bed. He squinted at the sunlight flooding the room. He sat up to find Mary seated at the mirror wearing a slip and applying makeup.

Mary heard Al stir and turned to him. She gave him a warm smile. "It's after eight. I promised my parents we'd meet them at the nine o'clock Mass, so you'd better get moving."

"Not a chance!" Al exclaimed. He rolled over. "Call them back and tell them we'll meet them at 11 o'clock Mass. I will never leave this room while you are still a virgin! Never!"

Mary gave Al an appraising glance.

"Oh, my lord and master of fourteen hours is giving me orders."

Her inflection sounded somewhere between a statement and a question. But Mary obliged. Al overheard her calling her mother back to tell them to meet at 11.

When Mary came back to Al, she broke into a huge smile and joined Al in bed. With the full light of day streaming in, Mary had no shyness about slipping off her slip and panties. As his hand explored Mary's body, he suggested that she lay back and, not only spread her legs, but also raise them off the bed.

In a romantic exercise mixed with gymnastics and determination, Al once again attempted to enter her. Al's fingers probed a proper path that might lead him to the "Promised Land." Mary gasped and moaned. She lifted her parted legs onto Al's shoulders and arched her body to meet his thrust, and Al finally was inside. Mary's body suddenly recoiled as she gave out, first, a gasp of pain and then a relaxed sigh. She shuddered, feeling his semen pouring inside her. They laughed, hugged and kissed with a certain pride in their somewhat belated accomplishment.

"Did that hurt you bad, sweetheart?" Al asked where they lay together for a moment.

"It hurt me, all right, but it hurt good, not bad."

They rolled slowly out of bed past the spottings of blood, sweat, and semen.

"Al, do you think I'm pregnant?" Mary asked as they soaped each other down in the shower.

Al remained stunned for a moment by the sobering thought.

"I guess you could be, Mary. But, according to the literature I received from Fathers Reilly and Walsh, it is not likely you can get pregnant if you're within a week or so from the end of your period. They call that the rhythm method, I think."

"I'm told that rhythm is a myth. It simply doesn't work," Mary said with a giggle. She applied more soap to Al's body.

They talked about Mary getting pregnant while they completed their shower. Their final choice was to try the rhythm method for just that week. The following weeks they would try to use the rubbers again.

"I'll be well broken in by then," Mary suggested with a conspiratorial smile.

A few minutes later Al was dried off, dressed and on the phone to Western Union. He told the clerk to send the following message to his parents, Mr. and Mrs. Samuel Gordon in New York City: "We're married. We're ecstatic. We'll arrive in Penn Station, Tuesday at 10:40. Love Mary and Al."

Mary's parents stood waiting in the parking lot of Saint Anne's Church as Al and Mary drove in. All four of them greeted each other happily.

"We went to the ten o'clock Mass," Mrs. Monahan explained. "Since your train is at two-twenty, everyone - your grandparents, uncles, aunts and cousins - is waiting at our apartment. By the time we get back, we'll have a buffet set up. There's not a lot of time. Do you really want to skip Mass today?"

"I may not have been married in a Church ceremony, so I may be denied the sacraments in the future, but I have so much to thank God for this morning. I really want to attend Mass," Mary said.

Mary kissed her father and mother. She promised she and Al would be home immediately after Mass to say good-bye to everyone.

Upon finding their seats, Mary got down on her knees on the kneeling bench. She closed her eyes and clasped her hands. Al sat next to her thinking she had entered a trance as she prayed.

After a few minutes, Mary sat back in her seat. She grasped Al's hand tightly and whispered, "I have thanked God in my own way for sending you to me and for making me your wife. There is no reason why we should stay for the Mass. We can leave now if you want to. You'll have to put up with my family for a while until we're alone on the train."

Al kissed her beautiful white cheek. "I can put up with your family for an hour or so. You'll have a week to put up with mine when we get to New York." Mary and Al rose and left the Church hand in hand.

The two hours they spent with Mary's family seemed like an extension of the wedding reception the night before. The only difference was that the Monahans' apartment seemed more crowded.

Aunt Cora took a moment hugging and kissing Mary, wished her every happiness. After stealing a glance at Al, Aunt Cora politely inquired of Mary if she had money for train fare home in case Al's family in New York "impossible to deal with."

Grandpa Porter immediately stepped between Mary and Aunt Cora. "Cora, I've heard you say some stupid things in your life, but I think this beats them all," he said sternly. "Do you think for one minute that Al Gordon here is going to let anyone make things difficult for his bride? I've only met Al one time before, but I'm proud to have him in the family. One of these days I'm going to meander up to New York City, myself. I'm eager to meet Al's parents and see out what kind of people could bring up such a nice, smart, successful young man with so much good sense." He raised his voice for all in the room to hear and told the assemblage, "There are those who said this family was going to the dogs when Opal Mae married Bill Monahan twenty years ago. But, I want to tell you I'm proud to have Bill Monahan, be he Catholic or not, as my son-in-law, and I'm just as happy to have Al Gordon as my grand-son-in-law. I don't care if he's a Jew or even a Buddhist. All I have to do is see that happy glow in Mary Jean's eyes to know he is the right man for her. And, I won't have you Cora, or anyone else putting Al down."

Cora fumed a little. Mary threw herself into her Grandpa's arms and began to cry. Al put an arm around Grandpa Porter and patted him on the back to thank him.

The whole crowd of relatives then escorted the newly married couple to the train station where everyone could wave and shout their goodbyes. From their drawing room car on the train, Mary waved out the open window. Al suddenly realized Mary had started to cry as the train pulled away.

"Why are you crying? Have I made you unhappy?" Al wondered tenderly. He kissed her to try to quiet her.

Mary started to laugh and cry at the same time.

"It suddenly occurred to me that my life has changed. I'm a married woman and not my Daddy's little girl anymore. I'm happy, but, at the same time, I'm a bit weepy about the life I'm leaving. Can you understand that?"

Al said nothing, but they clung to each other. Mary continued to weep a few minutes more.

"You know," Mary said when she became composed. "They served lots of champagne last night. I was too excited or nervous then to enjoy a glass. Would it be terribly extravagant if I ordered a champagne cocktail as we start our trip?"

"It might be, but you're lucky enough to be married to a man with close to $700 in his pocket and a new job paying eighty dollars a week," Al teased. "So, let's celebrate."

In the bar car, a black porter in a clean, starched white uniform poured their champagne and then excused himself.

"Though I love the flat grassy plains and the scrubby tumbleweeds of Texas, here's a toast to our new futures together. From New York City to the Rocky Mountains of Denver!" Mary said, lifting her drink.

They clinked their glasses together in a toast and enjoyed this romantic moment. They became entranced in their private world which they created at their table, just sipping champagne and watching each other's eyes.

Later, looking out the window, Al and Mary broke away from their glances to see a whole different world passing before their eyes. The so-called "Hooverville" shanties of the poor spread along the railroad tracks on the outskirts of Houston. Al and Mary sipped their champagne again. It occurred to Al that drinking champagne while passing a group of homeless and presumably hungry people was a strong argument for socialism. But Al knew he could do nothing for the thousands of wretched squatters. His mind turned away from such harsh realities and he hoped never to be in such a predicament himself.

Robert Miller

CHAPTER 56

Back in their compartment, Al pulled down the shade and enfolded Mary in his arms. They quickly began undressing each other.

"Do you think we'll ever be able to have sex with me on top"? Mary asked.

"We'll not only accomplish that someday, but we'll accomplish it today," Al said as he kissed her. "Tell me your sexual fantasies, and I'll try to make them all come true before this train leaves Texas." Al's voice and face showed determination, but his heart hoped he could fulfill his promise.

The bunk bed turned out to be too cramped to be very comfortable for them. Al and Mary positioned and repositioned themselves several times. Finally, they had reached a position with Mary on top. Al immediately felt how her whole body gyrated wildly and pushed down on his. The intensity became overwhelming and they both experienced orgasms simultaneously, with Mary collapsing onto Al. Soon, they fell into a satisfied, happy sleep in the cramped bunk.

When Mary woke, she could not believe how dark it looked outside. With hunger pangs pulling at her stomach, she nudged Al awake to ask, "Do you think we missed dinner?"

"Are you really so hungry? Or, do you simply want to escape the sex maniac you have in your cabin?" Al teased, while stretching his free arm and leg.

"Now which of us do you think is the sex maniac?" Mary teased.

They shared laughter and kisses.

"Now, listen," Mary interrupted. "This is our anniversary! We've been married exactly twenty-four hours. And, I'm a lot happier, hungrier, and more relaxed than I was at this time last night. It's time to celebrate. Let's order steaks, champagne and pie a la mode." Mary giggled.

"I'll go for that!" Al exclaimed. "I guess once in a while we do have to put our clothes on to go out to the dining car."

Clash of Cultures - The Al Gordon Story

The rest of the journey on the train was one of lovemaking, experimentation, interrupted from time to time by short periods of sleep and the porter's courteous knocks on the door either to announce meal times, or the arrival at St. Louis where they had to change trains.

By the time the train pulled out of North Philadelphia for its final run to New York, Al and Mary felt like seasoned expert travelers knowledgeable about all the train's comforts.

Mary's mood started to tense the closer they got to New York. "Sweetheart, you are to me my Jewish 'Greek god,' but do you think your parents will like me?"

Al said nothing, but held her close for a moment. Suddenly, the brightness outside disappeared as the train headed into a tunnel that would take them into Penn Station in New York City.

Mary started to tremble. "Will your parents be at the train to greet us?"

"I think my mother will be there. Dad will probably have to stay at the office. The other cast of characters you probably won't meet until tonight," Al said reassuringly as he hugged her.

Once the train came into the station, Al and Mary stepped off onto a mostly empty platform. Al spotted his mother nervously eying the disembarking passengers. His sixteen-year-old sister, Shirley, showed an apparently neutral impatience, waiting to see what would happen. Al called out to his mother. The sight of Al brought her running up to him and Mary.

Al's mother hugged him, looked him over and then turned her attention to Mary. She looked Mary over, appraising her for the first time and then broke into a warm smile.

"Mary, Al told us that you were beautiful, but he didn't tell us how truly exquisite you are," Mrs. Gordon said. "Welcome to New York. Welcome to our family." She then introduced Mary to Shirley. Mary kissed and hugged each of them.

Al saw relief and joy in Mary's face as she met the first members of Al's family.

Mrs. Gordon took Mary's arm and started leading them up the platform. "My son the cable desk editor," Mrs. Gordon started. "My son the married man. My son the big shot." Mrs. Gordon laughed. "Allie wanted to get married. He asked Selma, a girl from the Bronx, to marry him and go to Texas with him, and when she turned him down, he found you right away."

Mary stiffened. Al had never told her that he had proposed to any girl. Now the damage was done.

Mrs. Gordon kept on talking with a pat to Mary's arm, "I want you to know that I really think that you and Allie are too young to be married, but I want you to know that now that I've met you I think he made a good choice."

Robert Miller

Al pondered his mother's words, especially about the other "proposal." They had not even left the station, and his mother already had placed suspicions in Mary's mind. He wondered if her comments were simply thoughtless, or if they were a calculated attempt to undermine Mary's confidence in him.

Mary said nothing to Al about the other girl from the Bronx, as the four of them made their way to 34th Street and Eighth Avenue. They proceeded up some steps to the loft over Riordan's Bar and Grill that was occupied by the Gordon Advertising Agency.

Al's father greeted Al and Mary as they came in. He had an unusually big smile that lit up his entire countenance. After pumping Al's hand and welcoming his son home, he turned to Mary to drink her in for a few seconds.

"Al, you have got yourself a real Irish beauty. I'm overwhelmed. May you both always be as happy as you are at this moment!"

Mary kissed him and told her father-in-law how happy she was to be there with Al's family.

They all stood awkwardly for a while talking to each other, between phone calls and customers walking in and out. Al explained to his mother that he had made arrangements to stay at the Concourse Plaza Hotel.

Mrs. Gordon seemed shocked and taken aback by this news. But it was agreed that they would all assemble later at the Gordon's apartment at 7:00 and have dinner there.

Before Al and Mary headed uptown to the hotel, they walked with Shirley over to the Automat on the corner of Thirty Third Street and Eighth Avenue. Mary was amazed at the compartments, each filled with its own specialty - sandwiches, bread, cakes, puddings, fruit slices, side dishes - things that could be bought for one, two or three nickels. She was entranced with the machine that dispensed coffee for a nickel dropped into the slot on the wall. Unlike Morrison's Cafeteria back home where customers paid a cashier directly, the purpose of the lone cashier was to exchange dollar bills for rolls of twenty nickels. Mary was mesmerized by the whole Automat way of doing things. After Shirley left Al and Mary outside the Automat, as they made their way back to the train station to get their luggage, Mary looked sternly at Al.

"Just which girl did you ask to marry and go to Texas with you? I fell in love with you, left my home, my family, my Church to marry you and share your life. I gave you my virginity and now I have come to New York to find that I'm your second choice, and that you only married me because someone else turned you down. I have a good mind to get back on a train this afternoon and go home to Texas and beg forgiveness from my parents and my church."

Al stopped right at the station stairs and put his arm around her.

"Mary, it isn't true that I proposed to anybody else. I did not want to get married. Not to anyone, but you. I came back to Texas just one month ago. Because I realized I couldn't live without you, I never thought about marriage before nor of marrying anybody but you. I don't know where my mother ever got that foolish notion in her head, or if she said what she said just to hurt both of us. Please don't pay any attention to what she said. You are the only girl I ever wanted to marry. Please don't think of ever leaving me. I love you and we're on our honeymoon. Let's enjoy it."

Mary seemed only barely satisfied with this.

"All right," Mary finally said. "I won't go home — I'd be ashamed to. But, I'm not one bit happy about being your obvious second choice."

Al held her close. When he reached over to kiss Mary, she turned her face to avert his lips.

"Let's just get our bags and head for the hotel," Mary told him in an icy controlled voice.

CHAPTER 57

In the taxi uptown to the Concourse Plaza Hotel, Mary's interest brightened as they drove through Harlem.

At the hotel, a short, round, middle-aged, white-haired desk clerk scrutinized the couple, perhaps wondering if Al, and the very young lady were really married. The clerk finally agreed that they could have the bridal suite, but it would cost $12 a night.

In the suite, Al gave the bellman a dollar, an enormous tip, and then he and Mary were alone. Al tried to take her in his arms but she turned away from him.

"Al, I am very unhappy with you," she told him firmly. "Just leave me alone for awhile. I want to take a bath and be by myself."

"I was hoping we could take a bath together, Mary."

Mary stepped back from his outstretched arms.

"Not now, Al. Not yet. I've got to get used to the circumstances I find myself in."

"Mary! For God's sake! Don't be so dramatic. My mother said something stupid to you. Something stupid and untrue. I never ever asked anyone to marry me but you. Never ever."

Al pulled her to him as Mary made a mild effort to push him away and kept her face averted so he couldn't kiss her lips.

"Just leave me alone for a while to think things through. God knows I want to believe you. So please."

She stepped away from Al and went into the bathroom. Al waited momentarily, then walked into the bedroom and plopped on the bed. He laboriously rubbed his forehead, trying to figure out how to handle the situation. He did not want his wife leaving him to go back to Texas.

Mary started the water running in the bathroom.

Al could not just sit. He paced the two-room suite anxiously for some time, taking notice of the mirrors, including one over the bed, and the flowers and a fruit basket.

Unable to concentrate, Al tore open the cellophane wrapping from the basket. He carefully picked out one green plum and sat down. He positioned the plum to bite off half of it. His tooth clamped down hard on the hidden pit. He winced in pain. Just then, Mary demurely came out of the bathroom dressed in a white negligee he had never seen.

"Is something the matter?" Mary asked.

"I thought I had broken my tooth on the damn pit," Al said with a dumbfounded look. He saw a concerned look on Mary's face. His eyes roamed the rest of her naked body showing through the transparent negligee.

"I have decided to forgive you," she told him in a soft voice. She dropped into his arms and onto his lap as he sat waiting on the couch. She kissed him with her mouth open.

Al took the cue and picked her up. He carried her over to the bed. They made love spontaneously, but now like experienced romantics who knew just what they were doing.

Thirty minutes later Al had almost drifted off to sleep when he felt Mary's chin on his chest demanding his attention.

"Now, I want to hear about that former girl friend of yours. What is her name?" Mary asked pointedly. Her voice brought Al out of his after-glow and abruptly put him on his guard.

"What girl are you talking about?" Al asked.

"You know what girl I'm talking about. I'm talking about Selma. Did you really offer to marry her if she would come with you to Texas?"

"No, I did not," Al defended. He tried to explain to Mary that he, indeed, loved only her and no one else. Mary was not mollified.

"I want to know if you proposed to her before you came to Texas!" Mary almost screamed. "I want to know if you only decided to marry me because she turned you down."

Mary got up and walked towards the living room. Al followed her.

"You asked that question six times," Al exclaimed. "And, six times I've answered it. Please listen to me. I love you. That's why I married you. I don't love anyone else. You are my first choice. My only choice. For God's sake, get a grip on yourself. Don't spoil our honeymoon. Don't destroy our marriage and our happiness!"

Mary's haughty indignation brought Al to tears. He became terrified that Mary would walk out of his life. He felt the first real threat that could break up his marriage and cause Mary to go back to Texas.

Mary looked shocked to see him crying. She ran to him, threw her arms around him and began crying herself. The two of them stood naked, clinging to each other and bawling. Between their tears, they begged each other for forgiveness for their mutual stupidity. Too exhausted to cry anymore, they began laughing over the ridiculousness of their situation.

"Al, sweetheart, it was so beautiful when we made love. I've spoiled it with my silliness. I want you to know I'll always love you," Mary said apologizing.

"I love you and only you," Al reassured her again. He dabbed away the tears from Mary's wide, wet eyes. Al concluded that they now had made peace, and, in the process, humbly learned something about the strangeness of women and of love.

By 6 that evening, Al was giving Mary a walking tour of the sights and experiences of the Bronx. He proudly pointed out Yankee Stadium and he helped Mary push herself onto the most crowded train she had ever seen. Later, back on the street, Mary and Al walked past apartment houses that rose above the street level restaurants, shops, vegetable stands, bakeries - and endless collections of small businesses block after block.

Mary commented to him on the surprise of seeing so many women sitting around on the stoops, benches, milk boxes, and bridge chairs. The women constantly chattered with each other amidst occasional screams at their raucous children to be careful.

"What are all these women doing on the street?" Mary wondered aloud. "Why aren't they upstairs making dinner?"

"I don't really know. People here tend to spend time outside. They probably get tired of being cooped up in their apartments all day," Al said. Mary, being new to the scene, was questioning things he had taken for granted all his life. And while Al expected Mary to be impressed by the Grand Concourse, which Al thought this was the finest, most elegant and widest street in the world, she seemed unimpressed.

Al guided Mary into the courtyard that separated two adjoining buildings and up the stairs to his family's apartment. Al rang the doorbell. The door opened quickly and there stood his grandmother. Al hugged her tight and kissed her cheek. "Grandma, I want you to meet my wife, Mary."

Al's grandmother squinted her eyes behind her thick glasses as she tried focusing on Mary's face, then she reached up and kissed Mary. "To tell you the truth, I thought Allie was too young to get married. Now that I see how beautiful you are, I can understand why he couldn't wait."

Mary seemed pleased and hugged her. She told this short elderly lady how much Al had talked about her. Al gave an astonished look, because he didn't remember talking to Mary about his grandmother.

Mary was introduced next to Al's Aunt Mollie, who looked Mary over and then offered a greeting with outstretched hands. "Welcome to New York and to our family, dear. You are a long way from home. We have heard so much about you and are so glad to finally meet you."

While Aunt Mollie's words were warm, her tone contained the clear understanding that she would keep her eye on Mary for quite a while before she granted complete approval.

Shirley greeted Mary now like an old friend. They hugged and kissed each other once again, and Shirley had lots of questions about the accommodations at the bridal suite.

Shirley had helped set the table for dinner, but there would be no meal until Al's parents arrived at 7:00 laden with packages of food. Then Mary took a turn at helping Al's mother and Aunt Mollie in the kitchen.

"You may not be familiar with this food," Mrs. Gordon said to Mary, as they unwrapped the packages. "We call this food appetizing. We have lox, which is smoked salmon. Here's smoked sturgeon, pickled herring, smoked whitefish, bagels, onion rolls, and Jewish rye bread. Is any of this at all familiar to you, Mary?"

"Well, no, Mrs. Gordon, not at all before I met Al," Mary explained, inspecting the food. "But Al and I have eaten at smorgasbord restaurants in Houston where they had smoked salmon, herring, and whitefish, too. And we had many meals at Schwartzenberg's, Houston's Jewish restaurant, and we ate food like this there. I love this food."

Al's mother gave a look to Mary and began to laugh. "Mary, you are a sweet girl. I'm happy to hear you say you like Jewish food. I know that is your way of trying to show us friendship. I appreciate that. I may have made an unthinking and cruel remark to you when we first met. I want you to know that what I said wasn't true and certainly was unwise and unkind of me. Will you forgive me?"

Mary didn't say a word, but embraced Mrs. Gordon. They were in tears, while hugging each other tightly with hands that were sticky and smelled of fish.

"Mother Gordon, I love Al so much and I know that I will come to love everyone in his family. And, even if I don't really love lox and herring, I promise you I will develop a taste for it," Mary said softly, smiling.

Robert Miller

CHAPTER 58

As they sat around the table that evening, Al marveled at how everyone seemed to get along. While Al's grandmother sat back with a withdrawn quietness, she seemed to hang on Mary's every word. Al felt that his mother's and aunt's misgivings of him marrying a girl from Texas, and a Roman Catholic, were all falling away as they became charmed by Mary's beauty and sweetness. Al looked over at his grandmother, wearing her shabbos dress, and saw her trying to focus her eyes on Mary. He noted that she, too, was smiling happily and proudly at Al's new bride.

Even Al's taciturn father got into the act. He suddenly expressed his belief that the country would not have gone through a depression if Al Smith had been elected president. Al was amazed to hear his father express his various political views so openly, since his father was reserved in such conversations at home.

After dinner, a procession of Shirley's friends came in to see Al's new bride. A couple of her friends had been one-time girlfriends or momentary flirtations of Al's in the past. Mary was sociable and happy to meet all of them — She knew how to charm everyone, and soon ended up disappearing into Shirley's bedroom with her and her friends.

While the girls were out of the living room, Al talked about his experiences working at *The Houston Press* and about his anticipation at going to work at the *Rocky Mountain News* in Denver.

Then, when Mary and the girls came out of Shirley's room, Mary appeared especially radiant to Al. She seemed to be happy to be the center of attention among these young women who were almost her age and she'd found much common ground with, so as the girls returned to the living-dining area, where coffee and cake was ready, Al walked over to Mary and put his arm around her to hold her close. Mary smiled at him, but squirmed out of his grasp. Al assessed her smile was less than her typical glow that usually lit her eyes. Her eyes were now cold and she looked back at Al while she stepped away.

Al was confused. He enjoyed a piece of cake, but kept an eye on Mary. After watching his wife disappear into the kitchen, he followed her there. Al came up behind her and tried to encircle her in his arms.

Mary looked around to make sure no one else was in the kitchen.

"You're a lecher," she whispered sternly. "That's what you are."

Al stood with a dumbfounded look trying to understand her criticism. "What have I done now?"

"How dare you bring me here and subject me to all your old girlfriends?" Mary went on. "Are all of your sister's friends your former girlfriends?"

Al smiled in a relaxed way, confident there were no old girlfriends that had to be taken seriously.

"Sweetheart, none of them were ever girlfriends of mine. None of them," he repeated. "I may have flirted with them from time to time, but I never had any serious designs on any of them. And, even if I did, you are the girl I married. You are the girl I chose. You are the only girl in the world for me. Don't you understand that? You have no reason to be jealous of anyone."

Al felt her body relax. Tears formed and slid down her cheeks.

She put her arms around Al and rested her head on his shoulder. The tears stopped and she wiped her face.

"Oh, Al. I don't know why I act this way. I'm tired and far from home. And, so afraid you won't always love me. I get confused. I really like your parents and your aunt and especially, your grandmother. Though, I'm not sure about Shirley. Do we have to stay here much longer? Can we go back to the hotel?"

"Ah, the lovebirds. The honeymooners," Al's mother exclaimed when she walked in on them in the kitchen. She came over and hugged Al and Mary separately. "I hope you will always be as happy as you are today." Turning to Al, she emphasized, "You found a real beauty there in Texas. Be good to her, Al, and you will each surely have a happy life together."

Al explained that they were both tired and would be returning to the hotel. Within a few minutes, Mary was busy embracing, kissing, and saying goodbye to the Gordons and Shirley's friends. Al was, once again, amazed by the continuous transformation of his Mary. As she told everyone goodbye, she appeared to be animated and happy, not a bit like the upset, self-doubting person she'd been just a few minutes before in the kitchen.

Al and Mary decided to take a long, slow walk along the Grand Concourse back to the hotel. Hand in hand, Al enjoyed pointing out the landmarks along the way - P.S. 70 where he attended school through the eighth grade, the Lewis Morris apartment building with its imposing doorman in front of the building, and the small parks where older people and youngsters were obviously escaping the heat of their apartments.

Mary looked about her as they passed the older apartment houses that flanked the Concourse, where people were sitting out in front of their buildings, sometimes conversing with people who leaned out their windows on the first and second floors.

"Are these what you call tenements?" Mary asked with a voice tinged with wonderment.

"No, sweetheart, tenements are much older buildings. These are elegant buildings. Tenements are in the poorer sections," Al explained casually. He proudly showed her a large Catholic church and then the Adath Israel synagogue. Then, passing an automat, they could not resist stopping in where forty cents worth of nickels bought them sandwiches and coffee.

The walk had been good for both of them. Al felt happy reacquainting himself with his neighborhood, while Mary seemed so amazed at the many ways of living that New York seemed to offer.

Back at the hotel, their night was interspersed with lovemaking, conversation, mutual reassurance, and sleep. Al drifted into dreams, immensely proud and pleased with himself for having captured a beautiful young charmer, a gal with her Texas accent. Yes, he really had brought her to his hometown, which he proudly saw as the biggest, best and brashest of all the cities in the world - New York!

CHAPTER 59

Time moved faster as Al tried showing Mary all of the many New York City neighborhoods and its events. Al splurged on double-decker bus rides, a trip to the Statue of Liberty, a baseball game, and a Broadway show. As they walked along New York's Great White Way at Times Square near midnight, Mary became speechless at the throngs of people walking around under the glittering neon lights.

The Gordons held one last party in their apartment before Al and Mary had to leave. Mary enjoyed all who came, but her secret concern was to know which of the girls who once might have been one of Al's girlfriends. She used her own canny intuition to analyze this female competition.

Robert Martin, one of Mr. Gordon's friends, confessed to Mary and Al that his name had been Martinelli, until he married Sylvia Goldstein, and that, although he had always lived among Jews since then, he had never forgotten that he was born a Roman Catholic. He encouraged Mary to always keep her faith in God, no matter what happened or what people said.

Al's friends from New York University were impressed, not only with Al's beautiful wife, but with his capture of a semi-managerial job in Denver. Al puffed his chest that evening proud to show his old friends in the Bronx that he had "made it."

One of Al's NYU friends brought Joan Fleischer, now an aspiring actress and also a friend of Shirley's, and someone whom Al really had seriously flirted with a few years ago. Joan's first impulse in entering the apartment was to hug and kiss Al. She greeted Mary and told her offhandedly, "Al once promised that he'd write a play for me, one that would make me a star. I hope that his being married to you will not preclude that."

Mary mumbled something, but Al, excited by his own sense of importance, threw himself at taking up the idea again. He herded Joan and his friends over to his typewriter in order to start writing the play right then and there.

That bit of banter and bravado got Al right back into trouble. He was well aware of it when Mary turned and stomped off towards the kitchen alone. Meanwhile, Al, Joan, her date and six others retreated to a bedroom where Al sat down and wrote two paragraphs. Without Mary, Al's showmanship stopped dead. He excused himself and went out looking for his sensitive, distraught bride.

Al found Mary in the kitchen and put his arms around her. "Why does it upset you to meet old female friends of mine? You are the only one I love. You're the girl I chose and for whom I agreed to forsake all others."

Mary glared at Al long enough for him to hear her unspoken message that she wanted nothing to do with those others. "I didn't like that Joan from the minute she walked in here dressed to the nines." Mary's voice was low. "The nerve of her running up and kissing you and asking you to write a play for her. And, then you act like a jerk and sit down and begin to write one with an audience gathered around you. And I'm supposed to like that? I don't like her and I'm not one bit sorry I got mad. I have to protect you from women like that. Do you get the message?"

"I get the message and accept it with pleasure," Al said, as he enveloped Mary in his arms, while she rewarded him with a soft kiss.

Back at the Concourse Plaza Hotel that evening, Al and Mary found that they had been ejected from the bridal suite to another suite, one slightly smaller. As the clerk tried to explain diplomatically and half-jokingly, they were now the veteran, "old" married couple. The bridal suite had been given over to an Irish couple who had been married just this morning and whose reception was still going on in the ballroom.

Mary suggested playfully to Al that they should peek in at the wedding party. Al agreed and followed her into the ballroom. They scanned the large room looking for a party, but all that remained was a small group of people, an obvious remnant of a larger group that had started the celebration many hours ago.

"My God," Mary quipped as she looked around. "They look like my aunts and uncles from Ohio. Look this crowd over and you'll see the same faces when you meet my relatives in Lima."

The bride and groom had left hours before and were apparently now enjoying their bridal suite. Mary smiled devilishly at Al, took him by the hand and led him upstairs for the last night of their Bronx honeymoon.

The next morning Mary was fully dressed by the time Al stirred.

"Get dressed, sweetheart, I want to go to Mass this morning. I saw a Catholic church as we walked down the Concourse last night and they have an 8 o'clock Mass. Will you go with me?"

"I'd rather stay here and you join me in the bed so we could make love one more time," Al responded.

Mary giggled, came over to the bed, and enjoyed a laugh. "My playful, loving husband. We've made love enough this week to last a lifetime," Mary said with a gleam in her eye. "Now, it's time for church and for me to thank God for the happiness He has showered on both of us. Then, we can come back here and make love, if you want. Or, we can save it for the train tonight."

Al smiled, knowing, either way, he would have the full excitement of his beautiful Mary.

Robert Miller

CHAPTER 60

The final good-bye to the Gordons was not complete without a lunch on the West Side at Mr. Gordon's favorite spot - Mama Leone's Restaurant. The family gathered for a 2 o'clock luncheon. Not only were there electric fans to keep the restaurant cool, but the whole front was opened to 48th Street so the customers could enjoy the afternoon's summer breezes. A pianist sat at the window and played romantic Italian music. Inside, the place was a bright mosaic of glittering colors.

As the family sat down for lunch, the table was virtually littered with massive amounts of bread, cheese, tomatoes, celery, radishes, and condiments. Of course, Mr. Gordon had no need to look at the menu. He knew exactly the best choice to order.

"You have to try the antipasto," Mr. Gordon told Al.

"Dad, I don't know what antipasto is, but I have developed a taste for shrimp," Al said.

Al's father laughed and then glowered at his son, "Do as I tell you. Order the antipasto. You'll get more shrimp than you'd get in a shrimp cocktail and half a dozen other things. Take my advice and try it. It's like a meal in itself. Then you get spaghetti and salad and, by the time the main course comes, you won't be hungry any more."

So everyone ended up ordering the antipasto. Lunch at Leone's had the family laughing and rejoicing as, one after another, a train of waiters lavished huge helpings of various kinds of food onto their tables, heaping plates of shrimp, potato salad, salami, sardines and even some assorted delicacies of which Al had only a vague awareness of what he was tasting. All the Gordon family oohed and aahed at the food, like visiting tourists might.

After the antipasto and the spaghetti, the waiters brought Al his main course of veal parmesan and Mary her veal scaloppine. After everyone had finished as much as possible of their meals, they all had a new appreciation of the word stuffed. But, then, the table was cleared and suddenly more slabs of cheese and whole tomatoes appeared on the table with light, fluffy powdered Italian cakes. The luncheon measured up to Al's idea of a Roman feast.

As Al's parents and Mary leisurely finished with coffee, Al had to settle his stomach by drinking a glass of seltzer water. Then Gene Leone, the host, came over and greeted Mr. Gordon, who proudly introduced Gene to "my newspaperman son, Al, and his new Irish wife, Mary." Mr. Leone congratulated the newlyweds and told them that the hostess who had seated them was "my Irish wife."

The lavish luncheon feast was a most memorable way of saying good-bye to a week with the Gordons and the exciting city of New York.

At Grand Central Station, Al and Mary headed down the ramp to the train that would take them west. Each step they took meant they were finally heading out on their own on a new adventure. As they neared the bottom of the ramp, a momentary melancholy hit them as they turned and gave the family a final wave. The Gordons were craning their necks to see better and waving back and forth. Al's mother had a handkerchief that she held to her mouth, but Al and Mary were too far away to see her goodbye tears.

As the train headed out of Grand Central and stopped briefly at the 125th Street station, Al reminded Mary that this was where he and the NYU football team had boarded on an autumn afternoon almost two years before to head down to play in Texas. Now his life had made a full circle - he had met Mary and brought her back to the Bronx as his wife.

Al and Mary sipped champagne cocktails in the club car. They watched the sun in the west fade over the Hudson. After they finished a couple of champagnes, they wobbled their way back to their Pullman car. Al watched Mary getting ready for bed. He thought how, so far, half of their lovemaking was taking place on moving trains.

CHAPTER 61

At the Lima, Ohio, train station early the next morning, a delegation of eight Monahan relatives, led by Mary's grandmother, greeted Mary and Al. Al initially found the Monahans somewhat remote and not as warm and expressive as he had expected.

If Al had been surprised by the sparsity of food on the Monahan table in Texas as compared to the Gordons' table in the Bronx, he was absolutely astonished at Grandmother Monahan's table that morning, weighted down by mountains of eggs, pancakes, waffles, ham, bacon, white bread, and potatoes. The old house abounded with prodigious quantities of both food and relatives. The relatives were all pointed out, rather than introduced to Al, as Mary embraced her Murphy and Monahan aunts, uncles and cousins one by one, as adults and children came and went with heaps of food on their plates and disappeared into other rooms.

Conversations circled around family members who were sick, had lost jobs and ones who just got new ones. Al got the impression that Lima lacked one important element, one that caused much suffering in the family - work. Family members had gone as far as California to find employment.

Al came to realize that Bill Monahan, Mary's father in Texas, had come to be held in awe by the family members in Ohio. For not only had Bill achieved success as the head of a pipeline crew, but, over the years, he had been able to hire many of the Monahans, Murphys and other relatives for his work projects.

The men of the family had to go where they could find work, but, as a rule, the women stayed behind in Lima, often for months and, sometimes, for years, while the men worked elsewhere to support their families.

Mary's grandmother, whose name was also Mary Monahan, boasted to Al that she had been born four miles from Lima and had never been further away than Marion, Ohio. She explained how part of the family history went back to her father who came from Ireland to work on the railroads. He had been forced to serve in the Union Army and came back alive and she added, "thanks be to Jesus."

Al remembered how Grandpa Jim Porter's father had fought for the Confederate Army. He became struck by the awesome thought how a Porter and a Monahan could have somehow fought each other and tried to kill each other during during a skirmish. Mary corrected Al's idea as "unlikely" because great-grandfather Monahan fought in Virginia while great-grandfather Porter fought mostly in Tennessee.

Rose Murphy, a cousin, introduced Mary and Al to her boyfriend, Tony Constantino. Rose whispered to Mary, "I didn't tell Grandma I had an Italian boyfriend, but, when she told me that your new husband was Jewish, then I told her Tony was Italian!"

Mary and Rose enjoyed laughing at the foolishness of it all, realizing that they found the prejudices more daunting in their imaginations than in reality. The two cousins laughed over their joys about being in love as they whispered to each other, gossiping about their men.

Al never knew exactly when breakfast ceased to be breakfast and began to be lunch. He assumed that the transition occurred when Uncle Jim King brought in a couple of pitchers of beer. Soon after, the eggs ceased to be served and, instead, cold cuts and white bread made their appearance.

Mary's grandmother and her Aunt Kate presided at the table, looking more like sisters than mother and daughter. They both practiced the trait of greeting people in loud voices and then, almost simultaneously, mumbling something under their breath that contradicted what they had said out loud. Aunt Kate did this by greeting a Mrs. Delaney and telling her how well she looked, while mumbling to Mary that she'd seen many a corpse who looked better.

Al came to enjoy this whole episode as a typical happy day of celebration in the Irish neighborhood, a "guaranteed" celebration, whether for a visitor, a wake or a wedding. By 3:30, the whole event had ended with jokes, laughter and handshakes. As Al and Mary headed to the railroad station to catch the train heading west, a party twice the size that had met them that morning escorted them back.

Upon boarding the train and finding seats in the parlor car, Al and Mary looked out at these relatives they might never see again. Al noticed Mary's thin arm waving happy farewells to each of her relatives. Al joined her in waving good-bye from the train window.

Mary leaned into Al's arm and asked, "Aren't they wonderful? Weren't you glad we had at least a few hours to meet all of them?" She paused to smile. "And aren't you glad you're leaving them too?" Mary had to laugh.

"Yes. Yes! Yes!" Al repeated quickly to all three questions.

From Texas to New York City to Lima, Al knew that their relatives and friends had finally given them their blessings, said their goodbyes and would soon be hundreds of miles away. He and Mary would be completely independent of their family roots and would have to rely on themselves to make some sort of simple, successful life out west.

A sunbeam flickered off Al's champagne glass in the dining car where he and Mary settled in for one last celebration. The two of them held hands, saying nothing. And, there would be a lot more hours like this on the train as they watched new vistas of farms, hills, valleys, small towns, prairies unfolding like movie scenes as they headed toward the great Rockies.

Al thought ahead to Denver and hoped that all would go well for himself and his new wife. He hoped nothing would ever come between them, and he even prayed a moment that he and Mary would have such happy days forever.

Part II

Robert Miller

CHAPTER 62

The honeymoon was over.

Al and Mary arrived in Denver at mid-morning and were quickly impressed by the metropolis nicknamed "the mile high city." Denver had started as a mining town during the Pikes Peak gold rush of 1858 and just kept growing. The view of the mighty Rockies ten miles to the west could not be ignored and the grand mountains beckoned to be explored.

The couple checked into the Brown Palace Hotel. After a few hours, Al made his way to the *Rocky Mountain News*.

Bill Wannamaker greeted Al warmly and asked him about Mary and their honeymoon trip. Then, he arranged for Al to start a day earlier than planned.

Al found Mr. Wannamaker much more loquacious than before and exuding a new urgency.

"Denver's an interesting place, and the newspaper has potential all over the plains and the mountains. There's not an important paper west of Kansas City or south of Minneapolis and St. Paul. And the paper in Salt Lake City is dull as dirt." Mr. Wannamaker sounded like a man just starting a new career. "The national election is coming up and it will sell plenty of papers, if we handle it right. That Hitler guy in Germany will make news and, probably, one day start a war somewhere. These next years will be important for newspapers and, with your help, I want to make the *Rocky Mountain News* number one in Denver."

Al found himself being swept along with Mr. Wannamaker's urgency to get started. Mr. Wannamaker walked Al around the newsroom, introduced him to various people and told them that Al would take over the cable desk as of that Sunday afternoon.

There would be no lolling around in Denver, Al thought, as he exited the newspaper building.

Back at the hotel, Al told Mary the good news that he would be starting work on Sunday. Mary took her turn to tell Al her good news, that she had found an apartment.

After that exchange of happy tidings, Mary lifted her dress over her head, hung it in the closet and, then, clad in a slip, bra, and panties pressed herself against Al. "Unless you have other immediate plans, I want you to make love to me one more time and then take me out to dinner."

"I want to spend the next four days with my clothes off making love to you," Al said, hugging Mary tightly.

"Listen to that insatiable man talk," Mary snickered, something similar to what he had heard from her grandmother in Lima, but then Mary added a thought that sounded out of character; "Sure, and the man keeps talking when he could very well be fucking instead."

Al couldn't remember having heard Mary express herself in such explicit terms. Her words excited him and he managed to get his clothes off as fast as possible. He performed as Mary had hoped he would. Then a few minutes later he was spent and fast asleep.

When Al woke up, his contentment immediately disappeared. Mary sat across the room staring at him with a look that expressed somewhat less than her usual total devotion to him.

"Is something wrong?" Al asked with a worried tone.

"Didn't I tell you I was hungry?" Mary answered with a question. Then she shared something else that bothered her. "And what did you do? You got your clothes off and had your way with me and then, poof! You immediately lost all interest and went off into a deep, exhausted sleep without even giving a thought as to whether I was satisfied or nor."

This was astonishing to Al. "Are you not satisfied with our lovemaking?" Al asked.

"Darling, I love our lovemaking," said Mary. "I love being able to satisfy you. But...what I'm trying to tell you, is that sometimes you bring me to the very brink of a peak of excitement and then you have your orgasm, just as I'm about to reach mine. Just as I'm beginning to get to the point where I feel I'll explode, you huff and puff a little, shrivel up, roll over and fall asleep, making me feel left in the lurch."

Mary paused for a few seconds, as she waited for the effect of her words. "It had to be said. I want us to be able to bring each other great pleasures in bed and talk to each other frankly about these things. Now will you get dressed and take me out to dinner?"

Al showered, still reviewing Mary's words and thinking what he would have to do to keep her satisfied. He had been happy in Denver up to the point when she informed him that she was not having orgasms when they made love. He realized, once again, that Mary may have inherited some outspoken traits from her midwestern relatives.

Later that evening, Al and Mary were happy to have another try at mutual satisfaction. And, they did make progress. He helped her achieve her release, which had always come so quickly and surely to him.

Moving into the apartment, Al learned from Mary that setting a piece of furniture down was not her idea of setting up home.

"It's perfect," Al said, scanning the new furniture.

Mary agreed, to a point, but then she had Al spend the whole afternoon rearranging the furniture. It took a few hours for Mary to give her final approval to the placement of the furniture.

"Mary, darling, isn't the room exactly as it was when we started?"

Mary's response was quick and decisive. She picked up a pillow and threw it in Al's face, let out a Indian war hoop that he imagined came from some Cherokee ancestor, ran to him and pushed him onto the bed. She promptly fell on top of him and assaulted him with tickles, kisses and other activities that eventually thoroughly drained his already worn-out body.

Sunday morning began with Mary's request that Al take her to Church. Al agreed, and remembered the Catholic churches he had attended in Houston and in the Bronx. Denver's Cathedral was within walking distance of their new apartment. The ten o'clock Mass was officiated by an Archbishop in a magnificent satin robe.

After a quick lunch, Al left Mary to go off to work. It was 10 hours later when he returned. Mary greeted him with tears and jumped into his arms.

"I'm so glad you're home," Mary cried. "I have never been so lonely in my life!"

After she calmed down, Mary suggested to Al that she should find a job that would coincide with his hours.

Al explained he would be working six days a week, Sundays through Fridays, and his hours would generally be from the late morning until nine or ten at night. This didn't matter to Mary, as long as she could do something.

She also said she needed a radio and a telephone to get through any lonely hours at home alone. Al agreed, and Mary had her radio the next day, and the telephone company installed a phone within the week.

Robert Miller

CHAPTER 63

Within two weeks, Mary found a job as a waitress serving lunch and dinner at a luncheonette. She enjoyed it a few days, until the smells from the kitchen suddenly began to make her sick.

"I never get sick to my stomach," she said in agony when Al came home from work and found her throwing up in the bathroom. "Something in that restaurant makes my stomach queasy."

Mary's waitress career was short-lived. With her continued queasiness, she had to give up the job. A doctor gave his diagnosis - Mary was pregnant.

Mary felt thrilled that she was going to be a mother. She called her parents and the Monahans seemed pleased, but the Gordons as Al had expected, were less than ecstatic.

Then, a week later Mary warmly and lovingly greeted Al coming home. She told him the news that she had visited a priest Father Curry, that afternoon. She wanted Al to meet him. She reassured Al he did not have to become a Catholic. But if he agreed to the very things he had already agreed to before, in Houston, Father Curry would give him instructions compatible with making him the husband and father of a Catholic. Mary's face lit up more as she explained the really good news. After that, they would be able to be married by a priest in the rectory of the Cathedral and, thus, their baby could be baptized.

"Will you do it, Al?" Mary asked softly and added, "You know that it is important to me."

"If it is important to you, Mary, you know I will do it."

Mary kissed Al and gave him her gorgeous smile. "It will make me very happy. I want our marriage blessed and recognized by the Church. That means our baby can be properly baptized."

Mary took Al to meet with Father Jim Curry the next morning. He turned out to be a very young priest, maybe five years older than Al, but he looked even younger. As soon as Mary and Al came into his office, he appeared open and friendly. He frowned and turned somber when Al recalled for him his experiences with Father Wall in Houston. Father Jim grimaced when Al told him how he had resented being called a heathen, not once, but twice by Father Wall. Al felt Father Curry showed pain as he listened. The priest listened without a word until Al finished.

"Al, I'm not going to call you a heathen," Father Jim began. "I promise. Mary told me exactly what happened. We want Mary back in our church. We'd be proud if you decided one day to join us, but, for the moment, it is enough if you agree to learn about us so you can be a fit husband and father in a Catholic household. I promise you will be treated with no disrespect."

"Thank you, Father Curry," Al said. "But, would the same thing apply if I were Lutheran, instead of being Jewish?"

Father Curry became puzzled, "Of course, Al, why do you ask?"

"Well, I was reading those pamphlets you gave Mary yesterday and some of them don't show much respect for Martin Luther."

Father Jim's face curled into a broad grin. He glanced from Mary back to Al. "I'm going to enjoy working with you, Al. You're a clear, incisive thinker, and you give me a fresh viewpoint. Our criticism of Martin Luther is not personal. He was a Catholic priest who saw fit, for his own reasons, to challenge the basic doctrine of the Church. Our disagreements with him are purely ecclesiastical — but you may be right that some personal bitterness might have crept in. We're not perfect. Our priests are also sinners and penitents. But, we are the true Church. That is the important lesson for today. You have now completed the first of eight instructional sessions. Will you come back next Monday morning at the same time?"

After Al agreed, the young priest told Mary, "Next week let Al come here on his own. It will be just he and I, one on one. And, I, too, am looking forward to it. Al will learn from me, and I think he also has some things to teach me."

Outside the rectory, Mary felt relieved. She felt hungry for the first time in a while, so they indulged in a large lunch. They parted company on Colfax Avenue, Mary heading back to their apartment on South Logan, Al heading over to Weston Street to work for the next ten hours. Al knew as long as Mary did not have a Church wedding, she would always feel that something was missing. By not disappointing her on his "lessons," he knew there eventually would be a Church wedding, thus helping her find a little spiritual happiness.

Al did go back to see Father Curry the following Monday, and for the next few Mondays. The instructions turned out to be one-on-one, give-and-take discussions, about the Church, combined with a very skeletal outline of its doctrines and traditions. Father Curry patiently listened to Al almost as much as he talked to him. Their conversations ranged widely on many subjects, including the forthcoming elections, the Ku Klux Klan, Jewish family values, fascism,

Nazism, communism, and the basic similarities and differences between Judaism and Catholicism.

"When will we begin the formal instructions?" Al came to ask on the sixth meeting.

Father Curry smiled and then furrowed his brow as he referred to his yellow pad. "I'm just checking my notes to make certain that every subject has been covered. I'd say the instructions have been satisfactorily completed and that you can be considered a fit husband for a Catholic wife and a fit father to a Catholic child." The priest rose, clasped Al's hand as Al stood up and said, "I've enjoyed these meetings, and hope you will not be a stranger. Tell Mary to come and make confession any time, and that she can receive communion. Tell her to come in and talk to me. I'll see if we can dispense with the banns and have an immediate wedding ceremony. Good luck to you both...or, better yet, to the three of you."

Al called Mary from the first phone he could find and told her the good news.

Eleven hours later, Al arrived home after work. Her own phone call to the priest had kept her awake and excited all day. She shared the latest plans with Al. Father Curry would conduct the wedding in the rectory the following Saturday afternoon. Her parents would make the two-day drive and spend Friday to Sunday at the apartment. Mary lived for the Church's endorsement of her marriage, and could no longer tolerate being alienated from her religion.

That Saturday, Father Curry performed a short and very nearly civil service in the same room where he and Al had their instructional meetings. Bill Wannamaker acted as best man for the second time. One of Al's new friends at the *Rocky Mountain News*, Tom Dunn, the assistant sports editor, acted as the required Catholic witness.

Mary had made confession before the wedding on Saturday morning. On Sunday, she would receive communion for the first time since they were married in the civil ceremony. Mary's face revealed how complete and at peace she felt with the Church since the devastating meetings with Father Wall.

Like old spiritual habits, Mary could not just turn her back on the Church, a Church wedding or communion. Al understood that. And Mary's pregnancy only made her more intense in putting things right with the Church.

As Al watched Mary kneeling in prayer in Church, he respected his wife for her angelic qualities. How hard Mary tried to get Al to become more involved in the organized institutions, whether Catholic or Jewish! But the more she tried the more it rattled him. Al stubbornly held on to his basic tenet that he needed no religious institution in his life — the only saint Al needed or believed in was Mary.

CHAPTER 64

Al made friends with a couple of Jewish reporters on the paper. In fact, he met members of the rather extensive Jewish community in Denver. Al and Mary even talked about attending one of the synagogues in Denver, but Al worked on Friday nights when services were usually held. So, instead, they attended the eight o'clock Sunday Mass at St. Agnes Catholic Church, allowing Al time to leave for work by eleven.

Having a steady, decent-paying job, Al took the next step in achieving the American Dream: He bought a 1934 Ford coupe. Saturdays now became a day for touring around Denver, up into the Rockies and as far north as Wyoming.

Their special friends were reporters and editors from the *Rocky Mountain News*. Tom Dunn worked as the assistant sports editor and Sid Bornstein worked the city desk. Tom, with his wife Anne, and Sid, with his wife Norma, fast became friends with Mary and Al. Although both of those couples were a few years older than Al and Mary, as natives of Denver, they provided helpful advice. They were both childless, but the other women took a great interest in Mary's pregnancy.

Having the Dunns and Bornsteins for friends made life much easier for Mary and Al because the three men all worked the same long schedule. The wives often got together for dinner and generally enjoyed their own company, and complained constantly about the havoc that putting out a morning newspaper had on dining schedules and the irregular eating habits their husbands endured.

Mary's friendship with Anne and Norma also took on religious overtones. Anne, like her husband, was a Roman Catholic. Norma, like Sid, was Jewish. Though Sid's attitude towards his Jewishness closely paralleled Al's, Norma was more traditional in her outlook. She was active in the synagogue, and observed traditional Jewish customs.

Both Norma and Anne took a further interest in Mary and the Catholic child of a Jewish father. The topic of circumcision inevitably came up in the women's discussions. If the child was a boy, Mary's obstetrician told her that circumcision normally was done on the second or third day after birth. Norma explained to Mary that the tradition among Jews was to have circumcision performed ritually on the eighth day, in a ceremony called in Hebrew "Berit Milah". The rite involved a Mohel (circumcisor), the father, the Sandek (godfather), and the Minyan (religious quorum). The three women considered for hours whether it would please Al to have some sort of party for the circumcision on the eighth day, without offending any of the Catholic regulations.

When Al arrived home tired one evening, Mary broached the circumcision subject. It was bad timing.

"For God's sake, Mary!" Al responded impatiently. "Do you think I much care whether our son is circumcised on the third day or the eighth day?"

Mary took offense at Al's angry reaction and began to cry. Al walked over to her and put his arm around her soft shoulder to soothe his wife's sensitive feelings.

"All I wanted to do was to please you," Mary said between tears. "I thought it might help you feel closer to your own people." She dried her eyes and cuddled up to Al. "I'm afraid that when I went back to the Catholic church you might have felt estranged from your own people. I feel guilty about that."

Al let out a low chuckle. "Why should you feel guilty? You're not guilty. Jews feel guilty because Christians tell us that 'the Jews killed Christ.' So, the Jews respond by telling the world they are 'God's chosen people.' The Jews, burdened with guilt, have the effrontery to make that ridiculous claim. The only thing more ridiculous and arrogant is the Catholics telling the rest of the world they are the one and only true church."

Mary looked at Al with horror.

"I can't believe that I'm hearing you say such awful things about the Jews and the Catholics. I don't believe what I'm hearing from you!"

She stalked off and walked away. Al laughed and followed her. He came up to her and put his arms around her to win her back.

"My sweet, devoted Mary. You are wonderful. You have no doubts about anything. God should have appointed you his Vicar on earth to set everything straight. This crazy world would be in a lot better shape if you ran things. There'd be no depression, no repression, no Hitler, no Stalin, just goodness and virtue under God's true church and supported by His chosen people."

Mary smiled and leaned against Al.

"Why do you make fun of me? Why do you go out of your way to vex me? Don't you know how much I love you and how dependent I am on you? I stay home alone all day and wait for you to come home. I think about things that I hope will make you happy. You come home tired and make fun of me and the things I believe in."

Al laughed and shook his head gently. Mary finally joined with a laugh. They both realized at that moment that the circumcision would be done unceremoniously without worrying about trying to honor any religious custom. Al learned, too, to remember, whether tired or not, to be patient with Mary's ideas and respectful of what she believed in.

Mary now ventured into another subject. "If it's a boy, I want to call him Alfred Emmanuel Gordon, Jr. Is that all right with you?"

Al put his arm around Mary and held her close before he dared to answer. "That sounds nice, Mary, but I was taught that Jewish people don't name their children after themselves or after living persons. They believe it is best to name a child after a departed relative, making the departed person's spirit watch over the child throughout his or her life."

"Do you believe that?" Mary wondered.

"No, I surely don't, but I think it would offend my parents and my grandmother if we named a child after me. Can't you think of another name?" Al asked.

"Of course, I can. We can. But, I want to name our son after you. You may be grouchy, and cynical, Al, but I love you and you are the boy's father and I'd like to name him after you. Don't my feelings count for something?"

"Of course they do, darling," Al said. He thought for a moment and added, "Maybe it'll be a girl and then we can name her whatever we want without offending anyone."

By the time the baby was born the following March, a boy, they had compromised and named him Selwyn Alfred Gordon.

"Selwyn" seemed perfect: The Gordon family once lived on Selwyn Avenue in the Bronx before moving to Eastburn Avenue, and Al's maternal grandfather, who had died when Al was nine, was called Shalman, and "Selwyn" seemed like a fair Americanization of it. Mary agreed to Selwyn Alfred, but he was Sel or Selly to them both from the day of his birth.

Sel was born on the first day of spring after a bitterly cold Denver winter. Mary loved the baby, who was big, blond, and fat. Al did not enjoy the problems of sharing an apartment that smelled of diapers with a noisy baby who demanded an enormous amount of attention from his mother. The noise and the clutter of baby toys and washed diapers added new frustrations and interferences to Al's original, comfortable, quiet lifestyle and took away the fun he and Mary used to have on Saturdays, his only day off.

Al loved the baby and was proud of his big, lusty son, even if he was noticeably jealous of the attention Sel demanded of Mary. The Monahans, who came every four weeks to spend time with Mary and the baby, added to the confusion.

The Monahans were doting grandparents. Al watched them hover over the baby while he treated his son with reserve. Bill Monahan admonished Al once to help Mary more with the baby.

"Maybe you enjoy changing a baby's smelly diapers, but I don't. There's no pleasure in that for me," Al snapped.

Al continued having difficulty adjusting to the baby. It seemed the baby had a way of making him feel inept, uncomfortable, and downright stupid when he held it. Sel noticed that and would wail when he rested in Al's arms as compared to the way he cooed and laughed when his mother or either of his Monahan grandparents held him. Al came to resent that, too.

CHAPTER 65

Although Al's parents had not been ecstatic over the news of Mary's pregnancy, they became eager to see pictures of their first grandchild and asked Mary and Al to plan a trip to New York during Al's summer vacation. "That's four days of hard driving each way. It would take up half our vacation just traveling. It doesn't make sense," Al kept repeating to Mary. The thought of driving close to four thousand miles round trip on his vacation was exhausting.

To Mary, it became imperative that all the Monahan and Gordon relatives get to know, love and hold little Sel. She knew one of Al's desires was to visit every state in the country at some time. To entice Al to drive east to visit the relatives, she spread out a map one night and pointed out how they could travel through states they had not been in, such as South Dakota, Minnesota, and Wisconsin.

Al finally relented to drive east, but suggested a more direct trip. He planned to go only as far as Pittsburgh to his aunt's home. His parents would take a train to Pittsburgh, allowing his mother to also have a good visit with her sister.

The trip across the country in 1938 was not easy. Selwyn slept all day and Mary had the job of trying to keep him quiet at night in the roadside cabins where they stayed, while Al tried to sleep. During the day, Mary was kept busy calming Selwyn and Al, besides changing diapers in the small backseat of their coupe. Mary developed the habit of throwing the diapers out the window.

"We're leaving a trail of shit from Colorado to Pennsylvania. If anybody is trying to follow us, they'll have no difficulty," Al said in frustration.

Al drove for many hours with the window open trying to bring in fresh air, to get rid of the foul aroma from Sel's diapers.

The destination was Aunt Fanny's, Al's mother's oldest sister. After her husband died, she moved from Virginia to Pittsburgh with her son, Sandy, Al's cousin, to be near her daughter, Hermine, and her son-in-law, Sidney.

Aunt Fanny's turned out to be a great place to meet. She was delighted to see her nephew and his family. Aunt Fanny's southern warmth immediately charmed Mary. Fanny and all the Pittsburgh relatives, including Al's parents, hugged Mary and fussed over the baby. Their dining room table abounded with Jewish favorites, including corned beef, tongue, and pastrami, plus Swiss cheese and an ample supply of lox and herring.

Sandy was a little grumpy because he could not get to Forbes Field to watch the Pirates play the New York Giants. He was a passionate baseball fan. He had traveled to the All Star game at New York City's Polo Grounds four years before. Like Al, Sandy adjusted to Sel's being the center of attention.

Hermine and Sidney showed a lot of extra interest in Selwyn and peppered Mary with questions about her pregnancy and the baby's birth. After several hours of waiting for the right moment, they admitted finally their secret to Mary - Hermine might be pregnant.

Al became absolutely amazed how his parents fussed over Selwyn, presenting a real turnaround from their attitudes when they knew about Mary's pregnancy. The senior Gordons had obviously been immediately captivated by the endearing charms of Selwyn Alfred Gordon. Once the Gordons' approved of Sel, their approval ratings of Mary and Al soared. Mr. Gordon pounded Al on the back and said, "You have a son to be proud of, Al, and we are proud of all three of you."

The pat on the back and his father's unexpectedly kind words were important to Al. His father never had been too complimentary. In fact, Al remembered that his father rarely had much to say to him through the years.

Al's mother began treating Mary with a great deal of respect and soon the two of them had their own special friendship as they shared laughs and jokes about Selwyn's antics. Added to Sel's presence the three sisters - Fanny, Mollie and Mrs. Gordon - laughed and talked incessantly like young girls again.

Al's father sat preoccupied with Selwyn and kept staring at him with devotion and wonderment. Selwyn, having found permanent admirers, reveled in all the attention from his newly found relatives in the next two days.

Shirley and Sandy, being impatient teenagers, managed to find relief from the baby by being allowed to go off to the movies and seek out other entertainment at an ice cream parlor.

By 9 P.M. Sunday night, two days after their arrival, Mary loaded a sleepy Selwyn in the cradle they had slung across the backseat of the car. With a flurry of hugs, handshakes, waves and kisses, Al drove west towards Denver. He felt pleased that the ordeal of the trip had included a happy gathering of his extended family. Selwyn, at his young age, had no awareness that he had brought parents, cousins, brother, sisters, and aunts together for a great bonding.

Al began to see Selwyn differently. He could no longer look into Selwyn's face and think of him as a miserable, interfering, smelly baby. Selwyn had established his own place in the family. He represented the link with the past and the future. Maybe Selwyn could be called a "blessed event," as God in His own way gives such blessings. Al remembered his father's look of love for baby Selwyn. It touched Al as he remembered how proud his father was of his first grandson. Looking through the rearview mirror, Al smiled at Selwyn in the backseat. Selwyn had gained new respect in Al's mind as he had become an integral part of Al's family heritage.

Robert Miller

CHAPTER 66

Back at work in Denver, Al found the world news more troubling week by week. Germany, Italy and Soviet Russia seemed to be using the war in Spain as a testing ground for their weapons and armies. Germany had embarked on a massive rearmament program, threatening its neighbors.

Troubling news came from Germany about the way the Nazis were treating their Jewish population. Al was repulsed by the pictures of elderly Jews in Germany being humiliated and forced to wash streets under the jeering scrutiny of armed Nazi thugs.

Al became more disturbed by the news of the "Anschluss," or union, of Austria and Germany in 1938. Then came the threat of war over the Sudetenland in Czechoslovakia that fall.

Al experienced uncomfortable feelings every night after work when he compared the tragic changes taking place around the world with his peaceful, almost idyllic life in Denver. When Al remembered the happy family gathering in Pittsburgh, he thought how life seemed so innocent back then only a few months ago. The current world events were rapidly destroying the sense of a secure, peaceful life.

By the summer of 1939, Al eagerly planned another vacation that would take them to Lima, Ohio, Pittsburgh, and New York City. On the trip east, they even managed to visit a new state, slowly fulfilling Al's determination to visit every state.

In New York, Al and Mary had occasion to meet some German-Jewish refugees. Both he and Mary became quite agitated to hear of the persecution these people had suffered and why they had to flee. The refugees gave Al and Mary a strikingly clear idea of the dangers facing Jews in Germany and the rest of Europe.

When Al got back to work at the newspaper in mid-August, the news reports constantly talked about Hitler's demands. He wanted Danzig and the Polish corridor to the sea. News of the Nazi-Soviet non-aggression pact clearly meant that Hitler could invade Poland. Speculation centered around whether Britain and France would back down from defending Poland, as they had done the previous year with Czechoslovakia or whether they would help defend Poland.

On September 1st, a Friday, Al got the news at the cable desk that Hitler had sent his army and air force to invade Poland. The British gave the Germans an ultimatum to cease their invasion. On Sunday, Al went to work early. The news came across his cable desk that Prime Minister Chamberlain gave a speech in which he said Germany ignored the British ultimatum and "consequently we are now at war with Germany." News of the sinking of a British ship, the Athenia, by a German submarine came across Al's cable desk the same day.

Al arrived home that Sunday night close to midnight. He asked Mary to sit down with him in the kitchen while he had a glass of milk. He wanted to tell her calmly what he had been thinking ever since the news about the treatment of the Jews started hitting every moral nerve in him.

"Darling, I must get into this war. I'll go to Canada to enlist."

Mary looked surprised.

"Al, I know you want to do something. But, why? This isn't our war. This country may never get involved in it. Why do you feel you have to go? And what about Selwyn?"

"Maybe it is about Selwyn. He's half Jewish. Maybe it's because I'm Jewish. I feel that Hitler has made war on everything we hold decent. He seized Austria last year, then Czechoslovakia, now Poland. And, look at how he treats the Jews. I want to do my part!" Al said with clenched lips.

"Your nobility is laudable, Al, but the timing, yours and Hitler's stinks!" Mary said with disgust.

"Why?" Al asked.

"I think I'm pregnant!" Mary said crisply.

Al was taken by surprise.

"I think Selwyn needs a brother or sister," Mary added. "And they both need a father. But, not as much as I need my husband. Al, I know how you feel, but, please stay here with me. Maybe, in your own way, you can do more to make people aware of how Hitler threatens, not only the Jews, but all of us, and, maybe in the end, that will make a greater contribution to the defeat of Hitler than you possibly could do with a gun in your hand."

Al had to contemplate the unexpected - another child. Maybe I am acting on impulse. Maybe I need more patience, he thought.

"Okay, darling, I will stay and not volunteer in the Canadian army," Al assured Mary. "But, if the United States ever gets into the war, I will enlist."

Al and Mary hugged. She felt at peace now that Al would be staying home to help with another baby.

Al felt no peace at work. He could see the reports of Europe falling apart under Hitler's onslaught - Denmark, Norway, Belgium, Luxembourg, Holland and France itself were all captured and held by Germany between April and June of 1940.

Al registered with the newly enacted peacetime draft, but he likely would not be drafted into the expanding peacetime army with two children. He spent his days caught up in the excitement of the raging debate about the war and the war in Europe, but at night, he became caught up in the excitement of another baby.

But Al could not rest easy as he read and heard about the war in news reports coming out of Washington.

The America First Committee, headed by Senator Wheeler, Father Coughlin, and Charles Lindberg, and joined by former ambassador to Great Britain, Joseph P. Kennedy, actively advocated American neutrality. President Roosevelt proposed a "lend-lease program" that would enable the United States to supply arms to Britain and her remaining allies. Roosevelt's program passed in March, 1941, after a long and acrimonious debate between the "America Firsters" and the pro-British elements.

Charles Lindberg made a nationally broadcast speech in which he blamed "the British, the Jews, and the Roosevelt Administration" for America's drift towards war. The very fact that this American hero singled out the Jews as being one of the three parties that were leading the United States to war shocked and troubled Al as he and Mary sat by the radio that night listening to the speech.

Mary put her arms around Al's shoulder, to comfort him. She kissed him and tried to assuage his hurt. "You've got to admit he puts the Jews in good company by combining them with the British and the Roosevelt administration."

Al took Mary in his arms and held her close. Tears formed in his eyes. An American hero had used his position to slander the Jews, rather than take a stand in their defense.

"Al?" Mary asked softly. "You're okay?"

Al started to laugh. The tears kept coming. He found it too hard to begin to explain why he felt so hurt.

Al took a deep breath. In some way, he felt distant from Mary and felt that he needed to try to explain why he was crying. "My country is being torn apart by those who feel we should do nothing and those who want to help the British. The Jews in Europe are being maligned by Hitler. They are the ones losing their jobs, their homes and their dignity. I can't believe that Hitler's vilification of the Jews is coming right over here into America. It frightens me and angers me to hear anti-semitic mutterings from not only blowhards like Father Coughlin, but, now, from a genuine American hero like Lindbergh. And who is left to fight the Germans? Only the British. If England loses its fight, the Nazis will take over the world."

Mary held Al close and suggested that things would look better in the morning. Al knew what he would face at the cable desk and that things would not be better.

1941 turned out to be Al's unhappiest year. The continued German victories in their onslaughts on Yugoslavia, Greece and the Soviet Union depressed him. By the start of December, 1941, he was in a state of constant depression over the world's news. The German hordes, which by now had been advancing into Russia, were reported to be stopped by the brutal Russian winter storms. Al held out hope that other news of growing antagonism between Japan and the United States might be worked out peacefully.

Al tried to forget his depression by attending to his son, Selwyn. It was the first Saturday of December, 1941. Selwyn would be five in March. Selwyn's excitement centered around telling his father how his friends had seen the new Walt Disney movie *Dumbo*, a full length cartoon, about an elephant who ears were so big that it could could fly. Selwyn's excitement guaranteed the inevitable. Al took the family, which now included Selwyn's two year old baby brother, Billy, to see *Dumbo* that afternoon. Al's spirits had lifted enough that he could laugh during the movie and afterwards with the two boys and Mary. *Dumbo* had provided the short escape that took him away for a few hours from his six-day-a-week job as cable editor reading the war news out of Europe.

Mary gave Al a surprise for Sunday's breakfast.

"Where did you find the lox?" Al asked with a surprised smile.

"I found a place that reminded me of Schwartzenberg's in Houston. I bought this on Friday to be a special treat for you."

"Treat?" Al wondered.

"For being so nice and going with me to Mass every Sunday. I thought you'd be entitled to a Jewish repast so you can be more comfortable when you enter the Catholic church," Mary said.

Al laughed. "It's the perfect breakfast before church. I can spend the boring hour of the Mass belching and trying hard not to break wind," he joked.

Mary gasped. "You're incorrigible Al Gordon. You should never be saying such things in front of the boys. I don't want them picking up your bad habits," Mary said firmly.

Al's eyes twinkled with mischievousness. "Then, let them pick up my good points," he said playfully.

He pulled Mary close to him and kissed her. She gave in to his loving kiss, while the boys watched and laughed.

Robert Miller

CHAPTER 67

That Sunday Al got to work and found news that had an impact on everyone.
"What happened?" Al asked a solemn group of co-workers.
"The Japs just bombed Pearl Harbor!" someone said.
"My God! We're at war!" Al exclaimed with shock.
Mr. Wannamaker walked into the newsroom a few minutes later and calmed everyone down. "Let's get to work. We're going to put an extra on the streets this afternoon. Press time will be 3 P.M." He turned to Al and ordered, "Keep the wires stripped and let's start to put out a newspaper!" He assigned reporters standing there to speak to local Japanese and to try to find families in the area who had sons at Pearl Harbor.
The newsroom came alive and the professionalism of Bill Wannamaker generated more of the same from everyone in the office. Al found a minute's respite and called Mary.
"You heard?" Al asked her.
"Someone stopped me on the street before I got home and told me the news. It's terrible, Al! I have the radio on now," Mary replied anxiously. "When are you coming home?"
"God only knows. We're putting out an extra edition now. There are new reports coming in all the time. I probably won't be home until very late. I'll be here if you need me. Kiss the children for me, sweetheart, and ask them to give you a kiss for me too. I love you," Al said.
"I wish you were here. I know you have your job to do. But, I'm frightened. I'm afraid you're going to join up and leave me here in this cold place with two small children. Please come home as soon as possible. I love you, Al, and I need you now more than ever," Mary said with a trembly voice before she hung up to let Al get back to work.

Clash of Cultures - The Al Gordon Story

Each bit of news generated a furor in the newsroom. There was scant information about damage and casualties. Al kept pulling the tapes and reading them, looking for new bits and pieces to put together.

>The Japanese embassy and consulates were burning papers and documents...
>
>People were spotting Japanese submarines and half a dozen other stories that were largely a result of panic...
>
>Men were gathering at enlistment centers to try to register...
>
>There were interviews with local people who had loved ones in Hawaii...
>
>There was an announcement that President Roosevelt would address a joint session of Congress on Monday morning...
>
>Vague news kept coming out of Pearl Harbor.

Al got home around midnight to find Mary still up. Her eyes were red. She told Al she had been talking to both sets of parents and they all agreed Al should not volunteer at this time. Her red eyes accentuated how shaken and frightened she felt. Al took her in his arms. She began sobbing.

"Please stop crying, Mary. We're safe here in Denver. We're thousands of miles away from the war." Al reassured her.

Mary continued to cry until her shoulders shook.

"I'm confused, too," Al admitted. "I've been ready to fight against the Germans. Now, our enemies are the Japs. The whole world has spun around in the last twelve hours. We have a whole new set of enemies. It's a crazy world and a crazy time, but, Mary, we have each other. Things will be all right. I promise you. Please stop crying," Al pleaded softly.

Al thought about fighting in the war. He let Mary have more time to cry.

"I know how much you and the boys need me. I won't enlist now. I probably won't even be called up. I have an important job as cable editor. I should be there for years and I might even get a raise," Al said softly.

Mary hugged Al's neck. "You always know the right thing to say to me," she said between tears that kept rolling down her cheeks.

The next morning Mary and Al listened as the radio carried President Roosevelt's speech to Congress. He called December 7, 1941 a date that will live in infamy. When he asked Congress to declare a state of war between the United States and Japan, the declaration of war passed almost immediately with only one dissenting vote.

After breakfast with the boys and Mary, Al left early for work. Mary could only hope that Al would not be drafted.

Al saw the news reports and realized the Japanese bombing of Pearl Harbor had been part of a premeditated assault on the Philippine Islands, Malaya and

Hong Kong. America and Great Britain found themselves allied in the war against Japan. A few days later Germany and Italy also declared war on the United States.

Al could not hold back, once he read Germany's declaration of war against America. His face grew red with rage. He wanted to spit in the German dictator's face. He walked into Mr. Wannamaker's office to explain what he had to do.

"I'm going to quit and join the Army Air Force," Al said as soon as Mr. Wannamaker looked up.

"Al! You've got a wife and two little kids!" Mr. Wannamaker exclaimed with a shocked look. He looked frightened as his face became very pale.

Al stood silent, enraged, his face red. He looked defiant.

Mr. Wannamaker continued. "You're important to me, Al. You stay with me and I'll make you my first war correspondent. World War One made war correspondents like Floyd Gibbons, Lowell Thomas, and Ernest Hemingway famous. Think of your future. Think of your wife and two boys," Mr. Wannamaker pleaded.

"Thank you, Mr. Wannamaker," Al said slowly. "What you say is true. And, I have much to thank you for. You gave me my start. You helped me to get the license to marry Mary. You gave me this job. But, I'm twenty-five years old. I'm healthy. I'm an American and a Jew." Al had rarely referred to his Jewish heritage to Mr. Wannamaker. Today his Jewish heritage gave him special cause to fight a truly evil enemy of not only the free world, but of his own people in particular. He could put himself in harm's way for his country and for other Jews. The decision was based on a connection to his Jewish heritage.

Mr. Wannamaker sat silently listening to Al.

"I want to join the Air Force and drop bombs on Germany more than anything else right now. That's my main objective. But, tell you what, Bill. If you need a war correspondent, I'll send you back war stories. You don't have to pay me. You've done enough for me and I can't tell you how grateful I am to you."

"When do you want to leave?" Mr. Wannamaker asked calmly.

"As soon as you can spare me. I'll take Mary and the boys to stay with her parents in Houston and I'll join up," Al said.

Mr. Wannamaker stood up and shook Al's hand. "I still think you're a little nuts. Yes, you are an American and a Jew. No, it is not your responsibility to take on the whole burden of fighting Hitler and the Japs. Al, I urge you to talk it over with Mary."

"God help me if I have to ask Mary," Al said. He managed a smile. "If I talk it over with her, I'm finished. Bill, this is simply something I have to do. With luck, I'll be back in a couple of years with hat in my hand and asking for my job back."

Mr. Wannamaker came around and gave Al a hug. "As long as I work on any newspaper anywhere, you know you have a job to come back to. Good luck, Al, and drop a bomb or two on those sons of bitches for me."

Al left the office and walked home through the bitterly cold Denver wind. He walked in the apartment and surprised Mary.

"What happened now?" Mary asked him as she helped him get his overcoat off.

Al mumbled something and took her by the hand. He explained that he had just learned that Germany and Italy declared war on the United States. Mary knew how strongly Al felt about Hitler and the persecution of Jews within Germany and the occupied countries. He had quit his job and was going to join the Army Air Force. He went on quickly to say that they would pack up and move back to her parents in Houston to make sure everyone would be safe.

Mary became hysterical. She cried for almost an hour, exhausting herself. After a while, Mary surprised Al by admitting that she really was proud of him, but she still felt so afraid of what might happen to him. "I'm so frightened about what might happen to you. You made such a decision like this without consulting me," Mary said, as she dabbed a handkerchief at her wet eyes.

"Believe me, sweetheart. It's not an easy decision. I'm going to miss the newsroom. I'm going to miss my home and the boys. And most of all, I'm going to miss the most beautiful woman in the world - you, my love. No, I had to come home with my bridges burned and the decision squarely settled in my heart. It was one I had to make by myself," Al said with a slow smile.

Mary began to smile, too. "Well, my love, like you told me once, I should become the church vicar to straighten out the world. Now, it's your turn to straighten out the world."

Her remark pleased Al. Mary had evidently understood what Al had to do. He was prepared to sacrifice himself to defend his country and his people against the threats of Hitler and the Nazis.

"Ever since I met you on the A&M football field, you've been my special hero, Al Gordon," Mary said. Her eyes were red and puffy with tears, but she gave Al a reassuring peaceful smile.

Mary thought of Al as fighting for freedom - the freedom to be a Christian or a Catholic or a Jew. Mary had thought about the world war. She understood Al's decision meant something special beyond patriotism. He had found a spiritual connection to his fellow Jews. He could not see them humiliated and destroyed. Still, she cried because Al had to leave her.

Robert Miller

CHAPTER 68

Back in Houston, Al thought he could simply walk into the Army Air Force office and enlist as an aviation cadet. Instead, he had to meet qualifications. The Army needed his college transcripts and then he had to take a written examination. No problem, Al thought. He did what he was told to do, to begin the process.

Al finally received a letter instructing him to report on Monday, February 23, 1942 to the Air Force Classification Center in San Antonio, Texas.

Preflight training took place at Kelly Field. Primary flight training was given at Bryan, Texas, where Al found himself in an airplane for the first time in his life. He loved flying from the first moment, but when Al's instructor turned the controls of the plane over to him, he felt less than comfortable. Al tried hard to master the rhythm required to fly, trying to pay attention to his instructor.

"It's like dancing," the instructor told Al.

"But, I can't dance," Al exclaimed.

After several days of practicing on the controls, Al was invited to have a beer with his instructor after a particularly exhausting session for them both.

"Al, I'm going to recommend you for navigator or bombardier training," the instructor told him during his second beer.

Al took the news reasonably well; he felt relieved because he was afraid he might not be able to learn to fly well enough to pilot his own plane.

Instead of further training, the Army Air Force reduced him to the rank of buck private. He underwent basic training at Shepherd Field in Wichita Falls, Texas. Al found himself in a group of Texans, mostly draftees, who were single and younger than he was. Al discovered Wichita Falls to be hot and dusty as well as remote and desolate. Al finished his basic training in mid-July and volunteered as an aerial gunner.

The Army then shipped Al to Harlingen, Texas, almost a thousand miles to the south, where he learned to shoot different kinds of weapons. He won marksmanship medals. He became editor of the base newspaper called the *Hags Howl*. (Hags stood for Harlingen Aerial Gunnery School.) The Army promoted him to sergeant.

The Commanding Officer at the gunnery school was pleased to have a professional editor for his base newspaper and asked Al to stay on at the base to edit the paper. Al thanked the colonel for the offer and explained that he got into the Air Force to fight the Germans. Al agreed to stay on at the base for another eight weeks while he waited to be accepted again for aviation cadets. The colonel's endorsement helped push Al's papers along.

Al's duties were twofold: to fly as a gunner on a B-26 on submarine patrols over the Gulf of Mexico and to edit the base newspaper.

While he waited, he had his family with him.

Al rented a house for Mary, Selwyn and Billy, where they enjoyed time together in the lovely subtropical Rio Grande Valley. While war waged in other parts of the world, the Gordons enjoyed almost idyllic lives in the south Texas summery weather. They explored the Rio Grande Valley, watched the boys build sand castles on the lonely beaches at Laguna Madre and made occasional shopping and dining trips into Mexico.

On one of the last days at the beach, Mary stared out at the Gulf waters. The terrors of war had been made vividly real to all Americans through photographs and cinema newsreels. Across the languid blue Gulf water, the world was in flames with people fighting and dying every hour in North Africa, Europe and Asia.

"Al, promise you'll build me a house when the war's over," Mary asked Al.

"Certainly, sweetheart. Maybe near the water," Al said confidently.

Mary needed the idea of the house to give her hope for the future. She could not stand the thought that she might never see Al again. She needed all the hope and faith she could find. Al was doing his heroic part, but she knew even the best of heroes need angels to help protect them. Mary said her daily prayers and went to Mass regularly, doing her part to help protect Al.

Robert Miller

CHAPTER 69

Ellington Field, Texas

Al's orders finally came through to report back to Shepherd Field. He was back in the aviation cadet program.

After twelve weeks at Shepherd Field, Al went on to the Cadet Center in San Antonio and was classified as a navigator. To his surprise, Al had been assigned to a preflight school at Ellington Field, Texas, just a few miles from Houston.

The Army Air Force thrust Al into the most difficult training period in his life. After years of soft living, Al pitted himself against the physical demands of the cadet program and the required classroom skills. One person kept him motivated - Mary. If he wanted his weekends off to be with Mary, he had to perform to the requirements successfully. And, he did.

Al helped edit the preflight yearbook, which gave him extra opportunities to run into Houston to visit the printer, and see Mary and the boys. The Army assigned him to Navigation School at Ellington Field, allowing him four more months to be close to Mary and the family.

Despite the rigorous training, Al found that, to his surprise, he was exceptionally good at navigating an airplane.

The Navigation School at Ellington Field had a substantial number of Jewish cadets and the base had a Jewish Chaplain, Rabbi Goldbaum. Al found out that Rabbi Goldbaum had been the rabbi at a synagogue on University Avenue in the Bronx before the war. Al and Rabbi Goldbaum bonded immediately. They reminisced about the Bronx neighborhoods they both knew and marveled at the fortune of finding each other, two New Yorkers in Texas.

"Al, I'm arranging for a Passover Seder on the base and would like for you to come," Rabbi Goldbaum told Al, after searching him out.

"I don't know if I should. I haven't really been observant since my Bar Mitzvah," Al admitted to the rabbi. "Not only that, but my wife isn't Jewish and my two sons are being brought up as Roman Catholics."

The rabbi looked at Al compassionately.

"In Germany, your sons would be considered Jewish. Your wife would be considered a pariah," Rabbi Goldbaum explained. "Your wife is married to a Jew. Your sons carry Jewish blood in their veins. Please invite them to the Passover Seder on the field. We would love to have them with us. It may be important to them some day to understand and come to terms with their heritage."

Al assured Rabbi Goldbaum he would discuss the matter with Mary. They went on to talk about the Bronx, discovering that they knew some of the same people. They also talked about the war, and the fate of the Jews in Germany. Rabbi Goldbaum expressed great fear for the Jews sent off to "resettlement" camps in the east. The ominous reports suggested the Jews were living under great privation, being systematically starved and worked to death, and there were some reports of worse atrocities on a major scale.

"Do you believe in human sacrifice?" Rabbi Goldbaum asked.

"Why, of course not!" The question startled Al.

"What is the difference Al when an ancient king throws a young virgin into a volcano to appease the gods or a modern dictator makes speeches against the whole Jewish people and wants to destroy them to make his country pure?" Rabbi Goldbaum reflected. "The death of the virgin appeases a volcano god, while the destruction of the Jews appeases the dictator, Hitler."

The rabbi's question had an strong impact on Al.

"I get so despondent to think that twentieth century man has gone backwards to the point of human sacrifice, without calling it human sacrifice, of course," the rabbi added softly. "Evil has an opportunity to control the world, sometimes, Al, and we have to show our moral strength to fight evil in any form it takes."

"I made up my mind to volunteer for the Army Air Corps was not on the day the Japanese bombed Pearl Harbor, but the day Germany declared war on the United States," Al said.

Rabbi Goldbaum breathed a deep sigh and gave a slight smile of approval. "You have a Jewish heart and a Jewish conscience. Maybe you're not lost to us yet."

Al appreciated the friendliness of the rabbi. He had not talked openly to a rabbi in years. The rabbi had reminded Al that their Jewish blood meant that they both shared a common heritage and spiritual bond.

"Please bring your wife and children to the Passover Seder," the rabbi urged again.

"Mary might feel uncomfortable, although she has attended Reformed Jewish services in Houston and Denver," Al said.

Robert Miller

Rabbi Goldbaum thought about Al's concern for a moment and then smiled. "Tell your Mary that I'm going to invite the base's Catholic chaplain, Lieutenant Donaghy, to attend our Seder. That might make her feel more at ease. Father Donaghy is a good friend of mine, and a very bright and caring young priest."

Mary and Al decided to attend the Passover Seder. When they arrived at the N.C.O. club on Ellington Field, they were surprised and amazed to find over 100 people there for the Seder. Attendance included almost all the Jewish airmen on the base as well as some who were not Jewish. Lieutenant Donaghy, the Catholic Chaplain, and Major Norton, the Protestant Chaplain, were there, along with Colonel Rockwood, the base commander.

A lavish table had been set on special tablecloths with matzos, grape wine and the other ceremonial objects of the holiday. All together, three wives and three children were there, including Mary, Selwyn, and Billy.

Rabbi Goldbaum greeted Mary effusively. He told her how happy he was that she and the boys had come and gave her credit for helping to make the Seder a celebration that brought together people of different faiths and rank, including the commanding officer and the other chaplains. Mary enjoyed the charms of Rabbi Captain Goldbaum from the Bronx.

"My dear," Rabbi Goldbaum said. "You may be a devout Roman Catholic and you may bring your boys up as Roman Catholic and you may even convince your husband to some day join your church, but, please, I ask you, for your husband's sake and your sons'! Never let your husband forget that his origins are from the same people from whom Jesus came, in fact, really the only people from whom He could have come. Your sons may not think of themselves as Jews, but it might be very important for them to know something about the people from whom their father came."

Mary smiled sweetly at the rabbi and assured him that there was no danger of Al forgetting his origin and background nor any likelihood that he'll let the children forget it either.

Rabbi Goldbaum introduced Mary to Father Donaghy, telling him that the Gordons were the couple he had told him about earlier.

Father Donaghy made the point to Rabbi Goldbaum and to Al and Mary that, as he understood Jewish law, there was no question that the Jewish religion considered Mary and Al's children as non-Jews.

"The Jewish people believe that either someone is a Jew or he is not," Father Donaghy commented. "Their position is that, if the child's mother is Jewish, the child is Jewish. We don't necessarily agree. We take the position that, if a Catholic man marries a Jewish woman, the children should be raised as Catholics."

"My good friend Rabbi Goldbaum and I might disagree about some things," Father Donaghy said, "But we both agree that these two are two lovely children.

And I, for one am delighted to have them and their mother share their faith with us."

"Yes, Father Donaghy, what you say is true," Rabbi Goldbaum told his chaplain friend warmly. "But, it is possible for a Catholic to have a Jewish heart. I have at times given you credit for exactly that, and these two handsome young boys are the product of a Catholic mother and a Jewish father. Whether they grow up to consider themselves Jews or not, others will likely consider them Jews. It is important that they understand their heritage and even the biblical relation of their heritage. How many of Jesus's original disciples were Jews?" The rabbi asked.

"All of them," Mary interjected.

"Of course," Al said. "There was no one else but Jews in Palestine in those days, except for the Romans and they were all pagans. Heathens as one of your colleagues once called me, Lieutenant Donaghy."

"I'm grateful to both of you," Mary went on. "To you, Rabbi Goldbaum for inviting us here, and to you, Father Donaghy, for also attending this Passover Seder. It's important to me to get Al to attend religious functions of any sort. I do drag him to Mass with me many Sundays, but he is a born cynic and skeptic. I love him so much and I worry about his immortal soul."

When the actual Seder began, Al joked to Mary about the long wait they would have before they could eat anything. Mary listened with great interest to the story of the Passover as Rabbi Goldbaum and others read from the Hagadahs, but Al reacted with his usual contempt for ritual. The two boys, Selwyn and Billy, were bored and hungry, but they were nonetheless happy to be on the base with their father and among so many men in uniform.

When the dinner was finished, the assemblage sat around the table and sang songs. Then, everyone, including the commanding officer and the chaplains, shook hands with one another and dispersed into the night.

The hard part for Mary and Al was that Al could not accompany Mary back home. He escorted her only as far as the car. He watched sadly as she drove herself and the boys back to Houston. Al turned and to head back to the rigors of life in the barracks with fifty men.

Robert Miller

CHAPTER 70

August, 1942

Al graduated as a Second Lieutenant. His first orders were to report to the assignment center at Lincoln, Nebraska. When he was granted a ten day delay en route, he quickly applied for and received sufficient gas ration coupons to take him and his family to New York City and back to Lincoln.

Al, Mary, and the boys crowded into the car and spent their ten days traveling across the country. They had two days in New York and one-day stops with the Monahans in Lima and Aunt Fanny in Pittsburgh. The houses they remembered as being so busy and full of people were empty since the Monahan and Murphy boys were now scattered around the world in the military, as well as Aunt Fanny's son, Sandy, and her son-in-law, Sidney.

The drive across the country served its immediate purpose. Al and Mary saw their relatives again, but the time spent seeing new sights served another purpose: It took their minds off Al's coming departure. The possibility of Al going away for a long time, and perhaps never coming back remained unspoken. Mary dreaded the solitude she would be facing without Al.

Back at Lincoln, Nebraska, Al learned that he had been reassigned to Biggs Field at El Paso, Texas. So, he drove there with Mary. Then he made sure Mary had enough gas ration coupons to get her back to Houston. After a brief and tearful goodbye at the gate at Biggs Field, Mary turned the car eastward and headed for Houston.

At Biggs Field, Al and the other navigators were billeted at the Bachelor Officer Quarters, two to a room. They were taken into an auditorium and assigned to crews which were into their Operational Training Programs but needed navigators.

First Lieutenant Jim Brogan, an Irishman from Boston, about Al's age, headed Al's crew. He was an experienced pilot who had graduated pilot training a year before and had been towing targets at the aerial gunnery school in Kingman, Arizona, ever since.

The co-pilot, Steve Johnson, a recent graduate of pilot school, was a stocky blond boy from East Paterson, New Jersey, who like Al, was a newly commissioned officer. He had recently married his high school sweetheart.

The bombardier, Lynn Kingston, was from Iowa.

Al met the crew and everyone tried to joke around to relax. Jim Brogan told Al they'd probably spend about a month at Biggs Field. Al also found out from Steve Johnson that Steve's wife had managed to find an apartment in El Paso to be near him.

"I was told in Lincoln not to bring my wife," Al said.

"They always tell you that," Steve said. "Most of us who are married have brought our wives here. God only knows when or even if we'll ever see them again."

Once free from the meetings, Al called Mary and made new plans.

She would leave the boys with her mother in Houston and join Al for the remaining weeks in El Paso. The next day Mary took a harrowing train ride that lasted almost twenty-four hours. When she got to El Paso, she was exhausted, but Al got a room for her at the Hilton Hotel. The next day Mary found a furnished room a few blocks from the airfield.

Al and his group flew days and nights, practicing bombing missions and navigation assignments. Near the end of the month, they flew in a huge simulated air raid on a target in New Mexico, while fighter planes from air bases along the way tried to break up the formations.

While Al and the crew were flying at 20,000 feet in the bitter cold, Mary and Helen Johnson, the co-pilot's wife, sat around the pool at the officers club in the dizzying heat of the west Texas desert. Al sometimes joined Mary at the pool in the 100-degree heat with his fingers still blue after nearly being frozen at high-altitude flying.

When the crews flew at night, Mary and Helen occasionally stood at the base's security fence to watch the B-24's line up and take off. If they thought a plane was close enough, they would wave frantically, hoping Al or Steve might see them.

Mary and Helen also spent time talking about the possibility of their husbands' deaths. Helen had no children. She knew she could start life over again with a new husband, if she had to. Mary had two boys, and she relied on her parents to help with the exhausting chore of caring for them with Al away. She found it inconceivable to think about falling in love again, starting over, trying to find new happiness and a new father for the boys as long as Al remained alive. Despite such talk of death and the war, the wives kept up a cheerfulness, as much for themselves as for their husbands. Mary and Helen enjoyed quick trips on their own across the border into Juarez, Mexico, for sightseeing, shopping, and dining on Mexican cuisine, while their husbands were told Mexico was off-limits at this stage of their training.

Early in August the inevitable orders came. Their shipping date was imminent. All wives and dependents were to be sent home.

Mary and Al gave up their room and moved back to the Hilton Hotel in downtown El Paso for their final weekend together. The past month had been like a second honeymoon. The last night in the Hilton was a bittersweet ending. The near 100-degree heat did not keep them from making love at all hours of the day and night. They clung to each other, knowing they had only this precious time to hold each other. Mary and Al didn't know when they would see each other again.

Al told Mary that Monday, August 16th, was the date his crew were scheduled to entrain for their "staging area" in Topeka, Kansas. The crews would be restricted to the base the moment they got there, and very likely, not no one would be allowed to make a phone call.

Mary and Al said their goodbyes in the bleak dark hours before dawn at the hotel in El Paso. While she stood naked before him, he stopped and held her close one last time before heading back for the last time to Biggs Field.

Later the same day, Mary took a train back home to Houston. Al was on another train that day with over a hundred and thirty other officers in the squadron, while more than two hundred enlisted men had to make do in day coaches during the twenty-four hour run from El Paso to Topeka.

CHAPTER 71

Steve Brogan and his crew were assigned a bomber - a brand new, factory-fresh unpainted beautiful silver B-24 Consolidated Liberator. The crew inspected the plane on Tuesday. Brogan, the pilot, had the honor of choosing the name to be painted on the nose. He chose Brogan's Boston Bean Dropper. Brogan and his beans had been immortalized on the nose of the B-24, which the crew dubbed the Bean Town Fart. The crew made a shakedown flight.

In Al's last letter from Topeka, he could not tell Mary where he was going because it was still a military secret and no one had informed the crew. But he did tell her about his love, longing and passion for her. He told her how happy she had made him and how much he loved her and the boys. At a time like this before going off to war and possibly to death, Al reaffirmed his love and fidelity for his precious Mary. What made their love more beautiful for Al, too, was Mary's unshakable and unquestionable love for Al.

On the morning of the third day at the Topeka base, Al got his final orders. Al was ordered to set a course for Presque Isle, Maine, a flight of some eight hours. He was to navigate the most direct course possible that would keep them over the United States at all times. Al plotted the course that would take them to Erie, Pennsylvania, with a slight variation northeast to Rutland, Vermont, then directly north to Presque Isle and on to their final destination.

He found the navigation easy. Al had a clear view of the ground. Flying the B-24 Liberator at 12,000 feet on the sunny day, Al's thoughts turned to Mary during his free time away the navigation charts. He took out some paper and jotted down a few lines of a letter to Mary. In the letter, he wrote that he was flying in a direction that took him farther away from her at the rate of almost three miles a minute. He wrote he would never be happy again until he was headed back to her.

Robert Miller

Some five hours after takeoff, Al announced to the crew that they were over Rutland, Vermont, and told the pilot over the intercom to make a course correction.

Jim Brogan acknowledged it and then began to wax eloquent to the entire crew about his New England. Normally not all that loquacious, the captain gave the crew a short history lesson of the area. He briefly told them that Vermont was the fourteenth state, and had been formed to ease a border dispute between New York and New Hampshire. He added that Maine, their destination, had originally been part of Massachusetts.

The crew had Presque Isle in sight exactly at the minute that had been Al's ETA (Estimated Time of Arrival). Al's precise navigation brought messages of approval from the Captain and the entire crew. Al was the newest member of the crew, the only Jew, the only New Yorker. But, he now felt that he had won their approval and respect.

They had left Topeka on Thursday morning and had arrived in Maine on Thursday night. Friday night they landed in Labrador. Saturday night they slept in Reykjavik, Iceland.

In Reykjavik, the Bean Dropper was inspected. The guns were checked and ammunition was supplied for their turret guns. The seemingly endless game of preparation was at an end. The B-24 was armed and ready to defend itself. Al was ready to test his determination to fight to the death so his wife and children could live free and be protected from hatred. Al was ready for war.

CHAPTER 72

The Bean Dropper and its crew spent two weeks in Scotland for another period of training. On a dull, rainy morning in mid- September, they joined the 311th Bomb Group of the Eighth Air Force at a base close to Tunbridge Wells, about forty miles southeast of London.

Despite all the months of training and preparation, Al felt nervous, as he attended his first briefing. The Briefing Officer gave the basic details. Al's notes were to the point. The target: Bremen. The flight: mostly over water. The greatest dangers: fighters to and from the target, flak over the target. The total planes on this mission: over a hundred.

The Brogan Boston Bean Dropper had been taken over by a senior officer and his crew. Brogan and his crew, which now included a replacement bombardier, Lietenant Fred Draper, of Kansas was scheduled to fly in a B-24 called Nazi Nemesis, a plane that has so far flown over twenty missions. Its position would be well back in the formation.

That morning Al and the crew spent over an hour in the B-24 before the pilot got the orders to start its engines. The crew sat another hour on the ground before takeoff, and then another hour circling into formation and climbing before setting out for the target.

Al's job was not to direct the pilot at all, only to keep track of the plane's position. If an emergency arose, such as an engine failure and they had to leave formation, Al's job would then be to direct the pilot of this single, lone plane back to the home base. All air crewmen knew that a single B-24 would be an easy target for German fighter planes. The rule for survival meant staying in formation and rely on the massing of the guns to protect the giant planes from the German fighters.

The cluster of B-24s assembled over England at 10,000 feet and climbed to 20,000 feet where the air temperature became frigid. Al's thought that air combat could be easier than ground combat evaporated. The temperatures

Robert Miller

heading to Germany seemed more frigid than the temperatures he experienced over Texas. The old B-24's heaters barely worked and supplied minimum heat. Wind rushed into the plane at 140 knots around the windows, turrets, and guns where the fittings were not too tight. Temperatures in the nose of the plane seemed to be worse where Al and the bombardier shivered. Al could only pat his arms against his body to try to stay warm as the bomb-laden plane kept droning on towards Bremen.

As the planes flew along the coast off the Frisian Islands of The Netherlands, one of the gunners gave a frantic call, "Unidentified aircraft at three o'clock!"

Al got his first sight of German fighters. The nose gunner, who was Catholic, gave a sign of the cross and prepared for battle.

The swarm of twenty German planes flew along at their altitude about 3,000 feet away.

"Be on your guns and be ready!" Captain Brogan ordered through the intercom.

Fred Draper, the bombardier and the only crew member with previous missions, came on the intercom. "Those guys are measuring our speed and altitude and they're giving that information to the antiaircraft batteries so they can get their range set when we approach the target. Those planes will attack us for sure, but not for a while yet, not till they get the proper count on us and feed it back to headquarters."

The B-24s were still over the sea. Al estimated they were about twenty minutes from their final turn towards the target and some twenty-five minutes from their estimated drop point.

The German fighter planes stayed off to the right of the bomber formation for what seemed like a long time. Then, suddenly they increased their speed, moved ahead of the formation, even as they climbed to a higher altitude. The bombers were approaching the point where they would be making nearly a ninety degree turn to the right. The bombers began to turn, exposing themselves to the fighters.

Al sat cramped in the rear of the plane's nose with a turret blocking his high view and the bombardier crouching over the bombsight below him. He could see clearly out to each side of the B-24.

"Here they come! Eleven o'clock high!" Steve Johnson, the co-pilot, yelled over the intercom.

Okay, Mary, keep your prayers coming! Al thought to himself.

Al could see little, but he heard the front turret firing and leaned over to the window on the left side of the plane and saw a Messerschmitt 109 coming at them with machine guns blazing.

"Oh, damn!" Al said. After his initial scare, Al wished he had a machine gun to fire back. The plane shook and shuddered from the impact of the piercing bullets. He held his breath waiting for a bullet to hit him. From his poor vantage point, Al could see other fighters diving through the formation, but he could not see if they were making turns to come back.

Other crew members called out a steady stream of warnings.

"Bomber going down! Bomber going down at four o'clock!" someone yelled in the intercom.

Al looked over to the B-24 that dropped out of formation with its guns still firing as it spiraled down towards the water. At one point, it opened its bomb bay doors as if to jettison its bombs over the water, but quickly closed them as the German fighters began to close in on the wounded bomber. Al quickly lost sight of the descending B-24.

"Their bomb bay doors are opening again. They're dropping their bombs! There's one, two, three, four, five and six parachutes!" the tail turret gunner hollered over the intercom. "They're going into the water. Hope they've got their Mae Wests and warm warm clothes on."

"It's got to be warmer in the water there than it is up here," the radio-gunner from amidship joked back.

The fighters had quickly disappeared, but Al knew what that meant. They would now face deadly German flak. Al watched with growing anticipation of the dangers ahead as they crossed the coast. He looked down only to see a flat green plain behind the coastal beaches. It was Nazi controlled territory, but the scenery looked like the coast of New Jersey from this altitude: lush, green, tranquil. He wished so much he and Mary could be together enjoying themselves on the Atlantic City beach right now.

Robert Miller

CHAPTER 73

The B-24 formation now approached Bremen from the northeast. Al peered out again from his side window where he saw the gray puffs that appeared no more dangerous than small clouds, but he knew the puffs were lethal. The bombers continued on course, buffeted by currents generated by the flak.

One B-24 just ahead of the Nazi Nemesis took a hit on one of its engines which started smoking. The damaged B-24 remained in formation for a while until the pilot shut down the engine, feathered the prop, lost a little altitude, but tried desperately to stay under the cover of the rest of the formation. It was a minute to the target and the drop point.

Al peered out the window to the right to see flak hit the wing of another B-24. The wing sheared off in a ball of flame. The bomber began spinning towards the ground.

"Look for chutes!" Jim Brogan told his gunners.

"No chutes," the ball turret gunner promptly reported. "They bought the farm."

"Did you see who that was?" Steve Johnson asked Brogan.

"I think it was Carlson's plane. Lynn Kingston was flying with him today," Brogan answered.

Al thought for a moment about Lynn Kingston who used to be the bombardier with this crew. It was Lynn's second mission and he was already gone. Al felt stunned and wondered why Lynn should die so soon. There are no rules up here, Al realized. One can die at any time. The bombardier's voice jolted Al out of his thoughts.

"Open bomb bay doors!" Fred Draper called through the intercom. Fred lay in the belly of the nose of the plane, constantly adjusted his bombsight and watched the planes ahead.

Al returned to his desk, plotted their present position and course. When he finished he took a note pad with him, attached his oxygen mask to a portable canister and left his station to climb onto the flight deck and back towards the open bomb bay. He was determined to watch the bombs that had only one purpose: to rain destruction on the ground below. He had seen two American planes shot down. Now, he wanted to see the bombs fall in retaliation.

As cold as it had been in the nose of the B-24, the wind blowing through the bomb bay was even colder and chilled Al even more. He was standing near the edge of the open bomb bay. Al did not have to wait long. The bombs started dropping to the target four miles below.

After the bombs were released and the bomb bay doors closed, Al climbed back to the center of the plane hoping to get a better view of where they actually hit. By then, the bombs from the Nazi Nemesis emerged and joined the hundreds of other bombs from the surrounding B-24s. Al could see that most of the bombs landed on the docks, railroad yards and some that fell into the Weser River.

Al felt a sudden rush of emotion. He and the crew had made it this far and dropped their bombs on Germany. He shook hands with the two waist gunners and proceeded back to the flight deck and solemnly shook hands with the pilot and co-pilot. By the time Al got back to his position at the navigator's compartment and connected his intercom, he heard Jim Brogan explode at him for walking around the airplane while they were on their bombing run.

"Stay alert everybody! Fighters are assembling again somewhere ahead and off to the left...at ten o'clock," Brogan alerted everyone through the intercom.

After dropping their bombs, the B-24s flew back west across the low lands of Germany towards Holland. The fighters did not take long to assemble and move to attack. This time the bombers, rid of their bombs, were lighter and faster. The B-24s were easier to handle and the pilots were able to keep them in tight formation.

The ball turret gunner screamed that he had hit a Messerschmitt 109.

Al could not see the action taking place under the plane. He wanted desperately to see what was happening. What he did see was a burning German fighter, apparently hit by a gunner from another plane in formation ahead of theirs, approaching on a collision course.

God, no! Al thought as he stared transfixed at the oncoming enemy aircraft.

The fighter plane missed them by feet, but came close enough for Al to see the helmet of the slumped pilot of the burning plane as it hurtled past them.

Ten minutes of the attack seemed like an hour. The fighter planes flew towards Al's plane with machine guns flaring bullets and passing by the bomber in seconds. The bullets missed.

The fighters disappeared and the remaining B-24s crossed the coast of Holland and flew out over the North Sea. About forty minutes later, the bombers began their descent to the warmer air at 12,000 feet and the crew rejoiced as they took off their oxygen masks and contemplated having survived their first mission.

Robert Miller

Fred Draper, the bombardier, who had not said a half dozen words to Al or anyone else when he first joined the crew that day, disconnected his intercom, walked back to Al and hugged him. Fred had suddenly become ebullient and loquacious.

"Thank you," Fred told Al. "You're bringing me home from my twelfth mission. I only have that many more plus one to go. I hope I can fly with this crew and this airplane. I think you're a lucky bunch. This has been my first 'no sweat-no scratch' mission and I want thirteen more just like this one." He motioned for Al to fold back his navigation table. He crawled up to the flight deck to thank their pilot and co-pilot.

Al thought about being shot at by enemy planes and how fate had let him survive. The period of sheer terror by the fighters lasted about forty minutes out of a total of eight hours of flying time.

Over the North Sea, the whole crew became totally relaxed. They would live to fly another time. And if they flew twenty-four more missions and survived, they could go home.

Back home, Mary and her parents listened to the radio and read the daily papers about the war, always eager to find a hint as to where Al might be headed. Sel and Billy were too young to understand the dangers their father faced, but Mary proudly reminded them their father was helping to protect them and other good people in other countries. She told them about the big bomber he flew in. They pretended to be helping their father by mimicking flying around in toy B-24s in their children's play.

CHAPTER 74

Al's detailed log during the mission became valuable to the debriefing officer by giving exact locations of the attacks and the flak locations. In fact, he gave a precise location of hitherto unknown German ack ack antiaircraft batteries. After the meeting, the officer offered Al a shot of whiskey. Though not a whiskey drinker, Al took the shot of whiskey and indulged in the pleasure of celebrating life over death. Al smiled as the officer complimented him with a "well done" on his first mission.

Al and Steve Johnson ended up at the officers' club. Over a couple of beers, they lamented the loss of Lynn Kingston. Their talk turned to the mathematical odds of surviving future missions. The idle talk about odds consoled them momentarily and gave them hope that they could survive. The statistics of survival meant counting - the total planes, the total shot down, the percentages and odds of getting shot down, the odds of being captured, the odds of getting back, and the odds of getting home. Air war seemed to be a game of percentages.

Al knew he would be sent out on his missions to go through the muddled fury of the attacks. God willing, his odds of making it would be in his favor.

"Four hours ago we were fighting for our lives. Now, we're safe and we'll sleep between clean sheets tonight," Al said. He and Steve clinked their beer bottles together to toast the thought. "It's strange how this air war is being fought."

Jim Brogan joined Al and Steve as they were finishing their beers.

"I hear that we're going to have a fighter escort on our next mission. The big raid today was on Hamburg and they had the fighter escort. We were the diversion. We were the bait to bring up the fighters. What do you think of that?" Brogan asked.

"I wonder if Lynn Kingston and the crew would get a lot of pleasure knowing they died to lure German fighters!" Steve wondered.

"I think his plane got hit by flak, which could happen to any of us," Al commented solemnly.

"We're not posted to fly tomorrow. I'm heading off the field because I've been promised an introduction to a lady in Maidstone," Brogan said. He finished off his beer in three gulps.

As married men, who were in no mood to party without their wives, Al and Pete chose to have dinner at the officers' club. Afterwards, Al found a quiet place to write to Mary. After writing about where he was and how his mission went, he drafted a story to send to Bill Wannamaker. He wrote and rewrote the story. Al then sought out the Base Information Officer, who was at the bar, introduced himself and explained that he wanted permission to send the story back home.

The burly Information Officer, Captain Arthur Fenimore, took the article from Al, and walked with him to a table to read through it.

Fenimore asked Al about his work at *The Rocky Mountain News* in Denver. Al told him that he'd promised to send stories back to Wannamaker. Fenimore kept the story to do some editing overnight.

The next day Al met Captain Fenimore at base headquarters where they went over the revised version of the story. Not much was changed, but the last names of Al's crew were deleted and somehow the story had been expanded to include the names of the commanding general of the Eighth Air Force, the Brigadier General in command of the 311th Bomb Group and the Colonel who had led the mission the day before. Those three commanders were prominently mentioned together with their home towns.

Captain Fenimore beamed when Al told him how impressed he was with the editing job. The captain told Al that he had worked for twelve years at *The New York Times*.

Al shared stories with the captain about growing up in the Bronx.

As the two men talked, the captain felt comfortable in sharing a secret revelation with Al. "Before I was Arthur Fenimore, I used to be Abe Feinberg. In 1931 when I applied to *The New York Times* for a job, I submitted two applications, one for Abe Feinberg and another for Arthur Fenimore. Which one do you think they hired? And, on top of that, the *Times* is owned and run by a Jewish family. It is a strange world we live in, isn't it?" the captain remarked with a grin.

Later that day, Al received a cable from Mr. Wannamaker through the direct wire services.

"Congratulations. Great story. Ran next to Ernie Pyle's column today and may run in Houston and other papers tomorrow. Send stories on each mission. Sending Mary $100 per story. Come home safe."

WANNAMAKER

Ten days later, Al got a letter from Mary in which was enclosed a copy of his article from *The Houston Press*. In the letter, she wrote about how everyone was terribly proud of him, but terribly worried too. Mary said she had sent a copy of the article to his parents, but they had already seen it in the *New York World Telegram*. *The Houston* article referred to Al as a brave Texan and the World Telegram story referred to him as a New Yorker. Al presumed, but didn't know for sure that the article in the *Rocky Mountain News* referred to him as being from Denver.

Al joked and celebrated with the others over some more beers.

"I now know my true identity. Besides being Jewish and having a Catholic-Irish wife, I'm really a brave Texan-New Yorker and Coloradoan. You can't beat all those combinations!"

Robert Miller

CHAPTER 75

Al's second, third, and fourth missions were called "milk runs" because they were over French and Dutch ports. The missions were "easier" only because there would be fighter support and less flak.

Al's fifth mission was with Colonel Hatfield. The target: Berlin.

The crew included the 311th lead navigator, Captain Ted Bolton, and their lead bombardier, Captain Bob Delapina. The co-pilot was also a captain. The plane they were to fly was Brogan's Boston Bean Dropper.

At the briefing, Al inquired why there would be two navigators.

"There are three reasons I know of," Captain Bolton said with a laugh. "You've become famous around here and everybody, especially Colonel Hatfield, wants to get their names in the newspapers. Second, this is my twenty second mission and my third over Berlin. After today, I'm going to draw three easy ones and go home. My job is to assess you as a possible replacement for me as lead navigator. Third, your file shows you're an aerial gunner. We decided to take one additional navigator and one less gunner. You're going to do the navigating, until we see our first German fighter. I'll be taking it easy and looking over your shoulder. This is a nice opportunity for you to work with the colonel."

"I've done a lot of navigating. I feel ready for the job," Al said confidently.

Delapina momentarily looked over his shoulder and back to Al.

"You put the Colonel's name in the paper, make him a hero, don't get him lost, and you're on the way to a quick promotion," Delapina said with raised eyebrows. "Shoot down an ME109 and you can get yourself a medal, too."

Al smiled as Delapina gave him a friendly jab with his elbow.

The rest of the time Al took notes as the Briefing Officer explained the details succinctly.

"Your target - a group of factories along the Panke River in the northern part of Berlin. Your route - over northern Holland and Saxony. You will have fighter escorts - from the time you hit the coast of Holland to a point north of Hannover, where the fighters turn back. No escorts - about forty-five minutes going to the target. Fighter escorts will be with you - when you cross the Elbe River and all the way to England," the Briefing Officer explained tersely.

Colonel Hatfield's B-24 would be in front of the 311th group of twenty-four planes, a little to the left and back from the mission group leader, who would be in the front of 144 planes. England's weather that morning was clear as the planes took off and climbed to their flying altitude over the picturesque countryside. The bombers flew such a tight formation Al could barely see the other twenty three planes from his vantage point in front of the aircraft.

The planes flew on towards the Dutch coast some forty miles north of Amsterdam. They encountered some sporadic but ineffective flak directed at them soon after they crossed the shoreline. At that point, the tail gunner reported fighters behind them, which turned out to be American P-47s. The P-47 fighters took up positions alongside the bombers for the next hour. When they had to leave, the P-47 pilots wiggled their wings to wish the bombers luck and headed back towards England.

Ten minutes later German fighters were spotted far off to the south of the bombers. Ted Bolton, who had been watching as Al plotted the course and checked off the landmarks, signaled to Al that he'd take over the navigation and that Al was to go to the waist gun to assume his position as gunner, to the rear of the plane.

Al plugged himself into the portable oxygen canister. He maneuvered his way back to the waist gun of the bomber. He checked out the fifty caliber machine gun, made sure it was loaded and in operable condition. Al had no time to think about how much colder the plane felt here compared to the nose. His rushing adrenaline warmed him. He felt a sudden urge to kill the enemy. His finger waited on the trigger for his first German plane. He had no awareness how fast his heart raced. He crossed the few feet to the other side of the plane where Sergeant Ed Bannister scanned the sky. The sergeant kept an eye on a group of German fighters assembling off the plane's right wing, far out of range. While Al and Ed watched those fighters, another gunner started shouting over the intercom.

"Bogies! Bogies! Coming in at twelve o'clock high!" the top gunner screamed.

Al grabbed onto the fifty caliber machine gun at his left waist gun position, but saw no fighters. The only aircraft he could see was the B-24 that was in formation with them, slightly behind and to their left.

Al followed the unseen air battle through his intercom. The German fighters concentrated on the planes ahead of them and on the right side of the formation. Al waited impatiently and tensely for something to fly by. He heard only the intermittent clatter of machine guns as the front turret and top turret gunners

Robert Miller

began to fire. Again and again the clatter continued, but Al saw no German fighters. Al strained to see anything to shoot, but all the fighting took place on the other side of the plane.

"This son of a bitch is heading right for us. I'll nail that bast...," the front turret gunner screamed through the intercom. His words went dead as the whole front of the airplane seemed to explode. The huge B-24 buckled and rocked turbulently before the pilot managed to regain control. "Who's hit?! Report in!" Colonel Hatfield shouted into the intercom. "Pilot to Navigator, please report situation in nose."

There was only silence.

"Pilot, this is Gordon at the left gun. I'll go to check on the nose!" Al yelled. He plugged himself into the portable oxygen canister and carefully stepped towards the nose.

When Al got to the pilot's cabin, he felt the bitter cold wind rushing into the plane from the front. Colonel Hatfield and the co-pilot struggled with the plane's controls.

Al lowered himself into the nose compartment where he found complete devastation. The front turret had been blown apart by the fighter's bullets. The bombardier crouched over dead. Captain Ted Bolton, the navigator, lay on the floor bleeding. Al thought the captain might be alive. When he rolled the captain over, Al saw the wound through the captain's neck and his eyes staring off into empty space. Despite the bitter cold, Al took off his sheepskin flight jacket and stuffed it into some of the broken plexiglass. He secured the front turret which rocked from side to side. He opened the turret with the thought of pulling the gunner out. The rushing wind blew blood and body matter back on him. He quickly closed the turret. His stomach soured as he looked at himself covered in blood and gore.

Al picked up the intercom and reported to the colonel, but he couldn't get through. The wires had been shot apart. He grabbed the log, maps, and chart from the navigation area and climbed back up to the flight deck.

"They're all dead up there," Al reported to the colonel. "It's one God awful mess. Are we able to fly?"

"We don't seem to have damage to our engines. We seem to be all right for the moment," Colonel Hatfield shouted. "The fighters have gone. We're approaching Berlin. You'll have to go back into the nose and drop the bombs. The flak will start any minute. You'll have to sit up there and watch the planes ahead of us and drop our bombs when they do."

"Roger," Al said. "The intercoms don't work. I'll need to tell you when to open the bomb bay doors."

"Don't worry. I can see the planes ahead. I'll watch their bomb bay doors. Just drop the bombs when they drop theirs!" Colonel Hatfield shouted firmly.

The Colonel patted Al on the shoulder. He saw the blood that covered Al's flak jacket. "Where's your jacket? You'll freeze to death."

"I had to stuff it in the shattered plexiglass," Al said as he hugged his arms tight to his body.

"Here! Put this around the plexiglass," Colonel Hatfield ordered while handing Al a canvas blanket. "Get your jacket on!" he ordered again. Then he waved Al to return to the nose.

Al climbed down from the flight deck into the horror that was now the nose section. The flak was heavy. The plane rose and fell as it rode the shockwaves and clouds of flak burst nearby. Al put on his sheepskin jacket and placed the canvas blanket between the jagged pieces of plexiglass. The jacket had blocked some of the freezing air; Al shivered for a few minutes. He pushed Delapina's body aside so he could position himself to watch the other planes in front drop their bombs.

Ahead of him, the formation flew through the puffs of flak. Below him, he could see the city of Berlin. When the other planes opened their bomb bay doors, Al felt a strange sense of calm. He blocked out the sickening scene of carnage all around him, the blood, tissue, body parts of formerly whole, living human beings. Instead, he experienced a new sense of purpose and determination:

By dropping bombs on Berlin, he would be helping to avenge the tortured, victimized Jews caught in the grip of the Nazis, and the three young men in the plane who had died that day. Whether he lived or died after this moment, this was his one personal moment to pound the Nazis into hell. He looked down on Berlin and wondered where Adolf Hitler was at that moment.

"Adolf Hitler! You son of a bitch!" Al shouted into his oxygen mask. No one could hear him. The three dead bodies two feet away only added to his fury. "Al Gordon from the Bronx is up here! I'm going to dump a load of bombs on you right now! Go to hell for me!"

When Al turned on the bombsight, the light began to blink. He was jubilant. When the other planes started dropping their bombs, Al hit the toggle switch. He felt the plane rising as the bombs left the bomb bay and dropped on Berlin. This moment his spirit had wings of its own. He had personally delivered some bombs to Adolf Hitler.

Robert Miller

CHAPTER 76

Al smiled to himself as he headed back to the empty bomb bay. The bombs had let Hitler know he and his kind could not rule the world. Al returned to the waist window to get a visual sighting of their location before checking his maps. Before he left, he grabbed his machine gun as the German fighters reappeared. The battle turned out to be brief. The Messerschmitts and Folk Wolf's had time for only two passes at the formation before they were driven off by a group of P-38s which arrived to escort the Liberators home.

What a beautiful sight to see those P-38s! Al said to himself after letting out an exhausted sigh.

Al returned to check in with the Colonel. "You have no idea of the devastation in the nose," Al warned him.

Colonel Hatfield signaled to the co-pilot to take control of the airplane. He went down into the nose compartment. When he returned, he shook his head silently.

"We are lucky," Hatfield said finally. "The ME 109 came at us from above. He hit us with a 20 millimeter shell that must have exploded in or just behind the nose turret and killed the three of them. We're lucky it didn't hit us in the flight deck or one of the engines. I can't believe our luck." The Colonel patted Al on the arm.

"How about my luck, Colonel! If I hadn't been in the back at the machine gun, I'd be where Captain Bolton was. The three souls in the nose ran out of luck today," Al said.

"Yes, they ran out of luck," the Colonel reflected. "But, so did the Nazis who were making torpedoes in that factory we hit today. We got hit, but we still went on. Put that in the story you write tonight and get it right! Meanwhile, I'm making you my navigator and promoting you to First Lieutenant. I've got three more missions after this one and I'm counting on you to get me to the target and bring me home each time." Colonel Hatfield had to shout to Al over the noise of the rushing wind and the plane's engines.

The Colonel called on the intercom for some of the crew to help carry the three bodies into the bomb bay and plug up the holes in the plexiglass. With the bodies in place, the Colonel returned to his pilot's position. Al remained for a while with the bodies.

Al's cool and detached demeanor vanished when he saw the three dead airmen, now cold, lying motionless. All the pent-up fear and excitement of the last hour came out unexpectedly, and he began to sob to till his body shook.

After a while, he began to calm down. He thought about how briefly he had known the two officers. He had not even spoken a word to the nose turret gunner, whose name he did not even know. Al knew there were many reasons to cry. He had three dead young men in front of him. He wondered again about his odds. He knew all the mathematics in the world could not predict the randomness of how death came in war.

A gunner came by to tell Al that the front turret gunner had been a tough Italian kid, Sergeant Romeo Terranova from Chicago, who was on his nineteenth mission.

The Colonel brought the plane back to the airstrip. However, the plane had to make a crash landing because the nose wheel didn't lock and then collapsed.

At the base hospital, the doctor ordered the crew to spend the night at the hospital for general observation.

With the Colonel's influence, the next morning, both Colonel Hatfield and Al were awarded Purple Hearts. Al was awarded an Air Medal for having flown five missions and was promoted to First Lieutenant.

The seven survivors of the Boston Bean Dropper were released from the hospital the next day and given a seven day pass to London. Al stayed behind to write his story. He did not leave until he had written a story about the raid on Berlin.

His lead read, "Ten Men left England in a B-24 Liberator to bomb Berlin yesterday and seven of them came back to tell about it."

Captain Fenimore checked over the story and told Al that his stories were being picked up by Scripps Howard newspapers around the country and probably going out on the United Press wire service too.

When the conversation came around to Colonel Hatfield, Fenimore became serious and gave Al some helpful advice.

"The Colonel's an ambitious man. He's one to share some of the glory with others, but in the end ambitious people will walk over anyone in their path, if it will help them get ahead."

"Does that include you and me?" Al asked.

"You and I are amateurs in the ambition department," Fenimore said with a raised eyebrow. "Colonel Hatfield and people like him are real killers. If you can help him achieve what he wants, and you've already started by telling this story about the Colonel, he'll do anything for you." Fenimore smiled suspiciously. "The Colonel just may turn out to be your rabbi to help you get safely through your next seventeen missions."

Before Al left for London, Captain Fenimore used his contacts and arranged a hotel room for Al. Al looked forward to a few days in London where he planned to buy souvenirs for Mary, the boys and other relatives back home. He had been writing to Mary almost every day. He enjoyed letting her know half-seriously that it might just be her Catholic prayers that helped get him though each mission.

Al had a list of things to tell Mary. He had survived the mission to Berlin and an emergency plane crash. He had to tell her how he had achieved the admiration and friendship of a powerful and determined colonel. He had to tell her about his articles being published in newspapers around the country. With more missions to fly, Al encouraged Mary to keep praying for him. He knew she would pray for him.

Clash of Cultures - The Al Gordon Story

CHAPTER 77

In London, Al visited the United Press International headquarters off Charing Cross Road. He walked in and was surprised to meet Roy Howard himself. Mr. Howard thanked Al for coming by and explained that he had planned to visit the base at Tunbridge Wells to look him up.

"Your account of your third mission went to all the Scripps- Howard Papers and got on the UP wire. It's dynamic stuff and we want you to keep writing them. How many missions have you flown now?" Mr. Howard asked.

"Five," Al answered. "I hope to make twenty more and go home. The last mission was difficult. We lost three men on board. The story has just gone out on the wire."

"The story's probably in our paper today. When I call New York later, I'll find out," Mr. Howard said. "By the way young man, I'd like to invite you to dinner tonight, okay?"

Al accepted cheerfully. As he left the office and waited impatiently for dinner later that evening, he thought of the old saying, "the pen is mightier than the sword." In his case, it was more the power of his portable typewriter. Al smiled to himself as he walked the streets of London. He had captured national prominence back home with his stories as well as the attention of the head of a major newspaper chain.

At dinner, Mr. Howard explained how the war was going.

"London was where everything was happening three years ago. But last fall the spotlight turned to Africa and now to Italy. The big show will be the invasion of Europe, probably early next spring. Then London will be where the action is all over again," Mr. Howard surmised.

In the midst of a few beers at the bar, Mr. Howard introduced Al to such lions of journalism as Quenton Reynolds, Ed Murrow, and Bob Considine, with the dramatic introduction of "the one-time cable editor of the *Rocky Mountain*

News, now with the Eighth Air Force, and writing articles on his bombing missions over Europe."

"All we're doing is writing about this goddamn war and this young fellow is both fighting the war and writing about it. How I envy him!" Mr. Howard said proudly to the other journalists.

Al returned to Tunbridge Wells ready to churn out more air war stories for Mr. Howard. He also had serious worries about surviving the next twenty missions. Steve Johnson, the co-pilot with Jim Brogan, spoke enviously to Al about his promotion. Al explained that on just one flight with the Colonel he got a promotion, a Purple Heart and an Air Medal. To make Steve feel better, Al suggested he would pass Steve's name on to Hatfield.

"Maybe it's better just to stick with Jim Brogan," Steve reflected. "I'd stay a second looey and come home safe from each mission. After all, Colonel Hatfield has lost three men and nearly totaled Brogan's Boston Bean Dropper," Steve added with a laugh.

Steve's tone changed from excitement to hesitation once he seriously started thinking about flying with the colonel. Al and Steve finally left for the night. Al wondered whether Steve had foreseen some pending calamity in flying with the colonel.

That evening, Al joined Colonel Hatfield and other officers in charge of planning the bombing missions. Though he felt uncomfortable among the top brass at the meeting, Al knew the Colonel had invited him there for a purpose. Near the end of the meeting, Al felt compelled to ask who had chosen this particular route to bomb Frankfurt.

"It was chosen at Eighth Air Force Headquarters," General Lamott, the commanding general, told Al sternly. "We would have the protection of the P-38s." Then he softened and asked the young lieutenant a direct question, "Do you have another suggestion?"

Al offered his strategic insights about a southern route that could fool the German fighters and ultimately offer less flak.

General Lamott and Colonel Hatfield turned to the map after listening to Al's suggestion. They huddled together for a private conference.

"Lieutenant, that's a helluva good suggestion. I like it. I'll pass it on to Eighth Air Force Headquarters. I'm going to suggest that we do it your way. Thank you," the General remarked.

As the meeting broke up, Colonel Hatfield approached the General and told him he would like to see Lieutenant Gordon promoted to a captain.

"How long has he been a First Lieutenant, Colonel?" the General asked.

"Just one week, sir," the Colonel said.

General Lamott laughed. "Well, let's see if we can wait at least another week before the promotion," the General said. The General looked at Al again.

"Lieutenant Gordon, you lead our planes to Frankfurt tomorrow and bring them all back safely, and you'll be on your way to a promotion. That's a promise."

Al saluted the General and added with a stiff smile, "Yes, sir."

The General returned the salute and then reached out to shake Al's hand. "Hit them hard tomorrow and then lead our planes back here safely. Good luck!" the General exclaimed.

When Al entered the tense calm of the briefing room early the next morning, he was astonished to see that the entire route to the target had been changed. The new route matched almost exactly the one Al had outlined to the General the night before.

"They were up half the night getting the flight plan changed. Let's hope that this route will work out and we have light losses today. If that happens, you'll be a hero," Colonel Hatfield whispered to Al as he leaned over to him.

"Won't you get the credit, Colonel?" Al asked.

Colonel Hatfield's eyes turned cold for an instant. He began to laugh and clapped Al on the shoulder. "You're learning, Al. If we fuck up, you get the blame. If we do well, I'll take some credit, but I'll see that you get your share too."

Al's southern plan worked. The twenty four B-24s avoided heavy flak fields and the German fighters were less of a threat. After taking only two passes at the bombers, the fighters left. The B-24s returned home triumphantly, without a single loss.

General Lamott stood on the runway tarmac where Colonel Hatfield's plane came to a stop, to welcome the flyers.

"Congratulations," the General greeted Colonel Hatfield. "This Columbus Day raid seems to have been the most successful raid we've made that deep into Germany. Maybe, just maybe, we've broken the back of the German fighter resistance."

The General shook hands with every member of the crew. When he came to Al, he said, "Young man, the route you suggested worked. I'll put you through for a promotion. When Major Wolfe is rotated back to stateside in a couple of months, you may be in line for his job."

Al flew two more missions with Colonel Hatfield on October 13th and 24th. They were milk runs because they were protected by P-38s.

General Lamott gave a party for Colonel Hatfield when he finished his twenty-fifth mission. The Colonel received the Distinguished Flying Cross and an immediate transfer to Eighth Army Headquarters for an imminent transfer back to the States.

Al envied the Colonel's chance to go back home. He missed Mary and the boys immensely, and lived for Mary's letters that kept Al informed of the boys' doings. Al knew he had seventeen missions ahead of him before he could begin to think about going home. A long cold winter loomed ahead for Al as he waited

Robert Miller

day by day for new flight assignments. Not all the ensuing missions were as smooth as the most recent ones.

On the same day they celebrated Colonel's Hatfield's safe completion of his 25th mission, a ghostly pall settled over the crews. Other elements of the Eighth Air Force attacked a ball bearing works in Schweinfurt in full force and were decimated. Sixty of the 300 B-17s, one out of five planes, had been shot down. The mission turned into a shattering loss.

A rumor, which proved to be true, had the airmen talking about the new German twin engine ME-210 fighters which were equipped with cannons that could destroy a bomber from well out of the range of the bombers' turret machine guns. The news of the more deadly new German fighters frightened Al and his fellow crew members.

CHAPTER 78

With Col. Hatfield gone, Al was put back with Jim Brogan'screw.

The next mission's target was the port of Antwerp. The route was largely over water and carried fighter protection.

The American bombers encountered intense flak over the target and some planes were hit, but all managed to drop their bombs and make it back to the base.

After the debriefing, the orders of the day included the promotions of Jim Brogan to Captain and Steve Johnson to First Lieutenant. Together with Al's promotion to Captain the day before, the three men had reason to celebrate.

"Al, you're one lucky goddamn son-of-a-bitch," Jim Brogan summed up his thoughts after two beers. "You fly with the Colonel and write about each mission. You get two promotions in a week or so. Then, you come back and fly with us and we get promoted. You were lucky you weren't in the nose of the Colonel's plane when that got blown apart. I'm sure you're going to make it through this goddamn war!"

Their gaiety over the promotions was tempered by the pervasive fear of the odds of surviving the missions yet to come.

"We're in a sort of purgatory," Jim Brogan pronounced in a lightheaded, beery swagger. "We're half way home. Get through the next half and we're sent home." He reiterated his mathematical philosophy in which they each had one chance in three of something happening. One in three of making it safely through the next twelve missions. One in three of being killed. One in three of being wounded or shot down. Yet all the statistics meant nothing if it was your turn to die. The airmen knew that the Germans would be trying to kill them before they reached home.

On Al's ninth mission, one of the twenty-four B-24s got shot down. The mission was still considered successful. Still, the loss of one bomber brought a pallor of gloom. Some officer had to pick up the effects of the airmen who did not return. He then wrote a letter to their next of kin. Worse, the other airmen had to look at the empty beds of the missing crew members, until new airmen came in to occupy them.

After his tenth mission, Al received an Oak Leaf Cluster for his Air Medal and was given a five day pass. The pass provided a temporary relief from the base, but it only extended his stay in England away from Mary and the boys.

Each flight had its periods of incomprehensible horror when the German fighters attacked and clouds of flak surrounded the bombers. Death's imminence had to be accepted philosophically, but it made for an air of constant tension for the crews. War became a macabre pattern - fly some missions; bomb targets in France, Belgium, Holland or Germany; pray that no planes are hit; then get to spend five days in London. The problem was that planes were shot down on most missions and some friends were lost.

When Al returned to Tunbridge Wells after one five day pass to London, he found that he had been appointed Wing Navigator, which meant he would fly fewer missions and be in on the planning for each ensuing mission. He was told he could fly one mission per week until he had completed his twenty five missions. When he flew, he would be in the lead plane of the squadron. After that, he would remain as Wing Navigator for another two or three months before being rotated home. By then, he would be promoted to Major.

But Al would have preferred to do without the promotion and get the missions done more quickly. With his new assignment, he wrote to Mary that he estimated completing his missions by early February and be back home by the end of June, 1944.

However, war is unpredictable and Al's plans could not be so easily calculated.

By the time Al completed his twenty fifth mission, Jimmy Doolittle had become Commanding General of the Eighth Air Force. General Doolittle changed the rotation period from twenty five to thirty five missions. Al had no choice but to continue as Wing Navigator, which involved long nights of intense planning and attendance at every briefing. He still flew one mission a week.

The night before one mission, Al found sleep difficult. He knew he had planned the missions as thoroughly as possible. He always felt terribly tormented that his luck would run out, that he might not just be killed, but that he could be horribly wounded and crippled for life. He couldn't decide which was worse: Being killed instantaneously, or being severely wounded. When he did sleep he dreamed that he'd fought off German fighters and flak. He woke frightened, disturbed, and tired.

Al's letters from his wife and mother during these months expressed their fears for him, but they also buoyed him greatly. They spoke of their pride for his missions and his stories that appeared in newspapers back home. Al received the first letter he had ever received from his father which commended him and stated how proud he and his mother were of his accomplishments in the air and in his journalistic endeavors.

In February and March, Al's raids began to change from forays into Germany to bombing the channel ports and defenses the Germans had been building on the French coast to repel a forthcoming Allied invasion. Everyone knew there would be an invasion, but nobody knew when or precisely where.

The skies had become safer. American bombers still got shot down on most raids, mostly by flak. The American and British fighters now dominated the skies over northern France. It was a rare day when the German fighters would rise to attack the bombers.

The planned raids were shorter and safer, which allowed most planes to return unscathed.

Al completed his 34th mission on May 31st and his 35th mission on D-Day when streams of heavy bombers attacked the German positions and rail yards along the invasion coast. Al's target was the Norman town of St. Lo. He flew over the invasion beaches. He was thrilled to participate in the D-Day invasion in his own way.

As his bomber headed back to base, Al knew his last mission was finished. He thought back over the eight plus months in England and the flights over Germany, France, Holland, and Belgium. He had earned seven Air Medals, a Distinguished Flying Cross, a Purple Heart, three promotions, which took him from Second Lieutenant to Major, and some renown both in his outfit and back home in the newspaper world because of the articles he had written for the Scripps Howard Newspapers.

On the flight deck, Captain Brogan gave Al a broad grin and a thumbs-up sign that everything was okay. Al smiled proudly and returned the thumbs-up sign. Al felt a little closer to home.

Robert Miller

CHAPTER 79

The following week, Al participated in the selection of a new Wing Navigator who would replace him towards the end of June, a captain with twelve missions. Al's orders were to transfer to Mitchell Field on Long Island. He was granted a twenty day leave that would commence on his arrival in the United States. Al hoped that he would get orders to fly back to the States in time for his eighth wedding anniversary on June 27, 1944.

Al missed getting back for his anniversary. Instead he had to report to Southampton, England on June 29th for sea transportation back to the States. He would be sailing back on the Queen Mary. The luxury liner had been transformed into a grey troop carrier that had just brought over almost 15,000 American soldiers to England and now was converted into something of a hospital facility as it carried back about a thousand wounded Americans with their doctors and nurses.

As a Major, Al was given luxurious accommodations. He was told he would have unlimited access to the main deck to soak up the sun. He could also enjoy the better meals served in the officer's dining room compared to the meals in the mess hall.

During his free time, Al interviewed dozens of American servicemen about their experiences fighting the Germans in France. There were soldiers who had been blinded or had lost arms or legs. Despite the suffering from their wounds, many were happily looking forward to returning home.

Al found out there were some German prisoners of war aboard and asked to interview them.

"It is strictly forbidden for anyone to speak to the prisoners," Captain Bert Cohen told Al.

Al thought about the irony of the situation. Captain Cohen was a Jewish soldier from the Bronx who was now in charge of the Nazi soldiers. The Captain told Al he had been spending the last year and a half escorting prisoners from

Africa and Italy to the United States on six occasions. This was his first trip escorting them out of England. Both men agreed there would likely be many more trips now that the invasion of Europe had started.

That night at dinner, Al showed Bert Cohen a copy of the article he had written. The Captain seemed quite pleased with what Al had written and asked where it would appear.

"Once it gets past the censors, it'll probably run in the *New York World Telegram*," Al said.

Captain Cohen was impressed. He mentioned to Al that a few of the prisoners spoke some English and maybe he could arrange for Al to talk to one of them.

Al spent much of the next day in the bowels of the ship talking to Master Sergeant Werner Koch of the German Tank Corps, the Panzers. Koch had fought in Poland, France, Yugoslavia, Russia, and again, in France. The German Sergeant thought the German soldiers were better than the Russians or Americans.

But the Sergeant conceded, "There are just so many of you. I don't see how we can prevail. I was on the cliff overlooking the American landing beach when your troops came ashore at Normandy. My commanders told us we could wipe you all out and I believed them, until I saw so many ships on the horizon. I think you had more ships than we had soldiers. It was like the war in Poland in 1939 all over again, except this time we were the Poles, outgunned, outmaneuvered, and with equipment not as good nor as much as yours. Three days of battle on Normandy convinced me that Germany was bound to lose the war. I am glad to be alive and on my way to America. I feel now that I will live to survive the war. So many of us are dead and so many more will die. What a pity."

"Do you hate the Jews?" Al asked, with the emphasis on the word "you."

"How can I hate the Jews?" The Sergeant looked at Captain Cohen and spoke softly. "I am under the command of Captain Cohen, an American soldier, and I presume a Jew. I went to school with Jewish boys in Stuttgart. I liked some of them and didn't like others. If Hitler wanted to sacrifice the Jews to build a better Germany, I wasn't crazy enough to try to defend the Jews. If I had, I'd have spent the last years in a tougher camp than where I am likely going now."

Al shook hands with the Sergeant, thanked him for the interview and told him his name would not appear in the article. The Sergeant was taken away by two guards and locked in the enclosure on the bottom deck that held the one hundred or so prisoners. Al went back upstairs and thanked Captain Cohen for allowing him to interview the German.

Al reflected on the fate of the German prisoner. The Sergeant had no future until the day the war was over and he could return home. What kind of home would he be returning to? What kind of country would there be? German cities were being bombed to oblivion by the very bombs that came from Al's plane. There would be a different government. Al speculated that Ike would lead the troops to victory in Europe, along with the likes of the determined General Patton. In the continued speculation of winners and losers, Al felt confident that the Allies would win. Many of Koch's friends and relatives might have been killed. All of Hitler's hate had amounted to nothing. Hitler had taken his own people down a dangerous road that had to end in self-destruction for millions of the German people. Al saw how the bulk of the Germans, like the Sergeant, had been too afraid to stand up to Hitler themselves. Hitler was on the road to destroying Germany.

On the other hand, Al had finished his personal goal of retribution by bombing Germany and Berlin. He was happy for a respite from the war and to be heading home to his wife, his children, a new life, and a new career.

CHAPTER 80

After a fine dinner in the officers' mess, Al played with the radio dials and found he could hear most New York stations, including WEAF, WJZ and WNEW. He peered out into the blackness and could see no sign of the shore, which he could sense was not very far away. Then he went back to his quarters, got his things together for an easy departure the next morning and turned in before 10:00 P.M. Whether it was from the excitement of coming home or the fact that he had slept so much in the sun the previous day, Al found it hard to drift off to sleep. When he awakened, he turned on the light and found it was barely past 3:00 A.M.

He tossed and turned for some time, then felt the rhythm of the ship change and he realized that the ship's engines were quiet. Al quickly got up, showered, dressed, and went out on deck.

He was astonished at the sight. The Queen Mary stood still in the Narrows between Staten Island and Brooklyn. After its lonely voyage across the Atlantic, it now seemed to be engulfed in a sea of ships in the harbor, all apparently being assembled for a convoy or perhaps the ships and convoy had recently arrived and were waiting to unload. The sight of all these ships thrilled Al. He looked around, first at the hundreds of ships he could see, then at the shore where he could make out Fort Hamilton to his right, Staten Island to his left and a dim, barely visible Manhattan some miles ahead. The Queen Mary remained in its place for awhile as tugboats approached it. Al assumed that a pilot was about to come aboard, but then he realized that a huge barge was being brought alongside with armed guards and he became aware that the German prisoners were being off-loaded.

Al thought for a few minutes about his interview with the German Sergeant and reflected on the differences of their situations. They were almost exactly the same age. The sergeant has been a soldier for some eight years, fought many battles, saw his comrades die, and now he is a prisoner in a strange and far away land and likely be a prisoner for two or three more years. Yet, Al is returning home a hero with a Major's gold leaf on his shoulders and a host of decorations on his chest. A beautiful and loving wife and sons were waiting to greet him. As Al watched the shuffling sullen German prisoners leave the ship and board the barges that were to transport them ashore, he thought of the planes that he had seen go down over Germany and the men who escaped the planes in parachutes only to face similar fates as these German prisoners.

Long before the first hint of sun crept into the eastern sky, the prisoners were headed toward Fort Hamilton. The ship remained motionless in the outer harbor until well after the sun rose at which point the harbor pilot boarded the huge vessel, which was soon guided by tugboats, to make its way slowly between the myriad group of ships in the harbor toward the Statue of Liberty. The Manhattan skyline became clearly visible in the distance as the Queen Mary turned toward the Hudson River. Al positioned himself on an upper deck to soak up the sight of his own home town on this bright sunny morning that marked the nation's one hundred and sixty-eighth birthday, July 4, 1944.

Al looked back at the Statue of Liberty and silently spoke to the great lady that guards the harbor that the United States was prevailing in this war and that indications were that the nation that had contributed the statue to New York harbor would very soon be entirely liberated by American, British, and free French soldiers.

As the huge ship moved ever so slowly north along the city's west side, Al began to wonder. How long will it take me to disembark? How will I get up to the Bronx? Should I surprise everyone? Then Al remembered that his mother had written that they now owned a car and Al suddenly was struck by the thought, What if they all went on a picnic somewhere on the 4th of July? How will I get into the apartment? How long might I have to wait?

After sailing north along the Hudson past the familiar landmarks as the Empire State and the RCA buildings, the mighty liner began to slowly turn to her right and, assisted by the tugboats, enter the Cunard slip on the west end of 54th street. Al saw and heard a welcoming band playing for them at pier side and he saw a fleet of ambulances and other vehicles awaiting the liner's arrival. As the ship slowly arched over to the pier, Al could hear the band playing *Stars and Stripes Forever*, and then *The Sidewalks of New York*, and he could see all sorts of activity in the pier area as the ship moved closer to its berth. As he peered out from the upper deck and looked into the bustling crowd, he heard a screech that carried over the noise of the band calling his name.

"Allie!" it shouted. "Allie, we're here on the balcony! Allie, don't you see us?!"

Al's eyes followed the sound of the scream and he was positively amazed to see his mother waving frantically from a small portico above the main pier, as she stood there surrounded by Mary, Selwyn, Billy, Opal Mae Monahan, Al's

Clash of Cultures - The Al Gordon Story

father, Shirley and Aunt Mollie. When Al recognized them, he began to frantically wave back. Mary now pointed Al out to the children as she lifted each of the boys so they could better see their father. Al managed to scream down to Mary to wait there, that it might take him some time to "clear" the ship, but for all of them to wait there. As the ship actually bumped against the berth, Al dashed back to his stateroom, got his luggage and papers, and headed ashore. He had to present his orders to an officer aboard the ship, who checked them and let Al disembark. He then proceeded down the gangplank to another desk where he presented his orders to the port officer.

The officer studied Al's papers carefully, then he told Al, "Welcome home Major. Your orders are to report to Mitchell Field on July 24th. I am extending your leave and changing your papers so that you will not have to report until August 17th. Now, go to the pay clerk at window #4 across the hall. They will pay you for the period since the last time you were paid through the month of August. Then you are on leave. Enjoy it. Welcome back to the United States of America, Sir."

Al walked over to the paymaster who, upon presentation of Al's orders, made some calculations and counted out several hundred dollars in cash and gave it to Al who then picked up his bags and walked towards a low barrier behind which Mary, the boys, and the rest of Al's welcoming committee were waiting. Al began to run, dropped his bags and didn't bother to retrieve them as he rushed towards Mary and enveloped her in his arms. As he held her close, he was informed that he would have to present his papers to the Military Policeman on duty there. Al temporarily interrupted his embrace, went back and picked up his bags, presented his papers to the M.P. and once more stepped through the barrier and back into Mary's arms.

Mary's hugs and kisses were warm and her eyes sparkled as she stepped back and let Al embrace the boys. Selwyn had grown much bigger in Al's absence of over a year and Billy didn't seem to recognize Al at all, and had started to cry as he saw Al's first embrace of his mother. Now Al picked up Little Bill who screamed even louder and Al handed Billy back to Mary, while he embraced his parents, sister, aunt, and mother-in-law.

Al then stepped back and knelt down to Selwyn's level and asked him if he had missed him and taken good care of his mother. Selwyn held his father close and asked him, "How many Nazis did you kill, Dad?"

Al laughed and told his son, "Not a one. All I did was direct the plane where to go. I didn't drop the bombs. Someone else did that. How many people were killed by our bombs I don't know and I'll never know."

"Mother read a story to me from the newspaper that said you dropped bombs on Berlin yourself," Selwyn said, and then asked, "Didn't you kill people that day?"

"I had forgotten about that. Maybe I did," Al told his son and then hugged him again. Al went to Billy and asked him if he had a hug and kiss for daddy. Bill hung back for a moment and then put his arms around Al's neck.

Al then turned to the group around him and asked, "However did you all know that I was coming on the Queen Mary today?"

Mary responded with a soft giggle and said, "We didn't know for sure, but your mother kept calling Scripps Howard and asking if they knew when you would be back and finally someone in their office managed to find out that you had been ordered to Southampton about the time that the Queen Mary sailed and he said you might be on it.

Then she got Scripps Howard to give us all press passes to get on the pier and welcome you. Aren't you glad we're here to meet you?"

"I sure am, but I never expected that. It's too much," Al laughed.

Al's father began counting heads. "I have a car outside and we all barely squeezed into it coming down. Let's put your bags into the trunk of my car and I'll drive everyone home except you and Mary. Here's a dollar for your cab fare. Treat yourself and take a taxi home to our apartment."

Al helped to load his bags into his father's 1941 Oldsmobile and watched the five adults and two children pile into it. The two children protested and wanted to come in the taxi with their parents and, in the end, Al and Mary relented and the children climbed out of the Oldsmobile while Al hailed a taxi. Al and his family clambered into the taxi and were on their way.

Al enjoyed a hug and a warm, wet exciting kiss in the taxi with Mary until she pulled away from Al and told him to "save that until later", and then commented on how well he looked. "I think you've actually gained weight. I thought of you as starving in England and lacking a decent meal." Al told her that any weight he had gained had been gained at the officers' mess on the Queen Mary during the past five days.

Mary informed Al that she had booked the bridal suite at the Concourse Plaza Hotel for them starting tonight, which, she told Al, got his mother's nose slightly out of joint, but, in the end, she said she understood, but asked that Al and Mary spend the day with them and get the children off to bed before they'd leave for the night. Mary also gave Al the sad news that his grandmother had died in January but that no one had wanted to write and tell him that while he was overseas.

Selwyn told Al that his article about the raid on Berlin had been read to his class at school and posted on the bulletin board in his classroom for the rest of the school year. Al could sense the boy's pride and was delighted with it. By this time, as the cab proceeded up through Harlem and into the Bronx, Billy was warming to his father whom he had apparently completely forgotten.

Mary seemed thinner and paler to Al, but her eyes sparkled. Al held Mary close to him as they bantered with the children who bounced around the back seat of the cab and seemed to be enjoying pulling out the folding seats in the spacious old DeSoto taxi.

Mary filled Al in on the happenings of her friends and family during the eleven long months since they had seen each other. Much of the news Mary had for Al was a rehash of things she had already written him, but she also gave him news that she had held back from him while he was in England, like the death of her friend Marjorie Leahy's brother, Ed Pat, who was in the Marines and was killed in the assault on Tarawa. She told Al of other boys she had known who were in various armed forces around the world, but Al was little affected by news of people he didn't know although he surely did remember Marjorie Leahy and her brother, Ed Pat, too.

When they approached the turn off the Grand Concourse onto Eastburn Avenue, Al saw his father unloading the car and all of the family and more than a dozen neighbors gathered around it ready to greet Al. When the taxi pulled up, they cheered. Al was shocked, but he realized that he must have been one of the first boys from the neighborhood to have returned safely home from overseas. He was overwhelmed with the greetings from people he barely knew. Many of them, mothers of people Al knew, told him where their sons were serving and at least two of them asked Al if he had seen Sheldon or Herman while he was in England. Al shook many hands before he was able to enter the apartment building and make his way up to his parents' apartment.

When he got upstairs, he found the apartment full of people. Al's parents were busy setting out food that had been delivered from the delicatessen. His mother prepared a cold lunch for the family and the steady parade of guests who arrived to greet Al and welcome him home. Al had eaten breakfast aboard the Queen Mary four hours before, but as he watched the delicacies spread out on platters, he suddenly realized how hungry he was. Mary and the boys were at his side every minute as he greeted the friends and neighbors who stopped in and then the various cousins, aunts, and uncles who began to arrive. Al found himself being greeted effusively by most of them.

Al realized his celebrity status was caused more by the articles he had written than anything else. People kept referring to them and asking pointed questions about individual bombing missions that Al had been on and had described in his articles. Standing in his mother's apartment, the place he had grown up in, eating a half sour New York delicatessen green pickle and talking with his father's brother, Uncle Dave, about a raid over Düsseldorf two months ago, Al felt truly bewildered. He just couldn't believe he was really home, in the Bronx.

Shirley's friends started coming in. They all made a fuss over Al, which he did not mind, but he felt Mary was getting irritated with the young girls' playful attention, so he disengaged himself from them and stayed close to Mary's side as the afternoon wore on.

Robert Miller

Al and Mary walked arm in arm from room to room greeting the guests; some stayed; others quickly arrived and left. As Al and Mary meandered around, clinging to each other and letting their bodies touch, the two little boys, Selwyn and Billy, trailed right behind them. Selwyn, especially, seemed bursting with pride that his daddy was home and enjoying the reflected glory of being the oldest son of the returning hero.

Al finally maneuvered Mary into a bedroom away from everyone else, closed the door and took her into his arms. "Did you say something about the honeymoon suite at the Concourse Plaza?" he asked her and then added, "What time did you reserve it for? Why are we hanging around here? Can we leave now?"

Mary put her arms around Al, pressed close to him and said, "Are you tired of your sons already? They have talked about nothing else for weeks than your coming home. You've been so busy flirting with Shirley's friends you haven't said two words to my mother or, for that matter, your mother, or Aunt Mollie who has spent the whole day in the kitchen slicing bread for this party in your honor. And you want to leave already? Not a chance. Not till the boys are ready for bed. Then you and I will go to the hotel and have all night to get reacquainted." Al pressed her close to him and ran his hands over her body and told her, "We have a lot of reacquainting to do and I want to start now." Mary kissed him and let him run his hands over her breasts and her buttocks. When he tried to put her hands on the bulge in his pants, she pushed him away and kissed him again. "Shame on you," she murmured playfully. "Honey, you're going to have to calm yourself down. I can't wait either, but we're here in your parents apartment, enjoying their party. I just need you to act like a respectable war hero at least three more hours." She gave him a deep, lingering kiss. When she broke away slightly, she added, "Tonight, we can begin to think of what we may have missed in the last eleven months and make up for lost time." Mary hugged Al again and began to laugh. "Oh, Al, I missed you so. I want to make love so much, but I can't do it here, not yet." She took a deep breath. "Please, go on now, my handsome war hero. Play with the children." She looked down and realized Al had grown uncontrollably excited from her kiss.

Al and Mary shared a giggle over Al's excitement for Mary. He told her, "Don't you wonder how I managed for the last eleven months without having you to tell me what to do and how to do it?"

"Why do you think I wrote you all those letters?" Mary quipped.

CHAPTER 81

Al and Mary stayed in the apartment until dark, which in those days of double Daylight Saving Time (called War Time) came well after 9 P.M. By then, the company had thinned out and the boys were ready for bed. Mary and Al packed a small case and started down the Grand Concourse to the hotel about two miles away.

Al saw a cab and hailed it. Mary began to giggle.

"Are you sure you don't want to walk?" Mary asked playfully as the cab pulled up.

As Al settled into the cab with her, he took her into his arms and kissed her, moving his hands over her body and guiding one of her little hands over his pants.

Mary touched the bulge in Al's pants and said in pretended innocence, "Oh, is that the reason for the hurry? Well, sweetheart, be patient a few minutes more, and we'll see what we can do about that."

They checked into the hotel and were ushered into the honeymoon suite by the same elderly Irish bellhop who had escorted them to the same suite on their honeymoon some eight years before.

Inside the suite, Mary leaned close to Al and put her arms around him. Her kiss enveloped his lips. Her mouth opened to Al's. Mary paused for a breath and told Al, "My hero is home. Let's get out of these clothes and make up for the last eleven months of misery." And, so they did.

In twenty minutes, Al was spent and fast asleep on the rumpled bed.

Al stirred awake later and found Mary sitting in a chair.

"Sweetheart, what are you doing out of bed?" Al mumbled sleepily. "Come back to bed and lie close to me. I haven't been this close to you in such a long time."

Mary turned out to be in the mood for earnest conversation, not lovemaking.

"Why did you pick the name Selwyn for our first son?" Mary asked solemnly.

"Why? I thought we picked it together. You wanted to name him Alfred Emmanuel Gordon, Jr., and I wanted to name him for my grandfather Shalman and we tried to find an Americanization of the name. Selwyn came to mind when I mentioned that we used to live on Selwyn Avenue before we moved to Eastburn Avenue. Why do you ask me now? The question seems to be coming out of the blue."

Al could see that Mary sat motionless. Tears formed in her eyes.

"I found some letters when I was cleaning your mother's closet. Maybe you want to call it snooping, but they were already open and addressed to you. They were from Selma. Why is she keeping them? Obviously you were romancing Selma at the same time as you were getting ready to marry me. I can't tell you how upset those letters made me feel. Then I came to realize that you named your first son after your old girlfriend, Selma. I was shocked," Mary said in a hurt tone. A pathetic look crossed her face.

Al laughed and reached out for Mary.

"Darling," he said tenderly and with more alertness. "How can you be so silly? I haven't thought of Selma in years. I surely never thought of her when we named Selwyn." He reached his arm out to her. "For God's sake Mary! Don't be silly. Throw those damn letters away and don't give them another thought. You are the only person I have ever loved and the only person I will ever love. Don't torture yourself with foolishness and don't torture me. I love you so much and I've missed you more than you could ever know. I've survived thirty-five bitter cold, frightening life-and-death missions to come home and fall into your arms. I don't want to hear another word now or ever about Selma or any another woman. You are my only love and my one true love. And, I want you to take that robe off and get back into bed beside me and let me hold you in my arms again and I want you to forget all that foolishness."

Mary shivered, got up and sat down on the edge of the bed next to Al.

"If you only knew how I want to believe you, Al. I've been so unhappy these last few days before you got home. I really didn't want to spoil your homecoming, but I can't get the thought out of my mind that you named Selwyn after Selma," Mary said softly.

"That is a ridiculous thought and simply not true," Al reassured her softly. "Please, Mary. Please come into the bed and lie down close to me and let me prove how much I love you."

Mary did as Al asked. Ten minutes later, after some more lovemaking, Al had fallen back to sleep. Mary nudged him again.

"What?" Al mumbled.

"What do you think that proved?" Mary asked.

Al tried to think of an answer, but he collapsed back to sleep before any answer occurred to him.

Mary remained unsatisfied, either by Al's answers or his hasty episodes of lovemaking that brought her to the brink but ended in frustration before she could reach an orgasm.

Al woke to find himself in a big empty bed with sunlight flooding into the room. He found Mary in the sitting room, fully dressed, looking relaxed, cheerful and perusing the *New York Times*.

"What time is it?" Al asked, squinting his eyes from the bright light.

"Time for breakfast," Mary told him as she got up and kissed him warmly. "You take a shower and I'll order from room service. What would you like for your first breakfast at home?"

"I'll have some more of your sweetness," Al replied happily.

Mary hugged him tight and commented, "My insatiable hero!" She kissed him again. "You flew thirty-five missions over Europe in ten or eleven months, and now you've already flown three missions last night and want a fourth now." She kissed him again and told him, "All right, Al. I'll take off my clothes and make love to you one more time, but you've got to do one thing for me."

"What's that, sweetheart?"

"Let me be the navigator. You be the bombardier. And, for God's sake, don't drop your bombs until I tell you to," Mary said firmly.

This time their lovemaking worked better for Mary. She restrained Al from having his orgasm until she had hers. They lay in each others' arms dripping in sweat as Mary laughed aloud.

"I have really found the secret," Mary said proudly. "If I fuck you enough to wear you out, you'll be able to save your load until I'm ready. If that's what I have to do to give myself real satisfaction, I'm just going to have to keep doing it for a lifetime. Is that okay with you?"

She waited for Al's answer. It never came. He had fallen fast asleep again.

Al felt amazed how Mary could act like a prudish little girl and then turn around to act like a passionate, real woman, the next minute.

Robert Miller

CHAPTER 82

After Al woke up, he and Mary joined the family back at the apartment. From there, they all went to the Gordon Advertising Agency's new address on 57th Street, where the Gordons placed classified ads in the *New York Times, Journal-American,* and the other six or seven New York daily newspapers.

Al accompanied his father over to Broadway for a short meeting at Hill-Martin Dealership to meet the two partners who were among his most loyal clients. On the way, Al's father invited him to join him at Gordon Advertising Agency. Al replied that the Gordon Advertising business, which was mostly designing newspaper ads for automobile dealers, had never really appealed to him, but that he would rule nothing out right now.

Al's father introduced Al to Bill Hill and Hank Martin, who appeared to be in their early forties. Since metal was needed to build airplanes, tanks and military equipment, new cars had not been produced since the early months of 1942. The partners simply sold used cars. They advertised that they wanted to buy cars from people who didn't need them or who couldn't get gas for them and wanted to get rid of them. Mr. Gordon used the opportunity to tell Bill Hill and Hank Martin that he had just asked Al to join the firm after the war.

"You have no idea how proud of you your father is," Hank Martin told Al. "He told us about your heroic accomplishments overseas. You know, your father is a wonderful man who has helped us build our business."

"You couldn't do better," Bill Hill assured Al. "Your father is one of the best. He's building a solid foundation for you."

Mr. Gordon went on to talk to the two partners about Al's two boys. Al saw for the first time how, away from his mother, his father seemed more animated and totally different from what he had ever seen at home. Al sat there enjoying the experience of watching and learning entirely new facets of his father's personality and character.

After getting back to the office in Manhattan, Mr. Gordon took the whole family to Joe Romano's, a small Italian restaurant on West 54th Street. He told Al the place had once been a speakeasy. At the restaurant, one of Mr. Gordon's friends came up to the Gordons' table and said a quick hello to the six Gordons and Mrs. Monahan. He joked, "I'm glad I don't have to pay your check for lunch."

Al's father beamed and said, "I'm delighted to host my son and his family for lunch. He just got back from England yesterday and we're so proud of him and so grateful for his safe return."

After lunch, Al broke away from the family to visit the Scripps Howard offices. There he met Bart Henderson, a short, squarely built middle-aged man with white hair who introduced himself as the managing editor of Scripps Howard's New York office. Their conversation came around to discussing the war in the Pacific. Mr. Henderson encouraged Al to take a tour of duty in the Pacific and send in more war stories from the Pacific area.

Al laughed at the idea of putting his life at risk again just to write newspaper stories. He had never been an adventure-seeking war correspondent.

"You're probably right," Al paused to reflect. "The war has sold lots of newspapers. It's helped make many newspapermen, like myself, more famous than we would have been without a war."

"The war's going on in the Pacific. You could give us some great coverage there," Mr. Henderson exhorted.

Al replied, "I've seen too many men die to get any satisfaction out of the war. Anyhow, I'm home for a while. I'm going to enjoy my wife and children before I put my ass on the line again to get a by-line in the newspaper."

Bart Henderson gave Al an understanding look and shook his hand as the conversation ended. "I deserved that, Al. You surely are entitled to your home leave. But, I want you to know I'd give my right nut to get an overseas assignment instead of sitting at this desk. I envy guys like you and the other war correspondents. Just keep sending me articles when you can."

Al asked Mr. Henderson if he could help him get some gas rations while he visited his family here and in Texas. The old newspaperman pledged to do more, starting with getting him airline priorities, reservations, and enough gas coupons to drive from Texas to New York and back with coupons left over.

Before Al left, Mr. Henderson put his hand on Al's shoulder.

"Listen, Al. Just keep writing. When you get out of the service, come back to us. We'll have a good and interesting job for you, maybe right here in New York, if you want it," Mr. Henderson said kindly.

Al felt elated by the meeting. He shared the good news with the family back at the apartment. Everyone encouraged Al to keep writing his stories, but the senior Gordons wouldn't give up trying to recruit him for the family business.

Robert Miller

The only disappointment for the senior Gordons came when Al and Mary told them they planned to fly down to Texas and take a leisurely tour of the country and visit various friends and relatives on the way back. Mrs. Gordon wanted to plan a big welcome home party for her son.

"I thought we had that party yesterday," Al joked.

"That was just an impromptu get together," his mother said. "We'll have a real party when you come back home."

Al and his mother agreed to set the date of August 13th for the official welcome home party.

Al, his family, and Mrs. Monahan had been booked on United Airlines. The twenty-one passenger DC-3 left LaGuardia Airport in New York and landed in Cleveland two hours later. After a thirty minute stop, the plane continued on to Chicago, and then to St. Louis, arriving there at midnight, where they had to wait for a Chicago and Southern Airlines plane to pick them up and take them in local hops about an hour each to Memphis, Little Rock, Shreveport, and Houston.

They arrived in Houston on Tuesday morning at about 8:00 A.M. It had been a long night for the children, but Mary marveled at how the airplane could make the 1500 mile trip in fourteen hours, compared to a four-day trip by car or a two-nights-and-a-day trip by train. The airlines spoke of having bigger planes after the war that would carry more passengers and fly longer distances nonstop, but the whole idea seemed fanciful.

Al, Mary, and the boys spent a busy week in Houston visiting Mary's friends, some of whom had lost sons or brothers in the war. Though they expressed happiness for Al and Mary, Al detected jealousy too in some of their eyes.

The children were delighted to be back with their grandfather Monahan, who had a way of captivating Selwyn and Billy completely. Al found himself wanting to establish his paternal assertiveness, but he ended up only being envious of his father-in-law's relationship with the children and, more than that, Mr. Monahan's uncanny knack of communicating with them so much better than Al. Al recognized that this was Mr. Monahan's time to enjoy being a grandfather. He felt sorry for his father-in-law when Mary and the boys had to pile into the car and head away at the end of the week.

Two days later, Al registered himself and his family into the Cosmopolitan Hotel in Denver. From there, Al went over to meet with Bill Wannamaker at the *Rocky Mountain News*.

In the newsroom, Bill Wannamaker rose and hugged Al when he came into the office. He had a photographer take Al's picture and a reporter interview Al about his experiences in flying thirty-five missions over Nazi occupied Europe. Al relished all the attention he received from his old friends and the new workers.

The story with Al's picture appeared on page one of the *Rocky Mountain News* the next day.

Clash of Cultures - The Al Gordon Story

The picture and story led to a call from General Hatfield, who was at Buckley Field a few miles east of Denver.

"I was pleased to see your picture in the newspaper," General Hatfield said, greeting Al on the phone. "Where are you stationed? What are your immediate plans?"

Al explained that he was on leave and would be traveling back to Mitchell Field on Long Island by his report date of August 17th. After that, Al explained he had no idea what would be happening.

"I'm organizing a photo recon group long range that is going to get B-29's and be sent to the Pacific Theater towards the end of this year. I have an opening for a Group Navigator and you're my man. It'll mean a promotion to Lieutenant Colonel right away and then you'll become a full Colonel as soon as I get my second star. We've been lucky for each other, Al, and I want you on my team," the General said firmly.

The General's comments flattered Al. They concluded the conversation by agreeing that Al would bring his family by Buckley Field tomorrow to visit the General for an hour. When Al and his family arrived there, they were accorded VIP treatment and escorted directly to General Hatfield's stark but imposing office. The General did all he could to charm Mary.

"I owe this young man a great deal," General Hatfield told Mary. "And, I want him with me when I go out to the Pacific in a big new B-29 in a few months. The General took Mary's hands and explained gently, "I know how happy Al is to be home with you and these fine boys. I want you to enjoy his home leave. But, I want you to know his destiny is to fly over Tokyo as we did over Berlin, only this time, we won't be dropping bombs. We'll be taking pictures to ascertain the results of our bombing."

Mary mumbled something to the effect that she hoped Al would get a safer job as an instructor or something like that.

The General laughed and told her, "Do you think it's any safer flying those crates they use in training than flying a B-29 over Japan? The B-29 flies higher and faster than anything the Japanese have. It's a great plane and it will be a clinical procedure...long boring flights and a few minutes over the target and nowhere near the danger we saw over Germany." Then his face softened. He smiled at Mary and asked her, "You wouldn't keep Al from doing his duty, fulfilling his destiny, building up his reputation as a newspaper correspondent, winning more medals and a promotion to Colonel, would you?"

"Do we have a choice?" Mary asked with a resigned smile.

"Of course you have a choice. Al can choose between going willingly or grudgingly, but I want Al to fly with me when I get out to the Pacific," General Hatfield said in a friendly but unmistakably firm manner. "I promise you, Mrs. Gordon, he'll bring me home safe and I'll bring him home safely. I promise you that."

Robert Miller

"When will you be leaving?" Mary asked.

"That's a military secret, Mary," the General said politely. "My guess is maybe November or December."

After enjoying lunch with the General at the Officers' Club, Al and his family packed themselves back into the car to head east to the Bronx. Al and Mary were silent for a time. Mary finally let out a sigh and said, "Well, I guess I'll have to cooperate with the General until I can get my husband back home."

"Just be patient, sweetheart. The war's not over," Al said softly.

Al's "destiny" came down to the General's wishes. He would be flying over Tokyo.

CHAPTER 83

Once Al and his family arrived back in New York City, Al became determined to make sure the family had fun, taking part in new adventures each day: Going to Jones Beach on Long Island, Orchard Beach, Playland, Coney Island, the Bronx Zoo, the Museum of Natural History, the Aquarium, and the Statue of Liberty, as well as attending three baseball games, all at different stadiums. He and Mary got tickets to see *Oklahoma!*, Broadway's biggest hit. They stayed at the Hotel Astor on Times Square for the night, which was not appreciated by the boys or Al's family.

Before they left the Hotel Astor, Mary came close to Al, kissed him and wanted to say something.

"Sweetheart, do you realize I haven't had my period? It's more than a week late."

"Could you be pregnant?" Al asked with a startled look.

"Well, in the light of the way we've spent a substantial part of the last month, I wouldn't be surprised," Mary said.

Her whole face then broke out into a bright smile that seemed to make the whole room glow for Al.

"Would you like a little girl?" Mary asked.

"Only if she'd be exactly the image of her beautiful mother," Al responded. Al reached out and enfolded Mary in his arms.

Robert Miller

CHAPTER 84

Al's new unit left for the Pacific early in December after flying nonstop from Salinas, Kansas, to Hawaii and then again nonstop from there to Guam. Al spent the following months on Guam with the 20th Air Force training to fly over Japan.

When General Otto Hatfield made Major General, a few days later Al was promoted to Lieutenant Colonel.

Mary was indeed pregnant. If it was a girl, they planned to name her Minella; a boy would be named David.

On Guam, Al enjoyed a reunion with his cousin Hermine's husband, Sidney, who was a staff sergeant on the same air base.

Al flew his first mission from Guam over Japan just before Christmas. The flights into combat on the B-29 were much different from his flights over Europe on B-24s. The B-29 was airtight and pressurized. The crew needed no oxygen masks. The heating system worked. Also, the long runs from Guam to Japan were over water, making the trips both comfortable and boring.

The crews reported no signs of fighters on Al's first mission over Tokyo. The flak was sporadic and never reached their level.

Al found himself in a B-29 converted into an elaborately finished photo plane with a darkroom fitted in what normally would have been the bomb bay. The photo plane had multiple purposes: photograph the target before bombs were dropped; go off to photograph another potential target; fly back over the original target to photograph the results of the bombing; and finally return to Guam at the tail end of the formation of superfortresses.

The added photography assignment required approximately 30 more minutes of flight time for each mission. The photo plane had to be modified to carry an extra gas tank. Al now found time to relax in the photo plane flying for eighteen hours at a time.

Al's plane led the formation of B-29 superfortresses. He took pictures of the target before and while the bombs were dropping. Another B-29 photo plane followed the mission and a photographer took photos of the results of the bombing. On the long tedious flights over the water, the photographs were developed, printed and enlarged aboard the aircraft. After six missions over Japan, the brass decided only one photo plane was required.

Al did his job of writing by sending back stories to Scripps Howard about the raids on Japan. The "Smoke Over Tokyo" story had been reprinted in newspapers all over the country that prominently mentioned Major General Hatfield who led that particular mission.

The Scripps Howard people were happy to be receiving Al's war stories and Hatfield was happy to be mentioned in each story.

When Al had time off, Sidney encouraged Al to attend Friday night services at the military tent where they were held. The Jewish chaplain, Captain Eisenberg, came from Brooklyn and, like Al, had served in the Eighth Air Force in England before coming out to the Pacific. Though Al attended Friday night services, he did so mainly to please his cousin Sidney, who actually shamed Al by telling him he was the highest ranking Jewish officer on the island and that it was his duty to meet and greet other Jewish airmen. But Al felt uncomfortable with the rituals associated with the services. Al wrote to Mary in his letters about his happiness at being reunited through Sidney with so many Jewish airmen.

Al only went so far in following Jewish religious customs. He made it clear after all these years that the whole idea of following rituals appalled him. He wrote to Mary about his basic belief in God, but he could never agree that God paid attention to rote and ritual as practiced by either the Jewish or Catholic religions. Al took on rituals as a burning issue, seeing them as "grievances" that man formulated and put in the way of the path to God.

Al explained his theories about religious rituals one day while having lunch at the officers' mess with Chaplain Eisenberg. The rabbi listened and reacted with a laugh, showing he had no pretense of offense.

"Colonel," the rabbi addressed Al. "You may have a Catholic wife and your sons may have been baptized as Roman Catholics, but you still have a Jewish heart. I think you carry some Yiddishkeit in your soul," the rabbi added jokingly. "That counts for points. Lots of them. God permits us to question, to disagree, to think for ourselves. What He asks from us is to be good to others and to love Him. I thank Sidney for bringing you back to the Jewish world and I welcome you to it."

"Does the Jewish world want me in it with my Catholic wife and Catholic children?" Al asked the rabbi pointedly.

"It certainly does, and there is no way you can ever escape it," Chaplain Eisenberg told him.

A question left up in the air that Al never asked himself was whether in any way he had been trying to escape his Jewishness. That question, once raised by Captain Eisenberg, bothered Al, but he found it easier to tuck it away in the back of his mind, left there for the time being. Was his antipathy to organized religion really his soul's rebellion, a rejection of his Jewishness? Or, was he trying to avoid anything that God expected of him, including certain observances and a contrite heart?

Al went on with his life and the war. He lived without finding answers to spiritual questions.

He continued to write news stories about his flights over Japan. Since the missions were not the tragic, awful, death-defying feats as the missions over Europe, Al found it hard to write exciting stories about his missions although there was a brutal enemy below that had to be destroyed as much as Nazi Germany had to be destroyed. He was simply not the same war correspondent writing about the war in Japan as he had been a year ago chronicling the horrendous battles raging in Europe.

By now, Al figured he was stuck on Guam as long as General Hatfield remained there. He continued to write articles about the General. Al received three more air medals for his fifteen missions over Japan. The General promised a promotion to full Colonel and a distinguished Flying Cross when he completed twenty-five missions.

Al spent much of his free time writing to Mary. He missed being away from eight year old Selwyn, and Billy who was approaching his fifth birthday. Minella, their baby girl, had been born in early April.

On May 7th, a month after their daughter was born, the war in Europe ended. The Army announced a point system by which people with the most children, the most medals, the most time overseas and the longest period of service would have preference for coming home. Al had enough points to get out of the service, but General Hatfield resisted.

"We're going to have bases on Iwo Jima and Okinawa that will make these flights easier and less boring," the General told Al. "You are my good luck charm. I won't sign that authorization. Stay with me until September and, if I still need you then, you'll get a promotion to Eagle Colonel. I'll then arrange leave for you in the States."

Al told the General that, of course, he would do what the General wanted him to do, but he admitted candidly his interests were in getting home permanently and resuming his civilian career more than becoming a full colonel.

General Hatfield smiled softly. "Why not consider a career in the Air Force after the war? One day the Air Force will be a separate service and will have missions that might include traveling the world. You can live the good life, serve twenty years and retire with good pay before you're fifty. It's something you ought to think about," the General suggested with a wily smile.

Al admitted to the General that it sounded inviting, but he ended by saying, "I'm a civilian newspaperman in my heart." Al thought it best to leave the

General with the impression that he would consider the options the General offered him.

Robert Miller

CHAPTER 85

Al settled into the routine of planning more missions that seemed about all the same and usually flying on those that the General decided to fly.

Between flights, Al spent time with Sidney and Chaplain Eisenberg. He also became friendly with First Lieutenant Tom Fahey, a young redheaded, Catholic Chaplain, from Worcester, Massachusetts. Al often had his meals with one or both of the Chaplains.

A tennis court had been rebuilt on the air base that offered some diversion from the tedious hours away from home. Father Fahey and Al spent more and more time playing tennis to the point that they were pretty proficient at the game.

Al counted his nineteenth mission over Japan on the last day of July as he flew with General Hatfield over the port of Yokohama with a load of firebombs.

His twentieth mission was over Tokyo on August 6th. A massive assault was going on at the same time as one plane, the Enola Gay, from Tinian dropped the atomic bomb on Hiroshima. That bomb changed Al's world, as it changed the entire world. Al overheard rumors that night about the big bomb when Al and the crew returned to their base on Guam. The full extent of the destruction of Hiroshima was not known until the official announcement the next day. The raids over Japan intensified in the following days.

General Hatfield and Al flew on a mission over Japan on August 8th to photograph the desolation of Hiroshima, which even from 25,000 thousand feet could be seen as almost total. After scanning the skies for possible enemy interceptors, the General brought the superfortress down to 12,000 feet to survey and photograph the dead city. Then they dropped farther down to 5,000 feet to survey the carnage that one bomb had caused. Vapor still rose from the gutted remains of buildings and from the ground itself.

Three days later, after a second atomic bomb had been dropped, this time on Nagasaki, the Japanese sent a delegation to discuss peace terms on Luzon in the

Philippines. General Hatfield found an excuse to fly to Clark Field in the Philippines to be near the action. He took Al with him.

Al found himself in his element. He was able to cover the important breaking news and was present with press credentials arranged by General Hatfield when the Japanese team arrived. He found out that the Japanese had nothing to negotiate. The Americans demanded one course of action - total surrender to the Americans and their allies. A surrender date was announced: August 14th. General Hatfield ordered his plane to be ready to fly back to Guam.

When they returned to Guam, the entire base seemed to be hung over after a wild celebration the day before. General Hatfield promptly ordered that his plane to be ready for another flight in two days. This time he ordered that all the extra weight be stripped from the plane and that it be fitted with new interior gas tanks for a long flight. It was obvious the General had plans other than sitting on Guam.

"Are we going somewhere I should know about?" Al wondered.

The General reached out to Al and actually hugged him quickly.

"To Tokyo! For the formal surrender. I'm in the process of getting clearance right now."

Al smiled in disbelief at the General's ambitious plans to be in Tokyo for such a momentous occasion.

"After the surrender," General Hatfield continued exuberantly, "We'll fly back to Guam immediately. I want my plane prepared to fly nonstop from here to Andrews Field in Washington, D.C. You are my luck, Al. We got through the war safe and sound. Your articles helped me get a promotion or two. Get me to Washington and I'll sign your papers so you can get out of the service and go back to that wonderful family of yours!"

After Al recovered from the surprise of the General's good news, he scrambled to get ready for the flight to the States. He selected Captain Tom Crawford as a backup navigator. Crawford's job was to plot the nonstop course to Washington, D.C., and to supervise the reconstruction of the photo superfortress into a lighter, faster plane to bring them to Washington.

CHAPTER 86

Japan was the place to be for an American General during those heady days when American officers poured into the city and prepared to take it over.

Al and General Hatfield stayed in adjoining rooms at the New Grand Hotel. The Japanese whom Al saw at the hotel were solemn, subservient, and extremely respectful of the newly-arrived Americans and their allies. Al found it perplexing to look at these gentle people and think of how he had perceived them as the ferocious enemies they had proven to be from Pearl Harbor to Okinawa.

Al ran into Roy Howard again, who recognized Al immediately and greeted him effusively.

"Our Colonel-Correspondent in the flesh!" Roy Howard exclaimed as he surprised Al with a quick hug. "Isn't this a great day? Will you be aboard the Missouri for the signing?"

Al shrugged his shoulders and said, "I presume that General Hatfield will arrange that for himself and for me."

"Good!" Roy Howard said. "But, I'm going to put you on my list too just to be sure." Mr. Howard changed the subject purposely. "What are your own plans? When will you get out of the Air Force?"

"Sometime next week, I think. General Hatfield and I may be in Washington by then. We're flying nonstop from Guam to Washington. He said he would sign my release papers in D.C.," Al explained. "I guess I'll be ready to go back to work full-time by October 1st." Al knew he had to ask for Mr. Howard's help at that moment. "Is there a job for me in New York, or Houston, or Denver?"

Roy Howard chuckled. He told Al that he could count on a job at whichever paper he chose, suggesting New York as the biggest and best opportunity.

"I'd give my right arm to hitch a ride with you and General Hatfield on your nonstop flight to Washington. Tell the General, if he takes me along, he can count on lots of ink on page one of all our newspapers."

Al gave him a big smile. He knew the notoriety would appeal to the General. The only hitch was that the General had planned to fly with a small crew to conserve fuel.

"You can also tell General Hatfield that, if he takes me along, I'll arrange for him to meet and, probably, get a medal from President Truman in the White House," Roy Howard added. The newspaperman knew when to lay his aces on the table.

"Knowing General Hatfield, I think I can speak for him and tell you that you'd be a most welcome passenger," Al said with a knowing smile.

When Al caught up with General Hatfield, he found his excitement tempered by some frustration. He was excited to be where history was being made. On the other hand, the General had become upset to learn that General LeMay, Commanding General of the 20th Air Force, had issued orders for all planes to remain in place. He had heard further that General LeMay was planning a nonstop flight from Tinian to the United States. General Hatfield did not want to appear to clash with or upstage his commanding officer, but he did not want to give up his planned trip to Washington either.

When Al told the General about Roy Howard's offer to come along in exchange for the major news value and a promised visit to the White House to see Truman, the General started pacing and thinking of his options. When he had calculated his options, he stopped to look at Al.

"Tell Mr. Howard that, if we make this flight, and I surely want to, he'll be my passenger and my co-pilot," the General said with a grin.

"If General LeMay doesn't want you to make this flight, how will you be able to do it?" Al asked with a puzzled look.

General Hatfield winked at Al. "I'll just have to find someone of higher authority than General LeMay to authorize the flight, won't I?" He patted Al on the back. "I'm going to see an old friend of mine at General MacArthur's headquarters. We'll see if we can't interest General MacArthur in having us fly back to Washington with the first photos of the Japanese surrender. You get busy in plotting a direct course from here to Washington," the General answered. He strode out to seek his contact.

In a few hours, General Hatfield met with Roy Howard and Al to explain the news from his meeting at MacArthur's headquarters. "I have informed General MacArthur that you will accompany us on our record flight and he will give you a copy of the surrender document, a personal memento, and a letter to President Truman to deliver to him on Monday. You will meet General MacArthur immediately following the surrender." The General turned to Al and asked, "How long will it take us to get to Washington?"

"About twenty-six hours," Al said.

General Hatfield's plan was set into motion. Al left immediately to make sure the B-29, which had been flown from Guam and was now being refurbished at the Atsugi Airport would be ready.

Tech Sergeant Joe Turner, the crew chief, greeted Al and explained, "We'll be lucky to get this sonovabitch off the ground as heavy as it is and as short as this runway is."

"How much gas do we have? How long can we fly?" Al asked.

"If we can get off the runway, we'll have gas to fly for some thirty hours with the new belly tanks we've installed. The goddamn plane will smell like a gas station. There'll be no room to sit or move around until we burn off the gas in the belly and jettison some of the empty tanks. But, the question is whether this fucker will lift itself off this short runway."

Al turned to Major Robert Cartwright, the co-pilot, and asked, "Will it lift off the runway?"

The Major responded like a man who didn't know how to worry about anything. "Colonel, if it doesn't, it'll be the biggest blast and fire to hit Japan since Nagasaki." Seeing the alarm in Al's face, the Major added, "Don't worry. The General and I will get the plane off the ground. It's up to you to direct us home."

Al relaxed and felt relieved. Al and Captain Crawford, the navigator, checked the course. If they wanted to arrive in Washington, D.C., at 7 A.M. on Monday, figuring a thirteen hour time difference, they would have to take off at 6 P.M. Sunday night Japan time. They navigated a course from Atsugi over the Pacific to Alaska, then over western Canada on a southeasterly course, over the Great Lakes and into Washington with a four hour reserve of fuel, in case of any unfavorable winds.

Al then reviewed the flight plan with Major Cartwright. It was decided that the crew would consist of seven members - three pilots, two navigators, Sergeant Turner and a radioman who would double as assistant engineer. Roy Howard would be the eighth person aboard for the record-making flight.

Before Al left the airport, he gave a long look at the massive B-29. He tried to size up his odds, that mental game of chances that he used to play between his combat flights over Europe. This flight amounted to one chance. The plane would make it or they would crash trying to make it home.

CHAPTER 87

Al had the papers from General Hatfield and the press credentials from Roy Howard. He would be aboard the Battleship Missouri for the Japanese surrender.

Mr. Howard had also left a note that he knew Al would appreciate. The note said Mary had been contacted and that she was flying from Houston to Washington on Sunday. She would meet him at Andrews Field Monday morning. Al could not believe how fast things were happening. As a skilled navigator, he loved calculating time, distance and the odds. He calculated that at 10 P.M. Saturday night in Tokyo it was 8 A.M. that morning in Houston. Mary would probably be on her way in about eight hours to Washington to meet him. She would probably be in Washington before he left Tokyo.

Al was seated with General Hatfield, his contingent, and Roy Howard aboard the Battleship Missouri as they waited to watch the momentous event of the two countries meeting to formally sign a peace treaty.

After the tedium of the long wait, suddenly General MacArthur, Admiral Nimitz, and General Wainwright appeared. MacArthur was without a tie and stood waiting as the Japanese representatives appeared before the three officers. General MacArthur tersely indicated to them where they should sign the instruments of surrender. They signed. Then General Wainwright signed. Then Admiral Nimitz signed. Then the representatives of the allied nations signed. The Japanese representatives left the Missouri. What was considered an awesome event lasted less than ten minutes. General MacArthur informed the group that "these proceedings are closed."

When the bulk of the audience had dissipated, an aide approached General Hatfield and escorted him and his party, including Al, into the ship itself. They were taken to a huge cabin where General MacArthur was holding court for a small group of major dignitaries. The aide introduced General Hatfield to MacArthur. General Hatfield then introduced MacArthur to Roy Howard, Al, and Major Cartwright.

Robert Miller

General MacArthur produced a copy of the surrender document for General Hatfield to take to President Truman and also gave him the pen he'd used to sign the document.

"You have witnessed a momentous event in world history today. Now, you are embarking on a flight which will set a new aviation record. I congratulate you in advance and ask you to convey my warmest wishes to President Truman and to the American people. Happy landings," MacArthur said to General Hatfield.

General Hatfield and MacArthur saluted each other. MacArthur shook hands with the crew and Roy Howard. An Army photographer took a picture of MacArthur with the crew and Mr. Howard.

On the deck of the Missouri, General Hatfield consulted with Roy Howard about the arrival time. Mr. Howard told the General that there would be a better picture if it was a day arrival, but a night arrival might rate some mention in the morning papers and more detailed coverage in the afternoon papers. A 7 A.M. landing, as originally planned, would be too late for any coverage in the morning papers.

"Let's go for it!" General Hatfield exclaimed to Al and Major Cartwright. So it was decided that the plane would leave at once.

When the General, his crew, and Howard got to the plane, they found they had another passenger, a naval officer from the Missouri who had just been notified his father had died in Bethesda, Maryland. He came with a letter from Admiral Nimitz, countersigned by General MacArthur, asking Hatfield to take Lieutenant Hannigan aboard the superfortress. Hatfield expressed his condolences to the young officer and ordered everyone, "Climb aboard!"

The way the plane lumbered into position Al could tell it was weighted down with a lot of fuel. General Hatfield pushed the controls forward and had the engines running at maximum speed before easing off on the brakes. The superfortress jerked forward. A moment of fear ran through Al. He calculated that everyone on board would know in one minute whether they would be in the air or this takeoff would end in a spectacular fireball. It was the longest takeoff roll Al had ever experienced. The nose of the plane slowly edged up and the super B-29's remaining wheels lifted off the runway at 11:59 A.M. Japan time.

Hatfield flew low over the sea as the plane slowly climbed to 1500 feet. He turned it to come back over the field and headed in an easterly direction over the Missouri and the great armada of American and Allied ships in the harbor.

The B-29 was up to 2,000 feet heading out to the Pacific as everyone on board watched the Japanese coast receding.

"What's the next land we'll see?" General Hatfield asked Al over the intercom.

"Kamchatka Peninsula in about four and a half hours," Al replied.

"Where in the hell is that?" the General asked.

Clash of Cultures - The Al Gordon Story

"In Soviet Siberia," Al said.

"I don't want to fly over Russia. Al, steer us around that damn place," the General ordered.

Al changed the course slightly to pass south of the Kamchatka Peninsula and east of the Kurile Islands. Once at this point, they changed to an easterly course that took them in the direction of Nome, Alaska, six hours away. They ascended to 20,000 feet as the skies darkened.

Al checked their position with aerial navigation and Captain Crawford checked their position by Loran. Their calculations came out exactly the same. They congratulated each other on the preciseness of their navigation. The plane was flying with the benefit of strong tail winds and their ground speed was approaching 400 miles an hour.

Al's basic assumption was that there would be a long tortuous night of flying, and they would end up in Washington at midnight. It came as something of a surprise to Al to see the beginnings of the grayness of the dawn popping up on the far horizon in front and to the right of the B-29. Seeing dawn breaking, Al felt confused about which day it was.

They had been flying eleven hours when they crossed the Alaskan coast. Al calculated the time about 11 P.M. in Tokyo, 11 A.M. in Washington, D.C., and 6 A.M. in Nome below, while still September 2nd in all three places. It dawned on Al that they had crossed the International Date Line. They would fly through a short day and into another night before landing in Washington, D.C., some eleven or twelve hours later.

Al took his turn to sleep in the empty space in the bomb bay that still reeked of gasoline fumes. When he woke up, it was full daylight. He had an awful headache and at the same time was ravenously hungry. He broke out two boxes of K rations. He sat there munching away on two candy bars, a small can of American cheese and a can of Spam. After a drink of water from his canteen and sprinkling some water on his face and back, he started to feel somewhat better. He climbed back into the front of the ship and relieved Tom Crawford. Crawford spent a few minutes filling Al in on their present position and enjoying some small talk.

Al took another time check: 2 A.M., September 3rd in Tokyo, 1 P.M. the afternoon of September 2nd in Washington and 9 A.M. where they were.

The last hours of the flight dragged on. They were flying over Toronto at 10 P.M.

The landing finally came two hours later at precisely 11:52 P.M. Washington Time (Eastern War Time) at Andrews Army Air Force Base in Maryland, a few miles away from Washington.

Robert Miller

CHAPTER 88

The landing was smooth. The crew was tired, but jubilant. The men in the tower congratulated General Hatfield on a record-breaking nonstop flight.

As the B-29 taxied to a position on the apron, they were greeted with lights and a swarm of people, including a horde of newsmen and newsreel cameras. Al and the others enjoyed a brief moment of celebrity. The commander of the air base greeted them and invited them to join President Truman in the White House the next day at noon.

Al searched the crowd and saw Mary waving excitedly standing behind the news people. She had on a new dress he had not seen before, a white summery form fitting dress with a wide brimmed straw hat that she kept holding as it fluttered in the night breezes. Al was temporarily prevented from getting to her by the wall of reporters and the time it took everyone on the flight to say their thanks. The General gave Al one last thank-you for a safe trip and, uncharacteristically, gave Al a quick hug with one arm around the shoulder.

In a few minutes, Al reached Mary. She fell into his arms and pressed her body against his. The General came over and reminded them that they were both invited to the White House the next day. Roy Howard and Mary greeted each other. She thanked him profusely for the help his news people had been in arranging her flight and the lavish suite, bedecked with fruit, flowers, and other goodies. Mr. Howard thanked her and he reminded Al to consider working for the Scripps Howard Newspapers.

Mary introduced Al to Dan Fogarty, an executive of the *Washington News*, who had kept Mary informed of Al's flight and coordinated all the plans.

"We are all so proud of you and everything you accomplished," Dan Fogarty said. He beamed broadly as he shook Al's hand. "We have a limousine that will take you both back to the Willard Hotel. Order everything and anything. Mr. Howard will take care of the bill. You are his guests. I'll meet you with another limousine at eleven tomorrow. I'll escort you both to the White House for your meeting with President Truman."

Al suggested that maybe he and Mary could walk to the meeting at the White House. Dan explained that it just wasn't done. He and Mary would not be allowed just to walk up the driveway.

Once in the limousine, Al and Mary kissed warmly. Their hands explored each other as if checking that nothing was missing.

Mary backed away for a moment to ask, "Don't you want to hear about your daughter?"

"I sure do," Al said as he continued giving her small kisses on the neck. "And the boys, too. When will I see everybody?"

Mary moved her neck slightly to allow Al room to continue kissing her neck. "The children are with my folks in Texas. We have to see your parents first and then mine."

"I guess we can go to New York tomorrow and to Texas the next day," Al said softly between the kisses. "But, I need to get you alone and make love to you, and then I need to sleep for a while," Al whispered seductively.

Mary laughed and asked why. She put her arms around him and kissed him once again. "It doesn't make any difference if my Allie has been awake for an hour or for forty hours. He wants to make love and go to sleep. Nothing has changed!" She became more serious after they shared a laugh. "Thank God you are home at last! And home for good!" She snuggled close to him. "I flew all night to get here. I'll need a little sleep later too." She put her head down on his shoulder and closed her eyes. Al did not want to disturb his sleeping beauty.

When Al entered The Willard Hotel suite, he gazed about. The luxury suite had flowers, an ice bucket of champagne, a bowl of fruit and a table set with cookies, coffee, tea, and milk.

Mary walked around the room opening her arms wide and expressing amazement at the size of the magnificent suite. "This reminds me of our honeymoon suites. Remember, love? The Warwick in Houston and the Concourse Plaza in the Bronx?"

Al remembered and gave Mary a knowing look. He moved over and opened the champagne which he poured, and they made a toast to each other, to their love and to their families. They sipped their glasses and then quickly they fell into each others' arms, removed their clothes, had a brief episode of reunion lovemaking and fell into an exhausted sleep.

Al woke to the sun flooding the room. It took him a moment to remember where he was and reached out for Mary, but he found himself alone in bed. He wobbled into the sitting room and found her in a negligee before a mirror combing her hair.

"Are you all right? Did you sleep well? What time is it?" Al asked.

"Yes. Yes, and ten after eight," Mary said happily.

Robert Miller

Al came behind her and ran his hands over her. "Sweetheart, why don't you come back to bed?" He urged.

"My hero is going to meet the President of the United States in less than three hours, but all he's thinking about right now is that wheedle worm of his." Mary turned and pretended a stern look, but softened and smiled. "I can see that with my husband around all the time I'll have to get used to his hot desires."

Two hours later Mary and Al were dressed and ready to meet the President. Before leaving, they made quick phone calls to say hello to the children and Mary's parents. Selwyn talked about how proud he was of his father's record-breaking flight and how frightened he had been that something would happen to him in the war in the Pacific. Al told Selwyn and Billy how proud he was of them for being good boys and for helping their mother. The call to Al's parents started out with Al's mother reprimanding him for not calling right away last night. After they hung up, Mary showed relief to be done with the call. She told Al that his mother was worrying about everything. His mother had even suggested to Mary that maybe Al had been wounded and the nonstop flight was to get Al into a hospital. Mrs. Gordon ended her conversations with Mary recently by saying that she could not rest at night until she saw that her son was all right and set eyes on him herself.

As Al and Mary waited to meet President Truman, Al remembered that he had been in Guam when he heard that President Roosevelt had died. The death of Roosevelt had shocked and saddened the whole country. He had been a great American leader. Al remembered the newsreels of Senator Truman at the 1944 Democratic Convention. He had not been impressed by Truman at all.

The group was ushered into the White House and escorted to the Oval Office at a few minutes before noon on Labor Day. Al was awed by his surroundings.

His first impression of President Truman, as the President came in and greeted the crew and Roy Howard, was how much he seemed to look like Mary's father, Bill Monahan.

President Truman shook hands with each one of them and then congratulated General Hatfield on his momentous record-breaking flight. Truman joked a little that he wanted to welcome the crew immediately while they still held the record. Then he told them that General LeMay was already in the air on a flight from Tinian that would lengthen the distance an airplane could cover on a single flight. He remarked that, whatever happens in the future, this particular flight will always be remembered because it was the first and because they had brought back a copy of the Japanese surrender document, and the pen that General MacArthur had used to sign it.

President Truman posed for a picture with the entire group. He shook hands with each member of the crew again. Mary was brought forward and Al introduced the President to Mary. She and the President exchanged friendly comments.

Truman looked back at Al and noticed his ribbons. "Young man, I want you to know that, if I had my choice of having all those medals you've earned, or being the President of the United States, I'd choose the medals."

"Thank you, Mr. President. I'm just a boy from the Bronx who tried to do his duty. But, given the same choice, I think I'd choose to be president."

Everyone laughed. President Truman now awarded Distinguished Flying Crosses to each of the participants of the flight and also awarded a Legion of Merit to General Hatfield, and the co-pilot, Major Cartwright, and the two navigators, Al Gordon and Tom Crawford.

As President Truman put the ribbon around Al's neck, he said, "One more medal for that boy from the Bronx. Congratulations."

"Thank you, sir," Al said proudly.

There were a few more photographs taken, including one of the President with Al, Mary, General Hatfield and Roy Howard. With the photographs completed, they were all ushered out of the Oval Office except President Truman and three of his staff members.

General Hatfield reached into a brief case he was carrying and gave Al his orders to report to the separation center at Ellington Field in Texas. He wished Al well and asked him to keep in touch. Mr. Howard then thanked Al for all he had done and told him to see him in New York in a couple of weeks so they could work out the specifics of his next job. He told Al that the newspaper would pay for his flight to New York. Al thanked him and expressed to him how much help he had been.

"It is I who am thankful to you," Mr. Howard said as he patted Al on the back. "Call my office in New York and let them know what other travel arrangements you will need."

By three-thirty, Al and Mary were on an Eastern Airlines flight from Washington for the eighty-minute flight to LaGuardia Airport in New York City.

CHAPTER 89

The greeting party at LaGuardia included Al's parents, Shirley, and Aunt Mollie.

When Al's mother finally got to hug him, she kissed and patted all the ribbons. She stepped back to scan him head to foot to see that he was healthy and uninjured. After the greetings, she said, "Thank God you're home safe! When will you be able to start work? Gordon Advertising needs you. You can build up our business and make it enormously successful in the years ahead."

Al put his arm around his mother and tried to explain that he was not an advertising man, but a newspaperman. He explained he could work anywhere in the country at the Scripps Howard papers.

"You're a celebrity," Al's father said. "I don't see how you could even consider living anywhere else than New York."

Al told his family that he surely loved New York, but had enjoyed the rest of the country starting the day almost eleven years before when he first boarded a train to Texas with the NYU football team. He mentioned that the decision where to live would be made jointly by Mary and himself together, alone, and very probably in their compartment in the next couple of days on the train to Texas.

Al's father packed all six of them into his 1941 Oldsmobile. They headed along the new Grand Central Parkway and across the Triborough Bridge into the Bronx. As they reached the Grand Concourse at 161st Street, Al asked his father to stop at the Concourse Plaza Hotel.

Al checked into the hotel's honeymoon suite for that night. The bellman, who had held the job since Mary and Al's first stay at the Concourse Plaza, greeted Al effusively. When Al tried to tip him a dollar for storing their luggage, the bellman refused and told Colonel Gordon, with the emphasis on Colonel, that it is an honor for the hotel to have Colonel Gordon stay there.

Clash of Cultures - The Al Gordon Story

When they got back to the Gordons' apartment, Al was treated to a feast of the foods that he had not seen for a long time - lox, cream cheese, Swiss cheese, whitefish, sturgeon, herring, and gefilte fish, together with pickles, tomatoes, cucumbers, and other cold delicacies.

Along with all the talk about the war, Al inquired about some of his friends, but nobody seemed to know much about them. Al realized how far removed he had been from the Bronx over the last eleven years. Shirley mentioned that Selma had gotten married over a year ago to a man from the neighborhood who, as far as Shirley knew, was still in the Army.

By late evening, Al and Mary walked back in the warm summer's night to the Concourse Plaza Hotel. Al interrupted the walk momentarily to stop at a candy store on 170th Street to buy the Tuesday morning editions of *The News* and *Mirror* for two cents each.

He also bought a bottle of Pepsi Cola for a nickel, which he and Mary shared to quench their thirst after their dinner of lox and bagels. They got back to the hotel, quite tired, but not too tired for lovemaking in their honeymoon suite.

Al awoke to the smell of coffee. Mary sat at a table that had been wheeled into the suite, where she ate bacon and eggs and drank coffee while she casually read the morning newspaper. The news gave prominent mention of Al's record-breaking flight. Both *The News* and *Mirror* had a picture of President Truman, General Hatfield, and Al Gordon. The caption identified Al as a New Yorker and the navigator.

Mary wore only her pink transparent negligee. Al looked her over carefully and saw that, at twenty eight and the mother of three children, she was still as beautiful and desirable as the beguiling young cheerleader he had first met so many years before. Al came behind her and slipped his hands inside her negligee, caressed her bare breasts and kissed her neck.

"Didn't you get enough of that last night and the night before?" she teased.

"Sweetheart, I'll never get enough of you," Al said softly.

"I'm going to hold you to that. And, if you want to make love to me now, you'll have to take your hands off my tits and let me turn around and put my arms around you...or, better still. Let me get this negligee off first and then I'll not only put my arms but my whole body around yours."

Al watched in awe and wonderment as she got up from the table, peeled off the negligee, lifted her nightgown over her head, pushed him back onto the bed and climbed on top of him. He had not expected this unusual, direct behavior. Al had never heard Mary refer to her breasts before as tits. He could not recall her so quickly removing her clothes, pushing him to bed and climbing on top of him in broad daylight in a sunny room with the curtains wide open. She dangled her breasts in his mouth as her whole body shook and absolutely convulsed over his and pressed him down into the bed as they both quickly reached orgasms together.

Robert Miller

"Now can I finish my breakfast in peace?" Mary said softly after her body fell onto his.

"Sure, eat your breakfast, but wasn't a little piece between courses delicious?" Al asked, as she lifted her body off his.

Mary's happy laughter was high pitched as she put on the negligee again and returned to the table while Al slowly headed for the shower.

When they went downstairs to check out, the hotel manager told them there would be no charge. When Al protested, he was shown a copy of that mornings Bronx Home News with his picture with President Truman on page one with a headline:

"Bronx Colonel Navigates B-29 Record Setting Flight and is Greeted by President Truman in White House." The hotel's public relations man took a picture of Al and Mary and interviewed Al about his prior stays at the hotel starting with their honeymoon. Al and Mary thanked the hotel manager again for his kindness. They got into a taxi and headed downtown.

Al and Mary had only a few hours left in New York. Al made a quick stop at the Scripps Howard Newspaper office to get help in arranging train tickets to Houston that night. He talked with Brad Henderson, the managing editor, about the possibility of working there.

After the short meeting, Al walked over to West 57th Street to meet everyone for lunch. The lunch turned into an occasion to celebrate Al's return and to try to persuade him one more time to join the family advertising business.

Lifting a glass of scotch for himself and as the others at the table held up glasses of rose wine, Mr. Gordon gave a toast.

"A toast to the future. And, to Al and his beautiful wife, to his safe return, a decorated war hero and now a world-renowned foreign correspondent of whom we all and most especially I, are immensely proud."

All sipped from their glasses. There was a ripple of applause from people at adjoining tables to the Gordon family. Al's father happily acknowledged their applause with a wave to everyone.

Al, too, gave a wave to the others in the restaurant and looked back at his father. Al had reached the age of thirty and his father had finally acknowledged accomplishments. Al was caught between feeling surprised and embarrassed, but he certainly felt pleased.

Being careful to show respect for his parents in their desire for him to join their business, Al said that he and Mary would have to make some serious decisions very soon. He had three career choices to consider - General Hatfield's, the Scripps Howard Newspapers, and the Gordon Advertising Agency.

Mary agreed with Al by explaining, "As Al says, we've got some life planning to do. That's what we're going to do on this train ride."

"We love you both and want you happy with your decision. But, use the time on the train to be together and express your joy for each other, too," Al's mother strongly advised.

Colonel Alfred E. Gordon found himself blushing.

CHAPTER 90

As the train left the station, his mother's words echoed through Al's mind as he sat in the train compartment. "You're back in the United States and out of danger, so why do I feel so sad to see that train take you away? I'm afraid you'll spend the rest of your life in Texas or Colorado or some other God forsaken place and that you'll forget your Jewish heritage and we'll never see our grandchildren again," Al's mother had told him.

"Do you think I'm anything like my mother?" Al asked as he turned to Mary seated next to him.

Mary threw her arms around Al as the train rolled its way through the dark tunnel out of the station.

"Al," she told him, "you are truly a unique one-of-a-kind person. You have your father's charm, a charm you never noticed before, and you also have your mother's confidence and determination. It's a rare combination. I hope some of it will rub off on our children. Now, do you think it is time for us to talk about their future, where they will live, and how they will be educated?"

"Yes, we must talk about those things, but not right now," Al said softly. He enfolded her in his arms, kissed her and held her close to him. He got up with his arms still around her and very gently led her to the narrow settee that lined one side of the compartment.

Twenty minutes later the train was speeding across the still sunny swampland south of Newark. Al and Mary began to get cleaned up and dressed again.

"Shall we talk now or shall we wait until after dinner?" Al asked.

Mary, who was readjusting her nylon stockings and smoothing out her dress, laughed loudly and told her husband, "Colonel Alfred Emmanuel Gordon, if we're ever going to talk about anything, it had better be in a public place. I'm not exactly hungry after that big lunch, but why don't we go to the club car and have a drink there and talk about the future."

They walked a couple of cars forward to find the club car. The car was quite crowded, but the steward greeted them and took note of Al's many ribbons. The steward asked them to be patient for a moment and he'd find them a place in the car for them to sit. How he did it, Al never knew, but in less than two minutes he was back and escorted them to two seats beside a small table that had dishes of peanuts and pretzels. Mary ordered a martini. Al asked if she'd rather have champagne. She declined the champagne and repeated her martini order. Al ordered himself a beer.

They talked in generalities. Al told Mary what Mr. Howard and Bart Henderson had told him about New York being "where the action was," not to mention the money.

Mary took Al's hand and told him, "Al, this is what we've been waiting for...the war to end and you to come home safely. That has happened and nothing else is important. I know it will break my parents' hearts to take the children away from Houston and I also know that your parents want us all to move to New York. In either place, we will have family to back us up and that's important. Then again, I wonder if we should be in Denver where we could lead our own lives apart from both families. Does Scripps Howard have a newspaper halfway between Houston and New York?"

"They have a newspaper in Evansville, Indiana," Al told her. "The goal of every reporter in Evansville is to be good enough to get to Chicago or New York. Evansville would not be a step forward in my career."

"All right," Mary decided. "It will be New York. The next question is Selwyn's schooling. Shall we send him to Catholic school or public school?"

"That's up to you, Mary," Al told her. "I agreed a long time ago to let you raise the children as Catholics and I'll not go back on that promise."

"I'm not sure Selwyn is happy at St. Anne's. He's eight years old and he gets into trouble with the nuns because they think he asks impertinent questions. He's got a lot of you in him, Al. I wonder if he'd be happier in a public school."

Al considered what she said for a minute. He gave her his answer, "That's a decision you have to make, darling. You base it on what you think serves Selwyn's best interest, and I'll always be one hundred percent behind you. Never doubt that."

Mary turned to look out the window. The train was going through Trenton, New Jersey, and slowing down as they approached the station. She ordered another martini. Al watched without saying a word as Mary quickly drank the martini and finished it off before Al finished his first beer.

"When did you begin to drink martinis like that?" Al asked.

"Two martinis before dinner is a medical prescription I got from the doctor," Mary told him.

"What doctor? What prescription?" Al asked in some alarm.

"Dr. Roberts in Houston," Mary explained with a smile. "Billy had a terrible earache last January. He was up all night screaming, and most of the day too. I took him to Dr. Roberts who prescribed some kind of medicine for him. He told me to give Bill two teaspoons of the stuff whenever he started to cry. Then he told me that, if it doesn't work, to take two martinis before dinner and I wouldn't mind his crying so much. It helped me. The two martinis prescription helped me to get through many a day with a crying youngster and all those nights my husband was away."

"I'm back now," Al said. "I'm home for good. Instead of two martinis before dinner, I'll prescribe one Al Gordon, taken vaginally, morning and night for the rest of your life."

Mary cackled with laughter and asked, "What about my time of the month?"

"It can be taken orally at such times," Al quipped.

Mary continued to giggle. She leaned over to him and asked in a conspiratorial manner, "Can it be taken rectally?"

Al was taken aback and momentarily speechless. "I don't know. It might be interesting to find out."

Mary leaned her face over to Al's and kissed him on the cheek. "It might at that, sweetheart. I've been so lonely for your so long I'm ready to be yours in any and every possible way."

"Let's skip dinner and go back to our room now," Al whispered.

Mary laughed aloud. "My husband, a night of great delights awaits you all the way from here to St. Louis. But, you do have to buy me dinner first."

They headed for the dining car, just as the train pulled into the North Philadelphia station. Al ordered a steak and mashed potatoes and Mary ordered the same, plus a third martini. Their talk through dinner was less of what they would do with their lives and had more to do with the delights that Mary was promising Al for the night to come. Mary ate about half her steak. Her voice became slurred as she finished her third martini and ordered a fourth. Al had another beer, finished his steak and ate what Mary left over. Mary became more quiet as the train sped on towards Harrisburg, Pennsylvania. Al ordered coffee for both of them. Mary didn't drink hers, but absorbed the aroma through her nostrils.

Al paid the check and began to steer Mary through the moving train back to their drawing room. Mary wobbled on the moving train as they threaded their way along the narrow aisle. Al wasn't sure if the martinis or the train gave her the noticeable sideways movements to her steps.

As they came into their compartment, now made up for the night with the bed set and the lights low, Al took her in his arms and reminded her of the promises she had made for a glorious night of ecstasy. Mary gave him an unfocused look as she kicked off her shoes and lifted her dress over her head. She dropped the dress straight to the floor. Clad in her slip, bra and panties, she threw herself on the bed. She murmured to Al that she needed to sleep for ten minutes, promised to wake up and make love to him as she had never had before.

Mary collapsed backwards on the pillow and immediately fell into a deep sleep.

Robert Miller

CHAPTER 91

Al awoke in a gray dawn the next morning as Mary climbed over him on her way into the small adjoining toilet and sink compartment. Her moans made it obvious she was not feeling well. She reported to Al she had a giant headache. She grumbled at him and held him responsible for her drinking all those "martoonies" and asked him to find her some aspirins and leave her alone. Al got the aspirins and sat down to read the newspapers while Mary intermittently slept and moaned before she got up to face the day two hours later. Al arranged for coffee and rolls. Mary started with the coffee, which she promptly threw up. It was midday and the train was somewhere past Indianapolis before Mary felt well enough to think about getting dressed and letting the porter in to clean the compartment. Though Mary was still shaky and with her headache still bothering her, she and Al made their way to the dining car to have lunch. Mary's eyes were red and she told Al she felt ashamed of herself.

"I've heard my father talk about hangovers," Mary said with a moaning voice. "He said when you wake up with a bad hangover, you're afraid you're going to live. When you reach the point you're afraid you're going to die, that means you're getting better." She paused to take in air and to stabilize her head. "So, why do I feel so rotten? Did I spoil your entire homecoming with all those martoonies? I'll never have another of those things as long as I live!" She patted Al's hand across the table and added, "Surely not more than two at a time."

Al chose not to say too much about the night before because a mother and daughter shared the table with them, and obviously their table companions were under strain and having difficulty communicating with one another. When the mother and daughter finally left the table, Al mentioned the many things Mary had promised him last night before she fell into a deep sleep. When Al repeated to her the exact words she had said about oral and rectal insertions, she looked at him blankly.

"I said that? Are you sure?" Mary asked with consternation and embarrassment showing on her face.

"Would I lie?" Al asked.

"Al, darling, I don't think you'd lie. I would never believe that I would have said anything about oral or rectal sex if I hadn't been under the influence of all those martoonies." She paused. "I do have a vague recollection. If you do three things, I'll try to make good on those unfulfilled promises tonight."

"And what are those three things?" Al asked with anticipation.

"One, let me have two martoonies, but no more before dinner."

Al nodded.

Mary's face couldn't conceal a blush as she went on, "Two, cut your fingernails. And, three, when we are in St. Louis this afternoon, go into a drugstore and buy some Vaseline."

Al reached for Mary's free hand, while her other hand held her head. He saw in her eyes she was trying to get rid of the last traces of her headache.

In St. Louis, Al and Mary spent two happy hours roaming and sightseeing the streets of the city before the train left.

Aboard the Missouri Pacific Texas Special that left at 6 P.M., Mary kept to her promise of only one martini before dinner and one with dinner. The dinner conversation centered around their plans for themselves and their children.

Mary first brought up the subject of her religion and her hopes that Al would take an interest in the children's religious development. She even went further by offering to give up Catholicism on the condition that they would find another religion for the family. She said she would convert to Judaism, if he would go to the synagogue with her and they could have a single religion for the entire family.

Al was stunned by the offer. He reminded Mary that he believed in God, but not in organized religion. He thought of himself as a free thinker and that he hoped his children would be the same. Furthermore, he was willing to keep his old promise to let Mary decide on the choice of religion.

Mary told him that it was one thing for a grown man of thirty to be a free thinker, but that children needed to be told what their parents believed. "If we give them a religion that they can see we both believe in and respect, it will give them a certain assurance of family stability. When they grow up, they can decide for themselves, but it's our responsibility to give them a basic religious background that they can later accept or reject," Mary explained.

Al thought about her ideas as he took the last bite of steak and watched the steward take away the empty plate. He reached across the table and placed his hand on Mary's before speaking.

"Sweetheart, I appreciate your offer to convert to Judaism. I really do. I know how difficult such a thing must be for you. But, the fact is that I don't want to be part of any organized religion, including my own. I wouldn't be any more

Robert Miller

comfortable in a synagogue than I am in a Catholic church. You know that I've never been exactly comfortable in any church."

Al's smile and patient explanation did not appease Mary's desires for a family religion, especially one where she could see Al an active happy participant. She felt a sense of hopelessness. His answer hurt her, but she decided not to show her true feelings. She just dropped the discussion and let Al enjoy his cup of coffee and ice cream.

The following morning, after breakfast in the dining car, the train rolled into Houston. Al and Mary found Selwyn, Billy and Minella Marie waiting for them alongside the platform with their Monahan grandparents. Selwyn and Billy greeted their father proudly and happily, especially as they inspected and enjoyed his military uniform with all the colorful ribbons. When Mrs. Monahan showed Al his blue-eyed five month old daughter, the little girl smiled shyly. She caught his heart and he was immediately captivated for life.

AN AFTERWORD

    I'd like to tell you that Mary and Al and their family lived happily ever after. It didn't happen that way. Not entirely. Al and Mary returned to New York with their family, and moved to the suburbs. After his experiences in Denver and in the war, his work on a marginal post war newspaper bored and depressed him. Caught up in the heavy drinking that prevailed in the 1950s, Mary moved towards becoming an alcoholic while Al became something of a womanizer. Their children grew rebellious and the realities of life in the fifties and sixties were a great deal different than the war years. The story of Mary and Al in the post war years changes dramatically. Look for the sequel, *Clash of Cultures II: The Post-War Years*.

Robert Miller

ABOUT THE AUTHOR

ROBERT MILLER was born and brought up in The Bronx. He graduated from De Witt Clifton High School in 1940 and attended New York University from the fall of 1940 until he enlisted in the Army Air Force in 1942. He was trained to be an air crew gunner and then attended navigation school and emerged as a Second Lieutenant and served overseas in the 91st Photo Reconnaissance Squadron. After the war he went into the advertising business. He and his brother Leonard joined a three person advertising agency run by their parents. He was married to Frances Fitzgerald, a Texan. They were married in 1944 and divorced in 1976. She died in 1978. Mr. Miller married the former San Gold in 1980. They have four sons, one daughter, twelve grandchildren and two great grandsons. The Millers have homes in New York City and in Ellenville, New York. He can be reached by e-mail: bobmiller@milleraa.com.

Printed in the United States
778400001B